THE
BEDLAM CADAVER

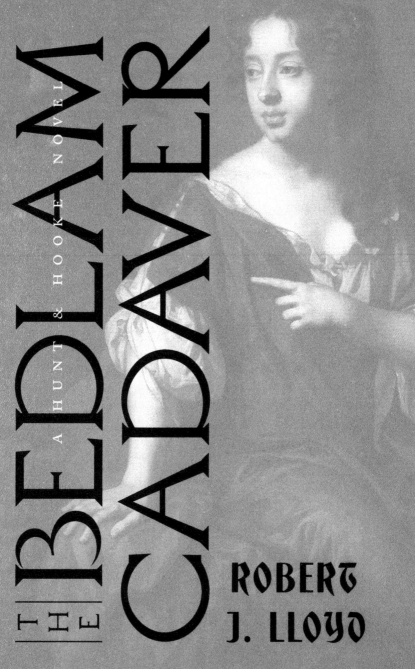

THE BEDLAM CADAVER

A HUNT & HOOKE NOVEL

ROBERT J. LLOYD

MELVILLE HOUSE PRESS NEW YORK & LONDON

The Bedlam Cadaver
First published in 2024 by Melville House
Copyright © 2023 by Robert J. Lloyd

First Melville House Printing: April 2024

Melville House Publishing
46 John Street
Brooklyn, NY 11201
and
Melville House UK
Suite 2000
16/18 Woodford Road
London E7 0HA

mhpbooks.com
@melvillehouse

ISBN: 978-1-68589-095-7
ISBN: 978-1-68589-096-4 (eBook)

Designed by Beste M. Doğan

Library of Congress Control Number: 2024933316

Printed in the United States of America
1 3 5 7 9 10 8 6 4 2

A catalog record for this book is available from the Library of Congress

To Stan and Vic, with love

CHARACTERS

MR. HENRY HUNT, Gentleman. (More usually, **HARRY**.)

MISS JANET WEBB, Harry's Maidservant.

MR. OLIVER SHANDOIS, Harry's Manservant.

M. HUBERT DIEUDONNE, Harry's Cook.

MR. ROBERT HOOKE, Secretary of the Royal Society of London, Gresham Professor of Geometry, Architect, and Surveyor for the City of London.

MISS GRACE HOOKE, Robert Hooke's Niece.

MR. THOMAS CRAWLEY, Observator of the Royal Society of London.

SIR CHRISTOPHER WREN, President of the Royal Society of London, Surveyor of the King's Works.

M. DENIS PAPIN, Acting Curator of Experiments of the Royal Society of London

MR. EDMUND WYLDE, Fellow of the Royal Society of London.

MR. JOHN AUBREY, Fellow of the Royal Society of London.

HIS MAJESTY CHARLES II, the King.

SIR JOHN RERESBY, Baronet of Thrysbergh, Justice of Peace for Westminster.

MR. JOSEPH FENN, Marshal's Officer.

MISS SEBILIAH BARTON, Bethlehem Patient.

DR. THOMAS ALLEN, Bethlehem Physician.

MR. JEREMY LESTER, Bethlehem Apothecary.

MR. JOSEPH MATTHEWS, Bethlehem Porter.

MRS. MILLICENT MATTHEWS, Bethlehem Matron.

MISS HANNAH MATTHEWS, Bethlehem Nurse.

MR. JOHN CARTER, Bethlehem Steward.

MR. WILLIAM JONES, Bethlehem Basketman.

MR. EDWARD LANGDALE, Bethlehem Basketman.

SIR BENEDICT CANTLEY, Deputy-Governor of the Royal African Company.

MISS DIANA CANTLEY, Sir Benedict's Daughter.

JAMES SCOTT, the Duke of Monmouth. (The King's Son.)

MR. THOMAS THYNNE, Member of Parliament for the Country Party and the richest Man in England.

MRS. ELIZABETH THYNNE (née Percy), Heiress to the Percy Estates.

MR. JOHN KIDD, Thomas Thynne's Gamekeeper.

MR. RICHARD SINGER, Thomas Thynne's Steward.

MR. JOSIAH KEELING, Salter and Oilman.

KARL JOHANN VON KÖNIGSMARCK, Swedish Count.

KAPITÄN CHRISTOPH VRATZ, Pomeranian Mercenary.

LÖJTNANT JOHANN STERN, Swedish Mercenary.

PAN JERZY BOROSKI, the Count's Polonian Servant.

MRS. SARAH UNSWORTH, Tailor.

MRS. RASZKA LEJBOWICZOWA, Tailor.

SIR PETER LELY, the King's Painter in Ordinary.

DHR. JAN-BAPTIST JASPARS, Sir Peter Lely's Senior Assistant.

DHR. PROSPER LANKRINK, Sir Peter Lely's Assistant.

DHR. JOSEPH BOKSHOORN, Sir Peter Lely's Assistant.

MR. KILL-SIN ABBOTT, a Waterman.

THE BEDLAM CADAVER

CHAPTER ONE

THE GRESHAM DISSECTION

An opportunity had arisen.

A woman had ended her own life at Bethlehem Hospital.

No family wanting her, the Hospital gave her body to the Royal Society of London for the Improving of Natural Knowledge—or, rather, to its Secretary, Mr. Robert Hooke. He was friendly with Bethlehem's Physician, and had, after all, designed the place.

Hooke summoned the Fellows.

About thirty of them gathered at Gresham College, jostling by the entrance to its repository.

Even in the shade of the colonnaded walkway, most stood hatless and holding their coats, for the midday sun was remorseless.

Sweat darkened the backs of their waistcoats as they waited for admittance. Some had removed their perukes.

Hooke promised an *extraordinary demonstration*.

☿

ALL THEIR TALK WAS OF THE forthcoming dissection. It was to be performed upstairs in the repository—more spacious than the anatomy room, or the Reading Hall, where most of the Society's experimental trials took place. Hooke expected more Fellows than usual; he was right.

Led by Sir Christopher Wren himself, the trial would reveal a brain and spinal cord. Then—by some method not yet divulged— Wren planned to impart movement to the limbs. The idea came from a meeting of Hooke's New Philosophical Club at the Angel and Crown a few nights before, when John Aubrey—his speech slurry from genever—had mentioned the mouths of those beheaded continuing to move in prayer. Anne Boleyn was one such. Her eyes had moved, too, roving around her from the straw.

May self-awareness continue even after the blade's descent, the person knowing of their own predicament?

☿

WORD WAS, HIS MAJESTY MIGHT ATTEND. At the Office of Works that morning, Sir Christopher had invited him. The King replied he was free and wanting entertainment.

Was this him now? The Fellows strained to see.

Red-faced from their load, two men carrying a sedan entered the quadrangle from Broad Street.

Once they had settled the chair, their passenger emerged and paid them; both looked gratified by the amount.

The newcomer wore a suit of blue silk, his waistcoat long, shirt-sleeves copious, breeches beribboned. He repositioned his hat—also blue, with a swan's feather curling around its brim. His peruke was a pristine creamy white, dazzling in the sunlight. His boots, of soft Moroccan leather, transported him silently across the grass, which had toasted over the summer.

Not the King, but Mr. Henry Hunt.

His appearance differed markedly from their last sighting; some Fellows did not even recognise him. Despite the news of his good fortune—rewarded handsomely by the Duchesse de Mazarin for services to her, and by the King for services to the Queen—they still expected the scruffy youth they knew as Harry, in the brown leather coat scarred by his adventures. Not this gentleman of sumptuous appearance. He had gained weight, too, his features softened by new flesh.

The door to the repository's stairway swung open, and out stepped Robert Hooke. Standing in his hunched fashion, dressed in habitual grey, he welcomed each Fellow as they filed in. All the men bowed and expressed their pleasure for the forthcoming demonstration.

A fragile-looking youth carrying a tray full of tools hastened past them. This was Thomas Crawley, Harry's replacement as Observator, about to assist Sir Christopher. Hooke patted his back as he went inside.

On spotting Harry, Hooke's demeanour changed. His mouth formed a sour line. Harry, feeling shame, knew why: over three months had passed since they last saw each other, on his last visit to Gresham.

Warily, the two men bowed to one another, then shook hands for old times' sake. Harry was careful not to squeeze too hard, for Hooke looked frailer than he remembered. Besides, all the rings Harry wore might cause him pain.

'Sir Christopher awaits,' Hooke said stiffly. His bulbous eyes, their irises mercury grey, held no warmth in them at all.

'I am gladdened to see you, Mr. Hooke,' Harry replied. 'I have been busy. My new house . . . its decoration, and choosing furniture.'

Hooke raised an eyebrow. Harry's voice had changed. Elocution lessons raised him up a class. His spectacles, Hooke noticed, were gold-rimmed.

'Grace made mention of your improvements,' Hooke said. 'I await your invitation to view them.'

Harry opened, then shut, his mouth, and gestured that he would follow Hooke upstairs to the repository.

Hooke smiled tersely. Even Harry's attempt at courtesy seemed superior. More a command that Hooke should walk in front.

☿

ONCE UPSTAIRS AND INSIDE THE REPOSITORY, Harry could see Sir Christopher on the dais at the far end of the long, narrow room, setting out the tools Crawley passed to him. The new Observator exhibited—to Harry's critical eye—a clumsiness about him. Between them and the assembling spectators stood a table support- ing the cadaver, covered over by a thin cotton sheet.

The Society's curios filled the repository. The Fellows nudged for spaces among the cabinets and chests of drawers.

Hooke went crookedly through the crowd of men towards Sir

Christopher. His stoop from the hunch in his back had worsened, Harry observed. Hooke was one of the few men in the room without a wig; his long hair, tied back, looked disreputably unkempt.

Denis Papin, now in all but title the Society's Curator of Experiments—at last, Hooke could concentrate fully on the Secretaryship—waved Harry over. Harry negotiated his way around a Roman statue of a woman dredged from the Fleet; the two men embraced happily.

'The prodigal son returns at last,' Edmund Wylde remarked in a stage whisper.

Harry ignored the gibe—which he knew to be good-natured, for he knew Edmund Wylde—and acknowledged him, and also John Aubrey, with a dip of his head. Wylde, leaning on a case full of fossils, shared an amused glance with Aubrey.

Nowadays—in appearance, at least—Harry was quite the gentleman.

At a hushing of the audience in readiness for the demonstration, they concentrated on the dais.

The tools—serrated knives, chisels, hammers—were by now arranged on a smaller table turned at a right angle to the one supporting the corpse. Harry recognised them from Gresham's anatomy room; he had used them himself when assisting Hooke.

Loud claps and a bellowed 'Lords, Sirs, Gentlemen . . . the King!' made everyone turn to the door. Despite their squash, the Fellows did their best to show their servility, all getting in one another's way as they made their bows, deep and sincere.

Sir Christopher, the Royal Society's President, descended from the dais and pushed his way through the company.

'Your Majesty, you do us great favour by your visit. You—'

'Let there be no speechifying!' The King sounded cheerful, glad of the distraction anatomy could provide. 'Sirs, I greet you all. I am most pleased with the invitation. Hmm. And, as you see, to accept it.'

He waved at the Fellows to settle them. Sir Christopher led him through the opening channel of men, all still bowing.

Unless occasion demanded, the King dressed informally. Today, in a russet-coloured suit. A head taller than most of the Fellows—his height further increased by heels and a full black wig—he looked over them as he walked towards the dais. Although the windows were open, the heat in the repository was considerable; he stayed cool and unruffled. His face, with its dark complexion and exaggerated features of his Medici forefathers, tended towards solemnity, but for now he was smiling, seeming free from the cares of Whitehall.

Hooke positioned a chair at the foot of the dais. With another happy look behind him, the King sat down to observe the dissection.

Returning behind the table, Sir Christopher tied on a leather apron. A smile played around his mouth as he waited for quiet.

Despite being nearly fifty, he was unlined and fit-looking, more like a man ten years his junior. He radiated energy and enthusiasm. Rare for him nowadays to undertake anatomy; as the King's Surveyor of Works, his time was greatly taken up with building. But his expertise with brains—had he not illustrated Willis's *Cerebri Anatome?*—made him the natural choice to lead the demonstration.

'May it please Your Majesty, my Lords, Sirs, Gentlemen, Fellows all,' Sir Christopher began. 'I shall reveal the brain, the brain stem, and its continuation through the bones of the spine.'

Applause broke out. Sir Christopher waited for it to quieten. His expression promised there was better to come. 'Perhaps we may animate the material of this dead woman's brain, its folds and undulations, into giving movement to her limbs. It is, therefore, a postscript to the investigations of Dr. Thomas Willis, with whom I had the honour to work.'

'You made the drawings for his excellent book!' Aubrey cried, unable to help himself.

'Yes . . . thank you, Mr. Aubrey,' Sir Christopher said, put out of his stride by the interjection. 'He had other help, too. Mr. Millington. Mr. Lower. The bulk of the work, though, was his—to say otherwise would do him disservice.'

All the men murmured their assent. Willis, dead five years, was one of the Royal Society's founders, and a well-liked Fellow.

'Willis studied the treelike arrangement of the *cerebellum*, and the *corpora striata*, the *optic thalami*, the parallel lines of the *mesolobe*. He numbered the *nervi craniales*. He discovered God's providential design—which we now call the Circle of Willis—allowing the blood's flow to proceed even if one of its arteries is blocked. He avoided the usual mutilation of autopsy by cutting at a brain from beneath. He invented ways of preservation, so putrefaction did not curtail his investigations. It was these preserved brains I drew, using Mr. Hooke's perspectograph.'

As more applause broke out, Sir Christopher gestured to Crawley.

Crawley removed the sheet, revealing the cadaver.

Before the dissection, Crawley had positioned the dead woman on her back. Her face was turned away from them.

All the Fellows wondered if she made a pretty corpse. None spoke the thought.

Her skin was the colour of cream. Her age, Harry guessed, was eighteen or so. She was slim—hipbones and ribs discernible beneath her flesh—and muscular, so obviously had been active. Released from under the sheet, a gamy smell arose; not yet too unpleasant, even in the repository's stifling warmth.

Crawley had already shaved her head. A pile of long dark hair—almost black—lay on the floor, shining glossily. The assistant swept it further under the table with his foot.

'Firstly, I shall expose the spine,' Sir Christopher announced.

All the Fellows shuffled forwards, as close to the dais as they could without bumping the King.

At another sign from Sir Christopher, Crawley positioned the dead woman onto her front, turning her away from the Fellows. By the loose way she rolled, Harry could see *rigor mortis* had faded.

Sir Christopher had arranged his tools as if set out for a banquet, in the order he considered he would need them. Crawley passed over the leftmost knife.

Naming them aloud as he did so, Sir Christopher soon exposed the muscles of the back. They gleamed wetly. He sliced through the long, deeper muscles on both sides of the spine, then scooped beneath them with his fingers to lift them away.

He cut through the V shape of muscles wrapping the neck and attaching to the skull.

All this took time; so absorbed were the men in Sir Christopher's work that few noticed the duration. Most were waistcoatless by now; hardly anyone still wore their wig. In the crowded repository, the smell of their sweat, and of the cadaver, was rising.

Using a chisel, Sir Christopher removed the top parts of each of the *vertebrae*. He named the *meninges*, cutting through them deftly with scissors to avoid severing the spinal nerves.

'Next,' he said, 'I shall remove the brain while keeping it still attached to the spinal cord.'

Starting above one ear and finishing at the other, he cut over the top of the skull. Crawley helped him peel back the dead woman's scalp, leaving her cranium covered by its fatty, fibrous tissue. Sir Christopher peeled this away, too, then cut through the muscles on each side of the head.

Crawley passed him a handsaw.

Sir Christopher sawed the forehead, working around the curve of the skull, being careful not to cut Crawley, who held it steady. Dust flew from the saw's teeth, catching the light from the repository's windows and then landing as a powder on the floor.

The dome of the woman's head came away. The tough layer covering her brain released from the bone with a ripping sound. Sir Christopher sliced through it. Wanting to escape the confines of her skull, her brain bulged, but it was still restrained by cranial nerves, connective tissue, and the optic nerves.

'You may observe the *encephalon*,' Sir Christopher told the Fellows as they leaned even further forwards. 'The *cerebrum*, the *cerebellum*, and the *truncus encephali*. Covered by the *arachnoid mater*. You see this transparent covering?' He lifted and tipped the head so they could see more clearly into the hole.

Having cut the covering away, he announced, 'I shall expose the whole of the *medulla spinalis*.'

He broke open the *vertebrae* at the top of the neck to reveal the final length of spinal cord, and cut the last attachments keeping the brain inside the skull.

'Mr. Crawley, please lift her.'

By now, Crawley looked pale, and seemed hesitant to touch the body. Sir Christopher narrowed his eyes at him. The Observator jumped forwards, placing his hands under the woman's shoulders to turn her. To prevent the brain from spilling, Sir Christopher cupped her head in his hands.

As Crawley brought the woman to a sitting position, for the first time she faced her audience.

She still kept her last colouring: the ceruse on her cheeks, now faded; the vermilion on her lips, now smudged; and the darkening on her eyebrows, now smeared.

Her eyes were half closed; she looked mistrustful of these men observing her.

Harry felt the blood leave his face. He was in danger of fainting. His legs threatened to collapse beneath him.

Knowing him to be squeamish, Papin looked at him sympathetically. Papin's face changed to astonishment as Harry began to wave his arms, shirtsleeves flapping wildly.

'Stop, Sir Christopher! Stop!'

In the silence of the great pause around him, Harry was conscious of the other Fellows, and King Charles II, all turning to stare at him.

'You must stop!'

A buzz of disapproval started up at his interruption of Sir Christopher's extraordinary demonstration.

'She is no suicide from Bethlehem Hospital,' Harry told them all. 'Her name is Miss Diana Cantley. She was my neighbour in Bloomsbury Square.'

CHAPTER TWO

THE NEW
JUSTICE

The Justice of Peace for Westminster and Middlesex, Sir John Reresby, owned fists a bare-knuckle boxer would envy. His broad back and broader shoulders strained the seams of his fustic-yellow coat.

He had hurried to the King's command. With him came the City Marshalman, Joseph Fenn, whose broken nose tacked up his gaunt face between a stern mouth and deep-set eyes. Fenn stood in his red uniform coat over by a cabinet displaying a monstrous lamb. To the Fellows' consternation, he had lit a Portuguese cheroot, whose miasmal smoke coiled around the exhibits.

Sir John, leaning heavily on his blackthorn walking stick—more like an Irish shillelagh—inspected the dead woman.

She lay on her back, resting on the wound along its length. While awaiting the Justice's arrival, Sir Christopher and Crawley had used tape to hold her cranium together. They had also covered her with the sheet, which Sir John had pulled back down to reveal her face.

'How was *Diana Cantley* delivered to the College?' Sir John asked the Fellows, peering at them indignantly as if they were to blame, and stressing the name for its unlikeliness. He had a booming voice, Yorkshire vowels, and a flat way of speaking that made his questions sound like statements. All of which, to Harry's ears, sounded rather threatening.

'Bethlehem's Physician, Dr. Thomas Allen, informed me of a suicide, and released her to us,' Hooke informed him. 'I instructed Thomas Crawley to fetch her.'

Crawley coughed to clear his throat. 'I went there last night, at about ten of the clock.'

At the Hospital, Crawley had barely glanced at her. She was only a body: the necessary receptacle of Sir Christopher's intent to reveal a brain and spinal cord. Besides, when he collected her, she was shrouded, her face covered.

Sir John glared at the young Observator. 'Another man, presumably—one less important than Dr. Allen—handed her over.'

'The Porter, Mr. Matthews,' Crawley answered timorously. 'And one of the Basketmen with him. I know not his name.'

'Basketmen?'

'They do the Hospital's fetching and carrying, and the keeping it clean. The Basketman placed the body on the cart. Then I drove it back to Gresham.'

'Straight there, straight back?'

'Up Winchester Street, through the Wall at Little Moorgate. Back the same way. Our stable yard's off Broad Street, so it's the quickest.'

'No distance to Moorfields from here.'

'Five minutes. Takes as long to harness the horse.'

Sir John's voice rose suddenly. 'A convenient distance if you need a body to dismember.'

'You speak as though we take all the Hospital's dead,' Hooke protested. 'We do not.'

'Taking a murdered girl was careless on your part.'

'She was not killed here.'

'Nevertheless, damaging for your reputation, Mr. Hooke—'

'Stop, Sir John,' the King intervened. 'Robert, you are not to blame. The Society is not to blame. Hmm? No suspicion may be laid at your door.'

Sir John made a grunting sound, suggesting *he* would decide where suspicion may be laid, but he bowed towards his monarch.

He turned back to Crawley. 'How did Bedlam's staff mistake Diana Cantley for their suicide?'

Crawley looked unhappily at Hooke, then as unhappily at the Justice. 'I couldn't know it was another woman. She was under the same sheet you see on her now—'

'Yes, yes. I grasp it. You do not quite answer the question I pose. No matter. You are merely a servant, who follows instruction from these *Fellows*.' Sir John said the word disparagingly.

'He is more than that, sir!' Hooke protested. 'An Observator needs a long apprenticeship. He is not just come in off the street.'

'Robert, calm yourself,' the King said. 'We must know who put her inside this sheet.'

'Bedlam's Porter would be a good candidate,' Sir John suggested, not taking his eyes off Hooke. 'Or the Basketman.'

'You must question them,' the King told him. 'Do it straightaway.'

'I have more questions to ask of these Fellows, Your Majesty.'

'Ask them, then. But cool your temper.'

Sir John forced a more measured tone. 'You had a hand in building Bedlam, did you not, Mr. Hooke?'

Hooke bridled. To use the term Bedlam disrespected the great care with which he had designed the Hospital, and the great care shown to its patients.

'It is the *Bethlehem Hospital.* And more than merely a hand. I am its architect.'

'The *Palace Beautiful*, I have heard it called,' Sir John said. 'A costly gaol for the cracked-brained.'

Hooke, deeply offended, straightened his back as much as possible. 'I designed it for the residents' comfort and recuperation. It is well-aired and filled with light. Its regime, under Dr. Allen, is greatly beneficial.'

'I have walked its galleries, Mr. Hooke. Residents, you say? Inmates, I say. Most are confined to their rooms. Shackled, even. Or else kept away from the visitors, down in the cellars.' The Justice snorted at Hooke. 'High walls surround it. It is a pretty prison.'

'None are kept down in the cellars—'

Sir John slowly drew apart his lips, baring his teeth. Halted by the expression—for it was animalistic—Hooke felt himself recoil from the man.

Abruptly dismissing Hooke, the Justice turned to Sir Christopher. 'And a place to obtain bodies for your cutting of them up.'

Sensing it was his turn to be insulted, Sir Christopher removed his apron, folded it neatly, and placed it on the table beside the dead woman.

'Here at the Royal Society, we investigate nature,' he said equably. 'The New Philosophy seeks new knowledge, and a new method of knowing, through experience and trials. As His Majesty exhorts us to do. We are his Royal Society. We wish to show and better understand God's creation, to further glorify Him and His work.'

The Fellows crowding the repository could hear the capital *H*s in Wren's reverent tone.

'By cutting it up, and breaking it apart?' Sir John swept his stick expansively at all the cabinets in the room. 'By keeping freakish monstrosities and memoranda of mortality? This child, for example, pickled in a jar? This man's skin, flayed off him like the Saint Bartholomew's?'

'Unlike that saint, he was dead at the time,' Sir Christopher said.

'It was a gift to the College,' Hooke added. 'We did not remove his skin. Also, those you call "freakish monstrosities" are part of God's creation. They are allowed by Him.'

Sir John angled his forehead towards Hooke as if ready to butt him. 'What new knowledge could you glean from opening this girl? This was an entertainment, nothing more.'

'We sought to stimulate her brain and spinal cord,' Sir Christopher explained, 'and her muscles, to impart movement to the corpse. We——'

Sir John banged his stick on the wooden boards of the dais. 'You would have her dancing, even after she was dead! You know well what she keeps inside her. Her meat. Her sinews. Her brain, where once her thoughts resided, her sadnesses and joys and her pictures of the world. You sought diversion from a melancholy occupant of Bedlam. Just as those who pay to see them still alive, in their torments, in their manias or mopishness, exhibiting their strange behaviours.'

'I wished to observe the brain microscopically,' Hooke said, indignation making his voice quiver. 'I have observed *animalcules* in rainwater a thirtieth of the thickness of a human hair. Think of the Bolognian stone, which retains its light to then release it in the dark. Does the material of the brain, similarly, withhold its memories? We might see them when we open the black box of the head. Perhaps memories—'

Sir John's expression was openly disbelieving.

'Our experimental trials are by the by,' Hooke huffed. 'We have a woman who should not be here. Unlawfully killed, certainly, but not here. *You*, Justice, are responsible for finding her murderer.'

'Unlawfully killed, yes. Of the here or no, I am yet undecided.'

Sir John looked down at the dead woman, his mouth curling with distaste at the sight of her violated head.

'Who was it, then, who recognised her?'

Both Hooke and Sir Christopher pointed out the flamboyant, fleshy young man dressed in blue. As all eyes in the repository had already swivelled towards Harry, it was unnecessary assistance.

Harry, straightening his peruke, advanced through the Fellows until he stood self-consciously next to the King and before the Justice.

'Diana was my neighbour in Bloomsbury Square,' he said. 'She lived there with her father, Sir Benedict Cantley.'

Sir John did not try to hide his surprise. This man's voice owned the sounds of a townsman. Not as abrasive as some—he had done some work to hide it.

Not the voice he expected from a Fellow of the Royal Society.

He pointed a stubby finger.

'I am Mr. Henry Hunt,' Harry supplied, knowing it was demanded.

Sir John looked down his nose at him, then flicked it with the same finger. He turned to regard the rest of the Fellows. 'None of you would have known she was not the girl from Bedlam? Unless *Mr.* Hunt had recognised her.' The *Mister* was stressed, placing Harry into a lower bracket.

The Fellows stood contritely, as if they were somehow at fault for Sir John's words being true.

'None of you?' Sir John repeated.

When they all assured him not, the Justice's expression was sceptical.

'London houses perhaps half a million people,' Hooke said impatiently. 'You cannot be surprised.'

'Can I not? I am surprised, a little, Mr. Hooke. Your number may be the real one, but moving among people of quality the place becomes far smaller.'

Harry noticed Sir John's glance at him as he spoke of 'quality,' and felt the heat rise in his cheeks. He thought of his old friend Colonel Michael Fields, who also had been bluff. But Fields had believed firmly in equality between men. Sir John's manner made him seem convinced of a unique superiority.

Sir John glared at them all like a fierce schoolmaster.

'No need to admonish them so,' the King told him quietly. 'Hmm? You are among gentlemen here.'

Sir John looked prepared to admonish even his King, but bowed his head instead. 'Your Majesty,' he said, which risked nothing.

'I knew Diana,' the King told him. 'Sir Benedict presented her at Court. In life, she was exquisite.'

'This news will undo him, Your Majesty.' Sir John sniffed, then redirected his attention to Harry. 'How well do you know the Cantleys?'

'Only since I moved to Bloomsbury Square, three months or so ago. I have spoken with Sir Benedict on a couple of occasions only. At our second meeting, Diana being with him, he introduced me to her. Nothing more.'

'You knew her well enough to identify her on the table.'

'Hence my stopping her dissection.' Harry paused, then added, 'I have also seen her riding, leaving, and returning to her house.'

'So, something more than nothing more.' Sir John chuckled bleakly. 'What was your conversation with Sir Benedict, on these *couple of occasions?*'

Harry shifted uncomfortably. He would prefer not to be questioned among the Fellows, but Sir John looked entirely unconcerned for his privacy. 'He is a merchant. I sought his advice on where best to invest my money.'

'You are deliberately imprecise. A merchant? He is the Deputy-Governor of the Royal African Company. I doubt not where he advised you to place your money.'

Those Fellows who paid money into the Africa trade shifted uncomfortably. But why should they not invest? The Company held a monopoly on all the ports for five thousand miles of the West African coast, from Cape Sallee to the Cape of Good Hope. The returns were spectacular, and almost always assured.

Sir John had not broken eye contact with Harry. 'Do you remember your conversation with Diana on the *occasion* of your introduction?'

Harry remembered it clearly. Until her father put a stop to it— by leading her off by her arm—she had been flirtatious. Even then she had looked back, holding Harry's gaze for a second.

'We spoke of living in Bloomsbury Square,' Harry said. 'And of the previous occupants of my house, who were mindful of their privacy. And of the fineness of the weather.'

Sir John turned to the King with a look of enquiry. Did he wish to ask anything more of this fop-dressed neighbour? The King, sitting elegantly with one leg crossed over the other, gave a little shake of his head. A permission to continue as the Justice saw fit.

Sir John resumed his scrutiny of Hooke. 'Did your dissecting of her show how Diana was murdered?'

Hooke cautiously moved around the Justice and further pulled down the sheet, revealing a large, ugly wound on Diana's ribcage. 'The method is plain. Her murderer used a pointed weapon, long and narrow.'

'I wonder if you should be in Bedlam, Mr. Hooke. For this wound is wide.'

'We cut around it, to follow its way and find its depth.'

'You say "we." Which of you opened her up, and which of you decided upon the method of her killing?'

'Me, Sir Christopher, and Harry—I mean, Mr. Henry Hunt.'

Sir John performed a doubtful twitch of his head. 'I know you are qualified for such work, Mr. Hooke. You are renowned throughout London for your experimental trials. Sir Christopher, too, I know of your prodigious interests. Natural philosophy, mathematics, anatomy. And your shared endeavours, both of you, in rebuilding the new London. But who is Mr. Hunt, that he should assist you?'

'I was Mr. Hooke's apprentice here at Gresham,' Harry answered for himself. 'Then Operator, then Observator, the role now taken by Mr. Crawley.'

'At first I took you for a gentleman. Now I learn you are not.'

'Judge me as you wish, sir. Whatever you think of me changes me not, neither one way nor another.'

Hooke looked approvingly at Harry for speaking up for himself, although he disliked the antagonism in the room. Sir John's belligerence provoked them all.

'You fear not the judgement of a Justice, Mr. Hunt?' Sir John said. 'We shall see, shall we not?'

'Sir John!' The King was exasperated. 'These are my cleverest of men. To denigrate them so is to do them disservice.'

'I would have liked to see the wound for myself, Your Majesty. I could have matched it to a weapon.'

'I commanded it.' The King left his chair and joined the men on the dais. 'The hole was a triangle, showing the weapon's cross-section.' He showed the size of it by gapping his finger and thumb. 'Diana's killer did not push far enough to poke it through her back.'

'It was a single stab to her chest,' Hooke said. 'Entering into her lung.'

'She needed little of your natural philosophy, did she, then?' Sir John scoffed. 'To discover what killed her.'

'No, indeed,' Hooke quietly agreed.

'She died quickly,' Sir Christopher added.

'We must be thankful for that, I suppose,' Sir John said. 'An *estoc*, then, or a tuck?' He mimed a thrusting action. 'There is no edge to those weapons. The danger is all at the point.'

The King nodded. 'Such swords are made to pierce armour.'

'A fencing sword, perhaps?'

'A little thicker,' the King replied.

'I thought, more like a smallsword,' Sir Christopher said.

Sir John's face fell. 'Half the gentlemen in London carry small-swords.'

'But almost all only gentlemen, as they are expensive weapons.' The King looked encouragingly at the Justice. 'A thin one, too. Thinner than most.'

Hooke produced a piece of paper from his pocket. 'Mr. Hunt thought to make a print from the original hole.'

'I put ink over the wound,' Harry explained, 'then impressed this paper upon it.'

For the first time, Sir John's voice suggested something near approval. 'This may confirm her murderer, if we find the weapon's owner.'

He bent back down to Diana, studying her skin, her colour, the way her face had settled. Her half-open eyes disturbed him. Her mouth, too, was slightly open, as if about to speak.

'Does your New Philosophy extend to knowing *when* she was killed?'

'She is no longer stiff, so I would say at least two days ago,' Hooke informed him.

'Although in this heat, it may have been yesterday,' Sir Christopher said.

'We stored her overnight and this morning in the anatomy room, which stays cool.' Hooke looked to Crawley for confirmation. 'It is difficult to be precise about these things.'

'Not as long ago as three days,' Harry said.

'You sound sure of it, Mr. Hunt,' Sir John said. 'Three days, no more?'

'Her decay would be more advanced. Her smell stronger.'

'So, yesterday, the day before yesterday, but not the day before that. Then kept at Bedlam until ten of the clock last night, as Crawley tells it.' Sir John looked in turn at each of the three men, then at the King.

'Who would wish Diana Cantley dead?' the King asked, looking around him at the men with him on the dais, and the other Fellows congregating before him in the repository. 'Hmm?'

'As yet, I have no answer for you, Your Majesty, but I shall find him. Have no fear of that.' Sir John's posture dared the Fellows to doubt him. These men who had come to watch a girl be unbraced and broken apart. Their not knowing she was Diana Cantley scarcely lessened his distaste for them.

'Mend her head, as best as you are able,' he said to Sir Christopher.

'Cover her, too. It is undignified for her to be left naked. Keep her here and lock the room until I fetch Sir Benedict. Your Majesty, I must now go to tell him of his daughter's death. I must inform the Coroner, too, of her murder.'

The King took him by the shoulder. 'I shall send a man to the Coroner, Sir John. The matter, to me, seems simple. Two women were exchanged, one for another. The unhappy woman at Bethlehem and Sir Benedict's daughter, Diana. Presumably, Diana was killed there, at the Hospital, by a sword's thrust. You must question the Porter. For he, I am sure, knows more. The Basketman mentioned, too.'

'Her father must be told first, Your Majesty, surely?'

'Bethlehem is but a short walk away. By the time you see Sir Benedict, we may hope you will already have apprehended his daughter's murderer.'

He increased his grip on Sir John's shoulder and steered him nearer to Harry. 'I have a further suggestion, too.'

Harry's heart sank. He sensed what was coming. And it would not be a suggestion. It would be a royal command.

'Mr. Hunt here is the perfect man to help you.'

Sir John looked dubiously at Harry, then at his King.

'He may not look like him, nor indeed, sound like him, but you should never judge a book by its cover. Hmm? Is that not what they say? Mr. Hunt has demonstrated his usefulness to me in the past.'

The King placed his other hand onto Harry's shoulder and stood between the two men. His expression now was jovial, as if the visit to Gresham had pleased him, proving more entertaining than expected.

'Together, I insist, you will find the murderer of Diana Cantley.'

CHAPTER THREE

THE BEDLAM
ALTERCATION

Injured as a child—a fall from a window disjointing his left knee, and another fall breaking his thigh—Sir John walked with a severe limp; nevertheless, he moved rapidly. He also had the habit of whistling as he walked. Harry recognised the tune, solemn and repetitive: 'An Old Man Is a Bed Full of Bones.'

Going through Little Moorgate, Harry donated a sixpence to a beggar in a soldier's coat, whose jaw had been partly shot away.

'A whole pig?' Fenn said in astonishment. It was the first time Harry had heard the man speak. In contrast to the Justice's boom, Fenn's voice was a rasping whisper, suggesting damage done to his throat.

'I had nothing smaller,' Harry answered, unsure if the Marshal-man approved of or deplored his act of charity. Sir John, evidently, disliked it; his brow was pronouncedly furrowed.

They turned to follow the wall surrounding Bethlehem Hospital's grounds.

Completed just five years before, the Hospital was vast. Nearly two hundred yards across, it comprised a pair of long galleries, one above the other, supported by a raised basement. At each end and in its centre stood grand stone-fronted pavilions, the walls between them built of brick.

As the three men approached it along the drive, to either side of them lay pleasant tree-lined gardens, and in front a large terrace. Their boots crunched on the raked gravel.

Two statues watched from above the gateway, one named *Raving Madness*, and the other, *Melancholy Madness*. Twins, only their expressions marked them apart. Both were modelled on a servant of Oliver Cromwell's—his Porter, Daniel, said to be seven and a half feet tall—after he found himself residing in the previous building.

At the top of some steps, the central pavilion's outer doors stood open. Going through them, the three men entered its tiled lobby. An interior gate—the 'penny-gate'—made of stout iron bars, was firmly closed, as was the door to the Porter's lodge.

Sir John scraped the bars with his blackthorn stick. After a few seconds of waiting, he struck each one of them in turn.

A burly man, nearly as wide as the Justice, appeared, wearing the Hospital's sky blue uniform. His anger at all the banging turned to uncertainty when he recognised the Marshalman. He did not know the bullnecked man clattering with the stick, nor the fop standing with them.

The fop knew him, though, for he called him Mr. Matthews. As Harry introduced the Justice, it dawned on the Porter who it was: the architect's young assistant, but for some reason in disguise.

'You come to see a patient?' Matthews asked them, unlocking the penny-gate. His voice was a bored baritone; he had said this a thousand times before. 'Or do you wish a tour?'

'We come to see you, Matthews,' Sir John said. 'For we must speak with you.'

'With me, Justice?'

'About a murder.'

'Why, I know nothing of a murder!'

'What is this *commotion*?' asked another man from inside. He was small, with a high-pitched querulous voice, and wore his peruke pulled too low on his forehead.

'We have business with this man.' Sir John placed the end of his stick onto Matthews's chest. 'This Cerberus at his gate.'

'What do you want with our Porter, sirs?'

'Why, sir, to question him. A girl was killed. He knows of it.'

'Who are you, sir? What is your authority?'

'I am Sir John Reresby, the Justice of Peace for Westminster and Middlesex. A Court Justice, appointed by the King. And who, sir— the fuck—are you?'

The man was too astonished to answer.

'This is the Hospital's Physician,' Harry supplied. 'Dr. Thomas Allen.'

Having attended his autopsies of dead patients, Harry knew Allen well. A Fellow of the Royal Society and on its committee, the Physician shared Sir Christopher's interest in the brain, seeking the morbid, material causes of lunacy.

Allen recognised Harry—despite his jack-a-dandy clothes—and welcomed him with an uncertain bow. The Marshalman, who visited Bethlehem from time to time, was familiar. Sir John he did not know—when the Justice had visited the Hospital, Allen was else-where—but Allen often dealt with patients far rougher. Recovering from the shock of the Justice's coarse language, the Physician assumed his calming voice.

'Let us not speak of this here. Come to my office. But please, no more *commotion*, or you risk distressing my patients.'

He beckoned them into the panelled lobby, which was decorated with marble tablets honouring benefactors, and cherub heads carved in wood.

Crossing its polished floor, Fenn walked close behind Matthews, as if expecting him to run.

☿

INSIDE, BETHLEHEM WAS AIRY AND LIGHT. Its plaster still appeared new, the paintwork still fresh. The full length of the down-stairs floor—the men's gallery—stretched away to either side of them, its furthest doorways a hundred yards off, appearing tiny. For the sake of coolness, the galleries were lit by the flatter light from the north. On the south side of the building were the patients' rooms.

The patients allowed the liberty of the gallery stood in desultory groups, or else preferred their solitude. Some pressed up to the win-dows, feeling the warmth of the sunlight; perhaps they longed for the freedom outside. Others sat in chairs, staring gloomily. One man remonstrated against Dissenters.

A straw-hatted man introduced himself to Harry. 'I am the Prince of the Air! I command an army of eagles!'

Another hopped, thinking the floor burned his feet.

There were other people, too, whose attire included hats and parasols, and who exuded the unmistakable air of content.

'It is busy with visitors,' Sir John observed, shaking his head. 'A strange entertainment, to seek diversion through these creatures' frenzical extravagancies.'

'Some visit family,' Allen replied. 'They do not all come to ogle.'

'And I might call my wig a wheelbarrow. You want their money.'

Allen made as if to speak, then stopped himself. Sir John looked satisfied at the Physician conceding the point.

A voice echoed, carrying from the women's gallery upstairs: a woman singing an aria. The sound made Harry think wistfully of childhood, although he could not grasp quite why.

Allen took them into a large office containing his desk piled with documents, a few simple chairs, an ancient workbench along one wall, and a tall glass-fronted cabinet filled with jars and bottles of medicines and mixtures.

As the Physician lowered himself into a large and comfortable-looking chair behind his desk, Harry noticed he had been careful to leave the door open.

'We are curious to know what took place last night,' Sir John said. 'Your Porter sent no suicide to Gresham, but instead a girl, murdered.'

'Sebiliah killed *herself*!' Matthews protested. 'With a needle!'

'A sword for this girl. I've seen the hole.' Sir John placed his walking stick across Allen's desk with unhurried deliberation. Allen's look of alarm showed he found the movement more intimidating than all his banging with it.

Harry felt sorry for Dr. Allen, whom he knew as a kindly man who cared deeply for his patients: he had forbidden the Fellows from using lunatics for their trials of infusing sheep blood. A close friend of Mr. Hooke's, Dr. Allen had worked together with him on building the Hospital from the first measuring of the ground.

'Sebiliah is the name of the suicide?' Harry asked him.

'Sebiliah Barton. Here for a year, or thereabouts. She suffered depressing passions. Pliable, though. Rarely a trouble for the staff.'

'We were all fond of her,' Matthews said. 'Despite her quietness.'

'Hannah discovered her,' Allen said. 'Last night.'

'Hannah's my daughter, sir,' Matthews explained, eager to show helpfulness. 'She's a Nurse here. Did her best to save Sebiliah.'

'The girl you gave over was Diana Cantley,' Sir John said. 'Killed by the thrust of a sword.'

'Cantley? She was not one of our patients,' Allen said, bewildered.

Sir John sneered at him. 'No, she was not. Yet Diana was the girl received.'

'You say Sebiliah died last night,' Harry said. 'The woman Thomas Crawley collected died at least two days ago.'

'And you gave her to him, Matthews.' Sir John smiled grimly. 'She did not, I think, venture from here alone.' He grasped the Porter by his uniform's collar. 'You gave over no Bedlam girl, but a girl of high quality. Sir Benedict Cantley's daughter.'

Matthews went to remove the Justice's hand, but the Marshal-man, Fenn, stepped in, pushing his face close to the Porter's and gripping his wrist.

'I gave Sebiliah to Gresham's man,' Matthews pleaded to Fenn's bent nose. 'Dr. Allen ordered it. I did it.'

'Another man helped you,' Harry said. 'A Basketman. So said Thomas Crawley.'

He motioned for the two men with him to let Matthews go. Sir John, after Fenn's enquiring look, nodded his agreement they should do so.

Matthews stood gasping, with spittle stringing between his lips and his eyes shiny with tears. 'William Jones,' he said. '*He* put her on the cart.'

'This was Sebiliah. You are sure of it?' Harry asked.

'God smite me down, I swear it! Hannah found her in her room. Up on the women's gallery. She couldn't stop her—from dying, I mean—so me and William took her—William Jones, the same man with me when your Mr. Crawley took her—to the room where we keep the dead. Then Millicent—my wife, who's Matron—washed her. We covered her over. It was all proper, sir, and respectful of the body—'

'Stop babbling, Matthews!' Sir John shouted.

'Sir John, we must speak with the Matron, and William Jones, who helped carry Sebiliah,' Harry said.

'I know that perfectly well, Mr. Hunt! Fetch them, Dr. Allen, so we may question them.'

'Have no worry, Mr. Matthews,' Allen reassured the Porter. Then he shouted through the open door in a startlingly carrying voice. 'Basketmen! To me!'

Immediately, they heard footsteps running, and another man shouting, 'Basketmen! To Dr. Allen!'

Three large men reached the office. All wore the same sky-blue uniform. One man was tall, and two were broad. All looked powerfully built.

Fenn looked to Sir John a little uncertainly. The Justice reclaimed his walking stick from the table.

'Mr. Carter, Mr. Jones, Mr. Langdale,' Allen welcomed them. 'Our Porter is in trouble. These gentlemen think him a murderer.'

The broadest of them—Carter, the Hospital's Steward—took a pace towards Sir John. 'What hog shit is this?'

Fenn blocked him with his arm. 'Stand down, Carter.'

'We ask questions, nothing more,' Harry said. 'I am Henry Hunt, of the Royal Society. This is the Justice of Peace, Sir John Reresby. Mr. Fenn, I see, you already know.'

'Do not speak for me, Mr. Hunt,' Sir John said hotly. '*I* will question these scoundrels. If *I* need to, and if *I* decide to.'

'You would do better, then, to speak politely,' Dr. Allen told him. Some steel had entered his voice. 'None of these men have done wrong that you know of. Yet you insult them.'

Sir John pointed his stick at the Physician. 'I will know of their wrong!'

Carter, Jones, and Langdale moved between Allen and the Justice. Fenn joined Sir John, shoulder to shoulder.

'A woman was delivered to Gresham College,' Harry continued, as if unaware of the altercation. 'For dissection. But not the woman who died here last night, as we expected her to be. You see why we are confused.'

'*I* shall speak with these men,' Sir John insisted. '*I* am the Justice!'

Dr. Allen lowered himself onto the chair behind his desk. 'Let us begin again,' he said. 'For we seem to have got off on the wrong foot.'

CHAPTER FOUR

THE BEDLAM SUICIDE

One of the gallery maids had fetched the Matron, Millicent Matthews, who now took up a chair next to her husband. Mrs. Matthews was barrel-torsoed and impressively hefty, and her countenance said little could shock her. She wore the same uniform as all the staff, its sleeves rolled up to show remarkable forearms, equal to any of the men's.

When Dr. Allen told her Sebiliah never reached Gresham, she needed it repeated. She was told again by the architect's assistant, young Mr. Hunt, who looked as if he had come into fortune. Instead, apparently, Sebiliah was exchanged for another woman, a well-to-do sir's daughter who lived in Bloomsbury Square.

The Matron still looked bemused, tutting loudly each time she thought of it.

Hannah Matthews sat with her parents. She shared their build, but had a more trusting face and a less careworn manner.

'I shall start with you, Dr. Allen,' Sir John announced. He sat in a chair, curling and uncurling his enormous fingers, his stick leaning beside him. 'Were you here last night, when your suicide was collected?'

'I had just arrived from my private asylum in Finsbury,' Allen told him. 'Mr. Langdale delivered the news of Sebiliah's death to me there.'

Langdale, the tallest of the Basketmen, taciturn-seeming and with a drooping eyelid, assented this was so.

'Why should you be fetched?' Sir John asked Allen. 'Is there need to call you, if you are elsewhere, whenever a patient dies here?'

Carter, the Steward, answered. 'I knew a body was required at Gresham College. I wanted Dr. Allen's say-so.'

'We discussed it right here, did we not, Mr. Carter?' Allen said. 'I share this room with the Hospital's Apothecary. Hence all the jars in the cabinet there. Mr. Lester worked in here last night, as did I. He shall vouch for me.'

'I shall speak with him,' Sir John said. 'If you need *vouching for.* You never saw Sebiliah dead, then?'

'I had no need to. Matron confirmed her death.'

'You do not quite answer my question,' Sir John said. 'Did you see her dead, or no?'

Allen looked abashed. 'I never did. I did not go upstairs at all. So not to where Sebiliah died, nor downstairs from where she was collected.'

'This was definitely Sebiliah Barton, not Diana Cantley.' Sir John looked around the room at all the other staff.

'There is no doubt,' Allen said. 'Poor Hannah here found her.'

'She was knitting. She used one of her needles,' Hannah said faintly, reaching for her father's hand.

'Sebiliah found the jugular vein, you see.' The Matron showed them on her own neck, a point just below the jaw.

'You allow the patients to knit?' Sir John looked astounded.

'The women are encouraged to,' the Matron replied.

'An activity conducive to their calmness,' Allen added.

'Hardly conducive to hers,' Sir John said. 'It was lax of you.'

'Over the past few weeks, she seemed serene,' Allen said. 'I never suspected her of intending self-harm.'

'That was your mistake, then.'

'It shall remain upon my conscience.'

Sir John was unconcerned by the Physician's conscience. 'So, you stayed in this office, where you arranged the delivery to Gresham College of your suicide, rather than bother yourself with seeing her.'

Allen raised his chin at the Justice. 'My staff know their business. I sent a messenger to Mr. Hooke. Sebiliah's father was a widower. He died not long after he brought her here. No other relatives, so far as we know. Nor visitors, apart from those who come from curiosity, and the staff who ministered to her needs.'

Harry, who was half leaning, half sitting against the windowsill, noticed Hannah glance at the two Basketmen, Jones and Langdale. They both stood in stonelike stillness, cousins of the statues over the Hospital's gates, directing their eyes at the wall in front of them.

Sir John missed the look. 'So she was yours to do with as you wished.'

'Too many are, who die within Bethlehem.' Dr. Allen looked wistfully into space, seeing an imaginary, better world. 'I wish it were not so.'

'Does it not make you queasy, giving over bodies for the cutting of them up?'

'For the dead, my care is over,' Allen said. 'The Lord shall take them then. We who study anatomy must necessarily find bodies. By the law, we may dissect only criminals and lunatics.'

'If so serene, why was Sebiliah still here?' Harry asked him. 'Your list must be long of people needing admission.'

'She could not have coped with the world outside. Here, she led an ordered life, which gave her no worry.'

'Perhaps she hid her torments, knowing you would relax your watching of her.'

'I cannot refute you, Mr. Hunt. We are given only the external signs to show the workings of our patients' minds. It is these we must interpret. Otherwise, how would we make our judgements upon their wellness? If not for aberrant behaviour, we would never know the insane from the sane. If Sebiliah's equanimity had continued, we would have released her—properly so—to make way for another.'

Hannah shifted in her chair spiritlessly. 'She was well, and getting better.'

'Did you see Sebiliah use the needle?' Harry asked her.

Allen did not wait for the Nurse's reply. 'You infer the hand of another?'

'He does not,' Sir John said. 'We seek the facts of Diana Cantley's murder—which yet we do not know. Mr. Hunt, we are not here about the melancholy woman.'

Ignoring the Justice, Matthews, the Porter, also spoke for his daughter. 'Hannah found her already bleeding.'

Hannah put her face in her hands, trying not to sob. 'I only happened to walk past . . . She died a minute after I got there. Then my mother came.'

'At what time was this?' Harry enquired, looking at Millicent Matthews rather than her daughter.

'In the evening . . . just after nine,' the Matron answered.

'Only an hour before Crawley came to collect her. You know it for certain?'

'The nine o'clock bell had sounded. We ring it so the patients know to go back to their rooms. The same bell clears the visitors.'

'Who rang the bell last night?'

'I did,' the Steward, Carter, affirmed. 'And promptly so.'

'But the gathering of the patients, the taking them to their rooms, and the locking of all the doors must take some while.'

'Not all are allowed the liberty of the galleries,' Mrs. Matthews said. 'About half of them, I'd say, at the moment.'

Her husband nodded his agreement. 'Even so, it can take a half hour or more, if any are being difficult.'

'Were there such difficulties last night?' Harry asked him.

'The usual pickle of getting lunatics into their rooms.'

'Did you have many visitors that late?'

'It was still busy, yes. They get under your feet, sometimes.'

'So, the patients were returning to their rooms, and visitors were leaving.'

Sir John scowled. 'Mr. Hunt, you are still distracted. We must know when Diana Cantley was exchanged for the Bedlam suicide.'

'I think of Diana. You recall the cosmetics on her face? I think she came to Bethlehem as a visitor.'

Sir John rubbed his chin. 'It would explain her presence here. But who did she come to see? Dr. Allen, were any of the visitors here last night people of quality?'

'As I said, I remained in my office. Mr. Carter? Mr. Matthews?'

'The day before, I think,' Harry said. 'Diana Cantley has been dead two days or more.'

The Porter and the Steward shrugged at one another. 'A few during the day. Not any that evening, I can think of,' Carter answered.

'You cease to notice them after a while,' Matthews said. 'Unless they get in your way, or interfere with the patients.'

Sir John gave him a hard look. 'Interfere?'

'Sometimes the visitors cause them disquiet, to see how they respond. They insult them, or prod them, or push them.'

'Or worse,' Carter muttered.

'We ask them then to leave,' Millicent said, wringing her hands. The muscles on her forearms flexed impressively.

'Our patients' well-being is paramount,' Allen said.

Harry gave him a sympathetic nod. 'How did you know a body was wanted at Gresham?'

'I attended Mr. Hooke's New Philosophical Club, at the Angel and Crown the evening before last. I promised a body to him when one became available.'

'How fortunate one was,' Sir John said. 'And so soon.'

'It is not suspicious, Justice,' Allen protested.

'I find it so! As I find all you medicos and natural philosophers who desire dead bodies for your . . . undertakings.'

Sir John pinched the bridge of his nose and let out a loud sigh. Then he turned his attention to the one man in the room who had not yet spoken.

☿

WILLIAM JONES WAS BROAD AND BIG-BELLIED, and his head was newly shaved. His full beard, uncombed and untidy, reached his sternum; when he spoke, it hid the movements of his mouth. His eyes were black and shrewd, with thick eyebrows arched over them constantly, as if he delivered the punchline to a joke.

'You are one of the Basketmen,' Sir John told him, although he knew.

Jones pulled at his earlobe. 'Fetching and carrying, I do, the cleaning, and delivering of messages.' He had a strong and expressive Welsh accent. 'And the feeding of the patients. Cutting up their bread, their cheese, the like.'

'The carrying you do includes the carrying of the dead,' Sir John said.

'When needs be, yes,' Jones replied.

'Mr. Matthews said you helped him bring the body down from the upstairs gallery.'

'Helped him? I did not.'

Matthews was open-mouthed and wide-eyed.

The Justice regarded Jones hopefully. 'But he said you helped him carry Sebiliah down the stairs.'

'Lying, then, he was.'

Matthews looked murderously at him. Jones's eyebrows raised further. 'I did not *help* him, see. Carried her down, I did. On my own. Mr. Porter walked with me. I did not *help* him. Mr. Porter did not *help* me.'

'Do not test me, Jones,' Sir John growled.

Jones arched his eyebrows even higher.

'You shall not laugh in my lockup, Jones. So, *you* brought the dead woman down the stairs from her room.'

'Yes, Justice. Over my back.'

'An undignified way to treat a body.'

'The quickest way. A stretcher's more awkward on the stairs.'

'Where did you take her then?'

'Down the stairs. To the room for the bodies.'

'The mortuary, you mean. Was Matthews still with you?'

'Walking by me, he was. Not *helping*.'

'You left her there. In the mortuary?'

'The room for the bodies, yes, Justice.'

Sir John puffed out his cheeks. 'Definitely Sebiliah?'

'No doubt.'

'There, on her own?'

'No, Justice.'

There was a pause. 'Well, continue, man! At some time, the two women were exchanged. This may have been the occasion.'

'Other people with her, there was, Justice.'

'Who?' Sir John demanded. 'Who were these people?'

'They was dead people with her, Justice.'

'Fenn, we'll take this pudding with us.'

'You asked. I answered, Justice.'

Dr. Allen pointed an admonishing finger at the Basketman. 'You are being obtuse, Mr. Jones, as well you know. Help the Justice, so he may be on his way.'

Jones looked barely contrite.

'It was both of you who handed her body to Mr. Hooke's boy,' Sir John said.

'Put her on the cart, *I* did, Justice,' Jones answered. 'Stayed by the door, *Mr. Porter* did. Opened the gate, *I* did. Locked it after, *I* did.'

A silence making him think he could bring the matter to a close, Allen lifted himself from his chair.

Harry disappointed him. 'Was any paper signed for Sebiliah's conveyance?'

Sir John's face brightened as the Physician slumped back down. 'You would have a bond, Dr. Allen, to admit a patient, and a certificate of recovery to release one. A similar paper, surely, must cover their deaths.'

'I have not yet prepared the note,' Allen said, looking disquieted.

Sir John guessed why Allen had neglected to do so. 'Given the nature of many of your patients, suicide must happen here often.'

'Even so, we do not care to broadcast such news.'

'Especially so, since you gave her the knitting needle.'

'We can't watch all the lunatics all the time,' Millicent Matthews complained.

'We cannot,' agreed her husband. 'The mad are ten times as many as the staff.'

'I am surprised you class them apart,' Sir John said, eyeballing Jones.

'Did you see Thomas Crawley leave with her?' Harry asked the Welshman.

Jones thought for a second. 'No. Closed the gate, I did. Heard him move off, mind. The horse. Its hooves. On the ground.'

'You saw Mr. and Mrs. Matthews wrap her in the sheet,' Sir John asked him, in his telling way.

'Mrs. Matron undressed her and washed her. Sent us pair out, thinking it more proper, like.'

'You do not quite answer my question,' Sir John said, exasperated. 'Did you see it?'

'The last of it, I saw.'

'It was Sebiliah inside the sheet. You saw her.'

'Yes. Saw her face.'

'Why did she need to be undressed, Mrs. Matthews?' Harry asked.

'For her clothes, sir,' Millicent answered. 'They belong to the Hospital. And I washed her because of all the blood.'

'There must have been a lot of it, if she pierced the jugular vein.' Harry spoke softly, showing her a sympathy lacking from the Justice.

'The sheet's the Hospital's, too,' she said. 'I'll send a gallery maid for it.'

Sir John stamped his boots on the uncarpeted floor. 'You worry about a sheet! Mr. Jones, I ask you this: Did you put another woman on the cart?'

'I cannot rightly say.'

'It is a simple matter of yes or no!'

'Not simple, is it? Not simple.'

'Yes? Or no?' Sir John was almost shouting again.

'I cannot say,' Jones repeated. 'By then, she was wrapped inside a sheet.' Even under the beard, his smirk was evident.

Sir John turned to the Marshalman. 'Place the manacles on him, Fenn.'

'Please, Justice,' Allen said. 'Jones has a manner. It is his Welsh way. We have told you all we can.'

'It was Sebiliah put on the cart,' Matthews insisted. 'Or else, let God blind me! If someone else arrived at Gresham College, we are not the cause.'

Sir John examined each of the Bethlehem staff in the room. Physician. Porter. Matron. Nurse. Steward. Basketmen—especially William Jones, who stood imperviously behind his beard.

He sighed wearily and leaned sideways to pick up his stick.

'Show me where she died, then take me through the whole of her last journey, before the cart.'

CHAPTER FIVE

THE WOMEN'S GALLERY

Dr. Allen led them to the Hospital's western pavilion. At the foot of the stairs leading up to the women's gallery, a padlocked gate stopped their way. Allen had sent his staff back to their duties, apart from Jones, who remained in the Physician's office with Fenn guarding him, and Matthews, who made a labour of sorting through his keys and unlocking the gate.

While they waited, Harry went to the nearest room and peered through the viewing hatch let into its door. Inside, a man pushed his forehead against the wires stretched taut across the window. The patients' windows were unglazed for the free passage of air, known to be therapeutic.

The man hummed the same two bars of music over and over.

'He suffers from furious paroxysms,' Allen told Harry, noticing his interest. 'This is a *lucida intervalla*—he is calm for now. Musicians are vulnerable to maladies of the mind.'

'I hear the woman singing, up the stairs.'

'She was famous, in her time. Musicians. Artists. Teachers. All are prone. There are many soldiers here, too, who cannot rid themselves of the fears they felt in wartime.'

Hearing the jangling of the Porter's keys, another man, sleepy-faced and with whey-coloured skin, joined them from a nearby room. He carried a tray laden with dishes of powders, a jar of leeches, and Indian hemp.

Allen introduced him. 'Mr. Jeremy Lester, our Apothecary.'

'Perhaps you saw the dead woman being taken?' Sir John asked Lester.

'Sebiliah did not arrive at Gresham,' Allen explained, after Lester looked stupidly at them.

The Apothecary's head jolted back at the news. 'But we sent her,' he said, as if one must lead to the other.

'Were you here yesterday evening, Mr. Lester?' Sir John asked.

'I said so earlier,' Allen said testily. 'He was.'

'Take a care, Dr. Allen, or I shall think you help him.'

Lester rubbed at his eyelids, which were swollen and dark, as he tried to recall as long ago as yesterday evening. 'Every day's the same among melancholics and maniacs, when you've forgot the variations. I spent most of yesterday in our room—mine and Dr. Allen's. Preparing vesicatories and cantharides.'

'You do not quite answer my question, I note,' Sir John said. 'The evening, particularly.'

Lester shut both eyes tightly, let out a great yawn, then seemed to decide. 'All evening, too, I was there.' He swayed, as if on a ship at sea. 'I prepare the medicines,' he added resentfully. 'Cheaper than buying them in.'

'Were you alone?' Sir John asked him, wondering how reliable this somnolent man would prove.

'Why, no, sir. I was with Dr. Allen, who worked on his papers.'

They left Lester yawning and swaying with his tray at the gateway, and climbed the stairs to the female gallery.

☿

ONCE THROUGH ANOTHER GATE ACROSS THE top of the stairs, Harry could see the full length of the gallery. Identical to the one below, it had the same long line of doorways to the south and the same north-facing windows lighting the corridor.

The same arrangement of patients, too. Some together, some alone. More visitors moved among them, looking in at the sadder patients either confined or preferring the solitude of their rooms.

Upstairs, the woman's singing had become a clear soprano. All her notes were exactly hit, and unstrained as if she performed at half effort.

'I recognise *that* melody,' Sir John said contentedly, looking into the air as if feeling the sound on his face. 'From Cambert's *Pomona*. Pomona sings when hiding from Vertumne.'

This was a side of the Justice Harry had not suspected.

'I knew Cambert,' he went on, seeing Harry's tentative smile of surprise, 'when he ran his Music Academy in Covent Garden.'

Unabashed by the interlude, Sir John pointed his stick for them to follow Allen.

☿

IN THE FIRST ROOM THEY PASSED sat an aged woman, who was naked and completely still on her straw-covered bed. Her bones were made of glass, Allen explained, at least in her delusion; she dared not move for fear of them breaking. She heard her own bones cracking when she did. She could not dress, or be dressed. Chewing food would shatter her teeth; she existed on soups swallowed carefully.

'There are one hundred and twenty cells here,' Allen told them. 'Hers is but one story among many.'

The next cell held a young woman barely out of childhood. She was manacled and gagged, her head shaved ready for blistering. When Harry caught her eye, she squirmed violently on her mattress. He could see she existed in a state of terror.

Spotting unfairness, Sir John waved at her with his stick. 'Why does she get a mattress, the other woman straw?'

'Straw is more hygienic for the dirty patients,' Allen explained, looking slyly amused at Sir John's revulsion.

'Why the gag across her mouth?' Harry asked.

'She utters profanities, nasty enough to raise Satan's eyebrows.'

A third woman sat on her cell floor, her shoulders jerking constantly. Another paced in circles, making loud guttural noises through her tightly pressed lips.

More cells. More stories among many.

During it all, constantly, was the noise of the woman singing.

☿

NO ONE HAD YET REPLACED SEBILIAH BARTON, so her room stood empty. Like all the patients' rooms, it was high-ceilinged and measured nine feet by twelve. Marks across the wall and floor showed where they had been scrubbed. New sheets covered the bed.

'Rather than have a gallery maid do it, Millicent mopped up the blood herself,' Matthews told them.

'Where is the needle?' Harry asked him.

'Back with the others. They're all the same.'

'Will you fetch one?' Sir John asked him. The Porter nodded but didn't move. 'Now, I mean.'

Taken by surprise to be allowed away from the Justice, Matthews looked to Dr. Allen for confirmation, then hurried away.

Harry went to the window and gazed out over the Roman wall and the rest of the City down to the Thames. In the pellucid air he could see Southwark sharply, still bearing its fire's scars from five years before.

Below him, in the Hospital's airing ground, patients were taking their exercise. The charity cases wore plain uniforms, the same sky-blue colour as for the staff. Others wore clothes of better quality, brought to them by family or friends. Some patients, lacking benefaction, had clothes so tattered they were little more than rags.

This had been Sebiliah's view, day after day, for the long and dreary year she spent here.

Matthews returned brandishing a knitting needle. Sir John took it, examined it, and passed it to Harry. 'We are agreed?'

'Not near thick enough to have killed Diana Cantley.'

'You allow visiting gentlemen their swords,' Sir John said to Dr. Allen.

'Yes, for their own protection against violent patients. Besides, when we insisted weapons be deposited in the lobby, there were too many complaints. Swords got mixed together. People took the wrong ones.'

Sir John flicked his nose. 'Matthews, take us the way you walked with William Jones, when he carried the body to the mortuary.'

CHAPTER SIX

THE BEDLAM MORTUARY

At the top of the stairs, they waited while Matthews unlocked the gate, and waited again while he relocked it. The same routine repeated itself at the bottom. Allen led them across the men's gallery, where Matthews opened yet another gate, enabling them to descend the next flight of stairs.

It was far darker down on the basement floor; the windows were narrow horizontal slots at the level of the ground outside. It was notably cooler, too; Harry shivered, even with his waistcoat on. Almost overpowering were the smells: cooking from the kitchen; soap and steam from the laundry; all the pepper stored in rooms rented by the East India Company.

The corridor was eerily empty. Only a few staff occasionally crossed it. Allen led them all the way from the western end of the building to the eastern.

Sir John's limp grew more pronounced as they went. 'William Jones carried her all this way?' he asked.

'If he says so,' Matthews answered sullenly.

'Did he, or no?'

'He did. I walked beside him.'

Eventually, they reached the mortuary. Allen showed them in after Matthews had unlocked it. Deep shelving lined its walls. There were two tables and a large sink. One body lay on a shelf, wrapped to be taken for burial. Sir John asked Matthews to reveal the face. An elderly man. A longtime patient, Allen told them, dead from the rising of the lights.

'You came with Jones carrying the woman,' Sir John told Matthews. 'He put her . . . ?'

Matthews indicated the nearer table.

'Then your wife, the Matron, undressed her. Where were you and Jones?'

'I went back upstairs, to my lodge by the main entrance. He must have gone to change his clothes and wash himself.'

'Mr. Jones would have been bloodstained,' Harry said.

'He looked like a butcher,' Matthews told him. 'A lot of the blood stayed in Sebiliah's room, mind. My wife cleaned all that. Langdale, the other Basketman you met, mopped the rest. The stairs, this corridor.'

'No blood on you, then,' Sir John said.

'I stayed clean,' Matthews said, as if ashamed of it.

'Where did Jones change his clothes?'

'I don't know, Justice. I'd hazard up on the attic floor, where the staff have their rooms. Langdale, most likely, would know. He must've gone to change, too.'

'By the time Jones returned to help wrap the body, he was changed and clean.'

'He didn't return to do so, exactly. He arrived as Millicent finished. I'd got back just before him.'

Sir John, leaning on his stick, spent some time inspecting the room, although what it contained could be taken in at a glance. 'Then where was the body put?'

Matthews showed them the space on the shelving, a distance away from where the dead man lay, against the adjacent wall. 'From habit. We knew she'd be fetched before long. We could have left her on the table.'

'When Gresham's boy arrived, where did you take her?'

'We've a door to the outside. Crawley knows it. A carriage can pull up close.'

'How long was she in here before he came for her?'

'By the time we'd brought her down, and Millicent—my wife, sir—had cleaned her, and wrapped her . . .' Matthews thought through the timing. 'A half hour, perhaps?'

'She died just after nine, away by ten?'

'Easy.'

'Crawley said he took her at ten,' Harry said.

'Gresham is only five minutes away,' Allen said. 'I sent my message to Mr. Hooke as she was being prepared.'

On the edge of losing his temper, Sir John raised his voice suddenly. 'Prepared, you say. For her dissection. You thought her to be

Sebiliah Barton, who was still warm! But this was Diana Cantley!'
He paused, breathing heavily. 'What is this room next door?'

'My anatomy room,' Allen told him.

'Open it up, Matthews,' Sir John said.

'One key I don't have,' the Porter replied. 'Dr. Allen keeps it.'

'It is up in my office, locked inside my desk,' Allen said. 'The
room has simply a table, a sink, and benches for onlookers. It also has
my tools, which is why I keep its key. I use the room when a patient's
dying is difficult to explain.'

'I have been inside,' Harry said. 'It is just as Dr. Allen describes.'

Sir John thought of the journey back to Allen's office, the tiredness in his thigh if he had to wait for long, and his duty to tell Diana's
father the sad news of her death. 'Never mind,' he decided. 'The
room was definitely locked last night?'

'I had no need for it,' Allen answered.

'You do not quite answer—'

'It was locked,' Allen said.

'Where is this outside door?'

Allen led them out of the mortuary, then turned along a short
passageway. Before Matthews could get to his key, Allen unlocked
the external door with his own, and opened it wide.

They faced the Roman wall and a neatly flagged courtyard in
front of it. A shingled roof over the door provided shelter from the
weather and also gave some privacy.

Matthews showed them where Crawley had parked the cart, and
the gate Jones had unlocked, then relocked after Crawley left with
his load.

'I am little the wiser,' Sir John confessed. 'Dr. Allen, I will take
your Basketman with me. Stewing in my lockup for a day or two

may teach him a more English helpfulness. Mr. Matthews, you know not of the dead women being swapped, I am sure of it. And nothing your wife said makes me think otherwise of her.'

☿

BACK IN THE HOSPITAL'S LOBBY, FENN gripped William Jones's collar. Manacles forced the man's hands in front of him. Jones showed only indifference, although he still insisted he knew nothing of Diana Cantley.

'We have learned little of import, I fear, of Diana's murder,' Sir John said aside to Harry. 'Now we must inform Sir Benedict. We shall go to Africa House to do so. He may well be there, and it is closer than Bloomsbury. Mr. Fenn, take the Welshman to my home in Leicester Fields and place him in the lockup.'

Dr. Allen, looking pained, bowed to the Justice, shook hands with Harry, and nodded to Fenn and the manacled Basketman with him.

Matthews waited to lock the penny-gate. Beside him, painted the same sky blue colour as Bethlehem's uniforms, stood a large box with a slot for coins, and an inscribed brass plate.

Pray remember the poor lunatics.

CHAPTER SEVEN

THE GRIEVING FATHER

Only ten minutes' walk from the Hospital to Africa House, but a while since Harry had taken such exercise. Although he carried his hat—its feather wagging behind him like a tail—he still had to blink away his sweat. His feet ached. Through the thin soles of his Moroccan leather boots, he could feel every jagged stone.

Passing a courtyard, Sir John—energy now returned—pointed out a line of people standing inside it. 'That is the office to bind yourself to servitude on the plantations,' he said.

Most of those queuing were young men alone, but there were whole families, too, with thin children looking scared. Mean-faced men patrolled them, watching for a change of heart.

'At least they have some say,' the Justice continued. 'Spiriters lure many, using kidnap or false promises. I have argued for ships to be searched before their departure for those put aboard reluctantly. There is yet no law to prevent it.'

'Little choice, or no choice at all,' Harry said.

'A rogue's market,' Sir John replied.

By the synagogue on Creechurch Lane, Sir John gave Harry a complicit look as if they should both share his disapproval, then led the way along Sugar Loaf Alley, whistling '*If All the World Were Paper.*'

☿

ONCE THE HOME OF SIR NICHOLAS THROGMORTON, Queen Elizabeth's Ambassador to France, Whitchurch House was now the headquarters of the Royal African Company. Most people called it Africa House. It was large but nondescript, remarkable only for just escaping the Great Conflagration.

'I have thought to invest in the Africa trade,' Sir John said, slowing as they crossed the courtyard.

'At Gresham, you sounded disapproving,' Harry said.

'The reconstituted Company far outperforms the old. You hear claims of fine returns, nowadays, though I doubt the more excessive.'

'Sir Benedict told me that last year it paid fifty-five percent above the value of each share,' Harry said, glad Sir John had chosen to rest before knocking. 'But it suffers from the old Company's debts. Antagonising the Dutch cost it dearly. Once those monies are paid, he expects quadruple the return.'

'Still an enterprise too much of luck, to my mind,' Sir John said, resuming his way to the house. 'Vessels flounder. And with the distances involved, there is a wait for your profits. That has put me off it.'

'If you own stock, you spread your risk. There is no delay if you wish to sell your shares. And the Company now has rights from the Mine Royal, so earns from any gold it discovers.'

'Of course, there are those who talk against the trade, perceiving unfairness.'

Harry regarded the Justice quizzically.

'The Company has monopoly, which some rail against. Privateers, too, wish access to Africa's west coast.'

'We should not discuss it with the father now.'

'Another time, undoubtedly,' Sir John agreed.

☿

GUESSING THEIR NEWS, THE DOORMAN LED them with great solemnity up the grand stairway. He knocked at an office door and took them straight in.

Sir Benedict Cantley was gaunt, with a deep cleft in his chin. His eyebrows grew wildly towards a bald pate, the hair around its sides falling in a tangle. Once good-looking, now he was sixty or so his features had fallen; on the wall behind him, a portrait by Sir Peter Lely provided evidence of the change.

A large graze on Sir Benedict's forehead began to bruise.

Recognising Sir John, and—with some confusion—his new neighbour in Bloomsbury Square, Sir Benedict rose slowly from his chair. He dismissed the doorman, who pulled the door softly to. The room's curtains were drawn together against the sunlight; shutting the door put them into deep gloom.

'You bring news of Diana,' Sir Benedict said. He reached out a hand to support himself against his desk. 'Your faces tell me it is not the news I hoped for.'

'Benedict, sadly, we do.' For the first time since Harry had heard it, Sir John's voice was quiet.

Sir Benedict coughed to clear his throat. 'You have . . . found her?'

'There is no soft way to tell you. She was murdered.'

Sir Benedict froze. His face drained of colour. Sir John and Harry, both thinking him about to fall, stepped forwards to steady him.

He shrugged them away. 'There can be no doubt?'

'I have seen her,' Sir John answered gently. 'Mr. Hunt here—I believe he is your neighbour—recognised her first.'

'It is definitely Diana,' Harry said. 'My deepest commiserations.'

'She lies at Gresham College,' Sir John said.

Sir Benedict's confusion was apparent. 'Gresham? Why should Diana be there?'

Sir John steered around the news of her dissection. 'We must ask all you know of her movements.'

'When last I saw her, she made her way to Covent Garden. She never made mention of Gresham College. Not once in her life, as far as I recall.'

'When taken there, she was already dead,' Sir John informed him. 'We think she was murdered at Bedlam.'

Sir Benedict sat back down heavily, placing his head in his hands. 'Gresham . . . Bedlam . . . I cannot fathom either.'

'We must try to understand, if we wish to find her killer.' Sir John hardened his voice to bring the man out of his daze.

Sir Benedict looked up at them slowly. Instead of seeing them, he saw his daughter, imagining her dead body and her face forever stilled.

'How was it done?' he asked, his voice barely audible.

'By sword,' Sir John said. 'A single thrust.'

'She would not have suffered,' Harry added.

Sir Benedict did not reply immediately. Instead, he turned and reached for a drawer in his desk. He withdrew a letter from it, then went to the window and pulled aside the curtain.

'I paid them,' he said. 'Yet still they killed her.'

☿

THE LETTER WAS WRITTEN IN AN extravagant hand. Long verticals and horizontals, and decorative loops crossing through parts of words, made it difficult to read.

> *Be assured your Daughter is unhurt. So She*
> *shall remain if you follow our Instruction. 200*
> *Guinea coins will buy her back. You trade in*
> *Human Lives, you think this Sum modest and*
> *fair. Take the Money to the Bridge, at its*
> *Drawbridge at Dusk. Now her Safety is your*
> *Obligation, so not Ours.*

Each capital *S* was particularly ornate. Each *k* looked more like a figure *8*, each lowercase *e* and *n* were indistinguishable. If Sir Benedict had not helped them, it would have taken Harry and Sir John far longer to decipher.

'Each letter *u* has a loop above it,' Harry observed. 'Otherwise, you could not distinguish it from an *n*, or this curious *e*. Uncommon for an English way of writing. Also, does it sound quite like English? *You trade in human lives, you think this sum modest and fair?*'

'Many write their own tongue badly,' Sir John said, holding the letter close to his eyes. 'I agree, though. My first thought was of a Baltic style. Swedish? Polish? Or Prussian, perhaps?'

'I made my first real money importing Scandinavian wood,' Sir Benedict told them morosely, 'for London's rebuilding after the Fire. Their lettering is similar. Especially the *k* looking like the number *8*.'

Sir John passed the letter to Harry. 'You see how the pen moves upwards.'

Harry studied it, then nodded. 'Forced against its natural flow. The ink spattered as the nib's point vibrated on the paper.'

'Most turn a pen to move it more easily, or else they lift it.'

'An obstinacy of character revealed, perhaps.'

'Obstinate enough to write such a note, then murder my daughter,' Sir Benedict said. 'I little think the detail helpful in finding him.'

'It may prove pertinent,' Sir John said. 'We concur this is a foreign hand, anyways. We could show it at the Baltic coffeehouse, where their traders and sea captains meet.'

Harry undid the Justice's attempt to hearten Diana's father. 'Or it attempts to mislead us.'

Sir John tutted. '*Numquam ponenda est pluralitas sine necessitate*, Mr. Hunt. You recognise Ockham's words, I'm sure.'

'I do. But what if it is not the simple answer we seek, but instead a more intricate one?'

When Sir John rolled his eyes, Harry at last saw his own thoughtlessness. 'I apologise, Sir Benedict. We will find your daughter's kidnapper, and her murderer, and bring him to justice.' Meaning to convey confidence, he compressed his lips and performed a small shake of the head, just as it occurred to him that whoever kidnapped Diana might not have killed her.

Harry stayed silent.

'When was this letter delivered?' Sir John asked.

'Yesterday afternoon, here at Africa House,' Sir Benedict answered.

'Did you see the man who brought it?'

'The fellow you met at the doorway took it from him. You must ask him.'

'We shall. You gave over the money?'

'I went there last night to the Bridge, as I was told to do, with the two hundred Guinea coins. I waited until after darkness came. Then, I was pushed from behind. I fell. My purse was taken from me.'

'Hence the graze on your head,' Harry said. 'I wondered upon it. Did you see anything of your attacker?'

'A glimpse, as I retrieved myself from the ground. I saw only his back, as he ran off. He wore a hood.'

'Was he tall or short? Broad or thin?' Sir John asked.

'Something in between all of those. I have watched the event in my mind repeatedly. There is little else I can tell you.'

'Definitely a man?' Harry asked. He had been surprised before.

As if the question was stupid, Sir Benedict did not bother to answer.

'To which side of the river did he run?' Sir John asked.

'The same way I had come. Back towards the City.'

'So, from the drawbridge, then back under Nonsuch House.'

Sir Benedict nodded absently, rubbing at the wound on his forehead.

'Did you notice a weapon?' Harry asked. 'A sword, perhaps, hanging behind him?'

'You ask, since a sword thrust killed my daughter. This man carried none, I am sure of it.'

Sir John sucked his teeth, making his cheeks concave. 'What did you do then, Benedict? You must have expected your daughter's return.'

'I waited. A couple of hours or more. The letter omits to say when Diana would be set free. However, there I stood, thinking she would come. At last, I went home, thinking—hoping, more like—she would be there.' Sir Benedict exhaled loudly, his body shrinking down into his chair as his lungs emptied. 'But she was not.'

'This morning, you came here as usual,' Harry said.

'I knew not what else to do. Nor where else to be. So, yes, I came to Africa House. I have been unable to work, though, my thoughts being only of Diana.'

Sir Benedict's voice kept cracking. His eyes shone with tears, which he pushed away brusquely with the back of his hand. 'My funny, laughing, clever, generous girl . . . My first wife died in child-birth, my son dying with her. I remarried, and we produced Diana. The only darkness in her life was the death of her mother, some three years ago. To be murdered . . . I cannot bear it . . . I thought her kidnapped for marriage, which happens to girls born into wealth. When I read this note, I thought she would be returned. Two hundred Guineas! You cannot place value on a human life—any number you mention becomes absurd—but I would have paid far more.' He glared at them. 'Far more!'

'It is a cruel blow.' Sir John placed his hand on his friend's fore-arm, a gesture this time accepted.

'Is the insistence upon Guinea coins pertinent, do you think?' Harry asked them both. 'The Royal African Company's own coin, made from West African gold.'

'It has become common currency,' Sir John said, 'despite its changes in value.'

'The rate is currently high,' Sir Benedict said, his voice auto-matic and dull. 'About twenty-six shillings a Guinea.'

'Gold is accepted everywhere,' Sir John said. 'Including Scandinavia. Besides, they guessed the Deputy-Governor would have them readily.'

Harry noticed Sir Benedict studying intently the surface of his desk. 'You said Diana planned to visit Covent Garden,' he said, more to distract the father from his grief than for further information.

'She told me she aimed for the house of Sir Peter Lely, who has his studio there. I have little notion why. I have not paid for her portrait to be made.'

'People often visit to see the pictures, not necessarily to be painted,' Harry said. He knew the house well, having spent part of his apprenticeship there, learning to paint and etch. When Robert Hooke first came to London, he had been Lely's apprentice. The two men remained friends. 'This was two, or three days ago?'

Sir Benedict closed his eyes, which pushed a tear down his cheek. He let it continue its descent. 'Why would you not think it yesterday?'

'Cadaveric rigidity had fade—'

'Enough, Mr. Hunt,' Sir John cut in. 'Signs, Benedict. Yet you received the letter yesterday.'

Sir Benedict looked appalled. 'Diana was already dead? What is this letter, then?' He shook it at them. 'It is too cruel!'

'A heavy burden to bear, no doubt,' Sir John said. 'Tell me, when was it she set off to see Sir Peter Lely?'

'The morning of the day before last. About nine of the clock. Unusual, for Diana seldom rose early. I watched her get into her carriage. I saw you with her, Mr. Hunt.'

Sir John turned his hardest gaze on Harry. 'You took a care not to tell me, Mr. Hunt.'

'I exchanged only pleasantries with her,' Harry replied.

'You helped her into the hackney,' Sir Benedict said.

'I offered my arm, as any gentleman would do.'

By now, the Justice's expression was withering. 'I thought your certainty of the timing of her death stemmed from your knowledge of cadavers. From your *New Philosophy*.'

'We must question Sir Peter Lely,' Harry said stiffly, 'to know if Diana reached his house, or else was taken on her way.'

'Indeed,' Sir John said. 'For presently, I have *you* as the last person with her.'

'The hackney driver, too.'

'One of three thousand. Did you note his number?'

Harry tried to picture the vehicle taking Diana away. 'I did not.'

'Then you may as well try to count Aquinas's angels.' Sir John saw Sir Benedict's stricken face. 'We shall question your man about the letter's deliverer, Benedict. Then, I am sorry to say, you must come with me to Gresham.'

'I will come with you, too,' Harry said. 'I have questions for Thomas Crawley. If the two women were not swapped at Bethlehem, then it was done at the College.'

'No,' Sir John said sharply. 'You will go home, Mr. Hunt. I shall meet with you there later. If that conveniences you.'

Sir John's tone added, it would happen, if it convenienced Harry or no.

CHAPTER EIGHT

THE NECESSARY BUSINESS

Harry ignored the instruction to go home. There was some necessary business to attend to. And time enough, while Sir John accompanied Sir Benedict to Gresham College, before Harry would need to return to Bloomsbury Square.

Sir John Reresby made thinking difficult. His constant desire to probe for weakness made Harry feel more claustrophobic than in this crush of people waiting to get onto London Bridge. He still stung from the Justice's rebuke and unfair suspicion. Just from his helping Diana into her hackney.

He should not have kept the information back, but to think him involved was preposterous. After all, he had put a stop to the dissection. What murderer would do that, and bring attention to himself?

Sir John desired an easy end to his investigation.

Harry shuffled forwards with the crowd. The ugly column of the Morice Water House stood to his right. To his left, the still-steepleless St. Magnus-the-Martyr, the Bridge dwellers' parish church.

The first building on the Bridge was three storeys high, its upper floor extending over the roadway to create a dark tunnel. Light came from perpetually lit lamps, and from the windows of shops and offices. Harry could feel the vibration from the Morice waterwheels below him, as they pumped water up to the City. The smell from a tannery filled his nose.

The clatters and bangs of the carts and carriages, and all the apprentice boys shouting for custom—the noises all amplified in the enclosure—made Harry feel more at ease.

He reemerged into sunshine and onto paving laid to welcome the King on his restoration, now scarred from the ceaseless traffic. This part of London Bridge was cleared after a fire started in a needle-maker's shop fifty years before and never rebuilt upon. Wooden palisades stopped people from being blown into the Thames.

On both sides of the road, stalls pressed perilously close to the vehicles passing. As a cart laden with beer barrels, pulled by four oxen, rumbled by, Harry had to wait in a recess over one of the piers, next to a woman selling trinkets and cheap jewellery.

At the Bridge's middle stood the chapel of St. Thomas à Becket. Its windows had been smashed and its Papist decoration chipped away in Henry VIII's time. Now a warehouse and shops, it smelled of tobacco and cheese. Harry watched the water sweeping around the old stone of the starling below it. Fish floundered helplessly, trapped in the netting of the fishpond built into its structure.

Being on the southern half of the Bridge was like returning

in time, with its old, narrow-fronted houses leaning over him crookedly, their backs overhanging the Thames on massive struts.

He entered the section of roadway going through Nonsuch House, which was barely wide enough for two carriages side by side. The building was remarkable for being constructed in the Dutch Republic and taken apart, its timbers marked and transported, then rebuilt to straddle the Bridge.

He emerged at the drawbridge. When raised, it allowed larger vessels to dock at Queenhithe, or to pass through on their way eastwards, out to the open sea. And it was an obstacle to southern invasion.

Here was where Sir Benedict was instructed to buy back his daughter. Where he had waited was deceived—his daughter already dead when the ransom was taken—hit, then left sprawling in the road.

Earning the curse of a trader trying to manoeuvre his cart, Harry turned to study Nonsuch House. Elaborately painted, towers at its corners were each crowned with a white onion dome, gilded vanes gleaming on top of them. Its gables extended far out from the pier it rested on, reaching over the Thames on both sides of the Bridge. Not allowing any glimpse of its interior, its windows were trapeziums of cobalt blue reflecting the sky.

Nonsuch House would not lead him to the kidnappers and murderer of Diana Cantley. Neither would it bring him closer to understanding the mystery of her being at Bethlehem. All that put her there, though, was Mr. Hooke's expectation they would receive a dead woman from Dr. Allen. Instead, Diana had been delivered to Gresham.

Perhaps she was taken there from elsewhere. Not from the Hospital. Diana had told her father she planned to visit Sir Peter Lely's studio; perhaps she was taken from Covent Garden.

Her murderer may have killed her there.

Or anywhere in between.

Or anywhere else in London.

Harry blew air out through his cheeks, ending in a plosive, popping sound. He brought his watch from his pocket. It was just gone a half past five. Five and a half hours since he had arrived at Gresham for the dissection.

He had wanted to impress the Fellows by taking the sedan chair. Now, his decision embarrassed him. He had overdressed for the occasion, too. The Fellows were more polite, but at Bethlehem Hospital the looks from the staff, who knew him as Hooke's assistant, were mocking.

Well, he wanted to put the old Harry behind him. That it came at a cost he would have to accept. On the Bridge, in his finery, he had received appraising looks.

He felt again for his purse. Its coins jangled reassuringly. A trip west to Hounslow soon to buy a sword, he thought. One from the Board of Ordnance's suppliers there.

He steered his thoughts back to Diana Cantley.

The woman wrapped in the sheet and taken to the College— whether Diana, or Sebiliah—was stored overnight and for a morning. Thomas Crawley had left her in Mr. Hooke's anatomy room.

If Diana was never at Bethlehem Hospital, someone must have smuggled her body into the College. Which meant whoever had done so had access to it, and was able to reach its anatomy room unobserved while transporting a body.

For now, Harry put aside the possibility Diana was murdered at Gresham; too much went on there for a woman's murder and storage not to be noticed.

About thirty Fellows had gathered that morning for the noon dissection. All knew the College's interior, and where the anatomy room was. Who else kept a key? He would have to check with Mr. Hooke.

If Crawley had transported Sebiliah to the College, then it was impossible Diana was already in the anatomy room; Crawley would have seen her when placing Sebiliah there. Diana may already have been hidden, in another part of the College.

Far more likely, Harry felt, was that the two dead women were swapped at Bethlehem. But by whom?

At home in Bloomsbury Square—days often his own to do with what he wished—Harry had looked out for Diana, hoping to see her as she went for her morning ride. Most mornings, she left about eleven o'clock. He made sure to be in his withdrawing room then, looking down onto the Square. Moving back when she looked up towards his window. Wondering if she sensed he was there.

Harry had used his knowledge that she was still alive three mornings before to bolster himself in front of the Fellows, and the Justice, who was being dismissive of the New Philosophy.

But Sir John had already caught him out in a lie when he admitted he had seen Diana riding.

So, something more than nothing more, Sir John had said, mocking him.

Until Diana's visiting Sir Peter Lely's Covent Garden home was confirmed, Sir John would continue to suspect him. Harry must go there, if only to clear his name with the Justice.

It was foolish, though, not to have mentioned helping Diana into the hackney. His guilt from being attracted to his neighbour had stopped him.

Guilt, for he had an understanding—if not yet an engagement—with Grace Hooke.

Harry took a lungful of warm London air, and shook his head irritably. His thoughts had returned to himself once more. Diana Cantley had been murdered. The King had commanded him to help Sir John investigate. That was what he must concentrate upon.

What did he know? What could he be sure of?

That Diana's killer was callous was certain. Her death was no accident, rashly done, then concealed in a panic. She was murdered by a well-aimed sword thrust, which had killed her immediately. Afterwards, a ransom note was written and sent, and her father was robbed of his money. Lastly, her body was placed—however it was done—at Gresham College.

If Harry had not recognised Diana, Sir Christopher would have completed her dissection. Afterwards, she would have been buried in a nameless grave. Sir Benedict would never have known what became of his daughter.

Who took her to Gresham, then, if not Thomas Crawley? And, if not Crawley, who took Sebiliah Barton's body away from Bethlehem? Or perhaps she was still there—the place was so big it could hide a dozen bodies. Harry thought of Dr. Allen's anatomy room, which had remained locked. They left it so, because Harry and Sir John had already been at Bethlehem for some considerable time. The Justice seemed tired from all the walking. Besides, Sir John was anxious to impart the bad news to Sir Benedict.

All this was by the by if the two women were exchanged at the Hospital. Perhaps William Jones would have confessed by the morning. The matter would then be resolved.

What else did Harry know?

The ransom letter was written in an unusual hand. A foreign hand. Sir Benedict and Sir John both thought it a Baltic hand. This must make its author—Harry would not say kidnapper, as he was uncertain it was the same man—easier to find. Although, foreigners were hardly rare in London.

Another thing he knew: Sebiliah Barton's death was by her own hand. Nothing suggested otherwise. No one else had been with her in her room when she died; Hannah Matthews, the Nurse, would have seen them. Harry had no doubt Hannah had been honest with them. Her upset at Sebiliah's death was self-evidently genuine. The girl had been distraught.

What was that look, though, he had caught between her and the Basketmen, Jones and Langdale? Harry tried to remember what the conversation had been. Dr. Allen had been talking about Sebiliah's lack of family . . .

Even though Diana Cantley had been his neighbour—an alluring one, too—Harry found his thoughts kept returning to the Bethlehem suicide. He had no notion of Sebiliah's appearance. No one had described her; to his shame, he had never asked. He knew only that she had no family and suffered from a sadness so profound she killed herself to end it. And she was quiet, he remembered Dr. Allen saying.

What happened, he wondered, to drive her to such despair?

'Hey! Sirrah Clay for Brains!'

The Bridge Warden was looking at him with an amused scorn. Deep in his thoughts, Harry had not registered the warning bell; the drawbridge was about to be raised.

Ushered away by the Warden, going back under Nonsuch House, Harry knew he must reach Bloomsbury Square before Sir John. But first he had his necessary business to undertake at the Goldsmiths' Hall, on Carey Lane.

CHAPTER NINE

THE KIDNAPPED
HEIRESS

He almost made it home.

A red-uniformed man mounted on a handsome bay awaited him where Southampton Street entered Bloomsbury Square. The evening light glittered gold off the horse's coat.

On seeing Harry, the rider threw down the last of a cheroot and touched his swerving nose as a minimal salute.

'Sir John sends for you,' Joseph Fenn informed him in his throaty whisper. 'We're to go to Westminster, to see a Mr. Thynne. A Member of Parliament, if you don't know. A Member of Parliament, if you do. Important in the Country Party. The Duke of Monmouth sent the message, asking for you himself.'

Harry looked longingly at his house. 'What does the Duke want with me?'

'No clue, Mr. Hunt. But I do know this. Mr. Thynne's wife's been kidnapped.'

☿

BACKING ONTO THE THAMES, CANNON ROW was close—and therefore convenient—to Whitehall and Westminster. The Earls of Derby, Lincoln, Manchester, and Somerset all chose it for their fine town houses.

The Thynnes of Longleat had one of the finest. Elizabethan, substantial, symmetrical, it boasted a tower pavilion at each corner, chimneys of irrational height, pinnacles, turrets, and patterned brickwork. The family's wealth was further displayed by an unrestrained use of glass; the front of the house was more window than wall.

Sir John hit his carriage's ceiling with his stick to halt the driver.

The Justice had not yet mentioned Diana Cantley, nor Harry seeing her into a hackney. The Duke of Monmouth's summons seemed to have swept those thoughts away.

Once they stood on the pavement, after the Justice had instructed his driver to return home rather than wait for them, Sir John continued. 'The Lords Shaftesbury, Cavendish, Halifax, Buckingham, Bedford, and more are of the Country Party. Their aim is singular: to exclude the Duke of York from his inheritance and put in his place a Protestant.'

'That Protestant being the man who asks for us,' Harry said. 'The Duke of Monmouth.'

'He asks for *you*.' Sir John leaned closer to Harry, and dropped his voice. 'Do not let these men take against you, for they can bring you down.' He sounded almost kindly, as if he cared for Harry's future. 'Thomas Thynne is one of the richest men in the country. Possibly the richest. He promotes the Duke, paying for his progresses around the country to bring support for his cause. Thynne would buy the throne for him, if he could.'

'Those who fear the King's brother's Catholicism prefer his Protestant son, despite his illegitimacy,' Harry said, after acknowledging Fenn, who had ridden his bay before them, at Thynne's gates.

'Shaftesbury wants it,' Sir John said. 'You cannot avoid his processions, and the bonfires.'

'Another's planned for tonight, at Charing Cross,' Fenn whispered ominously. 'Green Ribboners, vexatious to the King.'

'It is a provocation,' Sir John said, as they crossed the gravelled courtyard. 'Right by the statue of the King's late father, blessed be his memory.'

Harry studied the vast facade of Thomas Thynne's house, its windows lined unpromisingly against them.

They climbed the portico's steps. Sir John lifted the front door's heavy brass knocker. He looked earnestly at Harry, then at Fenn.

'We must be wary. These are dangerous men.'

He let the knocker drop, alerting the household to their presence.

☿

DRESSED IN THE THYNNE COLOURS OF yellow and red, the doorman made them stand in the portico while he went to inform his master of their arrival.

'To keep us mindful of our station,' Sir John remarked.

After a well-judged wait, the doorman returned and led them inside. The interior was all dark panelling and tapestries. The library the man left them in, its candles all lit, faced the Thames and its curve as the water turned east.

Dusk was almost done. A last ultramarine blue clung to the horizon, the day's shreds of cloud rich cream and salmon. The moon rose. Venus was low over Whitechapel. St. Paul's Cathedral's ever-fattening bulk dominated the horizon, with the other church spires and the Fish Street Monument stabbing the sky.

Sir John looked idly at all the books.

'You know of the play by Shakespeare, called *Romeo and Juliet?*' he asked, managing to keep his voice quiet.

'I do, but have never seen it,' Harry answered, equally quietly. Fenn shrugged, uninterested; his focus was on watching the door.

'Well, the Thynnes made enemies of another family, whose name was Marvin. There were fights between them. Servants killed, and so on. Thomas Thynne's grandfather married a Marvin. A girl named Maria. Both families took against the match. For the speed of it, its unsuitability, and as both were just sixteen. Shakespeare took the story and made it into his play.'

'Sixteen is young. I had no thoughts of marriage then,' Harry said.

'You thought only of your master, Robert Hooke, I'd wager, and your work for him. Flaying dead men, pickling children, weighing the air, and so forth.'

'I have never flayed a man,' Harry assured him. 'This much is true. Mr. Hooke was everything I wanted to be.'

'Was, you say. Wanted, you say.'

'Sixteen is young,' Harry repeated.

'Thomas Thynne's wife is fourteen, and already on her second husband.'

☿

FOOTSTEPS APPROACHED, THEN TWO MEN ENTERED the library.

Sir John, Harry, and Fenn made their bows, none of them returned. Instead, the taller of the newcomers, a good-looking man whose stockings stretched over muscular calves, shook the Justice's hand.

'Your Grace,' Sir John said, amazed by the putting aside of the usual niceties of rank, to James Scott, the Duke of Monmouth.

'Address him as Your Royal Highness,' the other man told the Justice. 'For he is the King's son.'

This must be Thomas Thynne. His voice was sullen, and sounded childish to Harry's ears, an impression deepened by the way his mouth turned petulantly downwards as he spoke. He had an askew chin, wine-reddened features, heavy-lidded eyes, and a stature that suited his name.

Monmouth, conversely, looked fit and capable—as anyone might expect, for he had served in the English fleet in the second war against the Dutch, then commanded troops in the third, fighting alongside the French. Against the Scottish Covenanters, he led the troops who put down their rebellion, most decisively, at Bothwell Bridge. His clemency afterwards won admiration—not least from the Scots.

Both men wore suits of black silk. Monmouth's wig was black, too, whereas Thynne's was long, white, and freshly powdered, its dust settling on his shoulders.

Monmouth shook his head at his companion. 'Sir John, call me Your Grace without self-consciousness. I am not a royal Duke, nor am I a Prince.'

Monmouth spoke easily, with the same smooth cadences and familiar manner as his father. Although it was often said he inherited his mother's looks and his father's charm, he was also unmistakably the King's son, owning similarly dark eyes and dense eyebrows.

'You are a Duke twice over, of Monmouth and of Buccleuch,' Thynne said. 'Soon, you will be King.' The corners of his mouth twitched, as if from satisfaction at the words just passed through.

Monmouth caught Sir John's stiff look. 'Worry not. This is not insurrection. Thomas goes too far, as usual. I have no desire for the throne. We look to exclude my uncle, for his Popery threatens absolutism. It is the Catholic way to prefer arbitrary government, which we are against.'

'You are the obvious choice to succeed,' Thynne said.

'My father disagrees.'

'His Majesty has dissolved Parliament over it,' Sir John said.

'Yes, well,' Monmouth answered casually. 'Shaftesbury pushed too hard.'

'Shaftesbury enraged him.'

'He should never have said my father should divorce and remarry.'

'That he might have legitimate children.'

It was Monmouth's turn to look stiffly at Sir John. Instead of any rejoinder, though, he took a breath, then gestured to Harry.

Sir John remembered his manners. 'Your Grace, if I may introduce Mr. Henry Hunt, of the Royal Society? Your father commanded him to assist me in finding the murderer of Sir Benedict Cantley's daughter.'

'I heard of that. Sad news indeed.'

'Her taking may be connected to the kidnapping of Mrs. Thynne.'

Monmouth gave a soft 'hmm,' again sounding like the King. He studied Harry, observing the expense of clothes matching his own. He reached out his hand, and Harry took it, their rings clashing.

'You turned my father down, refusing to work with the Board of Ordnance, after you discovered the use of the bloodless boy.' Monmouth grinned suddenly, showing straight and white teeth. 'We are both disobedient, are we not?'

'I helped him a little, Your Grace,' Harry replied. 'He honoured me by leaving the choice to make.'

'Do not be falsely modest,' Monmouth said, wagging his finger. 'It is unbecoming of a gentleman. You also prevented the death of his wife, at her Consult. The talk at Whitehall was of little else, for you saved half the Court, too.'

'The Papist half,' Thynne said dismissively.

Monmouth ignored him. 'I heard the tale of the Sancy diamond from the Duchesse de Mazarin herself. And the killing of Sir Edmund Bury Godfrey—your predecessor, Sir John, as Justice of Peace for Westminster. Mr. Hunt helped with that matter, too.'

'Let us hope he's as useful with finding my wife,' Thynne interrupted. 'Which is what you're all here to discuss.'

Monmouth gestured to the sofas. 'Thomas, have your man bring wine.'

When Thynne's butler had brought and poured them claret, Monmouth raised his glass to Sir John and Harry in turn, and lastly to Fenn, who sat awkwardly away from them on a Jacobean chair, there not being room on the sofas.

'So, *Mr.* Thynne, your wife is kidnapped,' Sir John said, careful not to let his host notice him wincing at the wine.

Again, Sir John's stress on *Mister*. Despite his lands and his riches, Thynne had no title. The Justice cannot help himself, Harry thought; as soon as he begins a questioning, he seeks to needle.

'You expect an answer?' Thynne replied tartly. 'You know full well she is.'

Monmouth frowned at his friend before looking back to the others. 'We need your help to find her.'

'I would have preferred you kept out of it,' Thynne sulked. Harry was unsure if he meant them, or the Duke. 'I have my own men. They search London now.'

'Which men are these?' Sir John enquired.

Thynne's rubicund face looked as if the question pained him. 'Men. Competent men. My Steward and my Gamekeeper.'

'Your Gamekeeper?' Sir John looked incredulous. 'From Longleat?'

'A solid man,' Monmouth answered for his friend. 'Kidd served in the Army. Singer, too, has experience of soldiering.'

'Brothers of the blade, then,' Sir John said. 'Do they know where to start with looking?'

Thynne answered this time. 'Not where, exactly, but they know the man who has her.'

'Who is he, do you suspect?'

'I do not *suspect*. I know. I have a letter here from him.'

Thynne produced it from his pocket.

Mr. Thynne.

I would love Elizabeth if she had Nothing. I would love her if she came from Nothing.

You would stop her Happiness, keeping her to gain her Wealth.

For you, Elizabeth is the means to an end.

I love her for herself.

If Freedom means to follow the desires of her

Heart, then I wish to set her free.

She has given herself, Body and Soul, to me.

I declare before God and the World I love her

with all my Heart.

K

Sir John lifted his eyebrows ostentatiously and passed the letter to Harry. 'This missive says no such thing. Its author mentions no kidnap. Elizabeth has given herself, this *K* says, to him.'

Thynne waved his glass by its stem, spilling some of his wine. 'As she is my wife, he can make no such attestations! She is gone, this letter in her place.'

Sir John ignored him, directing his attention instead to Harry. 'You cannot doubt he is ardent. Look at the writing. You shall recognise it, I think.'

Harry spoke while reading. 'The same as the letter delivered to Sir Benedict. Each *k* looking more like an *8*, each *u* owning a loop above it.'

'The same forcefulness of the upstrokes, too, the nib of the pen not being turned,' Sir John said.

Harry glanced up from the letter at Thynne. 'You know who this man is? *K*?' He leaned across to Fenn, giving him the letter.

Thynne poured himself more wine without offering it around. 'The *K* stands either for Karl, or for Königsmarck. He is a Swedish Count. *Karl Johann von Königsmarck.*' Thynne overenunciated the name derisively. 'He murdered Sir Benedict Cantley's daughter, too, you say. And now he has taken my wife.'

'I said only there may be a connection. His words here say only that they love each other,' Sir John said.

After a silence, Sir John had to prompt Thynne. 'You have *summoned* us, so pray tell us what more you know.'

Thynne's petulant mouth was ajar, showing his wine-stained teeth. Monmouth encouraged him with an impatient wave.

'James—His Grace—summoned you, not me.' Thynne stopped to think through what to tell them, wiping at his mouth. Then he made a defeated, snorting noise. 'The terms of my marriage are complicated. My wife mourned her first husband, Lord Ogle. We were not to live together, nor consummate our marriage, for one year after his death. I honoured that agreement. I stayed here in Cannon Row, while she lived mostly in Syon House, the Percy family's home in Isleworth, or else at Petworth, their home in Sussex—'

'You talk of the Percy family's homes,' Sir John interrupted. 'That is not quite the whole truth, is it, Mr. Thynne? For when the last Earl died sonless, his fortune and estates went to his sole heiress. She was a child then, the Lady Elizabeth Percy—your wife, sir, as you call her, for you have not yet said her name—when she inherited Syon House, and Petworth House. And Alnwick Castle, and Warkworth Castle. And Spofforth Castle, although that was badly damaged in the Wars. Also, Northumberland House in the Strand.'

Looking indignant, Thynne rose from his seat. '*My wife's* father sought to protect his property from any husband of his daughter. In her minority, *my wife's* care was placed into the hands of her grandmother, the Dowager Countess. We made the contract, her grandmother and I.' He gave Sir John a long, haughty stare, which, to Harry's mind, quickly became ridiculous. 'The document's legality is not in doubt. I care little of your approval, or disapproval. What are you to me? A Justice. A mere baronet from the North.'

'Thrybergh is in Yorkshire, not Baffin Bay,' Sir John said, enjoying himself.

Thynne's nostrils flared. Monmouth put his hand on Thynne's arm. 'Calm, calm, Thomas.' He spoke as if talking to his horse. 'Continue on with the rest of it.'

Thynne swallowed more wine, then sat back down. Perspiration beaded his forehead. 'The year gone by, I insisted on my rights as her husband. My wife absconded. She left for the Dutch Republic. She broke the contract! I had made many concessions, and showed much consideration.'

'To the grandmother, or the granddaughter?' Sir John asked.

'Both of them, dammit! Seemingly, my wife met Königsmarck in the Hague. Some talk has them meeting before she left London, when he was here to offer his soldiering in Tangiers, against the Alaouites. He is a mercenary, nothing more.'

'It seems to me Elizabeth no longer feels bound by the contract. She wishes to be with another, whom she prefers.'

'Her *feels*, and her *wishes*, are of no account. She is legally bound!' Thynne wiped sweat from the end of his nose. 'I refuse to believe she prefers him. My fortune is by far the greater.'

'Considerably enhanced by the Percy estates.'

Thynne's face darkened. 'You have said Königsmarck murdered another girl. I will have my wife away from him, whether she is happy about it or no. I am her husband. Her safety is, therefore, my concern.'

'You seem to wish to make it mine. Yet there is nothing to show she has been coerced. And I am not yet ready to make an accusation of murder against the Swedish Count.'

'I order you to make it yours!' More wine spilled as Thynne swung his glass at Sir John. 'Be assured, I shall make life difficult for you if you do not.'

Despite his warning to Harry and Fenn about the threat of Thynne and men like him, Sir John looked studiedly unimpressed. He fiddled with his stick, apparently absorbed in the decoration on its silver handle—the Reresby three crosses, flowered at each end—and at the way the design had worn from his grasping it.

'I am the King's man,' he said, without looking up from the stick. 'A Court Justice, appointed by His Majesty. You foment opinion against his brother, so are out of favour. You proposed to bring the Duke of York before the grand jury as a common recusant. Your Country Party is the Anti-Court faction.' Only now did Sir John look up. 'You are in no position, I think, to order me. Nor Mr. Fenn, who is the Lord Mayor's man, through the Provost Marshal. Nor Mr. Hunt, neither, who is his own man, but who follows the wishes of his monarch.'

'Please, Sir John,' Monmouth implored, before Thynne could retort again. 'My father would wish a Percy safe, even if she is now named Thynne.'

Sir John spread his hands reasonably. 'You think this letter subterfuge, Your Grace? You think this Königsmarck means to do her harm?'

'If he murdered Sir Benedict's girl, I would not want Elizabeth with him. He may have enticed her with false words.'

Thynne stood up again and walked unsteadily towards a bookcase. 'She must be made to recognise her own foolishness.'

'It is definitely a tangle,' Sir John observed. 'What say you, Mr. Hunt? Give up your thoughts upon the matter.'

Wanting time to devise his reply, Harry played with one of his rings. 'I say, we must find Mrs. Thynne,' he started reluctantly, 'and elicit her opinion. She shall not wish to stay with the Count, I think, if she knows him a murderer. If Königsmarck killed Diana Cantley, the choice is no longer hers, as he will hang.'

'I require my wife back,' Thynne said.

'That should be her choice,' Harry said. 'Rather than yours. *Mr.* Thynne.'

Thynne laughed incredulously. 'Who is this asinego you bring to my house, James? Let my men Kidd and Singer find her. We have no need of these, these—'

'Calm yourself,' Monmouth said sharply. 'We want their assistance. The Justice has influence. Mr. Hunt has proved himself capable before.' He looked at Sir John. 'I shall speak with my father and appraise him of the situation. Are you unwilling to help us without his say-so?'

'I find myself with Mr. Hunt, Your Grace. We shall seek Elizabeth for herself. Not for Mr. Thynne.'

Monmouth leaned across the gap between their respective sofas and took Sir John by the hand again. 'You do us great favour.'

'To do so, we must start with where she last was,' Harry suggested. 'Your account last had her in the Dutch Republic, Mr. Thynne. When did she return to London?'

'A fortnight ago,' Thynne answered, as if he resented the timing, and still obviously affronted. 'She stayed with her grandmother at Northumberland House. Yesterday morning, about ten o'clock, she left from there to go shopping. But she never returned.'

'The Dowager Countess told you this?' Sir John asked.

'I visited her this morning.'

Sir John glanced at Fenn, sharing a private joke. 'You do not quite answer my question.'

Thynne harrumphed. 'She sent a man to inform me. I went to Northumberland House. My wife had left for the Royal Exchange's upper gallery, her grandmother told me, and the shops there. Then she intended to go to the Goldsmiths' Hall. She said, to its shops on Carey Lane.'

Harry looked at Sir John. 'I wonder if Mrs. Thynne is always so detailed when telling her grandmother of her day.'

'She had no luggage with her, if you think she planned to elope with Königsmarck,' Thynne said.

Ignoring Thynne, Sir John spoke to Harry. 'Her grandmother, after all, arranged a marriage to a man she thinks little of.'

Thynne looked murderously at them both. Monmouth answered for him. 'Elizabeth's page searched the Exchange, but could not find her. The Dowager Countess sent more servants out. They went to all her favourite places—tea shops, trinket shops, such places ladies go—then to Carey Lane. No one had seen or spoken to her. No sign of her, except for this letter from Königsmarck.'

'Has the search continued today, Your Grace?' Harry asked him.

'By the two men we spoke of. Kidd and Singer. At the Exchange again this morning, then Carey Lane this afternoon. Their intelligence has it that Königsmarck is definitely here in London.'

'We know he is,' Thynne said. 'We have his stupid letter. He is difficult to miss, for he has yellow hair down to his waist, and refuses to wear a wig. The better to show off his tresses, I suppose.'

'Where was he seen, do your men report?' Harry asked.

'In and about Holborn. Until he moved on, he stayed at the Black Bull. He has a second man with him. A Kapitän Vratz, who hails from Pomerania. Another mercenary.'

Monmouth nodded his agreement. 'Vratz commanded the forlorn hope at the siege of Mons. Only two besides himself—of fifty or so under his command—escaped with their lives.'

'These are dangerous men,' Thynne added, unaware Sir John had earlier used the same phrase.

The Justice pulled at his ear. 'I shall ensure Holborn's Night Watch is informed tonight.' He motioned at Fenn and Harry that they were to leave. 'Tomorrow, all of my men shall look. We shall find these two foreigners. They shall lead us to Elizabeth, I am sure. By your leave, Your Grace. And yours, *Mr.* Thynne.'

CHAPTER TEN

THE RHENISH WINEHOUSE

They had not eaten since breakfast. The day had taken them from Gresham College, then to Bethlehem Hospital, and for Harry and Sir John, Africa House, while Fenn went to Leicester Fields with William Jones, the Basketman. Harry had walked to London Bridge, then done his necessary shopping. Sir John's and Fenn's questioning of Jones was interrupted by the Duke of Monmouth's messenger.

Giving in to their hunger, the three men took the narrow passageway from Cannon Row to the Rhenish winehouse. Sir John whistled 'A Health to Betty.'

Once inside, Prior, the winehouse owner, soon had them settled at a table. The other customers all looked affluent: lawyers, merchants, men from the nearby Admiralty Office. One group spoke together in German; perhaps they had strayed from the Steelyard.

The winehouse had barely cooled since the daytime. Sir John, laboriously taking off his coat, directed Prior to send a messenger boy to the Watchhouse by Middle Row in Holborn. It was to block all exits from Holborn and look out for the Swedish Count.

Sir John ordered trout, Harry chose the oysters, and they agreed to share a bottle of wormwood wine. Meat being too rich for his stomach, Fenn wanted only vegetables and salads, washed down with Adam's ale.

Prior himself brought the wine, commending its properties of dissipating phlegm and drying the vapours of the stomach, and the water for Fenn.

Sir John poured a large glass for Harry, who was trying to find a place for his hat. 'Half the Night Watch will be at Charing Cross for Shaftesbury's bonfire. Nevertheless, we shall start the search in Holborn.'

'Most likely this man Königsmarck is already gone.' Harry rested his hat on a cross-member of their table, its feather protruding from under the tablecloth.

'I have heard of him before,' Sir John said. 'In Sweden, he has some importance. His uncle governs Pomerania. The letters we have, and the testimony, show he killed Diana and has taken Elizabeth Thynne.'

'The style of writing suggests it, you think, appearing Swedish.' Harry sounded doubtful.

'You do not believe it?' Sir John took a swig of his wormwood wine, then raised the glass to look at it appreciatively. 'Too much coincidence to suspect another. I shall pursue the simpler answer, at least for now.'

'The letter shows him guilty only of wanting another man's

wife,' Fenn said. Harry had to lean in to hear his whisper. 'And you can hardly call the marriage a real one, despite the contract Thynne spoke of.'

'To my mind, the letter seems suspect,' Harry said. 'Why write of your deepest emotions to a cuckolded husband?'

'You think Königsmarck's just another man after the Percy fortune?' Fenn asked.

'He may have kidnapped Elizabeth for marriage,' Sir John said, 'which happens to girls of her class.'

Harry thought for a moment. 'If the marriage is legal, as Thynne insists, then Königsmarck can make no claim.'

Prior returned with their food and began loading their plates.

'Keep Mr. Hunt's oysters away from me,' Sir John told the landlord, shielding them from view with his hand. 'For I dislike them strongly.' He looked down at his own plate. 'Well, all aboard!' Even before Prior finished dishing it out, Sir John attacked his meal. He chewed vigorously as he considered Harry's point. 'To find Mrs. Thynne, firstly we must find Königsmarck. We may ask her then, to know if she needs saving from him.'

'More like, she needs saving from her husband,' Fenn said, as Prior placed salad and cold potatoes before him.

'I despise that man,' Sir John declared. 'I am not surprised his wife has made him an Actaeon.'

'You oppose him for his politics,' Harry suggested.

'I oppose him for his character!' Sir John rapped his knife's handle against the tabletop.

The Navy men looked around, disturbed by his vehemence. Sir John answered with an apologetic hand.

'Before we met with Thynne,' Harry said tentatively, when attention had left their table and they were eating again, 'you warned me of him.'

'He once murdered a beadle, when the man objected to him laying waste to a bawdy house,' Sir John said.

'Yet he walked free?'

'You sound surprised, Mr. Hunt,' Fenn said, managing to make his hoarse whisper sound acerbic.

'The King pardoned him,' Sir John said. 'Others, too, who were with him. All aristocrats and rakes.'

Fenn grimaced. 'Lenience extends to such men. Let's hope his next shit's a hedgehog, eh.'

'You showed little restraint yourself, Sir John,' Harry said, beginning to realise how strong the wormwood wine was. The heat in his cheeks was rising.

'Well, I like to think I have some clout myself, you know.' Sir John and Fenn shared a mischievous look. 'Since tying himself to Monmouth, Thynne has lost the King's good will. I would be unwilling to assist him in anything which might incur His Majesty's displeasure, but the search for Elizabeth must now take precedence.'

'Over finding Diana Cantley's murderer, you mean,' Harry said, a hint of challenge in his voice.

Sir John scowled as he pulled aside the bony scutes of his trout with his fingers to get at its flesh. 'I have not forgotten her. Remember, I am close to her father. But, irrespective of her choice of husband, Elizabeth Thynne is a person of the utmost quality.'

'It sounds to me, she could not choose her own husband,' Harry said. 'Despite her quality. Others did that for her.'

'True enough,' Sir John agreed. 'Thynne and her grandmother coerced her into the marriage. Thynne wants her wealth. Presumably, the Dowager Countess receives some benefit.'

'She sold her own granddaughter, you mean.' Harry shook his head. 'Whatever the case, the wife has set herself against the husband.'

'Understandably so,' Sir John said. 'You have met the man.'

'Given her antipathy, why did she return to London? Only then to disappear with the Count.'

Sir John paused his fork in midair, pondering the thought. 'Perhaps she changed her mind and returned for the sake of her marriage. Then she was taken, against her will, as her husband tells us. Or did she, in the Hague, when away from her husband and family, leap into the arms of the first man who truly loved her? She had been bought and sold twice, first to Lord Ogle and then to Mr. Thynne.'

'Why is the grandmother her guardian?' Harry asked.

'Elizabeth is estranged from her mother, I understand, who opposed her first marriage. Her childhood, I wager, was a continual parade before potential suitors. Perhaps she married Ogle only to put an end to it. Then, she suffered the misfortune of his untimely death.'

'Only to be married off again, to one of the richest men in England,' Harry said.

'The rich sell their children to the highest bidder. You know, the Duke was married at just thirteen. His wife was only twelve. Passion is suspect with such people, if it interferes with suitability. I am hypocritical, for I, too, want the most for my children. My problems are different, though.' He grinned at them both. 'For I have five sons.'

Fenn laughed wheezily. Harry did so more dutifully. The wine was making him feel drowsy. He swallowed an oyster, which slid viscously down his throat. He had never made up his mind if he liked them. 'The Duke is impressive, I thought,' he said, to fill the developing silence.

Sir John pointed his fork at Harry; bits of fish fell back onto his plate. 'There, you expose the root of the problem. If only he were not! Monmouth owns a regal countenance, his father's bearing, and has shown himself brave in the past. His conduct at Maastricht, for example, where he led the final charge himself, against Dutch mines and heavy fire.' Sir John's fork was pointed again, this time generally at the room they were in and the people who sat in it. 'He finds popularity easily. Therein lies his danger.'

'The King sees it,' Harry said. 'Why he dissolved Parliament, of course.'

It pleased him to be conversing with men such as Sir John on matters political.

'Parliament favoured the Duke, being dominated by the Country Party.'

'Monmouth's followers form militias,' Fenn said. 'His Brisk Boys.' He lowered his whisper conspiratorially. 'Their talk's all of a Black Box, supposed to keep proof of the King's marriage to Monmouth's mother.'

Sir John regarded him with disdain. 'That box is a myth,' he said. 'The King himself has assured me of that.'

'The Brisk Boys believe anything which best suits them. Such a certificate would legitimise Monmouth and assure his inheritance.'

As he took another oyster, Harry thought that the Marshalman's nose really was extraordinarily bent, and wondered how its shape contributed to the broken sound of his voice. If the man was willing to undergo the procedure, it would be a simple thing to straighten it. Not knowing Fenn well enough to gauge his likely reaction, Harry did not suggest it. 'With such a certificate, even those who prefer William of Orange would accede,' he said instead.

Sir John speared a piece of carrot. 'As I say, there is no truth to it.'

'If the King were to change his mind, and steer the throne towards Monmouth instead of his brother, you would not object.'

The Justice allowed a mordant smile. 'I am His Majesty's Justice. I am his to command.'

Harry found himself warming to Sir John. When he was not bullying people, he became approachable. Fenn, too, was less harsh a man than he had first taken him for.

'I've read warnings in the broadsheets of another civil war, whichever side gets its way.'

'Imagine!' Sir John looked horrified. 'The country at war with itself again. Being too young, I did not fight in the Wars, Mr. Hunt. I know plenty who did. My father, for one. After some wrestling with his conscience, he in time declared for the King. He was captured at Newark and made a prisoner. Fairfax had him confined to his house for the rest of the war, for which I thank him, since it ensured my father's safety.' The Justice chuckled. 'An extraordinary man, my father. You know, he once had a leaping competition with the last King—God bless his memory—which he won. My father never used stirrups to mount a horse, preferring to jump into a saddle. He was clever, too. I think of him every day.' He pointed at Harry's meal. 'It was a plate of oysters that killed him, poisoning his stomach. I have avoided them ever since.'

Harry looked doubtfully down at his plate. His taste had suddenly faded, as if his tongue had lost connection with his brain.

'His Majesty, at least, now sees the threat his son poses,' Sir John continued, his eyes gleaming, amused by Harry's discomfort. 'He has stripped Monmouth of his appointments. The Duke no longer keeps his captaincy of the Life Guard, his governorship of Hull, or his Mastership of Horse.'

'He could have raised a considerable force against his father,' Fenn said.

'I had a friend, a Colonel who fought for Parliament,' Harry told them. 'Even in old age, he suffered from his memories of it.'

Sir John looked at Harry with a heightening interest. 'An odd ally for a young man such as you, I might think. I met once with Cromwell. Had I agreed with his cause I would have thought him the greatest of men.'

The Justice finished his food, wiped his greasy fingers on his napkin, and inspected Harry shrewdly. 'There is more to you than meets the eye, Mr. Hunt. You resemble any of the bloods in White-hall, all slaves to Monmouth in his style. It makes me wonder quite what it is you are.'

Harry took his time to answer. 'Most men are a mixture, are they not? Of certainties and doubts. I was Mr. Hooke's apprentice. I am lucky now to have money. Mine is not a complicated story.' The wine, in combination with the oysters, was making it difficult to swallow.

'Fair speech, fair spoken, Mr. Hunt. I know you were rewarded. The King praised you to me. Monmouth, too, knew of you. Of course, I had heard of the Queen's Consult, and the poison machine you found there.'

Fenn picked up a leftover potato and raised it at Harry to acknowledge the deed. 'Everyone has heard of the Queen's Consult,' he whispered.

Sir John rubbed the last of the grease slicking between his palms. 'Most men *are* a mixture, aren't they?' he observed. 'Those who are not make the most trouble, I find.'

To hurry the pair dining with him, he began to pull his coat back on. Fenn was quickest to respond, pushing aside his plate and rising from his chair. Harry drained the last of his wormwood wine. On top of Thomas Thynne's claret, it made him feel sluggish and queasy.

Clumsily, he pushed his chair back, and only just remembered to reclaim his hat.

'I wonder which one is Count Königsmarck,' he said, as they steered themselves towards the door.

CHAPTER ELEVEN

THE MONMOUTHITE BONFIRE

Wanting to check on the Holborn Night Watch, Fenn went to reclaim his horse. Sir John hailed a hackney up by the King's Gate, but its driver was reluctant to take them northwards to Leicester Fields for Sir John, then on to Bloomsbury for Harry.

'You make a show of refusal,' Harry said, 'to raise up your price.'

'I do not,' the man said, weary of the way such gentlemen spoke to him. 'There's trouble at Charing Cross. A bonfire's been lit, and a crowd's gathered.'

'The Green Ribboners,' Sir John said, settling himself into the seat next to Harry. 'Let us hope they do not become too dithyrambic. A temerity, this close to the Palace. More usually, their bonfires and processions keep to the City.'

'I saw the faggots placed there this afternoon,' the driver said testily, as if Sir John doubted him. 'A stuffed Pope, too, to be burned. Outside Northumberland House.'

'The home of Elizabeth Thynne, née Percy, the lady we seek,' Sir John muttered aside to Harry. Then, to the driver, 'Go through the Park, to avoid the protesting.'

The driver set them off, the clatter of hooves starting on the cobbles.

'There,' Harry called to him. 'That was not so hard.'

'Don't blame me if there's trouble,' the driver answered sullenly.

'You shall have a shilling for yours,' Harry told him, knowing he could not afford to refuse them.

The hackney's wheels rattled up King Street, past the buildings of Whitehall Palace and Scotland Yard. A lamp by the driver poked a feeble light ahead, into the nighttime darkness.

On land gifted by the King to Sir George Downing, a new street of houses was under construction. Downing, Cromwell's spymaster, had shown himself useful to the King by hunting down his former comrades, the Regicides. Designed by Sir Christopher Wren, the street was planned as a cul-de-sac, but the way still lay clear to St. James's Park. Seeing the bonfire's red glow through the opening of the Holbein Gate, the driver took the turn.

They could hear chants of 'For Monmouth! For Monmouth!' and 'Fear Papistry!'

If Monmouth was already home, after their meeting at Cannon Row, he could not fail to hear them; his house was on Hedge Lane, beside the Royal Mews.

'Monmouth would not show himself to them, surely?' Sir John said. 'It would be too flagrant.'

'He has no desire for his father's throne,' Harry said. 'Or so he told us.'

Sir John grunted. 'He would not turn it down if gifted to him. But he is more than Shaftesbury's puppet. Monmouth's is a balancing act. He wants to usurp his uncle without further offending his father.'

The driver went into the Park, which he was not supposed to do. Sir John reassured him, saying he would explain it, and besides, any local Watchman would be busy at Charing Cross.

'I have done enough policing today to allow this man across the Park,' Sir John told Harry.

Spilling into the Park from Cockspur, Monmouthites gathered. As the hackney drew closer to them, its lamp illuminated the protesters' green ribbons, which fluttered and dragged behind them, pinned to their clothes. Some in the crowd wore outfits entirely of green. Some had painted their faces the same colour. They appeared, then disappeared as quickly, dreamlike in the lamp's beam.

The driver encouraged the horses with a snap of his whip, although the protesters ignored him, all intent on reaching Charing Cross. As he cut the corner, his hackney bounced across the grass; he was anxious to reach the safety of Haymarket, the main thoroughfare to Piccadilly and the Western Road.

The crowd's noise faded behind them.

Arriving in Leicester Fields, Harry stopped the Justice from rising. 'I must tell you one thing more before you go.' He felt bilious from the meal and the journey. His lips were numb.

Sir John regarded him expectantly.

'A coincidence is all,' Harry continued. 'I know you felt I hid my seeing Diana, when she took a hackney to Covent Garden.'

'If she ever did,' Sir John said. 'We know only she told her father so.'

'I shall visit Sir Peter Lely to affirm it.'

'What is it you wish to tell me, Mr. Hunt?' Sir John asked, impatient to return home.

'After our going to Africa House, I went to London Bridge. I wanted to see where Sir Benedict went to pay the two hundred Guinea coins, and also for some time to think things through.'

'Some solitary reflection? I value the same. Although, I remember, I did ask you to return home.'

Harry made an apologetic face. 'Afterwards, I went to the Goldsmiths' Hall, to its shops on Carey Lane.'

When Sir John spoke, his words were measured. 'Where Elizabeth Thynne told her grandmother she planned to go. Where her husband's men searched again this afternoon.'

'Thynne's men did not question me. As I have never seen her, I could not have helped them, anyways.'

'You never have? Whoa, driver! You get me home.'

Instead of any goodbyes or further discussion, Sir John paid the driver, rapped with his stick on the coach's wheel to signal he was away, then glanced back once more as he crossed the pavement to his house.

CHAPTER TWELVE

THE BRISK
BOYS

'On to Bloomsbury, if you please.' Harry's voice sounded harsher than he had meant. He wanted to purge himself of the oysters, especially after telling the Justice of Carey Lane, but had no wish to ask the driver to stop.

'*If I please*,' the man said sourly, under his breath.

As they approached Cock and Pye Fields, another red glow flickered, this one across the facade of Newport House. More protesters had set alight barrels of pitch. Harry heard chanting again, this time of 'Brisk Boys!' Rough music was being played; pipes blown and drums beaten.

A sudden thud made him start.

'By God, you prick!' The driver used his whip for more speed.

Figures came out of the darkness. A man's pale face appeared at Harry's window. Someone else banged on the side.

'Stop!' a voice shouted gruffly.

'I shall not! On. On.' The whip again, but then, 'Whoo!'

The halt pitched Harry forwards on his seat. More faces appeared next to him, and someone hit the hackney's door with something hard.

'You shitten rogue!' the driver shouted.

'We would know if you be for Monmouth, or for York,' a deep voice said.

The door was pulled open. Two wild-eyed men looked in at Harry. One held a cudgel, the other a Protestant flail.

A green-painted woman pushed in between them.

The hackney's interior reverberated with the noise of their shouting. 'For Monmouth! For Monmouth!'

'What in the name of stars have we here?' the green woman asked gleefully. 'Will yer look at this bawcock?'

Harry scrambled to the far side of the seat. The woman grabbed at him; he knocked her away. The door on the other side was opened; more Monmouthites clamoured at him.

Pushed by unseen hands, the hackney started to rock.

'Away, whore's-son!' the driver cried as he was pulled down from his seat. Harry heard his body thud to the ground.

'Out!' This voice was high-pitched. Its owner had pinned green ribbons to his coat front.

The man with the cudgel raised it at him. 'Come out, or we drag you out!'

'I shall, I shall.'

Harry stumbled as he climbed down from the hackney.

'He looks plump in the pocket,' the woman said.

'And moist!' the man with the high-pitched voice observed. He pushed his face right into Harry's. 'Have yer drunk for Monmouth, or for York?'

The people, all festooned with ribbons, pressed around him. Another woman pushed Harry's shoulder, spinning him into the side of the hackney.

The driver leaned against the wheel, blood streaming from a split cheek.

A large tankard appeared; a Monmouthite poured wine from a flagon.

The deep-voiced man—who turned out to be small-framed and wet-lipped, with spittle stringing at both sides of his mouth—held the tankard towards Harry. 'You quaff to Monmouth,' he said implacably.

'Quaff to Monmouth! Quaff to Monmouth!'

'Brisk Boys! Brisk Boys!'

Reluctantly—too slowly for one of the men, who pushed him again—Harry took it.

Harry's heart thumped against his ribs. His hand shook so much, he could barely hold the tankard. 'You force my obedience,' he said, slurring his words.

'You're for York, then!' high-pitch shouted triumphantly. 'The King's brother, not his son!'

'I might have toasted Monmouth freely. Instead, you threaten me and bully the driver.'

'You're too nazy to get clever, bawcock.'

'It would waste both my time, and yours.'

A savage punch hit the side of Harry's head, catching the top of his ear; he did not even see who delivered it. The surprise and the pain made him vomit wine and oysters over his shirtfront and breeches, and on his Moroccan leather shoes.

His spectacles fell to the road.

'Break his peepers!' someone shouted.

Amid laughter and more shoves, Harry managed to grab them before anyone else could. He slid them back on, wincing with pain when the temple scraped the top of his injured ear.

A Monmouthite pushed the driver—who stood holding his face, blood leaking between his fingers—closer to Harry.

'Drink for Monmouth, then be on your way,' deep-voice said.

The driver raised his chin defiantly. 'The Devil fetch me, I shall not, as it means against the King.'

Harry winced. What was the man thinking? They should drink. These people were not open to reason, nor willing to debate. They proclaimed themselves Brisk Boys. Even the women.

'You are a Papist, then!' High-pitch was exultant. The driver got another swipe, this time across his throat with the flail.

'To support the King is not Papist, you turd!' the driver shouted, pain making him crouch on the ground. One woman went to kick at his head, but the deep-voiced man held her back.

'The King wants his brother to succeed him, does he not? And *he* is openly Catholic.' Deep-voice seemed to be respected; the others nodded in agreement.

'And the King takes French money from his Catholic cousin, so he may rule without Parliament,' said high-pitch. 'Now drink, you fucksters!'

Harry swung the tankard backwards, sending vinegary wine down his gullet, where it mixed with the taste of vomit.

'For Monmouth! For Monmouth!'

Trying not to choke, Harry passed the tankard to the hackney driver, who was doubled over next to him. 'Please, will you drink? This is not worth a beating.'

'Wise words, my friend,' deep-voice said, clapping Harry on the shoulder.

'Drink! Drink! Drink! For Monmouth! For Monmouth!'

The driver raised his eyes to the Monmouthites—Green Ribboners, Brisk Boys—milling around him, held out the tankard towards them in an exaggerated toast, then poured wine into his wide-open mouth. Plenty escaped, flowing down his chin until the tankard was completely dry.

He turned it upside down to show them.

'Say the words! You drink to Monmouth!'

'To Monmouth,' both men said together. 'We drink to Monmouth.'

'Now, kick away,' deep-voice said, taking Harry's hat and swatting him on his face with it.

Once the exultant crowd had melted away, the route the driver took to Bloomsbury Square was, to Harry's no great surprise, along Monmouth Street.

Outside his home, as well as the promised shilling, he gave the driver an extra sixpence for his trouble.

CHAPTER THIRTEEN

THE SINGULAR ISSUE

The next morning, Harry left Bloomsbury Square early.

He wore his tougher boots: yellow leather, better for walking, and clean. Dressed more plainly than yesterday, he had chosen his second-best peruke, this one black and shiny. The deep-voiced Brisk Boy had confiscated his hat; Harry decided to forego one.

The sun already baked the air. By the time he arrived at Gresham, he was sweating.

At Harry's knock, Hooke appeared and stood in the doorway without inviting him in.

He always has something of the metallic, Harry thought, as he surveyed the older man. Hooke's hair, long and untied, was silvery. Depending on the light, his irises were mercury, or tin, or pewter. Even in summer, and with all his walking around London as City

Surveyor, Hooke's pallor retained a tinge of grey, as if metal lurked in his flesh. Iron filings gathered on his chin and upper lip.

Hooke, too, took time to observe Harry. He paid close attention to Harry's blackening temple, wondering how much further the bruise continued beneath the peruke.

'Tell me of your yesterday,' he said eventually, by way of greeting.

Harry rubbed his sore ear self-consciously. 'I went with the Justice to Bethlehem. He arrested a Basketman. More for insolence than any evidence of guilt.'

'Dr. Allen dined with me last night, and told me of your visit. He was most offended. Sir John used ungodly language towards him.'

'When playing the role of Justice, Sir John can be rough. He has shown a smoother side.'

'Which is the truer reflection of him, I wonder?' Hooke did not expect an answer. 'The Justice came with the dead woman's father in the afternoon. Sir Benedict was inconsolable. He has engaged undertakers already, who took her last evening.'

'We told him the news at Africa House, which was horrible to do.' Harry regarded the empty quadrangle, its grass craving rain. 'I need to speak with Thomas Crawley.'

'He knows nothing more than he told Sir John yesterday,' Hooke said sharply.

'The staff at Bethlehem, I think, also know nothing more.'

Hooke made a pained expression. 'You think the exchange happened here?'

'I want Crawley to show me where he stored the body before the dissection.'

'You have seen the anatomy room often enough, Harry.'

'Is he here?' Harry persisted.

'We shall find him,' Hooke said, with a heavy sigh.

Harry looked up the stairs to Hooke's lodgings. 'Is Grace there with you?'

'You ask, since you have invited her to luncheon today, so she tells me, at your new house. Do the two of you have an understanding?'

The question's bluntness took Harry by surprise. 'Would we have your blessing, Mr. Hooke, if we did?'

Hooke cocked his head to consider his onetime apprentice, who was now very much his own man. A wealthy one, too, since his rewarding. Hooke felt keenly the loss of the boy, who had been deft and eager to learn. He felt awkward with the man—this replacement—unsure even how to address him.

Was he still Harry, or was he Mr. Hunt?

Harry was nervous, it gratified Hooke to see, so must still value his opinion.

'This is backwards,' Hooke answered. 'You have not yet sought my blessing, therefore I cannot give it.'

Harry's mouth was an O of surprise.

'The question you pose is conditional on your answer from Grace,' Hooke continued, oblivious to Harry's dismay, as if this were merely a chance to explain logic to a simple pupil. 'Which you hope for today, unless I mistake the purpose of this luncheon.'

'You *have* discussed it with her, I see,' Harry said, cheering a little.

'We guessed it together.' Hooke smiled wryly. 'Have a care how you ask. As her guardian, I have tried arrangements in the past.'

'I know very well how stubborn she is.'

'You are a pair, then. The both of you being stubborn may not be felicitous, in a marriage. I doubt not your feelings for one another. I do know she feels a little slighted. Your focus has been on your house rather than her.' Hooke waved away Harry's attempted interruption. 'I am cognisant as to why. You wish it made suitable for her domesticity.'

Although he would soften Hooke's term, Harry could not deny it. 'So, is she here, Mr. Hooke?'

'At the Royal Exchange. She begged money for a dress. Perhaps that augers well for your answer.'

Harry felt a pulse of concern. 'Is anyone with her?'

Hooke caught Harry's flustered expression, a frown creasing his forehead. 'Mary Robinson.'

'I ask, because yesterday I saw a ransom letter. Diana Cantley's kidnappers promised her return if they were paid.'

Hooke's eyes widened. 'Did Sir Benedict refuse to?'

'No. They took his money, on London Bridge.'

'Yet they murdered her?' Hooke's eyes widened further still. 'Hence, you worry after Grace.'

'Diana was already dead before Sir Benedict received the letter. Another woman has been kidnapped, too. Mrs. Elizabeth Thynne.'

Hooke stepped back, to distance himself from Harry and his news. 'Formerly, the Baroness Percy?'

'It is all the work of a Swedish Count. Sir John has men searching London for him, as does Mr. Thynne.'

'Will this Count murder Mrs. Thynne, too?' Hooke's grey face was even greyer.

'No, no . . .' Harry wanted to reassure himself. 'He seems enamoured with her, and her with him. Your mention of the Royal Exchange made me worry. That is where Mrs. Thynne was last seen.'

'Where did you learn this? I have heard no rumour of it.'

'From her husband, at his house in Cannon Row. I went there last night with Sir John. The Duke of Monmouth was there, too.'

'Monmouth is no legitimate heir, although Thynne would have him so. His supporters are seditious. Against the King, against heredity, and for Exclusion. You cannot move about London without demands for your signature to a petition. Ah, this singular issue . . . London—the whole country—disagrees over it. Every other man speaks in favour. Each man in between rails against.'

'There is a middle way,' Harry said.

'Limitation? The Duke of York would never accept it. He would overturn any constraints placed upon him.'

'Monmouth is popular. Last night I saw a bonfire lit, and there was trouble. Green Ribboners showing their support.'

'Did their *support* result in that contusion on your temple?'

Harry rubbed under his peruke. 'Brisk Boys, bullying concordance. They stopped my hackney. They hurt its driver, too. One of them took my hat.'

'It's not safe to venture out after dark nowadays,' Hooke said matter-of-factly, showing no sympathy, least of all for the hat. 'Shaftesbury and his Green Ribbon Club have stirred up the mobile.'

'Why should it not be stirred? The Succession affects all of us, equally. Parliament brought the King back from France. Why should it not choose his replacement?'

'The King's return was not the sea of democracy you suppose. No one had the heart to oppose General Monck, when he marched his men from Scotland.'

'The King had to promise appeasements.'

'And ever since, has worked to negate them. He keeps the power of prorogation. Shaftesbury turned Parliament against him, so the King stops its meeting. Shaftesbury risks the Tower, as when he offended the King before. Some say he authors Titus Oates's evidence, though I doubt it.'

Harry smiled slowly. 'We have rarely spoken of politics, Mr. Hooke.'

'Exclusion sucks us all in, does it not?' Hooke glanced up his stairs, still worried for Grace and her whereabouts, then turned back to Harry. 'Come, let us find Thomas Crawley.' He locked his door behind him. 'That brings a question to my mind. Where is the body of the Bethlehem suicide?'

Harry shrugged his ignorance. 'Sebiliah Barton was her name. Her death troubles me as much as Diana Cantley's. Since he is friendly with Sir Benedict, Sir John thought only of Diana. Now, though, his hands are full with finding Mrs. Thynne and the Swedish Count.'

'Is your involvement, then, at an end?'

'Sebiliah's death leaves questions.'

'Do not go causing trouble for Dr. Allen.'

'Things happen at Bethlehem without his knowledge.'

'You must not sully the Hospital's good name.'

'Better, then, for this matter to be properly explained.'

Hooke scowled, but made no further reply. He set off across the quadrangle, ignoring the path and walking straight across the sun-frazzled grass.

CHAPTER FOURTEEN

THE CHANGED MIND

Crawley braised metal in the workshop, putting together a sturdy-looking frame.

'For my signalling system,' Hooke told Harry, inspecting the joins. 'I am to show its usefulness to Mr. Pepys at the Admiralty Office. With one frame above my lodgings and another in Harrow, on the school there, the distance between them is fifteen miles. Far enough for the demonstration.'

'You showed me before, Mr. Hooke. I recall your symbols. More clearly discerned than the standard alphabet.'

Hooke indicated the symbols made from pine boards stacked against the wall behind Crawley. 'With telescopes, we could read messages originating from Portsmouth, or Chatham, and they would reach London in under a half-hour. My enemy is inclement weather. Especially fog.'

'Your signalling towers must be close enough together.'

Hooke swatted aside the obviousness of Harry's point. 'I expect the Navy to pay handsomely.'

'By the Navy, you mean its Commissioner, Viscount Brouncker. Who was, until Sir Christopher replaced him, the Royal Society's President.'

'Everything is politics, is it not?' Hooke gestured to Crawley. 'Pause, Thomas. Mr. Hunt wishes to see where you stored the body.'

Reluctantly, the Observator put aside his tools.

'Show me the way you brought in the cart,' Harry instructed him. 'And where you stopped to unload it.'

'I brought it through the stable yard.' Crawley addressed Hooke, making Harry bridle at the discourtesy.

They followed Crawley to the stables, then back across the quadrangle, until he reached the spot nearest the anatomy room.

'You left the cart unattended, to open the door.' Harry phrased his question like a statement. Sir John's interrogation style was infectious.

'That took only a moment. No time to swap two bodies.'

'You summoned help.'

'As it was late, it was quiet. I thought it quicker by myself.'

'You were able to lift her,' Harry stated again, comparing his memory of Jones, the bulky Basketman, to the gangly youth before him.

'She was inside a hamper,' Crawley said. 'That was heavy, so I removed her from it.'

Crawley kept licking his lips. Harry stared at his mouth until he noticed and stopped. The Observator coloured from embarrassment—or was it anger?

'Then you carried her from the cart,' Harry continued.

Crawley spread his hands, pushing the question away. 'I more . . . dragged her.'

'You risked damaging her.'

'I was careful when I lifted her down.'

'But then you pulled her . . . like this?' Harry mimed the action, crossing the covered walkway, walking backwards with an imaginary corpse whose heels bumped inaudibly over the tiles. 'Presumably, you held her by her armpits.'

Crawley nodded shamefacedly. Still walking backwards, Harry entered the anatomy room, where a black marble slab supported on trestles, and sloping to a cedarwood trough, served as the cutting table.

Hooke's dissection tools remained in the repository. Without them, the anatomy room looked bare.

'You lifted her onto the table,' Harry told Crawley. 'How so?'

Looking persecuted, his sharp Adam's apple bobbing up and down, Crawley took the invisible woman from Harry and hoisted her onto the marble slab. He positioned her head and shoulders first, then lifted her body, then swung her legs until she lay securely on it.

'You uncovered her to look at her,' Harry said.

Crawley reddened further. 'I have a proper respect for bodies. She stayed covered.'

'Then?'

'I locked the door and returned to my room. I did not see her again until the morning.'

'When you removed the sheet, in the morning, was she dressed or undressed?'

'I had to undress her.'

'What time was this?'

'St. Helen's had just rung eleven.'

'And it was the same woman dissected in the repository later. Miss Diana Cantley.'

'The same.'

'Did she wear a Bethlehem uniform?'

'She had on her own clothes, as some of the patients do.'

'Where are they, Crawley?' Harry deliberately omitted the *Mister.*

'On the pile, ready for burning.'

Harry flicked his head towards the College's rubbish pile, behind the stables.

Within a minute, Crawley had returned with the same mauve dress Diana wore when Harry had helped her into the hackney. Crawley had wrapped her shoes, her underclothes, and her hat inside it, making a pathetic bundle.

The dress was crusted with blood.

'Did you think her wound self-inflicted?' Harry asked incredulously.

Crawley looked haplessly at him, then at Hooke, hoping for support.

'You are the Royal Society's Observator.' Harry slapped his hand down on the mortuary slab. 'Observe!'

'Gently, Harry,' Hooke said.

'I did not think of it at all,' Crawley confessed. 'I thought only of the dissection and making her ready.'

'There's nothing else she had?' Harry's tone hardly softened. 'No bag? No purse?'

Crawley looked guiltily at Harry, then at Hooke. Slowly, he reached into his pocket. 'Only this,' he said. 'From around her neck.'

He held a simple chain. From it hung a small brass key.

Harry took it from him. The chain was silver; he decided to ignore why Crawley had kept it. 'Small for a door,' he said, showing the key to Hooke.

'For a jewellery box, then?' Hooke suggested. 'Grace has one like it.'

'Sir Benedict shall want it,' Harry said. He slid it into his own pocket, then changed his mind, hanging it around his neck, as Diana had done. Then he blew out his cheeks impatiently and marched back outside.

Crawley followed meekly, Hooke walking behind.

Harry gazed over Gresham's quadrangle, as if the answers he looked for floated in the shimmering air.

Without looking at him, he spoke to Crawley. 'You stopped the cart inside the stables.'

'It was late. No one was there.'

'You do not quite answer my question,' Harry said. 'Did you wait inside?'

'I rode straight through. I swear it.'

Turning to the Observator, Harry realised Crawley was trembling and close to tears.

Harry's questions had been like those of the Justice: harsh, dismissive, overly persistent. He had even slipped into Sir John's way of phrasing: *You do not quite answer my question.*

He stared down at his yellow boots for a moment, then lifted his eyes back to Crawley. 'I am sorry, Thomas. I have spoken far too roughly.' He looked at Hooke, who stood behind Crawley with his arms folded. 'The bodies were not swapped here.'

'Resume your work with the signalling frames, Thomas,' Hooke said. 'The second one is still to finish. Thank you for showing us how you brought in the dead woman.'

Crawley strode away, wiping at his face.

'You were too harsh,' Hooke told Harry. 'He will learn.'

'I shall apologise again. My puzzlement frustrates me. If some-one swapped the women here, it must have been in the morning. Which makes me think one of the Fellows is responsible.'

Hooke looked around the quadrangle as if to catch the Fellow still in the act. Then he returned his gaze to Harry. His eyes were dark; they looked more like gunmetal.

'When you were my assistant, then when I made you Operator, then when the Royal Society appointed you as Observator, you always looked up to me.' Hooke spoke very quietly; Harry had to lean in towards him, as he had with Fenn at the Rhenish winehouse. 'You were a whirligig in those days.' Hooke smiled at the memory. 'You, I believe, wanted to be me. To surpass me, even, for you are a competitive soul. Perhaps, one day, you shall. You may become the Royal Society's Secretary, or have a professorship here at Gresham. Or something greater. Who knows? What will you become? Who will you be? Certainly, you are capable of much.'

Hooke placed his hands on Harry's shoulders and brought his metal eyes uncomfortably close; the two men were almost nose to nose.

'Thomas Crawley's ambitions are not so high. He wanted only to be you, Harry. Today, I think, he will have changed his mind.'

CHAPTER FIFTEEN

THE SELF–SATISFIED MAN

This was Harry's favourite view.

From his first-floor withdrawing room he could admire Blooms-bury Square, with its gravel paths forming four square lawns, its well-laid pavements, and the neat cobbles of its roads. Across its opposite side stretched Southampton House, the hills of Hampstead and Highgate rising beyond. Houses of red London brick, like his own, lined the other three sides, although with a pleasing irregularity. All benefitted from the residents' anxiety to keep them as neat as their neighbours.

Free from the City's congestion and upwind of its smells and smokes, the Square boasted aristocracy and aldermen, and those made rich by commerce, speculation, lawyering, and doctoring.

And now it boasted Mr. Henry Hunt, rewarded generously by

Hortense Mancini, the Duchesse de Mazarin, for an assignment successfully undertaken, and by a King grateful for the saving of his wife.

At last, Harry felt worthy of Grace Hooke.

Throughout his apprenticeship, he had wished after her. A hopeless aspiration. Until now—until his reward, until moving into this house—he had never been near her equal.

A coach-and-four pulled into the Square. Harry hoped it carried her—Grace was later than they had arranged. Instead, it stopped outside Sir Benedict's house, next door but one. It carried an elderly couple, Harry saw. The Deputy-Governor's parents, possibly? They struggled out of the coach and made slow progress towards the house, helped by Sir Benedict himself, who looked pale and despondent.

The three disappeared from view, returning inside what had been, until so recently, Diana's home.

With a flush of shame, Harry thought again of his furtive watching of her through this window, retreating behind his India screen if he thought she had sensed his gaze.

The King had commanded him to help find Diana's murderer. Harry hoped Sir John would not want him also to help search for the Swedish Count, Königsmarck, and the other man Thynne and the Duke had mentioned, Kapitän Vratz, the Pomeranian.

The Justice had enough men of his own, surely?

From downstairs came reassuring noises of Harry's cook, Hubert, busy preparing the luncheon. They had spent much of yesterday morning deciding courses. With Harry's maid, Janet, Hubert then ventured out to Holborn market to find the necessary ingredients. Harry had left at the same time for Gresham and the dissection; he had given his last instructions from inside the sedan chair.

He could hear his servant, Oliver Shandois, in the dining room, setting out the cutlery. The gold rather than the silver.

On the new mantelpiece of Italian marble, over the rebuilt fireplace—the old one ripped out was too small—sat the box Harry had bought from the Goldsmiths' Hall.

Despite this business with Sir John Reresby, Harry was a very self-satisfied man indeed.

☿

THE NEXT VEHICLE INTO THE SQUARE had a driver he recognised. One of Gresham's stable boys, and the coach was Robert Hooke's.

Harry went to instruct Oliver—who had left his real name on the West African coast—to welcome Grace inside. A uniform for the boy would be good, Harry thought, recalling the splendour of Thomas Thynne's doorman. Some, he knew, gave their black servants silver collars engraved with their masters' names, which looked smart. After all, Oliver was Harry's representative to his callers.

Then Harry called for Janet to bring tea and the countess cakes Grace liked, made with marzipan and rose water.

Back in his withdrawing room, he settled into his purple velvet sofa and inspected the room again. That morning, Janet had cleaned every surface and straightened every object. Swept out the fireplace. Brushed the Turkish carpet and wiped the India screen. Polished the teak cabinets, the glass decanters, the silver candlesticks, and the walnut longcase clock made by Thomas Tompion. Shaken the linen damask curtains edged with lace to French design, which matched the upholstery of the chairs. Dusted the frame of his glowing landscape in oils, an English copy after Claude Lorrain.

Harry looked again—after a little burst of fear—at the box on the mantelpiece.

☿

OLIVER'S TRAMPLING UP THE STAIRS ALWAYS reminded Harry how Tom Gyles, Hooke's nephew and apprentice, used to move around Hooke's lodgings at Gresham. Grace's footsteps, contrastingly, were light. Almost silently so.

Harry stood as Oliver—who kept his face impassive at the pantomime of relaxed ease his master performed—showed Grace in. When Oliver left them, he bowed deeply, as if they were royalty.

In the light flooding through the window, Grace's fine blonde hair glowed. The day's brilliance made her pale cream dress appear lit from within.

Checking his servant was away from the door, Harry took her hands in his and kissed her proffered cheek, making her wrinkle her nose at the smell of his pomade.

'Spectators gather for the Tyburn Fair,' she said, gesturing towards the clock to explain her lateness.

Harry chastised himself; he had forgotten about the executions, even though Sir John had mentioned them yesterday on their way to Africa House.

Grace studied his long waistcoat. 'Peacock blue, Harry?'

'Azure, my tailor told me.'

'Azure it must be. With silver galloon, too. Silk breeches?'

'Silk moiré.'

Grace looked at him with concern. 'Whatever's the matter?'

Harry's face had frozen into a rictus smile.

'Nothing at all,' he answered with difficulty. 'It is wonderful to see you. Janet is to bring countess cakes. I know you like them.'

'I do like them.' Grace was looking at him, her head cocked to one side—the same pose her uncle used when thinking. 'I had them on my last visit here.'

'Less rose water than before.'

'Explain that bruise upon your head.'

Discomfited, Harry raised his hand to touch it. 'Ah. I met some Green Ribboners last night, who took against me.'

'I see they did.'

Harry had tried on his best peruke—the cream one he wore for the dissection—when changing after questioning Crawley at Gresham, but it sat too uncomfortably over his bruise. And, inside his house, with Grace for a luncheon, a wig felt too formal. She would think it preposterous. Instead, he had asked Janet to tie his hair back. Left to grow these past months, he had thought it long enough to hide the injury.

As Harry seemed unwilling to provide further detail, Grace pressed him. 'Uncle said you were hurt. At Shaftesbury's show by Charing Cross.'

'This was at Cock and Pye Fields. Away from the bonfire, I believed I was safe.'

'Why argue with them? You are hardly political.'

'They give me no chance to debate. If they had known I spoke with their darling only a short time before, they may have disliked me less.'

'Lord Shaftesbury, you mean? Or the Duke of Monmouth?'

'Monmouth. After the King commanded me to help the Justice of Peace for Westminster, our business took us to him.'

Grace looked gratifyingly impressed. 'Mary told me of Diana Cantley, murdered. She said you recognised her and stopped her dissection.'

'Mr. Hooke expected a suicide from Bethlehem Hospital. Instead, it was my neighbour.'

'Trouble finds you again, it seems.'

'I think Sir John is finished with me. He has the Watch searching London for the man who killed her. A Swedish Count, apparently. He has also kidnapped Thomas Thynne's wife.'

'Did you tell Uncle this morning?' The thought appeared to irritate her.

'I did. You were gone shopping, he said. Is that when you bought that dress?'

Grace ignored his question. 'Why did he not tell me of Elizabeth Thynne's kidnap?'

Harry felt relieved. It was her uncle she was irritated by, not him. He reached out to touch her dress. 'Very elegant, Grace. It suits you well.'

She jerked away from him, and the compliment, her hand smoothing where Harry had touched the fabric. 'By keeping from me what happens in London, I suppose he thinks he protects me. But how can my ignorance help me? It makes me less safe, not more.'

Grace moved to the window, and looked along the pavement below, towards where the Cantleys lived. To where Sir Benedict lived, she corrected herself. For now, he was alone.

She had known Diana slightly. Beautiful girl.

Still annoyed, she turned back to Harry.

'I have heard of Elizabeth's dalliance with the Count. If she is with him, it is willingly, by all accounts.'

'It looks as though he murdered Diana. He wrote a ransom letter to her father, delivered after she was dead, then took the money from him. There was a second letter to Mr. Thynne.'

Grace flinched. 'Thynne wants your help to fetch his wife back, I suppose.'

Harry wanted to discuss with her the differences between the two letters, but Janet arrived with a tray, which she placed on a small table by the window. Motioning at Grace to sit, Harry pushed her chair out then in for her, before sitting down himself.

Janet fussed with pouring tea and laying out plates for the cakes.

'Your girl is young,' Grace said, when Janet had left them.

'She is eleven.' Although Grace's tone was innocuous enough, Harry immediately felt defensive. 'Her family is glad of her wages.'

'Your African is young, too. He has no family, glad or otherwise, as far as you know, since you bought him at a Covent Garden auction.'

'His last master wanted younger. I did not buy him. I give Oliver a servant's wages, and also his shelter.'

'*Give* him? You are generous.'

'And I take an interest in his education. His reading improves every day.'

'A kindness to him? Or to you? Being able to read shall make him more useful to you.'

As she was being prickly, Harry deflected her questions. 'My cook is old.'

'Your Frenchman? Not that old.'

'You might say, being a cook, he is seasoned.'

Grace was unwilling to acknowledge his joke. 'What says he is?'

'A cook? Why, the letter recommending him. From the Chevalier de Fouville himself.'

'You take the document to be genuine?'

'Hubert cooks very well.'

'Then you have the evidence of your senses. As Uncle would require.'

They both smiled at this, but Harry's smile was forced. This conversation was nowhere near taking him to his desired destination.

'I have not invited you here to speak of my servants, Grace. Tell me how you have been.'

Grace widened her eyes and gripped his wrist, moving aside his shirt's abundant sleeve to do so. 'Have you not heard the news of my health?'

'You have been ill?' Harry said, his voice rising from concern. 'I am so sorry, Grace, I did not know.'

'Not at all. I have been perfectly well.' She released her hold. 'If you had not been so neglectful of our friendship, you would know. You have upset Uncle, too, by your absence from Gresham, and the lack of any invitation to your house.'

'You know what he is like. He would wish to put his mark on the place. Then take offence if I did not follow his suggestions. It is now completed, I think.' Harry took a nervous swallow. He should broach the matter of his intent. 'I hope to your satisfaction.'

'To my satisfaction?' Grace sipped her tea, then placed the fine china cup delicately onto its saucer. 'The last time I came here, I met with the man showing wall-stuffs. I spent an entire afternoon with him, as you had asked me to do. By the end of it, I was exhausted, he showed me so many.' She looked around the withdrawing room, then around it again, the opposite way. 'Yet I see none of my choices. Perhaps your house is not complete after all.'

Harry went to rest his hand on the back of hers, but she pulled away. 'You thought too much of their cost, Grace. He reduced his price for the best of them, so I purchased those instead. In here is flock on best linen. For value, I have chosen well.'

'You did not think his first price inflated, to pretend a saving?'

'You call him dishonest, with no reason to think so.'

'*You* did not think to consult me on your changes.'

Harry was at a loss for what to say. Her argument was unfair. He *had* considered her opinion, but the man's price became so reasonable he could not refuse him.

Grace had turned away from him, one shoulder now towards him, and had she pushed her chair further back, too?

This did not go well.

She spoke to the window rather than to him, the sunlight coming through it accentuating the cornflower blueness of her eyes. 'This house. These . . . things.' She fluttered her hand at all the objects in the room. 'Do you still pay for fencing lessons?'

The question threw Harry. 'Solomon Faubert is an excellent teacher. He was the Keeper of Horse to Louis Quatorze.'

'And so, expensive. You have dancing lessons, too. And elocution lessons. Your voice has changed.'

'I look to better myself, Grace. You cannot resent me for that.'

'I dare not guess how much your waistcoat cost.'

'Since my reward, I can better dress myself.'

'You must be near to spending it all.'

'There is still plenty aside. I have also looked at investments to increase it. The Africa trade. The East India Company. Canada furs. The Somers Isles Company, in Bermuda. The New River Company, whose pipes now supply half the water in London. You may go to the

Royal Exchange, to seek the merchants there, and come away with a dozen ideas of how best to use your money.'

'Who is this man before me, in his waistcoat with silver galloon, and his silk moiré breeches, and his maid bringing us tea and countess cakes?'

Harry glanced across at the box on the mantelpiece. Panic was rising. How should he answer *that* question? All his thoughts of future happiness felt under threat.

'Grace . . . you know how strong my feelings are for you. I bought this house for *us*. I have tried to make it fit for *you*. I want—more than anything—to offer you a comfortable and happy life. A marriage, both of us equal in our contentment. A home fit for our children.'

'We have never spoken of *children*,' Grace said, drawing out the word. 'We have barely mentioned marriage.'

'I thought we had an understanding.'

'Have you discussed this with Uncle?'

'As a courtesy, I first discuss it with you.'

'I thank you for your courtesy.' Her voice was coldly flat. 'Is that your proposal, then?'

Her eyes' blueness was transfixing. She turned straight on towards him. 'You behave as though you can buy me. I am not to be sold. There are other women in London for that.'

It felt like a slap.

'And scarcely propitious, to ask me on the day of the Tyburn Fair.'

'In truth, I had forgotten all about it.'

'How self-involved you have become.'

Seeing Harry's stung expression, and the points of redness on his cheeks which always appeared when perturbed, Grace softened her voice. 'When you were Uncle's assistant, you always were busy with helping him. His surveying and building. His experimental trials. You made his models. Drew his designs. You helped him with his clocks, his optics, his air-pump. You catalogued Gresham's library, and his own. And a hundred other things more. You made his marine barometer. The glider.'

'I broke my ankle landing it on the quadrangle.'

'I would not call that a landing.'

'It was the gentlest meeting with the ground I could manage.'

'I helped Uncle reset the bone.'

'As I recuperated was the first time we really spoke with one another.'

'You whined about it for weeks.'

'It hurt.'

Grace gave a sad, small smile. 'You used to think of nothing but Uncle's schemes. The New Philosophy. The Royal Society.'

'As well you know, I thought of you, too. I may no longer be Mr. Hooke's man, but I have not forgotten those things. Not at all. I have built my own elaboratory, out in the garden. I have not yet shown you.' Harry reached across the table again for her hand; this time she allowed him to take it. 'My work for Mr. Hooke could have been little entertainment for you.'

'Far from it. For I had set my heart on you. I turned down two others, if you remember, disappointing Uncle on both occasions. I had set my heart on his assistant, Harry Hunt, who rarely thought of himself. Most men think of little else *but* themselves. You did not worry yourself then with fashion. Now you even keep a blackamoor boy, like a courtesan with her pet. You were modest. You were kind. You were clever. You were *interesting*. At least, to me.'

Coming from the kitchen downstairs, they could hear raised voices. Loudest came Hubert's strong French accent, but Janet's and Oliver's sounded excitable, too.

'Do they argue?' Grace asked.

Harry looked at her disconsolately. His approach towards a proposal had been disastrous—he must await another opportunity, when her mood was less set against him—and now he was being humiliated by the disgraceful behaviour of his servants.

'I know not. I should go to see.'

The voices increased in volume, then heavy footsteps advanced up the stairs.

'I don't know if I like Mr. Henry Hunt,' Grace continued, although by now she was distracted and looking towards the door. 'I much preferred my Harry. I'm sorry. Truly, I am. I find I have no wish to marry the man you have become.'

Oliver, without knocking, rushed into the withdrawing room.

'Mr. Hunt, sir. You must come! You must come!'

CHAPTER SIXTEEN

THE GARDEN ELABORATORY

'Would you wait here while I attend to this commotion?'

Feeling completely dejected, Harry expected Grace to leave. After her rebuff, she would never stay for the luncheon. His determination to propose, his careful planning, and his nervousness all led him to ignore her mood, and had made him insensitive towards her.

He had pressed on when he should have held back. It was poorly timed and poorly expressed.

That he was rich, she could not hold against him?

Now his servants spoiled his proposal completely. Without the interruption, perhaps he could have argued her back towards him. Persuaded her she was wrong.

Grace stood up and rearranged her dress, straightening out its skirts. 'If these are to be my servants, it is a chance to better know them.'

His hopes were not dashed after all!

She was too complicated sometimes, Harry thought, and often left him behind.

Oliver motioned frantically. They followed him, venturing towards the noise downstairs.

In the kitchen, Hubert spotted them first and hushed a red-eyed Janet. When he saw Grace standing just behind his employer, his eyes widened in what looked like panic.

Plump, sallow-skinned, with wild hair over his ears and grown past his collar, Hubert stepped from behind a table laden with platters and salvers, a tureen, serving bowls, and the profligate luncheon he had prepared.

'Monsieur, I must you show.' The cook's voice dropped to a murmur, as if only now was there need for discretion. 'Will you arrive in the *jardin*?'

Harry sent a mystified look to Grace. She looked back at him, entertained at what she took to be Hubert's French eccentricity. Although, whatever was in the garden had clearly upset Janet.

Harry turned back to his cook. 'What is the trouble? You may tell me here.'

'*Non! Je dois vous montrer!*' Hubert beckoned Harry to accompany him.

Grace went with them, into the heat of Harry's sunlit garden with its brace of newly transplanted apple trees at its centre, espaliered fig and pear trees trained across its walls, and an ordered area for herbs and simples. Paths divided the lawn to make a scale model of Bloomsbury Square, intersecting between the apple trees, where a bloomery-iron bench and a life-sized bronze Athena faced each other in the shade under the branches.

A sweet smell pervaded the air. The abundant insects and birds in the verdant lushness of this particular London garden all went about their noisy business, disregarding the humans who had joined them.

'I arrive, *pour les herbes*,' Hubert explained. 'I see door for *l'elaboratoire. C'est ouvert!* I go to look inside. *Vous venez*, Monsieur, *vous venez.*'

Harry's new elaboratory was a copy of the one belonging to Isaac Newton, the Lucasian Professor of Mathematics at Cambridge University. When visiting there, Harry had seen it, built against the chapel in Trinity College's garden. Harry's was more solidly constructed, with thicker timbers on a firmer foundation, and lit by larger glass windows. In case of fire from volatile elements, he had positioned it well away from his house.

Forgetting his station as employee, Hubert pulled Harry by the arm. Harry allowed himself to be taken, crossing the lawn as the others stayed back. He could see Grace looking flummoxed, and Oliver and Janet both tearful and shocked.

The elaboratory's door stood open. Someone had forced its frame, leaving splinters of wood jutting out around the sturdy lock.

When Harry stepped through the door, the smell became almost too much to bear.

Inside was his sturdy table made of African hardwood. The equipment Harry kept on it had been pushed aside. His never-yet-used microscope, its box's hinges broken, lay on the floor, surrounded by the pieces of a smashed glass alembic. Boxes and jars, holding powders and metals for experiments not yet performed, had also been swept from the table.

In their place, wrapped in a white sheet, lay a body on its back.

☿

ALTHOUGH THE STINK MADE HIM GAG, Harry forced himself closer. Unwrapping the sheet exposed the corpse's head.

A woman. She had been undernourished; her cheekbones pushed against her pale, translucent skin. Unlike Diana Cantley's, her face was free of any powder or colouring.

Her eyes, purple-lidded, set deep in their sockets, were tightly closed. Her lower lip caught behind her upper teeth, as if in concentration. Her hair was a dull, mousy brown, tangled and matted with blood. Patches of her scalp were red and scarred, where she had pulled at her hair.

Unwillingly, Harry reached out and pressed the dead woman's cheeks. They moved easily, rolling over the bone. He felt for her legs under the sheet, squeezing her thighs and calf muscles, and flexing her toes. They, too, were relaxed, the last parts of a body to soften as *rigor mortis* released its hold.

Her pliability gave little help to tell when she had died. The summer heat trapped in the confined space of his elaboratory, and the woman's thinness, meant the process of rigidity, then relaxation, would have passed quickly.

Harry knew the time of her death, anyways. Almost to the minute.

He pulled the sheet down to reveal her neck.

There was the wound he expected to see: a puncture hole high on her neck, just beneath her jaw, with a shallower gash to one side.

Where she inserted a knitting needle into her jugular vein, then pulled at it to ensure the wound was fatal.

The way blood streaked over her skin showed she had been wiped with a cloth, but not thoroughly.

Both to distance himself from the sickening smell and to look at the full length of her body on his table, Harry backed away.

He studied the outline she made under the sheet: there was something he had not expected.

Since no one at Bethlehem Hospital had told him of it.

☿

THE SOUND OF MOVEMENT MADE HIM turn. Grace stood just inside the doorway, pressing her nose with her fingers.

'This is the woman who died at Bethlehem,' Harry told her. 'Her name is Sebiliah Barton.'

'The poor, troubled soul.' Despite the smell, Grace moved further into the elaboratory and stared over his shoulder at the body.

'She was destined to be dissected at Gresham,' Harry said. 'But Diana Cantley was put in her place.'

'She was not destined to be so. Uncle's wish for a cadaver—any cadaver—was to take her to Gresham. Also, your wish—as all the Fellows wished—to observe her being dissected.'

'You know the Royal Society's business, and its requirement for bodies.'

'I meant no disparagement,' Grace answered quietly. She was looking at the wound on Sebiliah's neck. 'I think of her anguish. All dead bodies who find their way to Gresham, I suppose, have their stories to tell. Whether they be criminals, or suicides.'

Grace's eyes were glassy. Harry remembered the way of her father's death and berated himself. Of course, the thought of self-murder would upset her. Let alone direct evidence of it, lying in front of her on his elaboratory table.

He reached out his hand for her. She held it tightly, gripping it with both of hers.

They were aware of the absurd picture they made, in clothes chosen for a luncheon both had known was really a proposal of marriage, standing in a cramped elaboratory with a suicide's corpse.

'Come, Grace, let us return to the garden.'

☿

BACK OUTSIDE IN THE SUNSHINE, OUT in the fresher air, Harry's three servants stayed back from them, unwilling to be nearer the dead body, or to break in on their discussion.

Grace still gripped Harry's hand. 'This woman died at Bethlehem Hospital. Why should she now be here, inside your elaboratory?'

'It is a mischief against me,' Harry said miserably. 'To incriminate me.'

'In what? She ended her own life.'

'In the murder of Diana Cantley. At least, in knowing of it. Already, the Justice suspects me. As far as he knows, I am the last person to speak with Diana, when she last departed her house.'

'You were on speaking terms with her?'

'I helped her into her hackney, is all. Before that, her father introduced us. Sir John also suspects me because Mrs. Thynne was last seen at the Goldsmiths' Hall. I was there, too, but a day later.' Harry slumped his shoulders. 'Now Sebiliah Barton is with me.'

'A day later? That can hardly show your guilt.'

'You do not know Sir John.'

'You must find where Diana went afterwards, from someone who saw her. Mrs. Thynne, most likely, is willingly with her Swedish lover.'

'I am in difficulty, Grace. The Old Bailey does not overly trouble itself with evidence. Being suspect is often reason enough to hang.'

'This is a crime against you. Against your reputation. It is too obviously a ploy. You must tell the Justice straightaway of Sebiliah. Deny any part. He will believe you, for you have the benefit of truth.'

His mind racing, Harry barely heard her. He had a wild thought of *not* telling Sir John. Of keeping Sebiliah's body in the elaboratory. Hiding her. Repairing his door with her still inside and locking it, never to be opened. Or burying her in his garden. Transporting her somewhere else. Grace never telling another soul. Swearing his servants to silence.

The impossibilities dawned an instant after each thought arrived.

In the instant after, he remembered his frightening, miserable time imprisoned in the Bastille, by order of Gabriel Nicolas de La Reynie, Lieutenant Général of the French Police.

He doubted he could face such imprisonment again.

But this time, he suspected, any such captivity would be short. That could be a blessing; he had seen inside Newgate Prison when visiting with Sir Christopher, who had designed it.

He groaned aloud.

There was no way of avoiding it. He must send a message to Sir John Reresby.

But first, there was something he needed to do.

A distasteful task. Mr. Hooke would have no compunction, and would set straight to it. But Harry had to stiffen himself against his own repugnance.

'Hubert,' he called to his cook, who stood with Oliver and Janet in the shade of the apple trees. 'Will you fetch me your sharpest knife?'

Grace grabbed his arm. 'What do you intend with that?'

'Nothing against myself,' Harry reassured her. 'Oliver, hurry to Bethlehem Hospital. Then return with its Physician, Dr. Thomas Allen. If he is not there, he may be at his private asylum in Finsbury. Bethlehem's Porter will tell you the way.'

Oliver nodded, and nodded again.

'Dr. Allen. Bethlehem Hospital. Or Finsbury,' Harry repeated.

Oliver smiled uncertainly, then left them, saying, 'I go, I go.'

'Will he get there?' Grace asked.

'He always does,' Harry answered her, shrugging. 'Dr. Allen will recognise Sebiliah, if it is her. I want to be completely certain before I inform Sir John.'

Holding a wicked-looking carving knife, Hubert reemerged from the kitchen; his initial speed turned to hesitation as he passed it to Harry.

'*Merci*, Hubert.' Harry turned to Grace. 'Do not come in. I need to make a cut.'

☿

INSIDE HIS ELABORATORY, THE HEAT AND the smell made the air thick and difficult to move through. Harry gathered the sleeve of his shirt in one hand and pressed it over his nose. With the other hand, he pulled the sheet fully away from Sebiliah's body.

He made several exploratory presses, then placed the point of Hubert's carving knife onto her lower abdomen. He pushed it through the layers of tissue and moved the blade across, opening Sebiliah from hipbone to hipbone. Cutting through the tougher tissue of her uterus, and opening it with his fingers, revealed what he expected to see: a delicate form inside.

By taking her own life, Sebiliah had also taken the life of her unborn child.

CHAPTER SEVENTEEN

THE BEDLAM
CADAVER

After a seemingly endless wait—Harry pacing in his withdrawing room and Grace trying to calm him—Oliver returned at last. With him came Dr. Allen, and also, to Harry's surprise, Robert Hooke.

'I am parched, Mr. Hunt,' Allen croaked, once upstairs in the withdrawing room. 'There is no keeping up with Mr. Hooke.'

Knowing the speed of Hooke's scuttling walk, Harry sent Janet for some weakened beer. Hooke always preferred not to go by carriage—especially if payment was involved—and had little sense of another's conception of distance.

Directed from Bethlehem by its Porter, Matthews, Oliver had found Allen at his private asylum in Finsbury.

'Your blackamoor's insistence persuaded me, though I grasped but half of what he said,' Allen told Harry. 'Wanting Mr. Hooke's advice, I detoured then to Gresham.'

'I was leaving for Pancras Wash,' Hooke said, studying the room they stood in, interested in the quality of the cornicing. 'The builders make repairs there after the flood, when cattle found themselves floating to Clerkenwell. They can do without me, for your need sounds the greater.'

'It is, Uncle,' Grace said. 'Harry is sorely used.'

Hooke brought his attention down to Harry. 'The Justice came to Gresham not long after you had gone. He spoke with me and Thomas Crawley.'

'He should be searching for Count Königsmarck and Mrs. Thynne,' Harry said. 'Why was he instead at Gresham?'

'I cannot say, Harry. He was brusque, as is his way. He wanted to know of your being at the dissection yesterday. I told him of seeing you at noon, with all the other Fellows. Thomas saw you enter from Broad Street, brought inside a sedan, when he fetched the knives from the anatomy room.'

Grace rubbed Harry's arm. 'Do not worry, Harry. You must tell the Justice the truth. Everything you know. He cannot doubt you.'

Allen's breathing, at last, was more regular. 'You have a body, your boy tells me. In your garden.'

'Inside my elaboratory,' Harry replied. 'Someone broke open the door and left it. Someone who means to do me harm.'

'What can you want of me?' Allen asked. 'It must pertain to your visit to the Hospital.'

'I wish to know if you recognise her.'

'You think I shall.' Allen looked glumly across at Hooke. 'As we surmised, as I followed behind you.'

'Is she the Bethlehem suicide?' Hooke asked. 'Now found herself with you?'

'I shall say no more until you have seen her.'

'Good, Harry,' Hooke said approvingly. 'Then we shall observe her without presumptions.'

☿

THE THREE MEN GATHERED AROUND THE elaboratory table, leaving Grace with the servants outside in the garden.

Allen studied the dead woman—still uncovered after Harry's incising of her—then nodded. 'It is Sebiliah.'

'With child,' Hooke observed. 'Was she delivered here already cut?'

'I cut her,' Harry replied, looking accusingly at Allen.

'The question was not asked, so I did not say,' Allen said hotly. 'As the dissection at Gresham was to be of her spine and head, her gravidity did not make her unsuitable.'

'Sebiliah was inside Bethlehem for a year,' Harry said.

'We have chastised visitors in the past.'

'Your staff should protect the patients better.'

'Too many patients, too many visitors, too few staff. Too little money coming in.'

Harry's cheeks flushed, and his fists were tightly clenched. 'The patients are vulnerable, and in your care!'

'Did she speak of the father?' Hooke asked Allen, who shifted from foot to foot, looking haunted.

'Sebiliah never spoke at all,' Allen answered.

'A mute, you mean?'

'She elected to be so. When first at Bethlehem, she was voluble.'

'Your mistreatment of her took her voice, then her life,' Harry said. 'Look how thin she is. Did she *elect* to refuse her food, too? And look at how she has pulled at her hair!'

But he did not give Allen the chance to. Instead, he grabbed the sheet from the floor and covered her.

Without looking at the other two men, he strode out of his elaboratory.

They went after him. Allen sheepishly, Hooke placatingly.

Back in the garden, as well as Grace, Oliver, Hubert, and Janet, there was also the squat, bullish figure of the Justice of Peace, Sir John Reresby. With him was the City Marshalman, Joseph Fenn, puffing smoke from his cheroot.

And another man standing with them.

CHAPTER EIGHTEEN

THE SUSPICIOUS JUSTICE

The blackthorn stick was pointed at each of them in turn: Mr. Hooke, the Royal Society's Secretary, hunched and looking surprised; Dr. Allen, Bedlam's Physician, sweating, wig too large for his head, and shifting guiltily; and Mr. Henry Hunt, bespectacled fop, once Hooke's assistant but now more difficult to define.

'What should I make of such a gathering?' Sir John asked.

'Not what there is not,' Hooke said sharply. 'Mr. Hunt wanted us here. Someone has left a body in his elaboratory.'

'A body, Mr. Hooke? We never meet without one.'

Hooke gave the Justice his steeliest look. 'Your arrival is fortuitous. It saves us from sending a messenger.'

'We shall see if it is fortuitous. For you, I mean.'

'I thought you searching for Mrs. Thynne,' Harry said to Sir John. With the Justice's arrival, his anger at Dr. Allen had turned into a gnawing worry. 'Why should you come here?'

'An inconvenience to you, I hazard.'

'Not at all. As Mr. Hooke says, it is fortuitous.'

Grace stepped into the group of men. 'Someone means Harry mischief, Sir John. Why else would a body be left here?'

'Well, Miss . . .'

'Hooke,' she told him.

'Ah, the niece. I have heard of you.' Sir John sniffed, which brought a wish he hadn't, caused by the fetor from the elaboratory. 'I can think of reasons, Miss Hooke.'

Sir John gestured at Harry, for one.

'It is Sebiliah Barton, from Bethlehem,' Harry told him.

'You seek to have her dancing, too.'

'Nonsense!' Robert Hooke protested. 'The woman was left here to do Harry wrong.'

Sir John bared his teeth at Hooke again. 'To my mind, you being here, Mr. Hooke, is suspicious. And you, Dr. Allen. The first to know of a corpse found so unusually might more often be a constable, or a beadle. Or a Justice, even.'

Harry saw the course Sir John had set for himself: precisely the one he had feared. 'I sent for Dr. Allen to confirm she is Sebiliah. Mr. Hooke came with him.'

'You knew full well who she was, Mr. Hunt. I think you all hid her from me when I was at Bedlam. Perhaps in that anatomy room downstairs, which remained locked up. After the first dissection was thwarted, you people planned another, to take place here.'

In his indignation, Allen took his wig off and flailed it ineffectually in front of him. 'You have it wrong, sir! I neither hid nor delivered her! Anywhere!'

'You suppose our culpability,' Hooke said. 'It leads you to error.'

Sir John leaned threateningly towards him. 'You wanted another body to cut.'

'I recognised Diana, so stopped her dissection,' Harry pointed out.

'Your feelings of remorse made you intervene.'

'You want an easy answer to one woman's murder and the disappearance of another,' Grace said. 'No crime has been committed apart from Sebiliah's, if you believe ending one's own life to be one. Harry had nothing to do with that.'

'It is an easy answer,' Sir John agreed. 'I am yet to decide quite if it is the right one. A spirited defence of your . . . friend?' Sir John looked at Grace as if her knowing Harry—however she knew him—discounted her from plausibility. 'This much is beyond dispute. Henry Hunt put Diana into the hackney coach. So where did he send her?'

'I have no idea where she went,' Harry insisted. 'Her father said she headed to Covent Garden.'

'We know nothing of her being there.'

'You have not yet asked.'

'I will, be assured. You had friends inside the hackney, perhaps. After they killed her, you took advantage of the planned dissection, exchanging Sebiliah for Diana.'

'There was no time to do so. I arrived at Gresham only minutes before the dissection.'

'I spoke with Thomas Crawley this morning.' Sir John pointed his stick at Harry. 'He said you made a great show of arriving by sedan chair. He saw you while he carried the dissection tools, across the quadrangle there. You had already been there, with Diana's body. You even accused *him* of swapping them.'

'He did not,' Hooke said. 'I was with Harry when he questioned Thomas.'

Harry nodded gratefully at his friend. 'I only questioned him to know whose body he transported between Bethlehem and Gresham.'

'You know full well,' Sir John said airily. 'Also, you admitted to being at the Goldsmiths' Hall, where Elizabeth Thynne intended to go.'

'I *admitted* nothing. I informed you,' Harry said. 'Your suspicion is absurd. I went there the day after. Besides, Mrs. Thynne was last seen at the Royal Exchange. She never reached the Goldsmiths' Hall, as far as anyone has said.'

The man Sir John and Fenn brought with them, who had stood silently all this time—a constable or a beadle, Harry presumed—wanted to interject; Sir John stopped him by a higher raise of his stick. 'Your time to speak will come, Mr. Keeling.'

The Justice moved towards Harry's elaboratory, taking Fenn with him.

Harry went, too. 'See, the door was forced, and Sebiliah left inside.'

Sir John took no notice of the damage to the door. Instead, he recognised the section of garden wall next to the elaboratory.

'We have solved that mystery, Mr. Fenn,' he said to the Marshal-man. 'The other side is Silver Street.'

'I know nothing of Sebiliah being left here,' Harry insisted. 'See, the lock—'

'Shows nothing other than you broke it.'

'I have its key, so why should I do that?' Harry asked, knowing the Justice's response.

'Why, to divert suspicion from yourself and lay it on another.' Sir John pushed at the door; his face creased from the smell. 'I had better take a look at her. Accompany me inside.'

But the Justice could not bring himself to go much further than the doorway, from where he could see Sebiliah on the table.

'What is that cut across her belly?'

'She was pregnant,' Harry told him, pushing past. 'The foetus is half-grown, I think, or thereabouts.'

'You blame others for leaving her here. Did they leave her like this, do you say, sliced open?'

'I made the cut, to confirm my suspicion.'

'You brought her here to dissect her. Mr. Hooke and Dr. Allen observed.'

'I opened her before they arrived. If you refuse to believe them, Grace—Miss Hooke—shall confirm it.'

'She watched you as you opened up the womb?' Sir John looked aghast. 'Being Mr. Hooke's niece should not expose her to such abhorrence.'

'No, she was outside. I insisted upon it.'

'I am glad of it. So, she cannot vouch for you, then.'

Harry clenched his jaw. Sir John was determined not to take him at his word. This version of the Justice was far different from the affable, discursive one in the Rhenish winehouse.

'Inside the Hospital, Sebiliah was cruelly abused,' Harry told him. 'Dr. Allen says visitors are often left unattended with patients.'

'Abused, you say? Call it what it was, if you suspect it. The word is *rape*, Mr. Hunt. An ugly word, but the right one. Who would want a child in such unhappy circumstances?' Sir John sighed as another thought occurred. 'The baby would have been taken from her, anyways.'

'Things happen at Bethlehem that should not.'

'I am sad for the woman, but I seek Diana Cantley's murderer, and Elizabeth Thynne. You are implicated, somehow. I am sure of it.'

'Helping Diana into her hackney and being at the Goldsmiths' Hall are no solid proofs for suspicion against me.'

Sir John wiped his great hands together and backed away from the elaboratory.

In the garden, the summer heat was intense, reflecting off the brick walls and stone paths. Everyone else sheltered under the apple trees, all with faces of concern and upset.

'I know nothing more than you of Diana's murder,' Harry said. 'Other than her body being at Gresham, and what we heard at Bethlehem, at Africa House, then at Mr. Thynne's house. I know nothing, either, of Mrs. Thynne. Yesterday, I assisted you, as the King wished. Today, I find myself accused. Sebiliah's being left here implicates me, as she was exchanged for Diana.'

'But she was not left here by another's hand, was she?'

'It was not by my hand.'

'I have a man with me, says it was.'

CHAPTER NINETEEN

THE FALSE WITNESS

The man Sir John called Mr. Keeling wore a black doublet, very plain, and no wig. His white shirt's overlarge collar over the black gave him a religious look. He was not much older than Harry, perhaps in his mid-twenties. Resembling a lobster-tail helmet lacking its ear guards, his hair was long at the back and cut straight across at the front.

'Say again what you said to me this morning,' Sir John instructed him.

Keeling looked everywhere but at anyone. His eyebrows sloped down to meet above his nose, giving him an owlish look.

'In your own time,' Sir John added, his tone saying *straightaway*.

'Yes, Justice. Last night, I performed my duty, as part of the Watch.' Keeling's voice was fluting, some words overemphatic, as if preaching to a crowd. 'Others pay to have their duty done for them. I prefer to do my own.'

He makes a virtue out of his poverty, Harry thought. Many bought their way out of the Watch. Nowadays, parishes employed professional men.

'We need no prologue,' Sir John told Keeling. 'Begin at Hecuba.'

Keeling's gaze swivelled around the garden, sliding past any eye contact with his audience. 'We were told to look out for a Swedish Count, easily known for his long and yellow-coloured hair. And another man with him, also a stranger. A German.'

'Pomeranian, in fact,' Sir John said. 'Kapitän Vratz is Pomeranian.'

'Truth be told, we were suspicious of any foreign tongue, Justice. Anyhow, the yellow hair gave the Swede away.'

'You saw Count Königsmarck?' Harry asked him.

'Yes, and the Pomereranian'—he looked at Sir John for confirmation—'with him.'

'Pomeranian,' Sir John corrected. 'Tell us where you saw them.'

'Along Silver Street, Justice. Which lies . . . the other side.' He pointed theatrically at the garden wall where Harry's elaboratory backed onto it.

Harry felt relief flooding through him. 'So, these are the men who left Sebiliah! Count Königsmarck and Kapitän Vratz. There must be a connection between their taking Mrs. Thynne and swapping Sebiliah and Diana.'

'Our thoughts coincide, Mr. Hunt,' Sir John said. 'There must be. Continue, Mr. Keeling.'

'I patrolled past here about midnight. We would usually walk in pairs, but our searching for the Count sent us all over Holborn, so many of us went alone. We had orders to call if help be needed. We were warned these are dangerous men.'

'Yes, yes,' Sir John said. 'More concisely, if you please.'

Keeling bowed and coughed to clear his throat. 'I saw men pull up in a travelling chariot, room enough for two inside, pulled by a pair of horses, steered by a postilion. I say chariot . . . not a post chaise, definitely, for it had servant seats at the back.'

'Mr. Keeling!'

'Sorry. Sorry, Sir John . . . It was painted a dark blue colour. It would be easy to recognise again.'

Hooke looked doubtful. 'If you saw it late at night, how could you discern its colour?'

'They had a linkboy with them,' Keeling answered, aggrieved by the challenge. 'Lighting the way with his torch. Besides, the moon was bright, and barely a cloud in the sky. Their boy was not really needed. If I owned such a vehicle, I would have left him behind.' Keeling caught Sir John's look and went on hurriedly. 'As best I could, I took it to be blue. It had a box for luggage, positioned above the front wheels. Had the carriage not stopped on the other side of this wall, I would have taken little notice of it. And had the passenger not got out to help its postilion open up the box.'

'And from this box?' Sir John prompted him, drumming his fingers on the handle of his stick.

'A body!' Keeling said triumphantly. 'They struggled with its weight. That was when I got my first good sight of them. I spied, then, the hair we were told to look out for. Beneath the man's hat, but enough showed from under it to put a name to him. Neither man spoke a tongue I recognised. I thought it might be German.

Or Dutch. Perhaps it was Pomereranian. I would never know the difference.'

'*They* put Sebiliah here, Sir John,' Harry said, his optimism rising. 'We have the time they left her, the means of her conveyance, and the men who wish to embroil me in their crime.'

Sir John's strange, beady expression managed to show grimness and delight at the same time. 'Continue on, Mr. Keeling.'

'The linkboy's torch was useful in this regard,' Keeling said, flicking a spiteful look at Hooke, his inflections as histrionic as an actor on a stage. 'It lit up the man to whom they passed the corpse. I saw his head, appearing over the wall.'

He raised his right arm before him, directing his index finger at Harry. His voice dropped very low. 'It was *that* man.'

'It never was!' Harry protested. 'I was not where you put me! Not at all. I was in my bed by eleven.'

'It was *you*,' Keeling said implacably. 'I got clear view. You had on the same spectacles. Your hair was loose, though, not tied.'

A hard knot of fear had formed inside Harry's stomach. He felt unsteady, as if he had climbed a tree and its branches were moving in the wind.

'Hubert, were you still up at midnight?' he asked his cook. 'I bade you good night. I left you talking with Oliver in the kitchen.'

'*À cette heure tardive, j'étais dans ma chambre sous les toits.*' Hubert was so perturbed, he had quite forgotten his English.

'Oliver?' Harry implored.

'Bed, yes,' Oliver said sorrowfully, following enough of the conversation to know his employer was in trouble. 'First.' He pointed at Hubert, meaning he had gone to bed before the cook.

'Janet?'

'In bed by ten, sir, after my work was done.' In her agitation, Janet did a little curtsey to both Harry and Sir John. 'Asleep straight after.'

'If any man stood this side of the wall,' Harry said, 'he was not me. Mr. Keeling is either mistaken or dishonest.'

'I am neither, sir!' Keeling said. 'It was you. I would swear it on God's blood!'

'Well, sir, go on. Swear it.'

The man did not pause. 'I do! I swear it!'

Harry looked desperately at Hooke, then at Grace. Hooke had his head cocked to one side, busy studying the accuser, to get a greater sense of the man.

Grace's expression was an uncertain puzzlement.

She could not believe this melodramatic stranger over him?

'Grace! This was not me.'

She said nothing. Instead, she moved closer to her uncle and held his arm, needing his support.

'Has this man been dependable before?' Hooke asked Sir John, nodding towards Keeling.

'Before this morning, I have never met him, so have no reason to doubt his word.'

'Equally, you have no reason to believe it,' Harry declared.

'I have little reason to believe you over him,' Sir John said. 'You have been duplicitous in the past. Mr. Fenn, what think you of Mr. Keeling?'

'Unlike most, he chooses to do his duty with the Watch,' Fenn answered in his broken, croaky whisper. 'There's no reward yet for finding Königsmarck, which brings forwards those who mean to profit.'

'As Keeling puts me where I was not, I doubt his whole story,' Harry said. 'Was Königsmarck ever here at all?' A thought struck him. 'In what way did they struggle with the body, as you said they did?'

Keeling held his hand horizontally over his head. 'It was difficult for them to lift it over the top of this wall.'

'You saw Sebiliah, Sir John,' Harry said. 'She is malnourished from her time in Bethlehem. Mr. Thynne told us Königsmarck offered himself to fight in Tangiers. The Duke told us Vratz fought alongside the Germans, and was made a Kapitän for his bravery at Mons. Sebiliah's body would not have troubled two soldiers.'

'That is not enough to make me doubt him,' Sir John replied.

Harry had another thought, which gave him a glimmer of hope. 'When Keeling first told you he had seen me, how did he describe me?'

'Exactly as you are, Mr. Hunt. Young, bespectacled, richly dressed.'

Harry pushed his hair further back, revealing more of the injury sustained during his brush with the Brisk Boys. 'Did he tell you of this?'

'He did not, Mr. Hunt, it is true. Well, Mr. Keeling, did you see this man's bruise when you saw him over the wall?'

Keeling, for once, sounded uncertain. 'His face may have been turned away.'

'I doubt you saw Mr. Hunt at all,' Hooke said. 'At midnight, by the light of a linkboy's torch? And from where, so the Count with his accomplice did not see you?'

'From the other side of the street, it is true, to keep obscured from them in shadow. But I saw them clearly. I am sure it was *this* man who helped them.' Again, the overdramatic pointing.

Sir John sent a look towards Fenn, then addressed Harry, looking him squarely in the face. 'I have you putting Diana Cantley into her hackney, the last time she was seen.' He put up one of his enormous fists and extended its stubby thumb. 'I have you watching her when she went out for her horse riding, which you did not at first admit to.' Sir John raised his index finger, to join next to the thumb.

'I have you at Bedlam only interested in the suicide, deflecting from the matter which pressed. That matter being the murder of Diana Cantley.' Another finger rose. 'I have you at the Goldsmiths' Hall, where Mrs. Thynne was thought to go.' A third finger. 'Now I have you receiving a body—the Bedlam suicide, whom then you cut open—from Königsmarck and Vratz.'

By now, he had extended his thumb and four fingers; he next raised the thumb of his other hand. 'I also have you living in Holborn, where the Count and his men were last known to dwell.' He spread all the other fingers of this hand and turned it towards Fenn. 'Suspicions enough, I think. Let us put Mr. Hunt in my lockup. Away from his friends. We must convince him to divulge Mrs. Thynne's whereabouts.'

'You have the wrong man, Justice,' Harry said.

'You must convince me so.'

Fenn unfastened his manacles from his belt. His face held no trace of the friendliness shown at the Rhenish winehouse. With little other choice, Harry placed his wrists out; Fenn clasped the manacles around them and locked them with his key.

He led Harry into the kitchen, past the table and the uneaten luncheon, through Harry's house, and out onto Bloomsbury Square. Sir John and Keeling followed close behind them.

Hooke, Grace, Dr. Allen, and the servants, when also outside on the pavement—in view of all who lived in Bloomsbury Square—all stood together silently.

Grace still held on to her uncle's arm, looking just as shocked and dazed as she had in the garden.

Since he was being bundled into the coach by a briskly efficient Fenn, Harry could not be sure—but did Grace's face show she doubted him?

CHAPTER TWENTY

THE TYBURN
FAIR

As Sir John had said on the way to Africa House, the last Sessions had conferred death to more than usual. On this execution day, thirteen men and ten women were to die.

A bailiff who, when arresting a debtor, cudgelled the man's protesting daughter and killed her.

A woman for shoplifting lawn-cloth.

A man who killed a hackney driver after disagreeing with the fare.

Two unmarried women for infanticide. Neither could provide a witness to confirm their babies were stillborn.

Two men who together murdered a Watchman. They killed him with his own staff after he challenged them late at night.

A woman for stealing a silver tankard.

A Frenchman who tried to rob a gentleman, then stabbed his interrupting servant. The Watch found him drunk in the cellar of his victim's house.

A woman who stole from her employer, then set fire to his house to conceal her crime.

A man who used picklocks to rob a Lincoln's Inn lawyer, taking silverware and spoons.

A woman, already branded for shoplifting, who stole silks from a mercer.

Two sedanmen who obstructed a gentleman when setting down their load. When he berated them, they kicked him to death.

A woman for shoplifting forty yards of serge and a campaign coat.

Another for stealing sixty yards of taffeta ribbon.

A man for horse stealing.

A Frenchwoman who claimed her recently deceased employer had left her a silver watch and a diamond ring. Even though she brought witnesses to attest for her, the jury found her guilty of theft.

A man who stole redwood from a Royal African Company lighter.

A seamstress who, dissatisfied with her apprentice's work, thrashed the girl with a rod. And the man who held her down for the beating. To increase her torment, they both rubbed the wounds with salt. The girl died three days afterwards.

A case of High Treason: a man sentenced for clipping His Majesty's coins. When searching the man's house, the Watch had discovered his clipping board and shears.

Lastly, another case of High Treason: a Catholic priest, for perverting a woman from the Protestant to the Catholic religion.

As no women had been found guilty of High Treason, there would be no burnings today.

A little under three miles from Newgate Prison to Tyburn. Through the heaving crowd, with stops along the way, the journey should last three hours.

The noise was tumultuous. Hooves clattered. Wheels rumbled solemnly on the stones. Jeers, howls of anguish, chants, shrieks, songs, or prayers being loudly said. Church bells rang. Children raced between their parents. Apprentices, enjoying the holiday, competed with one another to make the most noise, banging pans or ringing handbells.

Accounts of the trials had already appeared. Spectators tried to pick out who was who. Most easily identified was the priest, dressed in black and supine on his sled. A well-aimed stone had induced a bloody gash on his forehead.

Most of the prisoners stared dully from their tumbrels, stupefied by thoughts of their oncoming deaths. The Frenchman sat hunched with his elbows on his knees, staring down at his fingers as he flexed them nervously, imagining them never moving again. The woman condemned for stealing ribbon chuntered with fear, her limbs jerking as if already on her rope.

The two sedanmen, both in their white wedding suits, waved at everyone. For them, this was fame, of a kind.

Sympathy from the crowd for the two girls condemned for infanticide. Doubt about their guilt, despite their misbegotten children.

No pity at all for the seamstress. As mean-looking a woman as everyone expected, she sat stiffly upright, one eye stuck shut from a stone's throw.

After Southampton Street—the turn into Bloomsbury Square—the procession reached its halfway point, the church of St. Giles-in-the-Fields.

☿

STUCK BY THE CHURCH, THE JUSTICE'S driver cursed. He could see no way through the crowd. The condemned were due their stop at the Bowl Inn, where many waited for a closer view. All the traffic had been halted by the front riders of the procession. Having taken Hart Street to avoid the crowd, he wanted to cross Broad St. Giles for Monmouth Street, the way to the Justice's house.

Up against the carriage, the crowd was impenetrable. It frightened the horses, making them fidget.

'Assert yourself through them,' Sir John demanded, banging the roof with his stick. 'We have timed this badly,' he grumbled to Fenn.

Sitting opposite them, Harry faced the back of the coach. Fenn's manacles pinched his wrists. The heat inside the carriage was unbearable, the breezeless air refusing to enter through the glassless windows.

To see who blocked them, people jumped up or even climbed onto the footplate. The Justice glowered irascibly at them, and pushed one near-comer away, using his great palm against the man's nose. Unless Sir John desisted, Harry worried, the crowd would take against them. Their carriage might be overturned.

The man Sir John had pushed appeared again. His large head, shaved badly so tufts of hair stuck out from his scalp, intruded through the window. A slack jaw kept his lips apart, revealing tobacco-stained front teeth, notched from biting his pipe stems. Despite the day's heat, he wore a thick black campaign coat. Sweat poured down his face.

He scanned the coach's interior, noting the passenger in manacles.

'Off with you, man!' Sir John barked. 'Get away!'

The man disappeared as suddenly as he had arrived.

From outside came the driver's shout. 'Be buggered!' Then the crack of his whip, and, 'Damn your blood!'

The driver went silent. Fenn and Sir John looked at each other. Both quickly reached for their swords. Sir John ducked his head through the window to see the trouble. He soon reversed, as the slack-jawed sweaty man opened the door and pointed a wicked-looking musquetoon at his chest.

Stepping back, Sir John tripped over Harry's feet, staggering into him. Harry pushed him off and edged sideways, away from the staring blind eye of the weapon's flared muzzle. Fenn kept his sword up—even against the musquetoon—until Sir John gripped him by his wrist to lower it.

The sweaty man motioned to Harry to step through the opposite door, where another man waited. At Harry's hesitation, he shouted, '*Wynocha!*'

'I see what this is,' Sir John said grimly. 'Your friends come for you, Hunt.' No *Mister* now.

Before Harry could reply, the door next to him was pulled open, and the second man dragged him from the carriage. Having his wrists manacled in front of him made him clumsy; Harry missed the footplate and lurched forwards.

The man caught him and hauled him upright.

Gripping Harry by the elbow, this second man cleared a furrow through the crowd, heedless of injured feelings as he pushed people aside. He aimed back towards Holborn, the same way the procession had come, then turned down Drury Lane. No longer shoulder to shoulder with people coming towards them—either aiming for the Bowl Inn or making their way to Tyburn—their progress was easier.

Harry took the chance to observe the man leading him along. Unlike the musquetoon bearer he was short and slender, and wore a three-cornered cocked hat. He turned back constantly to see if they were followed. His fingers dug into Harry's forearm; attempts to shrug him off only met with their tightening.

Harry looked for a way of escape. After all, the man had no visible weapon. But just as he decided to try to release the man's hold and run, the larger man caught up with them. Although lobster pink and sopping with sweat, he kept on his coat to conceal the musquetoon. Big and lumbering, his mouth still open, the man's eyes rotated slowly in their sockets, as if his brain could only elicit so much speed from them.

'Strażnik Pokoju nas widział! Śeiga nas!'

Finding an open doorway, the men shoved Harry through it. Harry found himself inside a cockpit, in a mixture of men, women, and children, all cheering a final game before the hangings. In the pit, a pair of blindfolded boys threw coins at a Pyle cock. One of its legs was broken, a hasty splint attached to prolong the contest.

Blood from previous bouts—including a battle royal where a dozen birds had fought to the last—stained the floor and flecked the sides, even spattering the foremost spectators. The boys threw hard, resulting in wild misses. The business of placing bets continued through the bout; gamblers risked foolish amounts of money on the outcome, as crazed by the risk as by the contest.

The large man propelled Harry along the topmost tier of benches, banging Harry's shoulder against the wall. Turning to remonstrate, Harry spotted Fenn, breathing hard, at the same doorway they had just come through.

Fenn saw them and drew his sword. 'Stop those men!' he croaked.

He knocked aside a couple standing by the door. On seeing his uniform, others let him past.

Harry was dragged along the wall, bundled through another doorway into the street's sudden brightness, then turned towards a coach—an expensive-looking calash with its roof folded back. The large man climbed into it, turned to grip Harry's collar, and pulled him inside. The smaller man went to the other side of the coach and also climbed in.

'We hebben hem!' this smaller man told the driver.

'*Ruszaj! Pospiesz się!*' the large man shouted.

As the calash's driver set off with an urgent bark to the horses—'*Macht schnell!*'—the men thrust Harry face down into the rear seat, anxious for him not to be seen by the chasing Marshalman. Harry doubted Fenn saw him being forced into the calash, for Harry's departure from the cockpit had been speedy, and the calash's leather hood must block any view of its occupants.

The driver wore a military-looking grey felt hat with a domed crown. Whenever he turned in his seat to look around him, Harry caught glimpses of his profile; enough to show a rugged competence and an unhurried air. Although he seemed careless of their safety— steering too close around other traffic, causing it to swerve out of his way—the pair holding Harry down looked completely at ease. The driver was expert, his horses obedient.

Once through Ludgate, the men allowed Harry to sit up, making no attempt to prevent him from seeing the rest of their journey.

They cut down to Knightrider Street—still busy with traffic heading for Tyburn—along Thames Street, and past the Queen-hithe Docks. Over Hooke's Fleet Canal. Past St. Paul's and all its bookshops, then the meat markets of East Cheap. To Aldgate by way of Crutched Friars—presumably, Harry thought, to steer clear of the Tower of London. Into the mazy Minories, dropping back south, next to the open space of the Pasture Fields. They followed the long street called Wapping Dock, with all its narrow alleys leading off it to the river stairs: Armitage Stairs, Wapping Stairs, Execution Dock, King Edward's Stairs.

The sunshine released the suffocating stink of Thames mud.

Here lived those who served and supplied the Navy: sailors, carpenters, ironmongers, mast and rope and sail makers, armourers, chandlers, brewers, bakers, dockhands, stevedores, and victuallers.

The road's surface was sticky. Dark stains reached up the walls. Every high tide brought water far up the streets, despite all the channels and the walls built against it. Many of the houses and stores were supported on stilts, or had their ground floors kept empty for the encroaching water; stairways led up to where their inhabitants lived. Flimsy planking walkways, elevated well above street level, snaked around the buildings, taking the place of pavements.

They reached a dismal alley too narrow for the calash. The driver called to bring his horses to a stop. *'Hör auf!'* For the first time since the journey began, he turned all the way around in his seat. His expression was laconic. 'Prusom's Island,' he announced.

Little knowing this part of London, Harry had no idea if he told the truth.

Disembarking from the calash, the large, lumbering man aimed his musquetoon at Harry's shaking back.

The driver, better dressed than the other two—he wore a patterned barracan suit—led the way. He removed his hat, showing that he went without a wig; his dark hair was long enough to make him have to sweep it regularly from his forehead with his hand.

Although Harry couldn't understand what the men said as they led him through the huddle of buildings, he heard the man in the cocked hat address him as '*cappitane*.'

These must be the men spoken of by Diana Cantley's father, Sir Benedict, and by Thomas Thynne and the Duke. What other foreigners would snatch him from the Justice in what was clearly a well-organised plan? None of them, though, with their Babylonish profusion of languages, spoke in Scandinavian—which Harry doubted he would recognise, but he did know some German, and some Dutch, and he thought the large man was speaking Polish.

None of this trio had the long blond hair Thynne had described, belonging to Count Königsmarck.

The man who had driven them slowed and signalled to a precarious-looking stairway, wanting Harry to go up it first. Even though Harry showed no resistance, the large man used his musquetoon to prod him painfully in a kidney.

On reaching the platform at the top of the stairs, the large man pushed past and pointed his weapon at the door. The *cappitane* performed a sequence of knocks, which were soon answered by the same sequence, but reversed.

The three men around Harry visibly relaxed. A fourth man opened the door from inside: gaunt, prominent-eyed, with blond hair so long it reached almost to his waist.

He punched Harry hard in the stomach.

CHAPTER TWENTY-ONE

THE SWEDISH COUNT

'*Ni blev inte förföljda?*' the blond-haired man asked.

'*Stadsvakten försökte hålla jämna steg med oss,*' the man wearing the cocked hat replied, '*men vi skakade av oss honom vid Shoe Lane.*'

'*Inga tecken av domaren?*'

'*Det var för rörigt för honom att följa efter oss. För många människor på väg till avrättningen.*'

'*Är det här mannen vi söker efter?*'

'*Han är mannen som Sir John arresterade.*'

'*Vi kommer snart få veta.*'

The calash driver gave Harry a firm push. Still winded from the punch, Harry saw the place he was forced into. Cheap accommodation, poorly built. If paid for in advance, such places could be found all over London, no questions asked. The ebb and flow of incomers was too much for the Watches to record.

Curtainless windows, their insides scrubbed with a thin lime wash and their outsides encrusted with soot, obscured any view, from either side. Someone had replaced missing panes with brown paper. Rippled floorboards showed around a threadbare rug. Plaster fell from one wall, exposing ancient wattle.

Empty bottles of wine and the remains of a meal littered a table. Contrastingly, the men's bedrolls and hand luggage were stacked around the room with military neatness.

The man in the cocked hat hefted a chair to the middle of the rug.

The large man placed his musquetoon on the table and took off his coat, revealing clothes soaked with sweat. He gripped Harry by the back of his neck and forced him onto the chair.

Harry was made to sit; his hands knocked against his thighs, reminding him that manacles still bound him. They had pinched and rubbed the skin; his wrists were pink and weeping.

All four men, their arms folded grimly, stood around him, regarding him for a long, intimidatory moment. Harry had to resist the urge to blurt out his innocence. Of anything they might accuse him. These men had not released him from the Justice out of kindness. But what did they want from him? He had not been near finding them to rescue Mrs. Thynne. If rescuing she needed—only Thomas Thynne's word said that.

No sign of her in this insalubrious room.

Why should these men deliver Sebiliah to his house, then leave her in his elaboratory, as Josiah Keeling had professed? But Keeling had lied about Harry taking her over the garden wall, so was his entire story a falsehood?

Harry wished his legs would stay still. They shivered as if he sat in a cold bath.

The blond-haired man brought his face level with Harry's. His hair hung lank and damp over his shoulders.

To project a semblance of courage, Harry stared into the man's eyes, which were a pale limpid brown, nearly beige. They stared back at him, with an intensity making them wetly bulbous.

'Who are you?'

His English was good, with barely a trace of an accent.

Harry was incredulous. 'You snatched me from the Justice, not knowing who I am?'

'We know what you have *done*.' The man raised his fist again, making Harry shrink backwards in the chair. 'Saying your name will save you some pain.'

The chair's back dug into Harry's spine. 'My name is Henry Hunt. I have *done* little. I was asked to help find a murderer. Thank you for appearing so promptly.'

'You think me a murderer?' The man looked equally incredulous. 'Who did the asking?'

'Commanding, more like. The King.'

At mention of His Majesty, Harry saw the other men knew English well enough to look at one another worriedly.

He addressed all of them. 'A woman was kidnapped, then killed.'

The blond-haired man—obviously the leader—turned to the calash driver, who raised his palms to the ceiling. He, in turn, spoke rapidly to the other men in what Harry thought was High Dutch, which seemed to be common between them. Harry could tell they were as perplexed as the driver seemed to be. The slight man with the cocked hat looked angry, not so much at Harry, but at the driver. The large, slack-jawed man darted fearful glances at them all.

The blond-haired man spoke to Harry. 'Betty is dead?'

'You know better than I. If by Betty, you mean Mrs. Elizabeth Thynne.'

'What? Tell me, damn you! Is she dead?'

'I hope not. According to her husband, she is with you.'

The man looked relieved, then frowned, and pulled at his ear. 'Why should you think so?'

'Because you are the Swedish Count he spoke of. Karl Johann von Königsmarck. Mr. Thynne thinks you took his wife, as you also took Diana Cantley, whose murderer the King wishes me to find.'

Königsmarck translated what Harry had said to his men.

The men all exhibited the same mixture of pain, confusion, and flat disbelief.

'Betty is alive, then,' Königsmarck said to Harry. Then his voice dropped to a sorrowful tone. 'But Diana is not?'

'You know Diana,' Harry answered. 'Knew, I should say, as you ran her through with your sword.'

'I did know her,' Königsmarck affirmed softly. 'She was Betty's good friend.'

Königsmarck straightened, then clicked his fingers towards the calash driver, who moved behind Harry and gripped him by the shoulders.

By the way the other two men answered to him, and how he answered to the Count, Harry knew he must be Kapitän Christoph Vratz, the Pomeranian mercenary.

Vratz spoke into Harry's ear as if their conversation were confidential. 'Who are *you* that the King should give you such a task?' His English, also, was good, but with an accent heavier than the Count's.

'I am employed by the Royal Society,' Harry lied. 'I have helped with other investigations, to His Majesty's satisfaction.'

Using the back of his hand, Vratz slapped him smartly on the cheek. 'Jerzy.' He addressed the large man, who started—disturbed from private thoughts—then moved in his deliberate way to the table where he had left the musquetoon.

Jerzy checked its load and pressed its dangerous end against Harry's chest.

'Do not lie,' Königsmarck said. 'Where is Betty?'

Unable to release Vratz's hold, Harry squirmed in his seat. Jerzy jabbed the musquetoon into Harry's torso; Harry wondered if he had broken a rib. Jerzy's finger lay dangerously over the trigger. Harry kicked his feet out. Showing more alacrity than he had so far displayed, Jerzy simply sidestepped them. The slender man took off his cocked hat and restrained Harry's arms, holding them as tightly as when taking him through the Holborn crowd.

If the musquetoon fired, Jerzy risked injuring his colleagues; Harry decided not to worry unduly until they moved from behind him. So far, these men played with him, he reassured himself. Even so, fear made him clamp his teeth shut.

Leaning over Harry, Königsmarck dripped sweat onto his face. 'Tell us, Henry Hunt.'

'In truth, I have no notion where she is!'

Jerzy jabbed hard again, this time into Harry's stomach.

'We know you have Betty,' Königsmarck said. 'That is why the Justice arrested you. Why do you think we risked taking you from him?'

'I do not!' Harry gasped. 'Mr. Thynne thinks her with you. He desired our help—mine and Sir John's—to help find her. Thynne has his own men looking for you, too.'

Vratz withdrew his sword from its scabbard.

Hearing its scrape behind him, Harry involuntarily moved forwards, tilting his chair, only to meet the musquetoon.

Vratz placed the flat of his blade across Harry's cheek. Its edge nicked his ear. 'Are you one of the men Thynne sent to Strasbourg, to kill us?'

'Strasbourg?' Harry answered, confused. 'No, no. I know nothing of that! Why send men to kill you?'

Vratz ignored the question. 'Why does he employ you to look for *us*?'

'Mr. Thynne showed a letter, saying it proved you had kidnapped his wife. I did not quite believe it.'

'You did not believe it because you know where she is.'

'No! Mr. Thynne wanted my help.'

It was Königsmarck who slapped Harry this time. 'That man is in no way her husband! Other than he has a piece of paper to say so.'

Königsmarck waved aside the men behind Harry. Harry heard them move away, and the sound of Vratz's sword dropping back into its scabbard.

Jerzy pointed the musquetoon at Harry's face.

'This is the last time I ask politely,' Königsmarck said. 'Where is Betty?'

Harry stared manically at each of the men tormenting him.

'I swear it, I do not know!'

He tried to rise from the chair, but Jerzy pushed him back with his weapon's muzzle. Harry grabbed at it, and pushed it away, but Jerzy simply stepped back and repointed it at him.

Harry, his eyes filling with tears, raised his hands imploringly at Königsmarck.

Königsmarck tugged at the lace of his sleeves. He gestured towards Vratz, his fingers performing a double tap as if pushing down a jar lid. '*Ze denken dat ik Betty heb.*'

'*Hij weet het niet,*' Vratz replied.

Königsmarck abruptly went to the table for one of the bottles of wine. He uncorked it with his teeth, drank from its neck, swished wine around his mouth, then shuddered with distaste.

'I agree with my friend. I believe you tell the truth. But where does that put Betty? And, I assure you, I know nothing of Diana Cantley's murder.'

☿

JERZY LOCATED A SAW IN HIS knapsack. After some diligent work and plenty of Polish swearing, he divorced the manacles from Harry's wrists. By then, Harry's waistcoat stuck to his shirt, and his shirt stuck to his back; he stood to readjust himself.

After thanking Jerzy, who gave him a slow, good-natured grin, Harry sat back down, attempting to hide his trembling from the men he found himself with.

'Why leave a dead body at my home?' he asked the Count.

Königsmarck took another pull at the bottle. 'I did not. Nor did any of my men.'

He passed over the bottle. Harry poured wine into his mouth, desperate for the moisture on his tongue.

'Late last night. Around midnight,' Harry said.

'I would remember at any time, I think. Last night we were here, together.'

'There are no more of you?'

'This is all of us.'

'A witness—his name is Josiah Keeling—described you. And your carriage with a luggage box big enough to carry the body. He said you delivered it to me over my garden wall. He lied.'

'If he lied about you, you may accept he lied about me. I have no such carriage. We have hired the calash, which has no such luggage box. Until my men brought you here, I knew not who you are, nor where you live. Hoping the Justice would lead them to Betty, they followed him. Instead, he took them to you.'

'Seeing him arrest you, we drew the obvious conclusion,' Vratz said.

Königsmarck looked ruefully at Harry, regretting his men's mistake. 'The dead body in the luggage box. This was Diana?'

'No, no,' Harry told him. 'Another woman. She died at Bethlehem Hospital. By her own hand.'

At Königsmarck's transparent confusion, Harry related the tale of the Gresham dissection. Vratz, in between taking generous nosefuls of snuff, took turns to translate for the others; Harry learned the man in the cocked hat was Johann Stern, who held the Swedish rank of Löjtnant, and the bulky man with the musquetoon was Jerzy Boroski, the Count's Polonian servant.

When Harry told them how Diana Cantley was killed, Vratz and Königsmarck showed him their swords. Neither matched the wound left in Diana's ribcage. Both Löjtnant Stern and Boroski were swordless; Königsmarck assured Harry—on the word of a gentle-man—the two men had brought no such weapons into London.

Two dead women, Harry explained, were exchanged. He told them of the King summoning Sir John Reresby, and of the visit to Bethlehem Hospital. Harry described the Basketman's arrest, and the sad duty of informing Sir Benedict of his daughter's murder.

And of the ransom note to the Royal African Company's Deputy-Governor, written in a Scandinavian hand.

At which Königsmarck found some paper and a quill.

Although his writing was as florid as the writing Harry had seen—the ransom note shown by Sir Benedict, and the love note shown by Thomas Thynne—and the shape of his *K* was almost identical, Königsmarck's was clearly a different hand. There seemed to be no subterfuge; the Count wrote surely and unhesitatingly.

Seeing Harry glance significantly at them, Königsmarck asked all his men to demonstrate their writing. The same piece of paper soon showed Vratz's style as all angles; Stern constantly broke his letters apart, leaving them lonely; and Jerzy wrote clumsily, the tip of his tongue protruding from one corner of his mouth as he did so. None of them used a quill the same way the two notes had revealed. Each man lifted or turned it smoothly—even Boroski—so leaving no spatter from dragging against the nib's natural slide.

Not wishing to jeopardise the truce sprung up between them, when Harry told of meeting Thomas Thynne he was careful to emphasise it was Thynne's conviction the Count had kidnapped his wife, and Thynne's refusal to believe she would ever join Königs-marck of her own free will.

Harry described Thynne's letter. 'It said something like, *I*—meaning you—*would love Elizabeth if she had nothing, or came from nothing. You*—meaning Mr. Thynne—*would stop her happiness. You keep her for her wealth, the means to an end. I love her for herself.* Something about freedom . . . *I wish to set her free, if freedom is to follow her heart. She has given herself to me. Body and soul,* I think it said. *I swear before God, I love her with all my heart.* It could have been *declare*, not *swear*.'

Königsmarck assured Harry he had sent no such letter.

'And besides, I never call her Elizabeth. Always Betty. But it tells exactly my feelings for her.'

He looked morosely at Harry, then at his men.

Vratz put a consoling hand on the Count's shoulder. 'We shall find her.'

'How?' Harry asked. 'Sir John and the Marshalman search for you. Following him, as you did before taking me, is now impossible. They have seen two of you. The Watch is alerted. Soldiers may be looking. And, as I say, Thynne, too, has men after you.'

Harry paused; a thought had struck him. 'What did you say before, about Strasbourg?'

'Knowing Betty prefers Karl, Thynne sent men after us,' Vratz answered. 'Four or five of them—it was difficult to see. They tried to ambush our carriage from the side of the road.'

'We travelled to see Betty in Amsterdam,' Königsmarck added.

'A long journey,' Harry said, thinking of the globe in Hooke's withdrawing room at Gresham College.

'Ten days, give or take a day.' Königsmarck looked frankly at Harry. 'Not long for the woman in my heart.'

'I shot at two of them,' Vratz said matter-of-factly. 'I know not if they lived or died.'

'How do you know Thynne sent them?' Harry asked.

'Two of them called one another by their names,' Vratz said.

'Which Betty recognised when we told her,' Königsmarck said. 'They were Thynne's men.'

'Kidd was one, Singer the other,' Vratz said.

'In that case, both survived,' Harry told them. 'Mr. Thynne has them here in London looking for you.'

'You could help us,' Königsmarck said to Harry. 'You know this city far better than we do.'

Harry was already shaking his head. 'Sir John thinks me your accomplice. I must prove myself innocent. Only then could I help you.'

'You think you can do so?' Königsmarck asked him, passing him more wine.

Harry nodded, exhibiting more assurance than he felt.

The Count looked more honestly doubtful.

CHAPTER TWENTY-TWO

THE HARD DECISION

When Harry woke up, there was no light in the room. His slide into consciousness came with the awareness there was also no noise. The sounds he expected—of four other men shifting or snoring—were absent.

When he called into the dark, there was no answer.

He uncurled himself from the mattress Stern had unrolled for him as they all bade their good nights to one another. The room had only marginally cooled in the night. Even with no blanket, he felt clammy. To cool himself, he pulled at his shirt; in the airless room it was of little use.

Noticing a sour, unpleasant smell, he realised it was him.

His tongue was leathery. He fumbled for his spectacles and put them on, then reached for a wine bottle, but it was empty. An ache from last night's drinking pressed his temples.

Once they had established an alliance—and Harry was convinced of the men's innocence of murder and kidnap—the conversation continued late, perhaps into the morning.

Kapitän Christoph Vratz was Pomeranian, he had told Harry, as the wine flowed. More exactly, a Kashubian. A gentleman's youngest son, inheriting only a small patrimony, he had opted for a life of the highway. Knowing Vratz would be modest, Königsmarck joined in his story at this point. Vratz, the Count said, had often proved his courage. Not least, by robbing the King of Poland, Jan III Sobieski, at the siege of Vienna. When the King, in disguise, left camp to observe the Turkish movements, Vratz waylaid him and relieved him of diamonds and gold, later selling them for eight thousand ducatoons.

One thing Vratz said was odd: after another great inhalation of snuff, he claimed he had died of his wounds at the siege of Mons. At first, Harry thought this a mistake of language—his English letting him down—but the Kapitän said it candidly, and his companions all seemed to believe it. The fact of his own death, Vratz said, brought him comfort, as it relieved him of worry. Quite how Vratz interpreted his existence after Mons, Harry did not know. Did being dead absolve him from everyday morality? Did he walk among the living in a dream state? But then, Harry reflected, he knew little of others' interior lives.

Whatever it meant for Vratz, it explained the way he drove the calash.

As for Löjtnant Stern, Harry discovered they could converse well in French. Stern spoke it fluently, and Harry had learned enough on his travels to get by. Stern was the bastard son of a Swedish baron. At fifteen, he left for Germany to further his education. At nineteen, he served in Pomerania as a soldier for the Elector of Brandenburg. His fighting took him through Poland into Bohemia, France, Austria, and Hungary. He fought for Louis XIV against the Protestant Dutch. All that warring had taught him compassion for his fellow man, he insisted. He had never indulged in cruelty and was always careful before God. The Treaties of Nijmegen—at their mention, all the men drew breath—brought peace between France and the Dutch and Spanish Republics, among others. Which was inconvenient for a mercenary.

Down on his luck, Stern decided on London, thinking to enlist with the King's Life Guards. Staying at the Amsterdam Ordinary in Broad Street, he met Vratz, and went into his service instead.

At the story's conclusion, the Löjtnant and the Kapitän raised their glasses to one another.

Wine had the opposite effect on Jerzy Boroski than on his colleagues, making him even more taciturn. As Königsmarck's servant, he worked for the Count at his Hamburg house. Königsmarck had summoned him to London to help rescue Betty from her husband. Now Boroski found his master was being blamed for her kidnapping.

☿

WHEN HARRY'S SIGHT HAD ADAPTED, THE glow of the almost-set moon through the translucent window gave him just enough light to see where Königsmarck and his men had slept.

Their bedrolls and luggage were gone.

Presumably the men had left to continue their search for Elizabeth Thynne. Perhaps they agreed Harry could not help them; that it increased the risk of discovery to have another fugitive with them. Or thought their Wapping hideaway would soon be discovered, so left him there to be arrested.

What best to do?

Go to Leicester Fields and give himself up? Explain himself again, and try to convince of his innocence? In the calm of his own house, Sir John might reconsider his too-quick verdict that Harry was guilty of kidnap and murder.

But with all the reasons the Justice originally had for suspecting Harry, there was now another man's testimony. Josiah Keeling, for whatever reason, was prepared to swear Harry had taken Sebiliah Barton's dead body from the same men Sir John sought for kidnapping Elizabeth Thynne. Harry recalled Grace saying he had truth on his side. But people were often convicted—sentenced to death, even—for far lesser crimes with far less evidence. One person's testimony could be enough to send you to the gallows.

The Tyburn Fair was evidence enough of that.

Sir John considered Sebiliah's body being inside the elaboratory as clinching evidence of Harry's guilt.

The Justice's opinion that he worked with the Count could only be reinforced by Stern's and Boroski's taking Harry at gunpoint. If only from their foreign speech, Sir John was bound to think them Königsmarck's men.

No.

Harry needed to clear his name. And find who really murdered Diana Cantley.

But how to do that while keeping clear of the Watch?

Anyone living nearby, on Prusom's Island, could have seen four strangers entering and leaving this room, and might have already reported them. The Watch was responsible for checking all visitors to their parish. A beadle or a constable might at any minute knock on the door.

He must leave, then, Harry decided, but where to go? Bloomsbury Square was out of the question. It was the first place Sir John would station men in case of his return. But if Harry went to Gresham, to hide in Hooke's lodgings, he risked incriminating both Robert and Grace Hooke. To Sir John's mind, their close association with him tainted them. Harry could not involve either of them further.

Harry recalled Grace's expression as Fenn had led him away. He must have misread it, he told himself. It could not be him she doubted. Her face displayed her bewilderment after seeing Sebiliah, and hearing Keeling's false testimony, and seeing the Justice arresting him. Anyone would be confused after such a sequence of events.

Who else might shelter him? His old lodging house in Half Moon Alley was impossible, as Mrs. Hannam still blamed him for the Colonel's death.

Having been appointed Hooke's assistant—although not yet given the title of Curator of Experiments—his friend Denis Papin now lived at Gresham, too. Edmund Wylde neighboured Harry in Bloomsbury Square, so Harry dismissed him. John Aubrey relied on the generosity of friends; Harry wasn't sure where he now resided. Sir Christopher Wren lived at Middle Scotland Yard, by the Office of Works. Too close to Whitehall Palace and all the men who guarded it, who by now would know the Justice's view.

How circumscribed his life was by his work at Gresham College. Most of the people Harry knew were through Mr. Hooke. Hooke's colleagues and friends, before they were his. Instrument makers, lens grinders, engineers, toolmen. Architects, carpenters, brickmak-ers, stonemasons. None he knew well enough to rely on for shelter and for safety, without word getting out of his whereabouts.

There was one notable exception: Hortense Mancini, the Duch-esse de Mazarin. She would have few qualms about sheltering him—Harry almost smiled at the thought, for the Duchesse thrived on such transgressions—but he rejected venturing to her home in St. James's Park. Too far and too difficult. He might make it there by oars, but it was too big a risk; his travels around London with Mr. Hooke made him too well-known to the watermen. A shame, as Mustapha would be with her. It was a while since Harry had seen either of them; it was not only Grace he had neglected by being so overinvolved with his house.

He longed to have Michael Fields's common sense and self-as-surance once more. Harry rarely dwelled on his friend's last days, when the Colonel had fallen into confusion. Madness, even, like the poor souls in Bethlehem. The Fields who had betrayed Harry was another man entirely—an imposter, like Bartholomew Slough, who pretended to be the dwarf, Captain Jeffrey Hudson.

If he were to travel anywhere in London, Harry considered, a disguise was necessary. But he had only the clothes he stood in. All expensive, brightly coloured, and made to draw attention. An azure—or peacock blue—waistcoat with silver galloon. A white shirt, although by now it was sweat-stained and grimy. His shoes, with their overlarge silver buckles.

He was too conspicuous. His breeches were black, at least, although made from lustrous silk taffeta.

And he had no purse. Therefore, no money. He had not had the time nor the forethought to collect it before being escorted from his home. He had his rings, though, which he could sell. But he would get nothing near their true value; any buyer would exploit his obvious desperation to their advantage, but, as they say, *beggars should be no choosers.*

Finally, Harry arrived at a decision. He would cross the Thames. But not by going over London Bridge, which risked arrest. In Southwark, he could find a room just as anonymous as the one he was in. There, he would hide, and have time to think. He hoped for an unquestioning landlord.

He must leave straightaway, while still under cover of darkness.

CHAPTER TWENTY-THREE

THE DAWN ROBBERY

Harry was relieved to find the door unlocked; he did not want the noise of forcing it open.

He descended the stairs to the street.

Eastwards, the sky brightened, but not enough to much help him as he approached the river. Along Cinnamon Street, he made a cautious way past the great timber yards, which were silent and still deserted. Without a lamp, he had to place his feet carefully; the road was rough, rutted, and pitted from Navy traffic.

Down towards the Wapping Stairs. Wherries could be hired nearby; he had done so with Mr. Hooke.

Dawn coloured the Thames a rich royal blue. With no cloud to disfigure it, the sky simply changed its black for blue, bleaching at the horizon. Storehouses towered over him. With little light yet to illuminate their shapes, they appeared like flat facsimiles of themselves. Harry could smell molasses, tobacco, turpentine, and hemp.

He clambered up some greasy steps. They creaked alarmingly under his weight, but led to a firmer path. Lashed together against a low wharf, wherries rose and fell with the water's gentle movement.

It was early; the place was still deserted. It was so quiet Harry could hear the river rippling against the ships in midstream, a packet boat and a coal barge waiting for room to unload at the wharf.

An early waterman might take him across. But Harry did not want to exchange one of his rings for a wherry ride. Perhaps he could use Mr. Hooke's name to persuade, with a promise of future payment; as well as being a frequent customer, Hooke was an interested one, always willing to converse on tides and flow. Knowing the distrustful nature of watermen, though, Harry doubted it. Besides, in his expensive clothes, would any waterman believe he was ever Hooke's assistant?

Across the river, Rotherhithe's lights looked far away. Harry realised he was breathing heavily; he told himself to calm.

Reaching the nearest wherry, he saw its sculls had been fastened over the seats with cords neatly tied. In all the fine weather, its owner had not bothered to cover it. Harry stepped inside it and worked at the knots. He had never rowed, but had watched plenty of watermen doing so. It could hardly be difficult. If the Thames took him further east than he wanted, he would make his way back by foot.

Having released the last knot, he unlooped the wherry's painter. The craft he had chosen was tied to its neighbour; he undid this last cord, too.

With an anxious look over his shoulder, Harry pushed away from the wharf.

At once, the flow of the Thames turned his boat, dragging it into a sharp left turn. He lifted the sculls to place them in the basic row-locks on either side. Designed to be pulled by two men, the wherry was heavier, more difficult to steer, with sculls far thicker, than he anticipated. As he tried to push aside the water, his hands could barely grip the sculls far enough around to keep hold. Having managed to drop both sculls into their places, angling their blades correctly proved impossible. Smoothed from use, their handles slid in his grasp.

Although it was early morning, already Harry felt hot. Fear at the stealing of the boat made his palms sweaty. He found, quickly, that lack of physical work had softened his hands. Already their skin was sore, and the pads of his fingers felt bruised from holding the sculls. His wrists, painful from Fenn's manacles, also bothered him.

As he tried to steer further out, away from the shore, the wherry resisted his rowing. At last, by pulling with one scull and braking with the other, he managed a clumsy turn, but the ebbing tide dragged his boat around too far and made it rock alarmingly.

What the watermen made look so easy was in fact horribly hard.

Thinking the wherry about to roll, Harry felt his panic rising. He pulled the sculls with all his strength, splashing wildly, trying to make the wherry face the south bank.

Slowly, the vessel began to obey him, but the effort to control it and keep it moving across the river was prodigious. His back and his forearms ached. He panted for breath. His palms felt as if they were on fire.

The sun balanced on the horizon, an orange semicircle illuminating the waves that chopped against his wherry. Soft greys and blues replaced the earlier blacks. Mist clung to the water, sending cobwebs across his vision.

Exhausted, Harry was now nearly in midstream. When he embarked on his voyage, he had looked across at Rotherhithe, with all its warehouses and wharves. The spire of its church, St. Mary's, had now moved way off to his right; instead, he faced sparse buildings and the open fields behind Jamaica Street. He could see Seven Islands, the rivers between them, and the remains of Edward III's manor house.

The wherry threatened to spin. At the limit of his strength, he tried to pull even harder.

He heard splashes that weren't his own. Coming from behind him. Unlike his haphazard ones, these were calmly rhythmical. He turned—as far as he could from the awkward position he was in— to see what approached.

Another wherry, moving easily and straightforwardly. Aboard it sat two men, both pulling at half the speed of Harry's strokes, neither looking troubled by their efforts.

The few boat-lengths between them became one. Then, they eased alongside him.

With a flood of relief, Harry recognised one of the watermen. 'Mr. Abbott,' he cried. 'Kill-sin!'

'Who are you, buggeranto, who strikes our property?'

'Kill-sin, I am Henry—'

The other man undid his oar and used it to poke at Harry's chest. Harry fell backwards, into the bottom of his wherry.

'This cull's a pageant,' Kill-sin said. 'It's a blood what filches our boat.'

Harry struggled to lift himself up. When he did, he saw his stolen wherry now rested against the watermen's. Kill-sin chewed imperturbably on tobacco. Both men looked at Harry with disdain.

Kill-sin scanned around them. 'Shall we put the fuckster in the river?'

'Don't wanna mill him,' his partner answered. 'Might catch up wiv us.'

'Crack his noggin. If the son of a turd can swim, all's well. If not, that's his difficulty, not ours.'

'You swim, blood?' the unnamed waterman asked.

Harry put his hands up to shield himself. 'I can. But please—'

Kill-sin looked at his mate.

'Crack 'im.'

CHAPTER TWENTY-FOUR

THE MALEVOLENT THAMES

Viscous and slimy water slapped Harry's face and filled his mouth and nose. He was gasping, but his lungs could not suck in any air.

He must have been knocked unconscious by the waterman's oar.

Panic gripped him. He could feel his heart's thumps, but happening separately from him; another man suffered while he watched on. Trying to raise his head—and to bring some rhythm to his breathing—he saw the low sun glancing over Ratcliff to his right. He knew he floated on his back, going headfirst downriver.

Harry tried to kick his legs, but they refused to obey him. One of his shoes had come off; this thought disappointed him most.

Mouth finding air, he uttered incomprehensible sounds, between groans and screams. Wanting to get his arms moving, he writhed from side to side. Full consciousness returned, but too slowly.

Ignore the pain. Think straight. Or Ratcliff would be the last thing he saw.

He tried to kick again, but a great spasm shook his whole body. He swallowed more water. His shoulders suddenly sank. His arms windmilled wildly. Rotating in the water, he was now sideways to its flow. Then, his feet went before him.

In the fast midstream he felt as if he slid down a hill, like sledging when a boy.

If only his waistcoat were not so heavy. He could never shake it off without going under. Knowing it would help him, he kicked away his remaining shoe.

Though still erratic, his breaths became more regular. He spat water to one side of him. Unless he got himself to the bank, the Thames might take him clear out to sea. If not, Harry wondered where his body would wash up. And who might find it?

The thought interested him. Would anyone discover him? He might simply disappear. All those who knew him would think him gone with Königsmarck's men and never heard of again.

For how long would Grace miss him?

She would wonder about it, until she stopped wondering.

Stupid thoughts. Stupid. *Wake up, Harry.*

Save yourself.

Past Shadwell now. Harry recognised its church, St. Paul's; the 'church of sea captains,' because so many were buried there. Beyond it, the waterworks overlooked the ponds left after draining the marsh.

He was on the river's curve where it turns to avoid Rotherhithe, preferring Limehouse. He must swim to the shore. He had not really swum since childhood. His mother, anxious he should learn, had taught him using the village millpond.

Cold, stiff, shaking, Harry's muscles had forgotten her lessons.

The ebb tide pulled him forcefully. He twisted in the water, hoping his arms could start a stroke. His legs felt like weights, anchoring him. He kicked them out feebly as he turned belly down.

His teeth felt as if his gums released them.

One by one, off they went, floating away in the water.

To take himself nearer the Rotherhithe peninsula, he heaved frantically at the water, to be startled by a curious pike. The fish stared at Harry blankly, showing him its own teeth, then slunk gracefully away.

As the water swept him around the river's curve, he managed some kicks, which brought him closer to the south shore. A clay-soiled and rocky beach presented itself intermittently above his view of the waves, with a few scattered cottages, and a floating dock with a tilt-boat inside it, hoisted up for repairs.

Fighting the malevolent Thames, Harry edged closer to the beach. Closer, closer. He forced himself to keep moving, keep pushing the water behind him, find some energy to do so. He wondered if he could yet put his feet down, if they might find a firm surface; he decided not to risk it, thinking he would be unable to bring his legs horizontal again. The current, though, seemed to change its mind; a sudden sweep of water pushed him nearer the tip of the peninsula, at its northernmost point.

At last, as he swam towards the shore, he felt something brush his knee, then his chest. Realising he was in shallower water, he let himself be taken by the waves, until he felt timber and stone beneath him: the causeway for the ferry, built so passengers could traverse the mud at low tide. Pushing with his knees—no strength left in his arms—he crawled along it, on algae-slippery stones, and found the causeway's head. There, he flopped down onto the beach's welcoming slope.

After wiping his spectacles—miraculously they had stayed on—he eyed heavenwards, thanking God and Mercy for his survival. He seldom relied on either.

For the first time since being oared and dumped in the Thames, he felt a welcome warmth. The morning sun on his face had never felt so good.

Shaking with cold, coughing up brackish, mud-tasting water, he hoisted himself upright, then stumbled further up the beach. Its mud was filled with reddish gravel, which jabbed uncomfortably into the soles of his stockinged feet.

Ahead of him, around the peninsula's nose, stood a tall pole like a ship's mast. Its base was submerged; it appeared to stand on the water. From its top projected two large pieces of timber, cut to resemble cow horns.

Harry had landed at Cuckold's Point.

CHAPTER TWENTY-FIVE

THE ROTHERHITHE TAILOR

Facing the beach, ablaze with morning pinks and golds, stood a row of wooden-slatted houses with red-tiled roofs, built on stone platforms to elevate them out of reach of the incoming tides. Slick steps led up to them from the mud. This same mud sucked at Harry's legs as he tried to muster some strength for the climb.

Wearily, he walked towards the houses, the changing angle bringing into view another mast-like structure along the shoreline. Fully revealed by the departing tide, it had a metal frame suspended from a cross-member. Swinging gently in the breeze, it was an iron-ribbed gibbet. Currently tenantless, it seemed to wait.

Beneath it stood a pair of anglers, their rods balanced on simple frames. The men watched Harry curiously but offered no greeting.

Not even a nod, as if a shoeless man emerging from the Thames was entirely usual in Rotherhithe.

Harry chose one of the sets of steps. On reaching higher ground, his progress became easier. Mud was substituted for a planking walkway. Too often submerged, its wood rotted and would soon need replacing.

With grasses verdant and lush, countryside opened before him, its boggy, rich ground crisscrossed with rivers and channels, ditches and sluices. Water mills and windmills stood sentinel-like, making everything from flour to gunpowder, or else pumping water from the land. Cattle grazed contentedly among them. Reed warblers and terns swooped between the trees and hedges. A pair of demoiselles circled each other above the grass. Harry, still shivering, paused to watch them. The male was a splendid, iridescent turquoise. The female owned paler, light green wings.

Harry stopped to pick gravel from the fabric of his stockings, then padded along the walkway, following the peninsula's curve. Soon, he stopped again, and looked back down at his hands. When he had seen to his stockings, they had felt different. Now he realised why: his rings had been taken from his fingers. After knocking him unconscious, the watermen had taxed him for stealing their wherry. His ride across the Thames had proved expensive. With no senti-mental affection for them—apart from as symbols of his newfound wealth—still he lamented the rings' loss. Their sale could have kept him for weeks this side of the river, if he kept to cheap accommoda-tion. Even if he received far less than their normal value. Now he only had the clothes he walked in, and no shoes.

He was too tired to grieve for long. Feeling a heavy resignation, he set off, aiming for the busier part of Rotherhithe.

He passed a dirty and dilapidated collier, then a couple of barges covered over with tarpaulins. A guard, well-wrapped against the overnight chill, watched him—the first person there since day-break—with suspicion, until Harry had passed far further along.

Enclosed by high fences made from sharpened poles, a woodyard was stacked high with timbers neatly aligned, mostly pine and fir. Baltic timber, presumably; it made Harry think of the Swedish Count and his band of mercenaries.

A shipwright's dock berthed an almost complete East India-man—or Royal African, there were no colours to tell them apart—with a double row of closed port-lids for its cannon. The lower row was false, being only painted along the hull. The masts were still to be set, and its ropes and tackle were missing.

Up and away from the river, where Lavender Street became Jamaica Street, was a large market garden planted methodically with rows of vegetables, mainly beans and spinach and peas. More tarpaulins stretched over wooden frames designed to be easily moved as the sun travelled across the London sky, to keep the worst of the sun from charring them.

Beside this garden extended the long, straight avenue of a ropewalk, with its trestles to keep the ropes being made up off the ground, and guides and machinery to twist the strands together. Stores, locked securely, held the finished ropes, with sisal and hemp to make more.

A family of foxes—a dog and a vixen, with lanky pups almost ready to make their own way—sheltered in shade beside one of these stores. Harry's approach made them wary; they monitored him closely, then slunk away when he drew too near.

Cottages gave way to tenements and warehouses. Here lived

the traders with the goods they traded and the shops from which to trade them. Here was kept, divided, and sold the sugar, the spices, the coal, and the timber, or any of the thousand other goods the ships brought into Rotherhithe. And more goods to be loaded inside them before their journeys to lands far distant, on voyages months long.

Signs projecting over the streets showed who sold what. Or merchandise was simply hung over the rails of the galleries which snaked around the buildings. Hatchways pierced the floors of these galleries, with ladders dropping to street level, or fitted with tackle to lift and lower goods. Windows were left open with wares draped over their sills, displayed between their iron bars.

Harry stepped aside for an early wagon laden with barrels, its horses led by a bullnecked man with enormous shoulders. He reminded Harry of the Justice, Sir John, but this man's expression was tranquil rather than fierce. The man gave Harry a once-over, then looked away; Harry's still-wet waistcoat and lack of shoes were not his business, unlikely to be of profit, and so of little interest.

Disturbed by the man's look and feeling fearful of the main street, Harry turned between some buildings backing onto the river. Their walls stained by slurry, these coarsely constructed dwellings formed narrow, mazy alleys between them. The tide running down had left murky puddles. Deep shadows—the sun still low—made it dark.

Not knowing what he aimed for, nor what he thought to do, Harry walked through this unwelcoming labyrinth. The smack from the waterman's oar still dazed him. When he touched where the blade's edge had impacted, his hand didn't come away with any blood. A surprise; it felt as though his head was split open.

An unsteady bridge allowed him over a ditch, one of the many inlets carving through the area. The tang of human waste made him flinch.

Reaching all the way to the riverfront, a long warehouse blocked his way and forced him back to Jamaica Street. By now, more people were emerging from their homes and shops. Harry received more looks, some speculative: a stranger in Rotherhithe, wet through, no shoes, the clothes he wore expensive.

After a while of searching for a tailor's shop, or any kind of shop selling apparel, he had to ask. He was told to go just after Shepherd and Dog Stairs, then turn left with a right soon after.

Finding the stairs, then the tailor's, took him up a steep stairway to a landing and no sign of life.

The door was locked. Harry knocked on it loudly.

After a lengthy wait, a rattling of a key, then a struggle with the door stuck in its frame, a middle-aged hawkish woman appeared. Her face was all greys and mauves.

Appraising Harry told her that this customer had no shoes but an excellent tailor. Recognising opportunity, she permitted herself a half-smile, and welcomed him in.

She opened some shutters, allowing sunshine into a shop kept scrupulously clean, containing a small, understuffed sofa, poor chairs, a counter, and shelving full of bolts of material.

Half the room was taken up by a waist-high platform, positioned by the largest window. Using its mini staircase, the woman stepped onto it, to pull back more shutters. Boxes of cutting tools and offcuts showed that this platform was where the sewing was done, although, being early, no one yet occupied it. Spectacles, presumably the woman's for close work, sat on the windowsill, their twin discs reflecting the morning sun.

Through an almost-closed door behind the counter reached the smells of fresh bread, coffee, and bacon being cooked. Movements sounded in what must be the kitchen; Harry knew they were not alone. He looked longingly towards the aromas, hoping the woman would take his hint.

Another half-smile, swiftly suppressed, showed she had caught his expression.

She went behind the counter and placed her hands on its top. The position immediately established a businesslike relationship between them.

'Would you take my waistcoat as payment?' Harry asked her. 'As I've no money.' He had altered his voice into a rougher version of his own before elocution lessons. The longer vowels and lazier consonants of a townsman.

'And no credit,' she replied. Her voice was deep for a woman's, with a slight quaver to it. And, Harry thought, not unkind. Able to see her in a brighter light, Harry noticed her mottled and dry skin, and the sags under her eyes. She looked as exhausted as he felt.

Harry took off his waistcoat, flicked off some of its dampness, and placed it on the counter. 'Look, silver galloon.'

Her expression told him he had said the most stupid thing she had ever heard a man say, from an abundant choice of stupid things men said. Shaking her head in disbelief, she went back onto the platform to the window with the spectacles and placed them on.

When she returned, she held Harry's waistcoat up to the daylight to inspect it. Afterwards, she placed it on the countertop and smoothed and folded it absentmindedly and automatically, as she had a thousand other garments before. She removed her spectacles and stared at Harry, standing with her head tilted and her chin raised. Her fists were clenched, her knuckles pale, the muscles along her forearms taut.

The woman was anxious, Harry knew. Perhaps even afraid. Of him being in the shop. Normally he would hasten to reassure, but in his present circumstances he thought he might use her fear to his advantage.

'I'll shout Rachel,' she said, and did so, towards the kitchen and its smells. She declined to add anything further for Harry's benefit.

There was a long and awkward silence while they waited.

CHAPTER TWENTY-SIX

THE NOTICEABLE WOMAN

Carrying a tray with two cups and a pot full of coffee, a second woman—Rachel, presumably—emerged through the door behind the counter. With the door's opening, the kitchen smells grew stronger.

Harry observed she was tall, and very thin. Her shoulders were spaced wide apart, giving her an angular frame tapering down to her narrow waist. Her cap, cream cotton with a stitched blue pattern, kept her hair back from her face, apart from one thick, dark coil which escaped it. Her bodice and skirt were the same yellow brown, the colour of wet clay. A neat apron had wide ribbons; an elaborate bow held it tight to her waist. All looked more expensive and more fashionable than you might expect from the modest shop they were in. An advertisement for her tailoring skills.

She observed a shoeless customer trying to make barter with his wet waistcoat, which—its dampness aside—was a far finer item than anything else in their shop.

Did he expect to receive *anywhere near* its original price?

Harry could almost hear her thoughts.

The first woman looked fondly at the second, who did a twitch of her eyebrows as if to say, he is at our mercy. No formality of employer and employee between them, Harry noticed. No suggestion of mistress and apprentice.

Wondering quite what the relationship was between them—they shared no discernible family resemblance—Harry coughed into his hand, both to signal his readiness to negotiate and to void Thames water from his throat.

'Two shillings,' the older woman told him before he said a word.

'I paid nearer twenty.' In fact, Harry could not recall what he paid; he had bought other clothes at the same time, careless of individual prices.

'You could have,' Rachel replied, for the first time looking directly his way. 'Fine waistcoat. Beautiful thing.'

She spoke in a clear, unhesitant monotone. Her accent sounded similar to the men's he had conversed with at the Steelyard, the Hanseatic League's kontor in Dowgate. Or Jerzy Boroski's—although his voice was far more gruff. She was much younger than the woman with her—younger than Harry first thought—but had the same weary look. Dark tiredness smudged her eyes.

He became aware he was noticing another person's details far more sharply than normal, without quite knowing why. By all the standards he was used to, Rachel was plain. Her features were too clearly defined—a too-firm jaw, too-dark eyebrows, and a too-pointed nose—and she had not nearly enough flesh. Her neck was too long. Her hands were too large, with their fingers too bony. They also looked chapped and sore. Capable, working hands, Harry thought, as his used to be.

'You'll really give me no more for it?' Harry asked the women, being careful to maintain his commoner tone.

'What fink you, Rachel?' the older woman asked.

Rachel poured coffee into each cup and passed one to her companion. 'Wet through, and far from perfect.' Cradling her cup rather than holding it by its handle, she took a tentative sip, wary of a scalding. 'You can tell by the taint it's been in the river. East of the City's the dirty side.' She took a glance at Harry. 'Half of London's shit lands here.'

Harry felt he should take offence at her implied insult, but was too tired to, and, also, in no position to.

The older woman guffawed. 'There's other tailors in Rotherhithe,' she told Harry—she said it as Rovverive—'Go see them.'

'We'll see you back here when none offer more,' Rachel said.

The older woman turned aside, tiring of the conversation. 'You mistake Rotherhithe for the Strand.'

Rachel leaned forwards and rested her elbows on the countertop, unashamedly inspecting Harry more closely. 'No purse, I see. No shoes, neither. Knocked on the head—there's the damage. Robbed?' She saw no need to pause for confirmation. 'Your pickle makes the garment cheap. So does the filth on it. You need money now, else you'd not wish us to buy the clothes off your back.'

'I want a fair price, is all,' Harry said, feeling self-conscious from her gaze.

'Charity, is what you want,' Rachel replied tartly. 'Is it not, Mrs. Unsworth?'

The older woman now had a name. '*Give to him that asketh thee, and from him that would borrow of thee turn not thou away*,' she replied. 'Though Matthew made a better apostle than a tax collector, I'd say.'

Harry recognised his mistake. These women were more than a match for him. He had nothing he could turn to advantage. Mrs. Unsworth's wariness of him had evaporated as soon as Rachel joined her. He wondered if there was a man of the household, or if, like so many women running their businesses after widowhood or separation, they kept the shop themselves.

Rachel looked at him slyly. 'A *disguise*, is what you ask for. Otherwise, you'd dry off in the sunshine as you make your way home. *Otherwise*, you'd have first gone to a cobbler, to put new shoes on your feet.'

She straightened up and stepped back from the counter. Looking up into her appraising grey eyes, Harry realised she stood taller than he did.

'But you can't go home, can you?' She blew across the surface of her coffee, then took a long sip. 'Two shillings is plenty.'

Then, after a moment to consider, she relented a little. 'But if you buy your clothes from us, we may show you the charity you're after.'

Rachel looked for her companion's agreement, which Mrs. Unsworth heralded by a reverse sniff: a derisive blowing of air down her nostrils.

'I can find you shoes, too,' Rachel said.

'I wasn't robbed. Not quite, anyways.' Harry had accepted losing his rings as the price to be paid for stealing a wherry. As Rachel seemed to have taken over the negotiations, he addressed her. 'Do you have anything like a soldier's uniform?'

While she thought, Rachel flexed her long fingers. 'You swapping those breeches?'

Harry smiled resignedly. 'They're silk moiré. Would they buy me some of your bacon, too? And bread?'

'Hear that, Mrs. Unsworth? Silk moiré, says the gentleman.'

'I 'ear it,' Mrs. Unsworth replied. 'What's your name, Mr. Gentleman? I don't do business with no one 'less I know what to call 'em.'

'William Jackson,' Harry told her.

He closed his eyes, wondering why that was the name he had chosen, and what it might lead to now he had. It had jumped into his head; it was too late now.

'Pour Mr. Jackson some coffee, dear, why don't you?' Mrs. Unsworth said to Rachel. 'He bin drooling since he first bin in.'

CHAPTER TWENTY-SEVEN

THE DELICIOUS
BREAKFAST

Again, Harry woke at dawn, given no choice by screeching gulls. All the birds of the Thames seemed to have gathered along this stretch of the river. Yesterday, while walking the length of Rotherhithe's bank, he had seen cormorants, grebes, and mallards, as well as the clamorous gulls. A heron, too, whose long legs and arch manner reminded him obscurely of Rachel in the tailors' shop.

His own legs were stiff and cold, despite the thickness of his new trousers—close-fitting labourers' trousers a bargeman might wear. The blackness above him brought with it the memory that last night he had sheltered under canvas. He had crept into the rope yard, sleeping where the family of foxes had watched him on his walk from Cuckold's Point.

He got up from his bed of rough sacking and wandered down to the river. There, he listened to the high water lapping against the wharves, and enjoyed the cool breeze and the fine spray scudding in the air, almost imperceptible on his skin. Across the Thames shone the lights of Limehouse—the side of the river he knew, which held everything he owned, where all was familiar.

But the north bank seemed mockingly distant.

Yesterday, he had spent his time skulking around Rotherhithe, doing his best to remain unnoticed. Rachel had promised to make him a soldier's coat, undistinguishable from the real thing. But with all their other orders, it would take three days, perhaps four, to do so. Wearing it, Harry hoped to pass unnoticed over London Bridge. He did not want to risk the Rotherhithe-to-Limehouse ferry—and certainly not a wherry—thinking he would be recognised.

Besides, he had no money.

There was one place he needed to get to, key to proving his innocence.

Rachel had provided him with a pair of stout leather shoes. For anonymity's sake, they were pleasingly scuffed; he had prevented her from shining them. They belonged to her husband, she explained, who had been impressed into the Navy. His shoes had not gone to sea with him. The press took him soon after the couple's arrival in London from the Polish–Lithuanian Commonwealth. Rachel's glower discouraged Harry from fishing for more information. The only further detail she volunteered was her real first name, with her surname: Raszka Lejbowiczowa.

At first, the shoes had seemed a good fit. After a couple of hours or so, though, of roaming Rotherhithe, Harry's heels blistered, and hard ridges dug into the soles of his feet. By the end of the day, he was hobbling.

A plain shirt—itchy after the fine fabrics he was used to, and with only an approximate fit—completed his outfit. It gave the camouflage he desired. To add to it, as he left the tailors' shop he had picked up some street dust and wiped himself down with it.

He had explored as far along the river as St. Mary's. Built of chalk and flint, the church owned a square tower with a crenellated top, and was easily the tallest building in its parish.

Standing in its graveyard, he had watched London Bridge's drawbridge lifting to allow larger vessels through. It was a shock to remember he had stood there, by Nonsuch House, where Diana Cantley's kidnapper had pushed her father to the ground and robbed him of his money, not even three full days ago.

Since then, his life had been turned upside down.

The rest of the day was spent resting, finding odd spaces between all the activity around him. In case he drew suspicion, he spent only a short time in each place. He tried his best to blend in, to avoid any kind of attention. How used he had become to being stared at when dressed in his gentlemanly clothes, taking such attention as his due.

By not meeting anyone's eyes, he found, and by looking casual, he could achieve a form of invisibility.

But he knew such inattention could not last. Someone, eventually, would ask who he was and what he was doing. Without money—the tailors had refused to part with any coins or tokens, saying his waistcoat and breeches did not cover doing so—he soon grew hungry. And thirsty, too, under the scorching sun. To minimise his pangs, he had resolved to sleep in the rope yard as soon as its last workers were gone for the night.

Today, he must do something. But what? Feeling his parched throat and empty belly, he thought to hand himself in. Make his way to Sir John's house at Leicester Fields. Most probably, he would be arrested as he went. But after Königsmarck's men had taken him, with threats from a musquetoon to do so, Sir John would take twice the convincing to acquit Harry from blame.

As Sir John had listed for him, an overabundance of evidence attested to his guilt.

Remembering Grace's expression brought a desperation to prove to her, too, his innocence. He still felt puzzled and hurt. He could not dismiss her look of doubt from his mind; the image brought with it a caustic feeling, unsettling and bleak. If ensconced in Sir John's lockup, how could he prove anything to her?

To trust others to do that for him—perhaps by incriminating themselves—was absurd. And how long might it take?

To improve his circumstances, he needed to take action; he could not merely hide forever. Did the Justice know he was here, in Rotherhithe? Perhaps Harry was already reported to the Watch. He remembered the two anglers who witnessed him emerge from the river. They must have been suspicious. Or the man guarding the barge who had seen him.

But before Harry did anything else, though, he must find food and drink.

He left the waterside, walking the same way as the morning before, towards Rotherhithe's centre. As nobody was around to see, he diverted into the vegetable garden. After climbing a fence, which wobbled worryingly under his weight, he stole some radishes. Brushing them clean of soil with his fingers, he crunched them as he walked, chewing mechanically; it was hard to summon the saliva to help them go down. He remembered the coffee and bacon wolfed down at the tailors' shop. Perhaps Mrs. Unsworth and Rachel could be persuaded to part with more. But what else could he barter? Perhaps Rachel would take her husband's shoes back. Swap them for a cheaper but more comfortable pair.

As he walked, the sky lightening with the onrushing day, he wondered what Robert Hooke was doing. Without question, his friend would be busying himself with some way of helping him. The thought cheered him greatly. If only Harry could get a message to him. Hopefully, Rachel would complete the red uniform coat sooner than she had said; he was unwilling to attempt a return to Gresham without it.

☿

FINDING THE TAILORS' SHOP WAS MORE complicated than he thought. The jumble of buildings looked different; he misremembered the route. When he at last recognised the right building, the stairs to the entrance seemed not as obvious. Once he had found the door, he paused for a moment outside it to gather his strength—or his courage, he was unsure which. Although the day was not yet warm, going back to the shop had made him sweat; he felt unaccountably anxious. Then it came to him why: he had worried that somebody had gone to the Watch, to inform of a stranger in Rotherhithe, but that somebody might be either of the women in this shop. As he had already given the two women his waistcoat and breeches, they had no need to wait for more payment.

To listen for impatient feet inside—male feet inside heavy boots—or the clanking of weapons, Harry placed his ear to the door.

The only thing he could hear was a woman humming. It brought to mind the melancholy singing in Bethlehem Hospital. With it came the smells of coffee and bread, but, this morning, no bacon.

Keeping his weight on his back leg, ready to turn and run, he tried the door. Just as he had found it yesterday morning, it was still locked. His shaking of the door brought a stop to the humming; afterwards, a long silence, then light footsteps across the shop.

After a labour to pull it clear of its sticking frame, Rachel opened the door—wide enough to show the shop was empty of any Watch, soldiers, or Marshalmen.

'Mr. Gentleman,' she said.

Rachel stood closer than most people would find comfortable. Her eyes—which reminded him of Robert Hooke's in their grey directness—looked unwaveringly into his. She had perfected, Harry thought, a way of looking that was completely neutral. As was her calling him 'Mr. Gentleman.'

Neither polite nor impolite. No trace of mockery or esteem.

Being so unusual, this neutrality soon brought Harry discomfort.

He stepped back from the doorway and bowed to her. 'I'm hungry, ma'am. And thirsty. But I have only the clothes I stand in.'

'The clothes you bartered for yesterday.' Neutral or not, she knew how to drive a hard bargain. Harry could only shrug.

'You find a place to sleep?' She asked questions as directly as she looked.

'At the rope yard, just past the vegetable gardens.'

'I know it.' She looked gravely at him. 'Mrs. Unsworth's not yet risen.' She thought for a second. 'She'll not mind if I feed you, I think. Perhaps you're more useful than you look.' Rachel flashed a grin as she said this, but put it away as soon as it arrived. 'There are things you could do.'

Harry found himself watching her mouth. Her teeth were bright. Her incisors were very slightly crooked and very slightly long. It occurred to Harry that he found them attractive. In the morning's heat—already sultry—a sheen of perspiration misted her top lip. Harry told himself to look at her eyes instead, but to avoid their insistent steadiness he ended up focussing on her glabella, the area at the top of her nose between her eyebrows.

He wondered if she might think him cross-eyed.

Hanging in front of one ear, the same tendril of hair as yesterday morning had escaped from under her cap. Thick, coiling, almost black.

She's too thin to be beautiful, and too weary-looking, Harry told himself. But why, then, did she make him feel so discomposed? A simultaneous thought was that he stood outside when he would much prefer to be inside, away from prying eyes.

Rachel sensed his unease; she looked past him along the balcony, at the view the shop's doorway afforded of its neighbourhood. To Harry's surprise, she then pulled him in by his arm and shut the door behind them.

'Stay there.' She motioned to the counter. 'I'll make you some breakfast. Then I'll decide how you'll pay.'

☿

EVEN THOUGH RACHEL HAD GONE THROUGH to the kitchen, leaving Harry alone in the shop, he still felt acutely conscious of her. Particularly her proximity at the door, when she had pulled him in. Even if only in thought, he knew his preoccupation with Rachel was a betrayal of Grace. A twinge of guilt afflicted him. As with

Diana Cantley, another woman had turned his head. This one was poor, undernourished, and Polish, working in Rotherhithe as a tailor. Married, too, he reminded himself, although her husband was at sea. Nevertheless, Harry ran his fingers through his hair to neaten it, as if by doing so he could rid it of its dirt. After his dunk in the Thames, his day of walking through Rotherhithe in the summer heat, and his night sleeping on sacking at the rope yard, he desperately needed a wash.

Ridiculous. To her, he was just a stranger divorced from his money, for reasons she had no way of knowing.

To distract himself, he looked around the shop, studying the equipment and materials. The women kept everything fastidiously stored. The floor and the platform were spotlessly swept. Kept beneath the platform, wicker baskets held scraps of materials. Larger pieces hung on hooks or frames. That the shop was busy was obvious, but he could only see two sets of tools. Organised by size on a shelf, brass and iron needles impaled long rectangular cushions. There were pots of thimbles, bodkins, and chalks, a couple of pressing irons, different types of scissors. Measuring sticks and lengths of paper for clothes ready to begin. Patterns, neatly folded.

Interested in its system, Harry studied more closely the way of marking the paper strips which recorded customers' measurements, but Rachel's return interrupted him.

With bread generously buttered, she brought little dishes full of honey and jam, and the same pot with coffee as yesterday. As Harry had seen her do with Mrs. Unsworth, they both leaned on the counter as they ate.

Harry could think of no food more delicious. His cook, Hubert

Dieudonne, had prepared him many fine meals; none inspired the bliss this breakfast did now. The taste danced in his mouth and made him feel faint from pleasure. Rachel saw his appreciation and laughed softly at him, knowing it to be far inferior to his usual fare. She swallowed the laugh, stopping it abruptly, as if it displeased her.

Some pinkness rose on her throat, Harry could see, and stained her cheeks.

CHAPTER TWENTY-EIGHT

THE WELCOME SHELTER

The breakfast's heartening effect did not last long. As the day went on, it made Harry melancholy, as it underscored that the safety of the tailors' shop had been snatched away from him. Mrs. Unsworth, whose first name, Harry learned, was Sarah, insisted he should leave, so she and Rachel could work in peace. To Sarah's noticeable displeasure, though, Rachel told him to return for a meal in the evening. It would be simple fare, she warned him, and there would not be much.

Rachel's generosity—even if not shared by her partner—gave reason to look forward to the evening. Until then, he must avoid suspicion. Most of his time he spent along the riverbank, walking the muddy beaches revealing themselves, then hiding coyly, as the tide dropped and rose. Having found a shady spot between a pair of boats waiting to be caulked, he whiled away the rest of the morning watching sandpipers and oystercatchers picking for meals in the mud. Eventually, an irate man, whose spot it apparently was—although there was nothing to show his ownership other than his temper—chased him away. As the man was far larger than Harry, it seemed sensible to move along.

The complicated disorderliness of the riverbank, with its wharves and jetties and rough quaysides, meant Harry soon found another place to stay out of sight. Or, at least, unbothered. He watched the business of the Thames, marvelling—as he always did—at the vast quantity of vessels.

Most people here had to work hard for their livings. Harry's inactivity was so unusual he was bound to draw attention to himself; he made sure to move from place to place. By the end of the afternoon, he had progressed around the whole peninsula. All the way between St. Mary's church—almost Bermondsey—to Rogue's Lane—almost Deptford.

Fatigued from all the walking and from having had no luncheon or anything to drink, and realising his skin prickled from the incessant sunshine, as evening at last fell, he made his way back to the tailors' shop.

☿

THEY SAT IN THE CORNER OF the shop, the table's small size bringing them close together. Harry was conscious of Rachel's hands as she ate. Also, her feet were bare. Even though they were safely under the table, he found the fact distracting.

They were tailors, not seamstresses, they stressed. Sarah had taken on the business from her dead husband, and Rachel paid towards their partnership.

They had been severe with their reckoning of his waistcoat's worth, with its silver galloon, but they were prepared to share their dinner with him. Yet Harry's first inclination was to whinge to himself about it; all the walking and sun made him irritable. The eels-and-oysters pie had more mace than he liked. The carrots were far too crunchy, which Hubert would never allow. The peas, too, were underdone, hard little bullets in his mouth.

But when washed down with Sarah's raspberry wine, the meal made him feel pleasantly sated. After his day navigating Rotherhithe, it was better than tolerable. When he was an apprentice, meals with Mr. Hooke—whose stomach was a tender thing—had tended to the plain. Harry had expected nothing more. Mrs. Hannam, when he lodged with her, made monotonous stews, but used great guile to vary her preparation of eggs. He had accepted her cooking as his lot, never thinking to complain. Although when Colonel Fields had joined the household, the two men shared humorous looks across the table.

Grace had said money had changed him; Harry saw how she might arrive at the opinion. And, he recognised, his fussiness made him far too dependent on other people. As he was now, having to swap his clothes for food and shelter, on terms far from favourable to himself.

Sarah must have caught something of his thoughts registering on his face. *'Beggars should be no choosers, but yet they will.'*

Rachel admonished her with a pretend slap on her hand.

Sarah was undeterred. 'Per'aps you'd tell us of yerself, Mr. Jackson. How d'you come to wash up on our shore?'

Chewing determinedly on carrot, Harry took his time to fashion his reply. Not generally one for deceit, he needed to clarify in his mind what his story should be. It should be a simple one, otherwise he risked becoming tangled in his own web.

Having heard of cases where people, after accidents or trauma, lost their memories of themselves—some even failed to recall their own names—he thought of feigning to suffer the same malady. But to base any kind of story on this idea was too ludicrous. Pretending such complete forgetfulness could only invite disbelief.

Instead, Harry stayed as close to the truth as possible.

'A man spoke falsely against me,' he told them, after swallowing the carrot. 'I need to clear my name. I promise you, I'm innocent of any wrongdoing.'

'Scarce is a man innocent of *any* wrongdoing,' Sarah said. She sent Rachel a look that meant something between them.

'What were his false words?' Rachel asked Harry, ignoring her partner.

Avoiding the truth, Harry stayed quiet. But the longer his silence, the more dishonest he must seem. What could he say, though? The clothes he had worn when first in their shop showed the women he had money, which often protected against prosecution. The crime needed to be serious enough that running from justice was feasible. So many offences were punished by execution, it was difficult to choose which one. He decided to be straightforward, hoping it would not dissuade them from sheltering him.

'I'm accused of kidnap and murder. I'm innocent of both.'

Slowly, Sarah put down her fork, which she had just loaded with food. 'I see why you must hide.'

'I say again, I've committed neither of these crimes.'

'What happened to your money?' Rachel asked him bluntly.

Harry blinked at her, then grinned, shaking his head. She had such a bracingly direct way about her, but it was difficult to take offence. Her accent—Poland meeting London halfway—was appealing, he thought, as was so much else about her.

'I lost what I had with me when I fell into the river. When reunited with the rest of it, I can pay you more than a waistcoat and breeches. Will you let me stay here while I think on how best to prove my innocence?'

'How d'you come to fall in?' Sarah asked him. After a life of living alongside the water, her tone showed amazement that anyone should do such a thing.

'I was running from a Marshalman who caught up with me in Limehouse, and opted to risk the water. I was lucky not to drown. As I washed up on the riverbank, I knocked my head.'

The women looked impressed at a swim across the Thames, but it was obvious they only half believed him, if as much as that. Silently, they conferred with one another, using looks, until Sarah gave an unenthusiastic nod. She picked up her fork to resume her meal.

'You will pay us more,' Rachel said, her grey eyes fixed on him. 'You swear it?'

'I swear it,' Harry told her. 'On my honour. And thank you. Thank you both.'

CHAPTER TWENTY-NINE

THE SLEEPLESS NIGHT

Normally if he woke up in the night, Harry got out of bed and wandered down to his kitchen, perhaps to read for a while at its table until drowsy enough for his bed again. Here, he did not wish to disturb Sarah or Rachel. As they had not yet invited him through it, he did not want to open the door behind the counter, which led to their private, domestic space. The particular noise of him doing so might wake them. So he lay in the dark, trying to calm his thoughts but finding it impossible to do so. For here, he was surrounded by noise.

The sewing platform creaked, sounding as if someone walked across it, which Harry found unsettling. The bedding Rachel had provided, using linen from the baskets under the platform, rustled.

Even the woollen blanket made a scratchy, rushing sound every time he moved.

Above and below him, the building's oak beams sighed, still shifting despite their age. A window shutter jittered on its hinges, tapping insistently. He could hear the river, and footsteps out on the street. And a bird with a strange hypnotic song, its notes rising and falling. Perhaps a nightjar, he thought, but he wasn't sure. Mr. Hooke would know.

Harry's restlessness demanded the soothingly mechanical sounds of time passing. His house in Bloomsbury was full of clocks, as were Robert Hooke's lodgings. Mrs. Hannam's house, too, had clocks upstairs and down. Sarah and Rachel had no clock in their shop. If there was one upstairs, or through in the kitchen, it was out of his hearing. All the shop's irregular sounds, and the random noises from outside, were too unpredictable.

Recently, disturbed nights had become more frequent. The previous night at the rope yard was an exception. After his time with Königsmarck and his men, then his unplanned swim and a day spent walking around Rotherhithe, he had slept a sleep of exhaustion, right through until the gulls woke him.

Tonight, he had awoken from a dream which had him walking down Fish Street Hill, the Monument to the Great Conflagration looming over him. The low sun as late afternoon turned into evening threw its shadow across Monument Yard. No one else was there, the scene unusually quiet for the City.

A second after, without the real world's work of climbing its stairs, Harry was up on the Monument's high balcony. He looked down over the rail, seeing a man's face drop away from him. The face—on a head which had no body attached—did not accelerate according to gravity's laws. Instead, it moved at a constant rate, leisurely and slow, throughout its fall. Its eyes, locked on his, had the same accusatory expression until the impact on the ground below.

As always—for he had had this dream before—it was the noise of bone breaking against stone that woke him.

CHAPTER THIRTY

THE UNWELCOME QUESTION

Both women were up on the sewing platform. Sarah sat in her chair in the morning sunlight. Preferring the steadier light and relative coolness, Rachel sat cross-legged in the shade. Again, she was bare-footed.

Harry watched Rachel surreptitiously from his place below, on a chair by the counter. She wore a richly patterned oriental-looking waistcoat. Perhaps of Polish design, Harry surmised; he had seen nothing similar before. The shift she wore beneath it had sleeves which stopped at her elbows. He observed her long, slim forearms, the muscles flexing under her pale skin.

Swift and relaxed, her fingers seemed barely to touch her needle. From time to time she needed to rethread it, placing the thread's end between her lips, looking as if she kissed her fingertips.

One time, Rachel caught his gaze. Her needle stopped dead and her face took on a masklike stillness. Her eyebrows lowered in a scowl.

But her eyes continued to look into his.

'If I were to ask, would you let me help you?' Harry asked her, to thin the atmosphere between them.

Rachel's needle continued on with its oscillation through the red material of the coat she made.

'Well, ask,' she said, after a while.

'Well, may I help you?'

'Can you sew?'

'I've used needle and thread often enough,' Harry replied. 'Though I'm nowhere near as proficient as you.'

'Then how can you help me, William?'

William. For the first time, Rachel had said his name. Even though it was not his real name—in fact, William Jackson was the name King Charles II used whenever out and about secretly, and was the name he used when escaping after the Battle of Worcester—Harry felt privileged, and oddly grateful.

Rachel made no visible acknowledgement of it.

'I can do something, surely,' Harry said. 'Even if not as speedily as you.'

Sarah made a dismissive sound, admonishing them both. Harry was unsure if she disapproved of what they spoke about, or that they conversed at all.

Rachel frowned at her, then at Harry. 'But I would have to show you.'

Interpreting this as an invitation, Harry climbed onto the platform and moved to her. She had bathed that morning; he could smell the olive oil in her soap.

'No,' she said. 'Let me continue.'

Her expression concealed either peevishness or amusement. Impossible to tell.

He returned to his chair next to the counter. Raised up on the platform like actors on a stage, both women concentrated on their work. The only sounds were from the shifting of the materials they sewed, and the needles piercing them.

Time passed slowly in the quietness.

Eventually, it became too oppressive. 'Rachel, will you tell me about your husband?' Harry asked.

Rachel's needle stopped again. She stared at him with what Harry took to be dislike.

'Leave me to my work,' she said.

He castigated himself for his clumsiness. His inconsiderate intrusion into her privacy. Calling him William was not the finger-post to an increased closeness he had taken it to be. He performed an apologetic bow and backed away.

Deciding to go outside, he put on the husband's too-small shoes, and closed the door behind him, struggling to close it as it caught again in its frame.

CHAPTER THIRTY-ONE

THE QUESTIONING MEN

The next morning when Harry awoke, the light's angle as it pried around the shutters told him it was late. Sarah should by now be setting up the shop, Rachel preparing breakfast.

Harry left his mattress of piled linen, came down from the platform to behind the counter, and put his ear to the door. Still, neither woman had invited him through it; it felt to him as though the door closed off a solely feminine preserve. He decided he should wait until they appeared, even though they might be upset at oversleeping.

Or, they had left the shop already.

He could not believe they had done so without waking him. The way the front door closed was noisy. That was something he could fix for them, he thought. Then it occurred to him that if they had gone, they had taken care not to wake him. He began to worry. Perhaps a reward was offered for his capture. If one was, Sarah and Rachel could use the money.

His bladder forced his next decision upon him. Going to the front door, he was relieved to find it still bolted. So neither woman had opened it. Or one had, and the other rebolted it after her, which he thought unlikely. He unbolted it, opened it, went through it after watching up and down the lane, closed it, then walked down to the privy, a shared shed backing onto the riverside. After relieving himself, he walked to the New River Company pump. He levered water with one hand into the other and sipped at the bowl of his palm. Then he washed himself. Face, hands, armpits.

He went to return to the shop.

While doing so, he overheard a harsh voice saying what sounded like 'Hunt.'

He froze, listening for the voice to speak again. He heard someone's muffled reply but could not make out anything clearly. After a long interrogatory pause, the harsh voice said its thank-yous. Then, asking someone else, a second voice definitely repeated 'Henry Hunt,' in among unintelligible words beyond the edge of Harry's hearing.

As quietly as he could, Harry padded back up the stairway. On the balcony, he turned to see people in the roadway. Two men were stopping them, wanting to know his whereabouts. Both had weathered, bronzed faces. One had a scar beside his nose, running down to his chin. It passed through his lips, deforming them, so they fitted awkwardly together. The second man was larger, built bullishly like the Justice.

Harry returned inside the shop and shut the door. His heart thumping, he saw Sarah up on the sewing platform. She had just pulled aside the shutters and was putting away his makeshift bed.

Her face fell when she saw him.

Harry stood with his back against the door.

'You bring trouble with you, William,' she said.

'I'm sorry—'

'I've seen the way you look at 'er.'

It took a second to comprehend her meaning.

'I want you gone.'

Harry felt suddenly cold, thinking again of Sarah and Rachel not being up when he had awoken. 'Did you call for the Watch, Mrs. Unsworth? Are they on their way?'

'I did not.' Her look was withering. 'Your story don't persuade me. But you've charmed her.'

'Rachel?' Despite the Watch being just outside, Harry almost laughed out loud. 'I've done far from that.'

Sarah made an exasperated sound, walked heavily down from the platform, and disappeared through the door behind the counter.

Waiting for the inevitable trudge of official footsteps along the balcony, followed by a sharp knocking, Harry stayed by the front door. When the sound of knocking came, a few minutes later, Rachel emerged from behind the shop. If Harry's standing there without opening the door surprised her, she hid it. She simply swerved around him to open it.

At the door was a small and decrepit man, his thin arms full of clothes needing repair. They looked like sailors' clothes. Despite being rinsed through, they still kept the tang of the urine used to wash them.

No Watchmen waited behind him, using the old man as a decoy to arrest the young man they sought.

CHAPTER THIRTY-TWO

THE FARAWAY SIGNAL

As a soldier rarely receives a well-fitting uniform, Rachel reasoned, she made the coat too large. And if Harry appeared lost inside it, she told him, people would think lack of food made him meagre; it would make their charity more generous.

They had dirtied the coat together. Rachel even put a tear in one sleeve. The cloth she had chosen was the same venetian red used by the British Army. Because of the variety of styles given out to the soldiers, from the many manufacturers, neither Rachel nor Harry were too concerned about exactitude; after last-minute doubts about the buttons, and a second bout of weathering, they were both happy enough.

The coat brought just the anonymity Harry hoped for, even along a Rotherhithe Street bustling with activity. He was nameless; he was only a beggar.

Few people wanted reminding how contingent on fortune their circumstances were—how easily they could slip from having plenty to having nothing at all. So charity, when it came, was given swiftly and furtively. Harry had received three copper farthings pressed into his hand, a ha'penny from a woman whose pinched face showed she needed it more than him, and a whole silver sixpence from a man in a sleek black coach, who sent his driver with it across the street.

At the shop, Rachel had also shaved Harry's head, using her husband's left-behind razor. As well as altering his appearance, it made him more difficult to age, she said, which might lessen any unwelcome curiosity. Although, he argued, his youth was not so much a problem; lots of young men returned from service injured or ill.

Looking in the mirror Rachel held steady, the difference in his appearance shocked him—although Harry was glad to observe he owned a regular and symmetrical skull. He worried he was too fleshy for the disguise to be completely convincing. But out on the street, as he was finding, few people looked at his face.

Most of the people around him were employed to fetch and carry, scurrying between the ships moored alongside the wharves and the offices and workshops and stores. There was a wide discrepancy in appearance between the masters—self-satisfied and slick-looking—and those they employed. Employees looked undernourished and harassed.

Other passersby simply shopped, carrying baskets laden with provisions, while speedy-legged boys delivered messages, making haste among everybody else, sometimes causing upset.

Keeping his head down—the sun making his newly bald scalp itch—Harry passed another rope yard, this one far larger than the one near Cuckold's Point. Two long rope walks reached south towards Bermondsey, both lined with workers spinning the strands. Buckets were positioned regularly along them, for quenching the fires liable to ignite from the hemp dust.

As Harry neared St. Mary's church, he slowed to look at the Watch-house. Its door was firmly padlocked, its single window shuttered. The men must be out and about, patrolling the parish and doing their checks. Perhaps they searched for him, as the two had searched for him that morning.

Or perhaps no one was interested in him at all, having already caught up with Count Königsmarck and his gang. Elizabeth Thynne might by now be recovered, and unhappily back with her husband.

Harry might be known to be innocent. The thought, which should have cheered him, came with a stab of loneliness. He wondered who might trouble to find him, to tell him so.

☿

WARY OF ANY CLERGY WHO MIGHT chase him away as a beggar, he sloped into the churchyard. Just as unwelcome, somebody might— from Christian zeal—invite him inside for sustenance and shelter.

An iron hook held the church door open, presumably to encourage air into the nave. Seeing no one for some time, Harry risked walking inside.

Sunlight streamed through the windows, patterning the floor and, as he walked through it, shimmering over him. He sat on a pew, thinking his noise would bring someone out from the cleric's office. He waited a full five minutes, but no one appeared.

The tower's stairs had an open door at their base. The staircase coiling behind it was so narrow he had to bring his shoulders in, and so low he had to stoop.

Halfway up the tower was the belfry. Through the ancient weathered stone that formed its louvres, Harry could see horizontal slices of Rotherhithe to the south, and to the north, the busy Thames. Dodging between the bells led him to another door, and a continuation upwards of the steeply wound stairway.

Once out on the roof, he was treated to a welcome breeze, which lazily flapped the church's Cross of St. George flag.

From here, Harry could look across the Thames to the City. To his left lay London Bridge. In front of him, the Wapping Stairs and the Pasture Fields. Between them squatted the forbidding bulk of the Tower of London. Behind that rose the Monument; its urn reflected the sun, seeming to blaze. Beyond them was Moorfields, spanned by the enormous Bethlehem Hospital; its roofline was clearly visible. Even further north—although it disappeared into summer haze—was Half Moon Alley, where Harry used to lodge with Mrs. Hannam. St. Botolph's spire stood nearby.

Bringing his focus closer, back to Bishopsgate, brought into view St. Michael's and St. Clement's on either side of Great East Cheap, and along Lombard Street, the church of All Hallows. Harry could identify Leadenhall, the Merchant Taylors' Hall on Threadneedle Street, and the buildings around Star Court. On past St. Helen's and the Leathersellers' Hall was Gresham College. Its high Elizabethan chimneys and the sharp triangle of the Reading Hall's roof made it easy to recognise.

All were so familiar to him. They produced an ache of nostalgia in his ribs, as if he had not visited for years. It was the part of London he knew best. He had come here only to look at it.

He could just make out the observatory platform built over Robert Hooke's lodgings. Squinting, as the light was bright, he could even see placed upon it the frame for Hooke's signalling system. Thomas Crawley had worked on its joints when Harry went to question him about fetching the dead woman—whether Diana Cantley or Sebiliah Barton—from Bethlehem. It must be up there ready to demonstrate it to Mr. Pepys. Another was to go to Harrow School, Harry remembered Hooke telling him, to exchange signals between them.

Hooke's pine board symbols hung from the frame, arranged in a square. From this distance, Harry could only discern their top line; at the limit of his eyesight and the power of his spectacles to correct, those beneath merged into the platform's hazy greyness.

At first, he could make no sense of them. Deciphering them was especially difficult because he viewed them from an angle. Each symbol was close to merging into its neighbour. He thought he must have forgotten the system, until he realised that each symbol presented its back to him.

Was that a vertical line with a horizontal line extending right from its base, like a capital *L*, that Harry could see? He decided it was. So, Hooke's symbol for an *H*. As it was hard to distinguish from the supporting frame, he was unsure what the symbol next to it might be, but thought it a single vertical line. If so, Harry remembered, it represented an *A*. The symbol following was as Harry expected, and repeated twice: a horizontal at its base turning to vertical, with another horizontal extending from its top, like an angular *S*. The last symbol he could make out was a diamond shape, representing a *Y*.

HARRY

CHAPTER THIRTY-THREE

THE SERVICEABLE GLUE

Blaming a headache, Sarah went to bed early. She left Harry and Rachel sitting together in the shop. Even though Sarah had pulled the door shut behind her, the noises of her climbing the stairs and readying herself for bed reached them, and at last the creaks of her mattress.

Harry leaned towards Rachel. 'Does Sarah own a second pair of spectacles?'

Rachel took the question's oddness in her stride, as she appeared to take most things. 'Only the first, as far as I've seen.'

'I want their lenses,' Harry said.

'She needs them. She couldn't sew without them. Use yours.'

'Mine won't work for what I need. I'm nearsighted, so my lenses are concave. Sarah's farsighted, so hers are convex.' He delineated the shapes in the air with his hands as he spoke, to show Rachel the difference.

'So, you need lenses which are convex,' Rachel said, sounding neither interested nor uninterested.

'Could you fetch them?'

'Steal them from her, you mean, while she sleeps?'

'Exactly.' Harry could not help but grin at her, amused by the absurdity of his own request, and also that Rachel showed no curiosity upon why he wanted Sarah's spectacle lenses, concave or convex.

'I'll return them in the morning,' he promised.

Rachel made a noncommittal sound. Not refusal nor agreement.

Harry looked around the shop. 'Do you have paper to spare? Large sheets, if possible. I can use smaller if need be. And I'll need to make some glue. Flour, sugar, some vinegar, and water make a serviceable glue.'

Rachel went to a basket stored under the sewing platform. She found one of the sheets of paper she and Sarah used to cut into strips and record their customers' measurements.

'I'll need more,' Harry said. 'Four sheets of that.'

Rachel's eyes fixed on his for a long second. 'Come through to the kitchen,' she said. 'We'll make your glue in there. We must be quiet, though. I don't want us disturbing Sarah.'

Taking some scissors from their shelf as he went, Harry followed her to the door behind the counter, and, for the first time, went through it. He felt as though barriers were being pulled aside. Rachel's impassivity made it hard to gauge what she felt about him, though. Did she feel closer to him, or further away? Did she care about much at all? She was willing enough to help him. But incurious enough not to ask what with.

Perhaps she reasoned the information would come soon enough. Perhaps she felt she already knew enough: Harry needed something, she could help him, and it cost her little to do so. Who knew? Her grey eyes told him nothing, keeping her thoughts opaque from him.

In the neat but cramped kitchen, with everything in it cleverly stored, Rachel found the ingredients for Harry's glue. She withdrew a bowl from a cupboard. 'A spoon?'

Harry nodded, and took the bowl. As he did, her fingertips touched the backs of his fingers, sliding along them. Despite being the briefest of contacts, the feel of her skin remained, as if she still pressed her fingertips against him.

Pretending to be fascinated by it, Harry stared intently into the bowl. Rachel, too, looked elsewhere.

'Tell me how much of each you want, and I'll mix it for you,' she said, after a silence between them.

'I'll do it,' Harry said, swallowing, putting the bowl onto the small kitchen table. 'I've made plenty before.'

Rachel looked just as grave as she usually did. 'Promise you won't break them. Sarah's spectacles, I mean. You said you want the lenses.'

'I'll have to break them, but I'll mend them again. With luck, she might not even miss them.'

'Promise.'

'I promise.'

'She could still be awake. She's not been up there long.'

'I've not heard her moving for a while.'

Rachel left the kitchen. Instead of mixing the glue, Harry listened to her light movements along the corridor. He imagined her treading on each stair. Her solemn expression. Her grey eyes. Her long limbs, and the way her dress moved over them as she walked. Her dark hair, which he had never seen uncovered.

Mix the glue, Harry. Mix the glue.

By the time Rachel returned, bringing the sleeping Sarah's spectacles with her, Harry had cut and glued the four sheets of paper together to make two thick ones. He rolled and glued them again to form a pair of tubes, one slightly narrower than the other. He had kept some paper back, which he folded and cut into strips.

Rachel watched him closely as he dismantled the spectacles, separating the lenses from their frames and placing them in the paper mounts he had made.

'When I mend them, she'll never know they'd been apart,' he reassured her.

He affixed the lenses, one at the end of each tube.

'I'll put these on the sewing platform,' he told her. 'It's so warm, I think by morning they'll be dry.'

They left the kitchen, manoeuvring around each other in the tiny space. Harry went through to the shop.

Rachel stayed in the doorway. 'Good night, William.'

'Good night, Rachel,' Harry said, pulling out the linen for his bed.

'She'd be upset if she knew.'

'I'll bring them back. I made a promise.'

The door shut quietly, leaving Harry on his own.

CHAPTER THIRTY-FOUR

THE SILK BREECHES

Harry gave back the reassembled spectacles. Rachel took them. A pressing of her lips was the only sign she was satisfied.

'She had me helping her to look for them,' she said. 'I made play of doing so.' Her voice was low-pitched, quiet, but also irascible.

'Now you can tell her you've found them, which shall please her.'

She went up onto the sewing platform and settled herself down cross-legged to sew, placing Sarah's spectacles next to her.

'You didn't have to help me,' Harry told her.

Rachel's dress was cool-looking cotton. She had only loosely tied the laces at the neck of her shift, leaving visible the dip between her clavicles. Harry wanted to place his fingertip into the enticing hollow.

'No, I did not.' She twitched her shoulders, a small movement, but it showed her vexation with him.

'I used our telescope. It worked acceptably well.'

She gave him the same flat gaze he was now used to. Trying an inclusive use of 'our' had not softened her towards him. Most people, he thought, would ask why he had made a telescope. But she showed no curiosity at all, even though she had helped him by providing its lenses.

Earlier that morning, being careful to keep clear of the Watch-house, he had returned to St. Mary's church. He left early, taking the telescope with him. It had not quite dried, dark patches still staining the paper, but was solid enough to stay together. He had had to wait for an official, perhaps the parish beadle, to leave the church. Up on the church tower's roof, placing one tube inside the other was diffi-cult, as they wanted to stick. To his relief, Harry managed to get his telescope to focus.

By pointing it just to the right of the Tower, Gresham College came into view. If the Normans had built the Tower any further east, Harry would not have had the sight line, so could never have seen the message. The telescope was not as powerful as he would have liked—nowhere near—but this time he could make out all the sym-bols on Hooke's signalling frame.

The top line still said *HARRY.*

Beneath it were Hooke's symbols for *SEND SIGN I FIND YOU.*

☿

'I WISH TO MAKE A FLAG,' Harry told Rachel. 'It's important. I'll need a large piece of material. Do you have any white? Then, I need a black symbol sewn onto that. Like a capital *L.*'

Rachel exhaled, as if summoning all her patience. 'What does it mean?'

Harry caught her eye, but she lowered her head back to her work.

'Well, confusingly, it means *H*. *H* for Har—for horse.'

'I know what *H* is, *William*.'

Her inscrutability made Harry doubt if he heard the stress on the name. Did she still give him shelter despite knowing he lied about his identity? And despite Sarah Unsworth's aversion to him.

'It's part of a code, you mean,' she said.

'Yes, a code. To be more pedantic, a cipher. It changes letters of the alphabet to symbols.' He saw her incomprehension. 'The symbol for *H* happens to look like another letter of the standard alphabet. Most of them don't. A *Y*, for example, is represented by a diamond.'

'So, a system,' she said. 'For secret talk.' She put down her needle, and the material she stitched. 'One day, I shall show you how we write Yiddish, using Hebrew letters.'

'I'd like that,' Harry replied. 'Very much.'

Again, the unreadable look, her grey eyes not warm nor cold, approving nor disapproving. 'We have linen. White enough? For the black . . . Why not your breeches? They are silk moiré.'

'But surely there's something cheap—'

Her laughter cut him off.

CHAPTER THIRTY-FIVE

THE MAKESHIFT FLAG

Rachel donated a square of cloth to make a simple bag. Inside it, Harry put the flag he had made—one sewing task Rachel was happy for him to perform—and a length of cord, and his telescope—Sarah's lenses restolen and repositioned inside the paper tubes—and tied a knot at the top. He put on the red coat, then went outside and rubbed the bag in the dust.

He went back inside to say goodbye to Rachel, and to Sarah, but she was too upset at having lost her spectacles again to pay much attention to him. Harry felt some guilt at how distressed she was by their second vanishing in as many days.

Then he made his way through Rotherhithe. The sun was too hot for the coat. Under his arms became unpleasantly damp. But he could not take the coat off, for its effect was dramatic. Wearing it, he could steer through the crowd attracting little notice. As before, most people pretended not to see him at all, averting their eyes—even turning their heads away—as they walked towards him. A few gave him subtle salutes. These came from older men who had soldiered themselves. Occasionally, a woman did the same. Harry wondered what stories and sad separations lay behind such acknowledgements, that they should be so friendly towards a veteran.

By the time he reached St. Mary's church, perspiration had created mini river systems on each of his cheeks, running down through the dust he had rubbed on them. The dust caked around his mouth and gritted his eyes. Sweaty, dirty, shorn-headed, Harry was far from looking like the gentleman sought for kidnap and murder.

The beadle from the day before was nowhere to be seen. Harry pushed open the church door, which this time was not held open, and let himself inside. The nave's chill was immediately welcome. He made his way up the narrow staircase again, through the belfry, and on up to the roof.

Back outside, he unknotted the bag and took out his makeshift flag. He had not used the silk moiré breeches to make an *L* symbol. Instead, Rachel had found some old cotton, dyed black with alder bark and vitriol. The church's Cross of St. George needed to be taken down, which proved exacting as the rope was old and stiff. His flag was easier to hoist. Having only a short length of cord, it was not as high as he would have liked, but St. Mary's bell tower was tall enough that Hooke must be able to see it. When the flag was secure, he let it go. At first it hung limply, but then the breeze shook it out.

As soon as the flag unfurled itself, Harry started to fret. Eventually, someone was bound to report a strange flag flying over St. Mary's. Or someone might notice it straightaway. If Hooke did not respond, Harry decided he would take his flag down rather than risk somebody removing it. Then he would try to smuggle it back onto the pole the following day, or the day after. Without knowing what story he would tell, he trusted his instincts to be able to evade the beadle's wrath; he did not think it a matter of interest to the Watch.

He waited for an hour, by which time he had become timid. Looking over the side of the crenellated tower brought glimpses of people who seemingly strode into the church to arrest him. Any man who looked as if he might be in the Watch, or who dressed expensively, or who wore a sword or anything resembling a uniform, made his heart lurch.

He decided to wait for one more hour. Longer than that, his nerves could not withstand. And besides, by then, the sun would start to drop.

An hour rarely stretched out for so long. At its end, studying Hooke's observation platform through his telescope, he saw no one had changed the signal. So, presumably, no one had seen his. Harry was disappointed but could hardly be surprised. Two factors counted against Hooke replying: Hooke was a busy man; London was large.

Harry untied his flag, folded it, and placed it and his telescope inside the bag. He would try again tomorrow.

CHAPTER THIRTY-SIX

THE NEW PHILOSOPHY

Footsteps on the sewing platform woke him.

'William, I'm tired to my bones. So tired, I can't sleep. I hoped you might talk to me a little.'

Hearing Rachel's voice from the darkness, Harry snapped into consciousness. 'If I speak to you, you're more likely to fall asleep?'

She chuckled, a low-pitched sound made in the back of her throat. 'It shall soothe me, I think. Otherwise, I lie thinking. The same thoughts, again and again.'

Harry sat up and made to ask what troubled her, but she cut across him. 'Tell me more of yourself. But quietly, so not to wake Sarah.'

But he could not tell her of himself, for to her he was William Jackson. He considered for a while. As he did so, Rachel squatted beside him.

'I'm interested in natural knowledge,' he told her. 'And the system of the world. How it works, I mean.'

'It's a place of such unfairness, I've never understood how it works.'

'That's to do with the people in it. I mean more, how the Earth we live on moves inside the solar system—our sun and the planets orbiting around it. And how our solar system moves among the stars.'

Rachel wriggled under the blanket and settled herself beside him. To Harry's alarm, he could feel his penis beginning to swell. He hoped she would not inadvertently touch it.

'Tell me something of all that, then,' she said.

Harry considered for a moment. 'We've recently calculated the speed of light as it travels through the æther.'

'We?'

'Well, Herre Rømer. He's Danish but works for the French, with Signore Cassini. Who's Italian. Herre Rømer found it out when observing Jupiter's moons. Their light takes shorter or longer to reach us when we're nearer or further away, as we go around the sun.'

'I never thought light might have a *speed*, William. I just thought it was all around us.'

'Then count yourself with Monsieur Descartes—a Frenchman—who considers light's transmission from one place to another to be immediate. But he's wrong, it seems. Mijnheer Huygens worked out the mathematics of it.'

'He is a Dutchman?'

'Yes, a Dutchman.'

'You place yourself in this group of men? Who come from everywhere. Do you flatter yourself to do so?'

'Not among them. I look up to all of them. It was a slip of the tongue.' Although they were both careful not to touch each other,

Harry could feel Rachel's warmth radiating across the space between them. His erection was now painfully distracting. 'Or instead, I could speak of attraction between bodies,' he suggested.

'I have no wish to be seduced,' Rachel replied. The way she said it was again flatly neutral, as were so many of the things she said.

'I had no thought of that,' Harry lied. 'By attraction, I mean gravity. By bodies, I mean stars, or planets, moons, and comets.'

She brought the thin blanket more tightly around herself, tucking it under her chin. 'Tell me of gravity, then.' Moonlight shone on the whites of her eyes as she turned them to his.

Harry swallowed and licked his lips. 'There's a man I've spoken to. He lives at Gresham College.' Sensing her lack of recognition, he added, 'In Bishopsgate, just north of the Leadenhall market. He—Mr. Hooke is his name—is its Professor of Geometry. Also, he's the Secretary of the Royal Society, which holds its meetings there. He was its Curator of Experiments, too, so he presented to the Fellows experimental trials, and explained their import. He inspected instruments, and tested trials made by others, most often suggesting improvements to be made. He still does these things, in fact, but has assistance. From Denis Papin. Another Frenchman.'

'You admire him,' Rachel murmured, snuggling even further under the blanket, her eyes now closed and her breathing becoming more regular. 'This Mr. Hooke.' Her forehead lightly touched Harry's shoulder.

'I do. I do admire him. I've spoken with him about how all the heavenly bodies—stars, planets, moons, comets and so on, I mean—attract one another. When we look at the night sky, it's easy to observe. The way our moon makes its journey around the Earth, for example, is steered by the same force which keeps us on this sewing platform. As gravity's insensible other than by its effects, to explain its cause is difficult. No visible hamous particles pull at bodies, nor do any push them down.'

Rachel half opened an eye. 'Hamous?'

'Hook-shaped. Gravity extends into the æther beyond the world's atmosphere, so we know the atmosphere can't be its cause. Mr. Hooke believes gravity's power decreases between bodies the further apart they are. By what proportion he has yet to ascertain. He thinks it may be reciprocal to the square of the distance. We've tried to measure its decrease or increase at different heights.'

'We?' Rachel asked again, but more drowsily.

'Mr. Hooke, I mean,' Harry said. 'And other Fellows with him. He told me he tried to measure it up the steeple of old St. Paul's, and at Westminster Abbey. He's used the new Monument to the Fire. We—he—counterpoised two weights on a pair of scales. If gravity increases closer to the Earth's centre, then the weight should be greater, but when we let down one of the weights, using a wire, equipondium remained. Most probably, two hundred feet gives us not enough distance to discern a difference, but—'

Beside him, Rachel snored softly. She had rolled over onto her side, so her back was to him.

Harry shifted to lie flat on his back, trying to relax enough to go back to sleep.

It was difficult.

CHAPTER THIRTY-SEVEN

THE NIGHTTIME ANGEL

The angel looks mundanely human, yet Harry knows he is one of the *malakim*.

A messenger from God.

The messenger walks towards him with a heavy step, becoming larger in his vision until all Harry can see is his face. Bathed in moonlight, this face is elderly, wrinkled, and unshaven. The angel is bald, with liver spots on his head like islands on a globe. When at his closest to Harry, he reveals his teeth, tapping the two at the front, and winks a conspiratorial wink.

Finally, the angel wakes Harry by saying loudly, 'So!'

THE SAME MOONLIGHT as in Harry's dream shone through the slit between the shutters. Colonel Michael Fields had visited him again; the comfort of seeing him always brought the hurt of his loss.

Harry clutched at his blanket, and squirmed on the linen beneath him, his rough bed on the sewing platform. Having turned from one side to the other to try to get back to sleep, he saw that the door behind the shop's counter was opening. The slightest difference of grey within the rectangle of the doorway was enough to tell him, or perhaps a movement of air from the passageway to the kitchen.

Then he heard the steps up to the platform being compressed by the quietest of footfalls.

Another greyness moved beside him. A soft shushing sound from the darkness. Rachel settled herself next to him, pulling some of the sacking under her.

The second night she came to him, for more of his New Philosophy. When he had awoken that morning, she had gone. Breakfast was in silence, which brought awkwardness for them both. In the afternoon, Harry had gone to the church again, to hoist up his flag. Only then had he looked at Hooke's observatory platform through the improvised telescope.

There was a new arrangement of the symbols.

TOMORROW ELEVEN

☿

HE FELT HER HAND SLIP BENEATH the blanket, then gently scratch his chest. She paused, waiting for him to respond. He stayed still. She lay her hand flat against his stomach. She trembled, he noticed.

Harry pulled the blanket more tightly over them both. She placed her head on his shoulder, breathing warm air onto his neck.

When Harry brought his hand to her face to stroke it, he felt tears on her cheek. He went to sit up, but she pushed him down again. Tentatively, she pressed her lips to his. They were dry; he could feel tiny ragged bumps along them. He licked them with the very tip of his tongue. Rachel sighed, sending her breath, tasting of wine—he wondered if she had needed some before deciding to leave her bedroom—into his mouth. Even in the dark, he could tell she was smiling. Without the cap he had always seen her wear, Rachel's hair trailed over his skin; the tickling sensation raised goosebumps. Still kissing him, she held the side of his face, stroking it with her thumb, then ran her fingertips over the stubble on his scalp. Her other hand found his and steered it between the opening of her thin nightdress.

His palm covering her breast, Harry had the notion he should feel guilty, or sinful. But he did not. The thought was easy to put aside, for how could what they were doing, in this dark corner of Rotherhithe, hurt anyone? As each gave permission to the other, what did they transgress? Rachel had come to him. She needed him, at least for this moment. Thoughts of what followed could be put aside. There might be more awkwardness in the morning.

Did she think of her husband, far away at sea?

What were his feelings for Grace Hooke?

Harry told himself to stop thinking. To concentrate on what Rachel was doing now, as her hand moved lower under the blanket. The moonlight caught the whites of her eyes, gleaming with wetness.

'*Du bist iung,*' she whispered into his ear. '*Du bist sheyn.*'

He started to ask her what it meant, but her mouth against his silenced him. As she kissed him, and he kissed her, a feeling of agitation, almost panic, overcame him. It felt as though the blood in his arteries and veins had changed to light, or fire—a dizzying, unsettling separation from his usual sense of himself. He had the direful notion that his heart was only a small pump, a muscle heedless of his thoughts or his wants. It needed no instruction from him to keep working, so equally, it needed none to stop.

Harry's thoughts finally slowed, then halted, as he wanted them to. His sense of himself became only this contact of his body with another's. Skin to skin.

Then, only pleasure, and Rachel's sighs, and more words he did not understand.

CHAPTER THIRTY-EIGHT

THE GOODBYE
KISS

In the morning, Sarah did not appear. It allowed Harry and Rachel to breakfast without her. Eggs and bread, with some small beer. They kept looking at each other, then looking away; their small talk frequently dried up in mid-sentence. Then they would grin, or give little sad smiles, with touches of one another's hands that were quickly withdrawn.

After Harry finished eating, he looked at Rachel for a long moment, trying to gauge her thoughts. Then he held her tightly to him, and kissed her on the lips. Absurdly, he began to say, 'Thank you,' but stopped himself. Thanking her was scarcely sufficient for all she had done. She had not merely provided him a service. She had welcomed him and sheltered him, stretching her friendship with Sarah to do so. She had trusted him, then shared herself with him.

For not reporting a stranger to the parish, she had risked arrest, and at the very least a fine.

He took Rachel's hands and put the flats of his palms against hers. Like that, they pushed against one another, leaning in towards one another. He gazed at her again, his eyes hot and stinging, feeling a tearing sensation in his chest at the thought of leaving her, and fearful of what the future might hold.

'When you look at me like that, William,' Rachel said, 'your eyes give nothing away. They never do. I could never guess what you're thinking. One day, I hope, you will tell me your secrets.'

CHAPTER THIRTY-NINE

THE WINE
DELIVERY

Leaning against a large, ornately carved gravestone in the shade under a tree, Harry could oversee the river and hopefully stay unobserved. If Robert Hooke came to St. Mary's by wherry, the vantage point gave a view of the Swan Stairs, the Church Stairs, the Elephant Stairs, and Redriff Stairs. The half tide revealed a stretch of pebbles and shale giving way to thick mud nearer the water. As this would be difficult to cross, Harry gave the same likelihood to Hooke arriving by road, having crossed London Bridge. The same spot overlooked Back Lane, by the church, and Elephant Lane a little further off. Both were busy, but he was confident he could recognise Hooke through the crowd. Or, of course, Hooke might send someone else for him. Thomas Crawley, perhaps.

The waiting wore on his nerves.

A skull on the gravestone grinned at him. The cancellaresca inscription remembered a life shorter than Harry's.

The churchyard was quiet, so no one to question his lurking there, although one self-important-looking man entering the church—perhaps another parish official—had looked at him suspiciously. Even though the man moved on, Harry's anxiety increased, especially when a sudden cacophony of the bells announced eleven o'clock. Where was Mr. Hooke? But Harry knew well how unpredictable travel around London was; journeys sometimes took far longer than expected, especially if London Bridge was on the way.

Agitated by the bells, he slunk a little deeper under the tree. Gnats wanting his spot bothered him; he flapped at them ineffectually and puffed them away from his mouth.

Various carts and carriages clattered past, but none slowed by the church. The man emerged from it, so presumably he was the bell ringer. Vessels glided by on the Thames. None came close to the Church Stairs, although a couple of wherries disgorged their passengers at the Redriff Stairs. Harry watched them clamber across the mud, their shoes making deep holes in it. The women lifted their dresses, doing their best to keep them clean.

After a half hour had passed since the bells, Harry despaired of Hooke's arrival. Pessimistic thoughts arose: of not having correctly understood Hooke's message, or of Hooke being found out—by Sir John Reresby perhaps—and prevented from fetching him. The Justice, instead, was on his way, or Joseph Fenn, or any of the Watch they could summon.

Although it was minor by comparison, another thought made Harry's heart flounder: What if Grace accompanied Hooke? What should Harry say to her?

Could he behave as if nothing had happened between him and Rachel Lejbowiczowa?

It would be impossible to maintain such dishonesty with Grace; she knew him more intimately than anyone. He should just tell her, Harry decided, with a tone of definitude in his internal voice. No, he should not. He should just keep quiet. No need for the story to be known by anyone but him.

And Rachel, of course. As soon as he thought of her, he could picture her with exactitude. Her tall, androgynous frame and thick, lustrous hair. Her teeth, with their slight pointedness and unevenness. Harry's throat felt scratchily dry; it was not from the summer heat. He thought of her mouth, and the way she had used it on him. Of the heat between her legs.

A madness gripped him, he knew. His time with the Royal Society, his knowledge of the New Philosophy, his intellect trained by Robert Hooke, had not prepared him to be possessed by such powerful emotion. *Call it what it is, Harry: it is lust.* Lust, pure and sinful. But, as he told himself so, around the edge of the thought peeked the knowledge it was more. Rachel had provoked a sentiment in him more subtle, more profound, more complicated, than merely carnal desire.

He craved her company. Her interest. Her understanding. Her time.

This was dangerous ground he walked on, described by another word entirely.

A rough cart loaded with casks, pulled by a pair of enormous Suffolk Punches, interrupted his thoughts, so he had to shrug them away. This was no cart he recognised from Gresham's stables, nor any of its horses. But the hesitant way it stopped outside St. Mary's suggested its driver's uncertainty. Obviously, a delivery, but why so many casks for a church? Anglicans only took a small drop of wine during Communion. Perhaps St. Mary's rector was thirsty.

Two other men sat behind the driver, both perching on the foremost casks. All three wore hats to shade them against the sun, so Harry had no view of their faces. Cheap clothes marked them out as labourers, but their postures did not. Difficult to say quite why, but these were not labouring men.

Looking left and right, checking no one waited for him in the churchyard, Harry moved out from his hiding place. As he walked towards the street, the cart's driver turned his head to look directly at him, revealing the face of Edmund Wylde.

Harry broke into a jog. Wylde recognised the man coming towards him, despite his dusty and torn red uniform coat.

'Make haste, Harry! Climb up!'

Putting aside the thought that it felt strange to be called by his own name again—for the first time in a week—Harry, helped by Denis Papin and John Aubrey, placed his foot on the top of the cart's wheel and pulled himself up. His three friends all beamed and exclaimed and hugged him, but Harry's joy on seeing them was muted. He still worried about the Watch, and Sir John Reresby, and Joseph Fenn. And besides, Papin was opening one of the casks, which had a lid newly fitted with hinges.

'Get inside, Harry,' Papin instructed. 'Mr. Hooke says to take you to Covent Garden.'

'So Mrs. Thynne has not yet been found?' Harry asked.

'She has not,' Aubrey told him.

'In which case, Covent Garden it is,' Harry replied. 'Mr. Hooke remembered. Will he meet us there?'

Papin nodded. 'He has arranged it with Sir Peter. Duck your head down, and I shall close this lid.'

CHAPTER FORTY

THE ARTIST'S HOUSE

Covent Garden piazza opened up before them—but not for Harry, for he still crouched inside the wine cask—revealing the ever-startling modernity of its houses, with their regularity and porticos. Their stone archways, rusticated by the patient work of masons wielding their chisels, stood two storeys high. The second and third storeys were of red brick. All gleamed in the afternoon sun.

The same sun told the residents and visitors the time. In the centre of the square was a gravelled area fenced off with low posts and chains, surrounding a Corinthian column supporting four separate sun dials.

The market's sheds and stalls were busy, with their stacked fruits, vegetables, roots, and herbs forming a baffling maze. Barrows and carts clustered around them, and customers weaved through.

Beyond the market was the high wall concealing Bedford House,

home of William Russell, son of the man who had paid for and prof-
ited from the development. Fifty or so years before, its inhabitants
had all been Earls and sirs and ladies, but the Civil Wars and the
Plague had driven most of these away. Nevertheless, still prohibi-
tively expensive, only the richest could afford to live there.

The house Wylde drove them to stood close to St. Paul's church,
on the western side of the piazza, whose clock agreed with the sun;
it was just gone half past noon. Lucky to get across London Bridge
before its drawbridge was raised, blocking those behind them, he
had made good time from Rotherhithe.

But rather than aiming for its grand front entrance under the
portico, Wylde turned along Hart Street, towards its coach houses
and stables. The alley by the White Hart Inn led to the back of the
row. They would go into Sir Peter Lely's house that way.

Inside his tar-black and alcohol-soaked cask, Harry dripped
with sweat. His legs had lost all feeling, and his tongue stuck to the
roof of his mouth; cruelly, he could hear a nearby tap running. His
friends took too much care. He should have ridden on the cart with
them. His red coat—he did not have the room to take it off—would
have diverted suspicion, as it had in Rotherhithe.

Human waste in the shared yard's house of office stank in the heat.

'Let us take him in,' Harry heard Wylde say. As Aubrey and
Papin hoisted up the cask with him inside it, Harry felt as if he had
left his stomach behind. Next came a painful judder as they landed
the cask on the ground.

'Take a care!' Wylde admonished them.

'You all right in there?' Papin asked. Harry groaned in reply. His
cask was rolled on its rim a short way, spinning him, then Harry
heard one of his friends knocking at a door. They dragged him inside,

then hefted him down some stairs. Harry could hear them grunting with the effort.

Then a further roll, and an eventual stop.

Aubrey opened the lid. Harry gingerly extended his legs, hearing his knees creak. Pulling himself out of the wine cask, assisted by Wylde, steadied by Papin, and blinking in the sudden brightness, he saw a spacious and well-equipped kitchen. It boasted a pair of Reigate Stone ovens, a pipe and cock for water, and expensive pans hanging neatly from racks. Taking up the room's middle was a trestle table, large enough for Sir Peter's staff—those who ran the house and those who helped with his business—to eat at it together.

One cook tenderised meat on a large butcher's block, and a second constructed a pie. Both affected to appear nonchalant, as if having men smuggled into their kitchen inside wine casks went on every day. An open door showed the way to Sir Peter's fully stocked larder, his dairy, and his scullery, where a maid noisily scrubbed at a pot.

Papin inspected Harry, found him wanting, and wiped at his face with the back of his hand. 'Mr. Hooke awaits you. I shall fetch him.'

'Why bring me down to the kitchen?' Harry, still in distress after his bumpy journey, felt a bitter flash of ingratitude.

'Too big a risk,' Papin told him. 'Mr. Hooke shall explain.'

'You are too dangerous a man to be seen with,' Aubrey said, as Papin left them to find Hooke.

Wylde nodded his agreement. 'Sir Peter's house is busy with visitors, any one of whom might recognise you.'

'You know I'm innocent of any wrongdoing,' Harry protested.

Aubrey looked apologetically at Harry. 'You are infamous as a kidnapper and murderer of women.'

'After you left with the Swedish Count, the Justice has half of London looking for you,' Wylde added.

'I've nothing to do with any of that!' Harry protested. 'And Count Königsmarck's men kidnapped *me*. I'd no wish to go with them.'

'I am certain of it,' Edmund Wylde assured him, spreading his palms as if surrendering.

'Mr. Thynne has upped the reward for you,' Aubrey said. 'Fifty pounds!'

'I knew not of any reward,' Harry said. Suddenly, all the times Aubrey had asked him for money came to mind.

'Until yesterday, it was only twenty,' Aubrey added.

'A tidy sum,' Papin said. 'I would be pleased to be thought worth that.'

'And I,' Aubrey said. He caught Harry's look. 'I would never divulge your whereabouts, Harry! I, too, believe your attestations of innocence.'

☿

AFTER A TOO-LONG-SEEMING WAIT, THE KITCHEN door opened and Robert Hooke walked in, Papin following behind him. Immediately, Hooke clasped Harry to him, then inspected him as Papin had done. Observing that Harry looked well, although with his recently shaved head markedly different in appearance, he forced a loud, violent cough. 'I worried you would not remember the system,' he said, when he had finished clearing his throat. 'Messaging you was facilitative. It convinced me to design further symbols to denote numbers, as to signal "eleven" took time.'

'I thought the same, Mr. Hooke,' Harry said, smiling at the older man's rejection of sentiment. That was as warm a greeting as Hooke would give. 'What have you told Sir Peter?'

'That we need his help to clear you from blame for Diana Cantley's murder. He says you may shelter here, in the guise of one of his Assistants.'

'You've not yet spoken with him of Mrs. Thynne?'

'Only a little. I left the rest of the tale for you. You were with the Justice when speaking with her husband, so you know more upon her disappearance. Curiously, Sir Peter recently painted her portrait.'

'It must still be wet. Mr. Thynne said she's only recently returned to London.'

'Sir Peter said he passed it to Mr. Bokshoorn, for him to complete the background.'

Abruptly, Hooke stopped speaking. An expression of intense relief passed across his face. 'You found shelter, I see. And clothes. And a zealous haircut. You must tell me of your adventures.'

'I shall. I've been all this time in Rotherhithe.'

'Grace shall be greatly comforted. She has worried about you. As have I, Harry. As have I. When you went missing, I succumbed to the darkest of thoughts.' Hooke reached out and touched the back of Harry's arm, as if to reassure himself of his friend's corporeality. 'Before going upstairs, take the red coat off,' he said. 'It is too easily noticeable. And too dirty for company. Sir Peter has his usual mix of visitors come to see him busy at his work, and to view his pictures. He has a drawing class scheduled, too.'

Harry pulled off the coat Rachel had made and placed it over the back of a kitchen chair. Despite smoothing it down, his shirt remained a mess of creases.

'Come,' Hooke said.

When apprenticed to Sir Peter Lely, Hooke was incapacitated by headaches from the paints and fumes. Instead, he attended Westminster School. But the two men stayed fond of one another. On recognising Harry's artistic prowess, Hooke arranged for him to serve part of his apprenticeship working in Sir Peter's atelier.

It would be welcome, Harry thought, to spend more time with the King's Principal Painter in Ordinary.

He said his farewells and thank-yous to Papin, Wylde, and Aubrey, then ascended the back stairs with Hooke. As they climbed, they nodded to various apprentices, only a couple of whom Harry recognised. Most of those he knew had moved on. Full Assistants were permitted to use the grand staircase.

From everywhere in the house, they could hear bustle. Sir Peter's grand front door opened into a voluminous hall, where a doorman received visitors. Through the wall separating the back stairs from the grand, Harry could hear a party chatting excitedly. Many visited to look at Sir Peter's paintings, either in progress or complete, or to view his collection of paintings by other great masters. Some came for instruction at his drawing school.

The first floor consisted of a line of rooms lit by the flatter northern light, as on the south the windows looked out at the portico and its high, arched ceiling. These rooms were used by Lely's Assistants, and were full of the tools of their trade. They were where materials were stored, frames were built, and canvases stretched.

By the time he reached the second floor, Harry felt breathless from keeping up with Hooke. On this level were the reception rooms, all richly furnished, their walls covered with paintings. Sir Peter also kept a fine library, filled floor to ceiling on all four walls by his binders of drawings, as well as his books.

Large double doors led into a room overlooking the piazza.

'We are to wait in here,' Hooke told Harry.

CHAPTER FORTY-ONE

THE WINDSOR BEAUTIES

In most of the other houses in the piazza, this was a withdrawing room. Sir Peter used it to display copies of his paintings. Prints brought in more money than portraits painted in oils; they could be reproduced in quantity and at different sizes, qualities, and prices. The room was empty of visitors, and more likely to remain so than Sir Peter's main reception room to the other side of the house.

Piled over the room's large table were aquatints and mezzotints portraying the Windsor Beauties: ladies of the court, depicted some fifteen years before, still selling all these years after. Sir Peter had made a fortune from their engraving, their printing, and their licensing to be copied by others.

Even more popular—some women appeared in both groups—

were the prints of the King's mistresses. The King believed firmly in equal opportunity, as long as a face was pretty. Most of his mistresses were aristocratic, but many, too, from humble backgrounds had taken his fancy. Some worked just around the corner, actresses at the Theatre Royal on Drury Lane.

Harry picked up Mary Davis, whom the King had left for Nell Gwynn. His Majesty paid for Mary and their daughter to live in St. James's Square. Nell had two sons by him. She—as the two women should never be nearer—was installed in Pall Mall.

Hooke showed Harry a print of Lucy Walter. 'The cause of our present predicament,' he said, shaking his head sorrowfully. 'The Duke of Monmouth's mother. There's talk of a box, keeping inside it documents proving her marriage to the King.'

'Lord Shaftesbury and his Brisk Boys believe it,' Harry said, remembering Joseph Fenn speaking of the box when they ate in the Rhenish winehouse. That conversation seemed a month ago rather than a week, or, more like, as if he recalled it from a dream.

'If Monmouth turns out legitimate, it changes the future of our nation,' Hooke said.

There were more prints. Elizabeth Killigrew, mother of the King's daughter Charlotte, and married to Robert Boyle's older brother—Robert Boyle, for whom Hooke had built and operated the air-pump. Catherine Pegge, whose two children by the King were imaginatively named Charles FitzCharles and Catherine FitzCharles.

Then Hooke picked up Winifred Wells. 'Someone at court, I cannot remember who, said she has the carriage of a goddess and the physiognomy of a dreamy sheep.'

Grinning, Harry looked at another print, this one of Barbara Palmer.

'The King has given her nearly as many titles as children,' Hooke said. 'Lady Castlemaine, Duchess of Cleveland, Countess of Southampton, and Baroness Nonsuch. Now turned to Catholicism and moved away to France.'

'You might say … she is out of the picture.'

Hooke did something he rarely did: he laughed out loud. His body shook as if he were inside a moving carriage. 'Mr. Pepys keeps several prints of her,' he managed finally. 'He showed them to me in his office. He hides them in a secret drawer.'

Louise de Kérouaille's Frenchness and her Catholicism, and her hold over the King, infuriated the public, which supposed she promoted French interests, which meant those of Louis Quatorze. Despite Hooke's insistence that knowledge should be based on demonstrable evidence, when he got to her picture he was more than willing to entertain scandal, even if it bordered on the treasonous. 'The rumour is, she helped broker a treaty between the King and his cousin, promising money if the King becomes a Catholic and he helps the French against the Dutch.'

The last picture they looked at was a detailed mezzotint of Hortense Mancini, the Duchesse de Mazarin.

'Well, we know all about *her*,' Hooke said.

Soon after they had finished their perusal of the prints, the door to Sir Peter's private studio across the hallway—away from the hubbub of the rest of his house—opened. Out came a girl, fourteen or fifteen, wearing a pink silk dress. She was Charlotte FitzRoy, one of the King's daughters by Barbara Palmer. With her was a chaperone and an Indian page boy.

As she passed the prints room, Charlotte honoured Hooke with the suggestion of a curtsey. Harry received only a perfunctory glance and a nose in the air, as she registered his shabby shoes, working-man's trousers, and grimy shirt.

Rolling back down his shirtsleeves, Sir Peter Lely accompanied her to the top of the grand staircase. After making preparatory drawings of her, chalk dust covered his fingers; he had wiped pale streaks on his shirt. He said obsequious goodbyes to her, and even to her servants, then ushered Hooke and Harry into his studio.

With a stool just before them, his easel and canvas stood in place, and there were some dark purple cushions where Charlotte and her page boy had sat. Easel and cushions formed two points of a triangle, the third being the generous window, the triangle's sides each a care-ful six feet long.

Declining the cushions, the men stood by the window over-looking Hart Street. Behind Sir Peter was his portable camera obscura, fitted with twin lenses to correct an image's inversion and reversal; Hooke had made it for him five years or so before.

Sir Peter had always managed his busy atelier, with all its Assis-tants specialising in different parts or techniques of the pictures, with an insistent vivaciousness. The last time Harry had met him he was plumply solid, lively and jolly, despite all the pressures on his time. But today, Sir Peter looked shrunken and pasty. Only in his early sixties, he looked far older. His posture was still proudly upright, but his movements were slow and stiff, as if they pained him to perform. All his adult life he had kept the same pencil mous-tache; now greyed and thinned, it contrasted with his wig, which was a lustrous blue-black, as dark as wet coal. His eyes were glossily mournful, as if he had only just received sad news.

He offered around the grapes used as a prop in his portrait of Charlotte.

'Mr. Hooke tells me you're in trouble, Harry,' Sir Peter said, once they were all eating. Though raised in Westphalia by his Dutch parents, nearly forty years of living in London had erased any trace of a foreign accent. 'Thought to have a hand in kidnap. And the murder of Miss Cantley. Knowing you as I do, that comes as a surprise.'

'I'm glad it does, as the rumour bears no truth,' Harry assured him.

'Good to hear it, Mr. Hunt.' Sir Peter smiled. 'You know, I'm so used to calling you Harry. It still seems odd to address you as Mr. Hunt.'

'While I'm here, and before I've cleared my name, can it be Mr. Jackson?'

Sir Peter's smile turned into a laugh. 'You use the King's nom de guerre. I shall do my best to remember.' His face turned serious again. 'It was harsh news about Diana. I know the poor girl's father, having painted him once. An exactly symmetrical supraorbital ridge, and widely spaced mentales.'

'I saw the picture,' Harry replied. 'It hangs in his office at Africa House. According to Sir Benedict, Diana planned to come here. To your house.'

Sir Peter looked at Hooke, then back at Harry. 'She wasn't murdered here, I'm sure.'

'She *was* here then?' Hooke asked, looking for somewhere to put down his grape pips.

'Sir Benedict didn't know why she should be,' Harry said.

'I can't tell you that,' Sir Peter replied. 'I've not seen her, so far as I know. But so many people come here whose names I never catch.'

'Perhaps you did see her. Tall, slim. Long and very dark hair.' Harry imagined Diana at her dissection with her hair shaved, next to her elderly father, last seen in his grief. 'She bears a close simi-larity to her father. Their skull shapes are similar. The same clefts in their chins.'

'It's years ago since I painted him,' Sir Peter said. 'Otherwise, I'd be able to lay my hands on the sketches.' He called through to one of the rooms further down the hallway, requiring chalk and paper. An Assistant hurriedly appeared with them. Within a few deft lines, Sir Peter had sketched a head; before them appeared an accurate likeness of the Royal African Company's Deputy-Gover-nor. Sir Peter put the drawing aside, then reached for another sheet. Having finished a second drawing, he revealed it to both men with him. 'Is this Diana?'

'It's very like,' Harry said admiringly, remembering Diana leav-ing Bloomsbury Square for her horse riding, rather than when she lay on Sir Christopher Wren's table.

'Young Kneller could never do that!' Sir Peter exclaimed, talking down his rival who lived across the piazza. 'She *was* here,' he contin-ued, waving the paper. 'Beautiful girl. As you said, thin. Thinner than's presently the taste.'

'But why was she here?' Hooke asked.

Harry, holding Sir Peter mostly responsible for the fashion gov-erning how women should look—which meant as much like the King's mistress Barbara Palmer as possible—took the drawing to look at it more closely. 'Sir Benedict said he never paid for her portrait.'

'Perhaps someone else did, without him knowing,' Hooke said. 'A suitor she kept secret from him.'

Sir Peter shifted his weight from one foot to the other. 'It's an uncomfortable thought. My home, one of the last places she was before her murder.'

'It may have been the last place,' Harry said.

Sir Peter looked even more uncomfortable. He called through to his Assistant again, this time asking for the diary. 'Is anyone in the antechamber?' At his man's assurance there was not, he looked quizzically at Harry and Hooke. 'More agreeable in there.' Not waiting for them, he left his private studio without looking back, assuming they would follow. 'Diana may have come here for a cheaper portrait,' he said to the air behind him. 'As my Assistants do those, perhaps her name escaped my notice.'

☿

HARRY AND HOOKE CAUGHT UP WITH Sir Peter by the double doors opening into a sizeable room with plush settees and chairs placed for conversation. Everyone in the house called it the antechamber. Its walls were covered with drawings and paintings. Sir Peter had amassed the country's finest art collection apart from the King's. There a Raphael, there a Caravaggio, a Titian, a Rembrandt, a Tintoretto, a Rubens. In every direction hung some fine example of European art. Sir Peter was particularly interested in drawings: Dürer, Mantegna. Romano, Franco, Vorsterman, Zuccaro. A large rearing horse by Leonardo. One of Van Dyke's sketchbooks lay open on a dresser.

Sir Peter used his collection for teaching, too. As the King's Painter in Ordinary, he often borrowed from the royal collection, and had his apprentices make copies. Harry had copied drapery by Correggio for him.

It was never quite clear whether copies or originals made their way back to Whitehall.

Displayed in front of the windows was a marble statue of a naked woman. Life-sized, she crouched on her circular base, looking over her shoulder and holding one arm across her body.

Harry went over to join her.

Sir Peter puffed out his chest proudly. 'Comely, is she not? As you'd expect a Venus to be. Later Roman, we suppose. Sir Peter Paul Rubens spotted her for our previous King—may God bless his memory.'

Hooke accompanied the living Sir Peter in a respectful dip of the head, whereas Harry stayed still. Hooke noticed, and sent him a narrow-eyed look.

'Rubens was in Mantua, there to find art for the royal collection,' Sir Peter continued, joining Harry at the statue. 'He arranged the sale, and had it sent to London. When Protector Cromwell sold all the King's goods, its price was very fair. I'd painted Cromwell, you see, and kept on the right side of him. Truth be told, I liked the man. Far more agreeable than many now pretend.'

Harry had heard the story before, as had Hooke, but both men enjoyed its retelling.

The Assistant returned with a substantial book, which was wrinkled and worn from use.

'Eleven days ago, she was here,' Harry said, recalling again helping her into the hackney.

Sir Peter leafed through the diary, then closed it with a bang. 'No mention of Miss Cantley.'

'So, not here for a portrait,' Hooke said.

Harry frowned. 'If not, why else?'

Sir Peter pulled a face to show his ignorance. Taking Harry back to the double doors, he pointed past the head of the grand staircase. On the other side of the landing was a short corridor leading to more workrooms. 'When I saw her, she stood there, outside the drying room.'

Harry walked into a smaller room with more portraits on display. The smell of oil paint, not yet dry, was strong. Sir Peter and Hooke came and stood with him.

'Don't touch!' Sir Peter warned.

'Did Diana come in here, or just stand in the doorway?' Harry asked.

'I remember, she looked down the stairs,' Sir Peter said, gesturing out to the landing.

'As if waiting for someone to come up them?'

'If I had the power to hear another's thoughts, I could tell you.'

'Did she appear concerned? Or scared, even?'

'As you can see from my drawing, I remember her face. But I didn't consider what she did, or who she was. If she hadn't been so pretty, I would have forgotten all about her. So many people wander through.'

As if to prove Sir Peter's point, a group of visitors, having climbed the grand stairs, arrived at the landing. To their flattered amazement, the famous artist himself was there to greet them. After introductions were done, Sir Peter called out again for help. A different man appeared this time, taking the newcomers to the antechamber.

Sir Peter's house was like Bethlehem Hospital, Harry thought, with all its unrecorded visitors, often unknown, passing through.

Perhaps inside a crowd was a perfect place for murder.

Sir Peter rejoined Harry and Hooke in the drying room. Harry stood in front of a portrait in oils: another girl, this one plump-lipped with a finely modelled nose, dressed demurely in a chocolate-brown dress. Her hair was curled and dramatically auburn.

Harry backed away to take in the whole picture. 'Who's this? I feel I recognise her.'

'It's no surprise to me that you do,' Sir Peter said. 'That, Harry, is Elizabeth Percy.'

Hooke did a silent whistle, as if everything had become clear. 'Now, Mrs. Elizabeth Thynne.'

'I accept the correction.' Sir Peter moved next to Harry and leaned forwards to inspect the painting. As it was not yet framed, the sides of the canvas pulled tight around its stretcher still showed. The light pink ground Sir Peter preferred was visible on its edges. He could not stop himself from wiping a perceived roughness of its surface gently with his thumb. Then, as the painting hung slightly askew, he straightened it. 'Her mother was a great patron of mine. I did several portraits of her. The daughter is a charming girl. Very witty. Interested in how paintings are made, which pleased me greatly. The grounds we use. How we polish them before the final paint is applied.'

'A painting's vivacity depends upon how it is primed,' Hooke said, quoting Sir Peter from long-ago memory.

'You both know it. You've both done it for me.' Sir Peter smiled at them affectionately. 'Mrs. Thynne even expressed an interest in how we put the pictures together. Stretchers, canvas, lacing them up, the way we then frame them. If she wanted only to charm me, it was perfectly judged.'

He sniffed the portrait, at where in the background perched a parrot in an orange tree. It was the last section painted, done by his

Assistant Joseph Bokshoorn. 'It's nearly ready for her new husband to take. I pray for her safety. Not because I doubt Mr. Thynne would pay for the portrait if she's come to harm, I hasten to add. Let's hope it's as the tattle has it, that she's eloped with her Swedish lover.'

'She hasn't,' Harry said. 'I've met Count Königsmarck, who's desperate for her return. Mr. Thynne's convinced the Count kidnapped his wife. I'm sure he didn't.'

'When did you meet with the Count?' Hooke asked him. 'Was it his men who extricated you from the Justice's coach, as Sir John puts about?'

Harry nodded. 'It was. They then took me straight to him. Königsmarck thought *I'd* taken Mrs. Thynne.'

Hooke wiped at his nose. 'Thinking it so, not irrationally, after your arrest for it. The same reasoning guides Mr. Thynne, who thinks you have her, and that you are in league with the Swede. Were there not letters proving Königsmarck's involvement?'

'One sent to Sir Benedict. One to Mr. Thynne. Both written in a Scandinavian style. Königsmarck denied sending them. He even showed me his writing. As did his men. None of them were the authors, I'm certain.' Harry pointed to the portrait of Elizabeth Thynne. 'She's the most likely reason Diana Cantley came here. Königsmarck told me Diana was Mrs. Thynne's close friend.'

Again, Sir Peter, looking astonished at Harry's revelations, called for help. A trio of his Assistants appeared; they held an earnest conference in Dutch. Harry recognised all of them: Dhr. Jaspars, Dhr. Lankrink, Dhr. Bokshoorn. At its conclusion, Sir Peter returned his attention to Harry and Hooke. 'We have the feeling Miss Cantley searched for something.'

'But what?' Harry asked.

'We don't know.'

'Whatever it was, would it have led to her murder?' Hooke asked, looking deeply perturbed.

'And to Mrs. Thynne's disappearance,' Harry suggested.

Hooke sniffed loudly, the smell of the still-wet paintings affecting his tubes. 'Diana Cantley was here. She disappeared. A ransom letter was written. Then she was murdered. By the thrust of a sword.'

'Whatever was she up to?' Sir Peter asked.

Harry examined again Elizabeth Thynne posed in front of her orange tree. Her expression told him nothing he needed to know.

'And who did she displease?' he asked, more to himself than the two men with him.

CHAPTER FORTY-TWO

THE FIVE WOMEN

After the sewing platform, the bed was a wonder of comfort. Even so, Harry slept only fitfully.

He had been given one of the garrets, where Sir Peter's servants and apprentices slept.

His thoughts circled relentlessly around five women.

Firstly, Diana Cantley, murdered after visiting Sir Peter Lely's house, then delivered to Gresham. He had stopped her dissection when he recognised her.

Secondly, Elizabeth Thynne, née Percy, the richest heiress in England. Her husband thought Harry conspired with a Swedish Count to kidnap her, as did the Justice, Sir John. For her husband, any affections Elizabeth held for the Count were by the by. Thomas Thynne required her return, and had capable men out searching.

Diana and Elizabeth had been friends since childhood; Count Königsmarck had said so. Diana had visited Sir Peter Lely's atelier. That she did so only to look at Elizabeth's portrait seemed a thin reason, to Harry's mind. That she did so just before her murder was too coincidental for his cause-seeking nature. Did Diana, knowing she was in danger, hide at Sir Peter's house from kidnappers who afterwards killed her?

Thirdly, Sebiliah Barton. She slid insistently into his thoughts. Meant to be delivered to Gresham after her suicide, instead she was stored—somewhere Harry did not yet know—then placed in his own elaboratory, at his home in Bloomsbury Square.

Seemingly, to incriminate him in the eyes of Sir John Reresby.

Sebiliah was pregnant when she died. At Bethlehem Hospital, she had suffered so much turmoil she chose to end two lives. Perhaps it had not really been a choice. At least, not a conscious one. Perhaps, to stop its own agony, her body behaved free from her mind, as Wren had wanted at his demonstration. Whatever the truth of this—Harry had no way of seeing into her thoughts, not even by dissection—Sebiliah had been hopeless, for herself and for her child.

He remembered the knowing look shared by the two Bethlehem Basketmen, Jones and Langdale, and the Nurse, Hannah Matthews. They had driven her to suicide; he was sure of it. Or they knew full well who had. Perhaps another of their colleagues he had not met. Or Carter, the Steward. Or Lester, the Apothecary. Harry did not believe it might be Dr. Allen, the Hospital's Physician. And the Porter, Joseph Matthews, had convinced Harry of his innocence.

That any of the staff had mistreated Sebiliah so badly sickened him. It also made him feel a piercing guilt. He played his part in a system which callously used people, even after death. Dr. Allen had been happy to donate Sebiliah's body to the Royal Society. *For the dead, my care is over,* Allen had told him and the Justice. Harry had been unquestioningly content to attend her dissection. Sebiliah's dead body was to have been made use of, just as it had been used when she was alive. Whoever had transported her to his elaboratory had used her, too, in their attempt to incriminate him.

The fourth woman Harry thought of was Grace Hooke. He had intended a marriage proposal. What a disaster that turned out to be. Disliking the man he now was, Grace had refused him.

When he was Mr. Hooke's apprentice, Harry had yearned for Grace. Knowing he was nowhere near good enough for her, he harboured no hopes of winning her. That did not stop him from wanting her. For years, he thought only of her; so tantalisingly close when staying with her uncle at Gresham College, so achingly far when back with her mother on the Isle of Wight. Careful of Robert Hooke's suspicions, Harry had resorted to secrecy, keeping from the uncle his attraction for the niece. This led to a distance between the two men, which Harry regretted.

When Harry became a Royal Society Operator—a position coming with pride but little money—he had still known he was unworthy of Grace. Her uncle, blind to her wishes, had arranged suitable and advantageous marriages. Sir Thomas Bloodworth, a wealthy merchant and Master of the Vintners' Company, and for a time London's Lord Mayor, had wanted her for his son. Grace refused the match, only to have her uncle arrange another, this time to Sir Robert Holmes, Governor of the Isle of Wight. As Admiral of the Fleet, he was famous for his exploits off the West African coast on behalf of the Royal African Company. Famous, also, for his fighting against the Dutch. His fireship attack had destroyed 150 Dutch merchant vessels in the Vliestroom.

But even Sir Robert's heroics had not been enough to convince Grace.

Instead, to Harry's complete disbelief—and to almost everyone else's around them—she had set her heart on him.

But he could not fend off the thought any longer: Harry's feelings for Grace were changing. This change came with a sense of panic, and a need to hold on to them; these feelings had steered the course of his life for so long. Grace's professed love for him had begun to feel like an obligation. Instead of a joyful, headlong rush into marriage and companionship and happiness ever after, he had buried himself in his house's refurbishment. Not to make the house ready for her, but to put off asking her to marry him. With the completion of the works came a pressing finality: now it was time to propose. The months of conversation Harry had conducted with himself, debating if marriage would make them both happy, and his doubts that it would, were at an end.

He had used Grace's doubtful look, as the Justice arrested him, as a way to blame her for the increasing distance between them.

☿

LYING IN HIS COMFORTABLE, WARM BED, looking up at a ceiling barely perceptible to his nighttime vision, Harry thought more of a fifth woman. She, presumably, lay in her own bed, back across the river in Rotherhithe. Or else, she could not sleep, and had wandered down to the shop, as she had wandered last night.

He kept imagining the feel of her against him: her skin's softness, her mouth's wetness. Her heat. Rachel Lejbowiczowa—another man's wife—had invaded his thoughts.

It made it difficult to focus on all the other matters confronting him. Even though his reputation—his life, perhaps—depended on doing so.

Harry had to free himself from the accusations against him.

Knowing he was unable to go back to sleep, he crept downstairs to the drying room, to take a long look at the portrait of Elizabeth Thynne.

CHAPTER FORTY-THREE

THE ATELIER'S VISITORS

The first-floor workshop overlooked Covent Garden piazza. Its window gave Harry a fine view of the portico's arched ceiling, but its position made the room gloomy. It was thought bright enough, though, for putting wood together.

He spent the morning constructing a support destined for a portrait of the Duchess of Richmond, famous both for being the model for Britannia—she was on all the coins—and for refusing to join the long list of the King's mistresses.

At first, a boy—whose apprenticeship began after Harry's time with Sir Peter—was suspicious of him. Once he saw Harry's competence with the materials and tools, he relaxed. Later, he left Harry on his own in the workshop, disappearing to replace the lengths of timber Harry had mitred.

When he had finished building the stretcher, Harry carried it to a room opposite, one far brighter. There, he cut an oversized rectangle of Dutch linen. Dutch, since such material—fine enough and wide enough for Sir Peter's requirements—was unavailable elsewhere.

To match their importance, Sir Peter's clients demanded large pictures.

After sewing the linen neatly onto the stretcher, then knocking wedges into each corner-joint to further stretch it, Harry found a knife and applied a thick oil-bound chalk layer, making sure to fill the material's weave. When dry, an Assistant would scrape it to remove any knots and bumps, and afterwards polish it to provide a smooth surface to paint on.

It was an enjoyably methodical activity, which enabled Harry to think. He needed to consider what to do next, and needed to be sure whom he could trust.

Once satisfied the canvas's priming was complete, he descended the back stairs to the kitchen. One of the cooks was busy killing an eel by bashing its head on the block. Even after several whacks the creature continued to writhe, refusing to accept its demise. The other cook skinned and chopped its already-dispatched friends, then fried them in a heavy skillet. A quartet of Sir Peter's apprentices and a couple of Assistants awaited their luncheon. When Harry came in, the second cook nodded towards steaming coffee, Turkish-thick and darkest black.

After generously served eel, with slices of lemon and freshly baked bread, Harry returned upstairs for something else to do. He would find Sir Peter's Senior Assistant, Jan-Baptist Jaspars, for instructions.

Going up the same way he had come down, Harry heard footsteps coming from the entrance lobby. Visitors arriving from the piazza. Heavy feet ascended the grand staircase on the other side of the wall. He had started on the back stairs ahead of them. By the time they reached the first floor, they were level; Harry glimpsed them on the landing.

Two men, both dressed expensively. With weathered skins bronzed by exposure to the sun, they had more the air of countryside than city. Or perhaps they were seafaring men. They had fallen into step with each other, as if marching. Their air of military competence compounded this effect.

Harry recognised them. One was the man with a scar running down beside his nose, continuing through his lips, and finishing with a raised whorl on his chin. The other was his bulkier partner. In Rotherhithe early one morning, they had searched for Henry Hunt. Outside Sarah Unsworth's shop, just before she told Harry she wanted him gone. Harry had assumed they belonged to the Watch.

They all reached the second floor together, where Harry had to turn towards them along the landing on his way to find Jaspars. Harry stepped nearer the wall and adopted the servile attitude required whenever a customer passed by. He expected the men to go through the large double doors which led into Sir Peter's art-filled antechamber.

Instead, they went along the corridor towards the drying room, where Harry and Hooke had discussed Elizabeth Thynne with Sir Peter. Harry tried to stay inconspicuous further down the landing. Inside the drying room, the pair spoke in tones too low to catch.

After their discussion, ducking his head back through the doorway, the scarred man called to Harry. ''Scuse me. You a part of Sir Peter's household?'

'How may I help?' As Harry approached the man, he could feel his own blood circulating around his body. He thought of Sir John's likely response to his reply, which would surely have been, 'You do not quite answer my question.'

'An odd question, this, you'll think, but I'll ask it,' the scarred man said. 'Has anyone showed an interest in this painting?'

Needing a moment to think, Harry decided to be obtuse. 'Sir Peter owns many fine paintings. Many visitors come to look at them. Titian, Veronese, Tintoretto. Some van Dykes.' Seeing the man's transparent contempt, Harry added hurriedly, 'You mean a particular painting. To view one, or to take one away?'

The man's grimace, made even more emphatic by his twisted lip, showed it made precisely no difference.

Harry went into the drying room, shrugging apologetically when shown which painting the man asked about. 'Not that I know of. As I say, Sir Peter has many visitors. And a large staff, too. One of the others might know.'

The second man, even more tanned than his partner, looked as strong as the stevedores who worked at the docks. He gestured irritably at the portrait. 'You know who this is, son?'

'I do. She's Mrs. Elizabeth Thynne.'

The scarred man nodded. 'Her husband—'

'Mr. Thynne,' the squatter man interrupted.

'. . . instructed us to take it,' the scarred man said.

'The wife's missing.'

'The husband's beside himself.'

'He wants her back. Not unreasonably.'

'Lacking her person, this picture'll have to do.'

Harry swallowed, his throat feeling narrow. 'It's not yet dry.'

Both men looked careless of his objection. 'I can only let you have it if Sir Peter's happy.'

'I know nothing at all of Sir Peter's disposition, do you?' the larger man asked his colleague.

'To me, his moods are a closed book.'

'But unless we know them, the boy won't let us have the picture.'

'Perhaps the boy means to interpose himself between us and our exit down the stairs.'

'Take the picture back from us, expecting no repulse.'

'Try to knock us down with those fearsome fists, thinking we'd not give him tip for tap.'

'I can smoke his opinion, though.'

'Oh yes. If everyone did the same, Lely would have no pictures left on his walls.'

Having had their sport, the scarred man made a show of counterfeit contrition. 'Perchance there's someone else you may ask if we may take the picture?' He said it overpolitely—mockingly so.

'Lely himself, even?' the other man said, using the same tone.

'Sir Peter's Senior Assistant is Dhr. Jaspars,' Harry said. 'I'll speak with him. Your names, sirs?'

The scarred man pointed first to himself. 'Mr. Kidd.' Then to his partner. 'Mr. Singer. Your name, son?'

Harry bowed obsequiously. 'Jackson,' he said. Then he paced downstairs to the room where he had built the stretcher. He was glad to see the apprentice had returned. Feeling guilty for doing so, Harry asked him to look after the two visitors; he did not want them simply taking off with the portrait.

Back on the second floor, about to continue up to the third, Harry glanced towards the drying room. Both men stood in its doorway, watching him intently.

His legs felt heavy as he went, from fear of being found out. Kidd and Singer were Thomas Thynne's Gamekeeper and his Steward. Harry remembered their names from the conversation at Cannon Row, and from speaking with Königsmarck and Vratz.

The third floor's layout was almost identical to the second, so above Sir Peter's main reception room—his antechamber—was a room large enough to serve as the main oil painting workshop. It was crammed with easels and desks, paintings at various stages of development, and every surface teemed with pigments kept in bottles, jars, bags, and boxes. All Sir Peter's preferred colours were either inside glass or on palettes bearing stalagmites of paint. His blacks: charcoal, ivory, vine, and lamp. Browns: Cologne earth, umbers both raw and burned. Siennas, raw and burned. Blues: ultramarine from lapis lazuli, and the lighter blue from its ashes. Smalt, and azurite. Reds: vermilion, ochre, lake, and lead. Yellows: lead-tin, ochre, orpiment, and lake. Indigo. Lead white.

More bottles stored Lely's various oils, each offering different finishes and drying times: linseed, walnut, poppy, safflower. Even with the casements wide open, the smell was so strong it made Harry's eyes sting.

Although Jaspars's strictness ensured the room stayed bafflingly tidy—all the pigments, brushes, knives, maulsticks, and scrapers kept fastidiously in their places—the room was difficult to navigate. Sir Peter's Senior Assistant sat at the far end of the room; from there, he could oversee everyone at work. Although sixty years old—the same age as Sir Peter—an aura of undimmed ferocity emanated from him. Initially, during his training, Harry had been terrified of him, but learned that all the gruffness concealed a generous and considerate soul.

Using another painting as his reference, Jaspars worked on a portrait. Recreating the folds of a dress, he was stippling with a tiny brush to replicate the texture of brocade. Sir Peter had finished the face, and—after the work of another Assistant—would revisit the hands. The background was sketched out in chalks, with a thin layer of underpainting in earthy browns and reds.

Beside Jaspars, an apprentice mulled azurite.

'Dhr. Jaspars, this is important, otherwise I wouldn't ask,' Harry said breathlessly, having steered across the room between its obstacles.

Jaspars, his brush poised halfway between his paint and his painting, peered at him from beneath unkempt eyebrows.

'Two men ask about the portrait of Mrs. Thynne.'

'Downstairs in the drying room,' Jaspars barked. Unlike Sir Peter, he had never lost his Dutch accent, despite all his years in London. 'Dhr. Bokshoorn finished the orange tree.'

'They're looking at it now. They say they're Thomas Thynne's men.'

Jaspars looked even fiercer. 'Before you let them take it, you must ensure they are who they say they are.'

'They ask a different question,' Harry said. 'They wish to know if anyone came to look at it. We must tell them no.'

Jaspars placed down his brush and wiped his hands with some rag. 'They must not know. You do, I imagine.'

'I do.'

'These men are dangerous?'

'If they take against you, then I would say yes.'

Jaspars raised himself stiffly from the chair. 'Then let us at least *seem* to be helpful, and get them gone on their way.'

He motioned to the apprentice to accompany them. Then, when out on the landing, he called into a second workroom. 'Dhr. Bokshoorn!'

Joseph Bokshoorn was a towering, cadaverous man with skin so pale it looked like the linen he worked on. After he joined them, Jaspars walked to the room that on the floor below was Sir Peter's private studio. 'Dhr. Lankrink!' Prosper Lankrink, the man Sir Peter employed for the quality of his landscapes, emerged. Both Assistants appended themselves to the group going to meet Thynne's men.

Downstairs, Kidd and Singer had moved to one of the workrooms, a room used to make the aquatints and mezzotints reproducing Sir Peter's paintings. They looked along its shelves, moving objects aside to do so, despite the protestations of the apprentice Harry had asked to guard them.

'Gentlemen,' Jaspars said, interrupting their search. 'I am Sir Peter's Senior Assistant. You wonder if anyone visited to see Mrs. Thynne's picture, I hear. No one did. I would have been told, I'm sure, especially with its being out of the way, in the *private* part of the house.'

Kidd knew he was being admonished, but was immune to Jaspars's reprimand. 'Anyone else you can ask? Lely himself, perhaps.'

'I should not like to bother him with a matter such as this,' Jaspars told him.

'You give less importance to this matter than us, then,' Singer said.

'Sir Peter is constantly busy,' Jaspars replied.

Kidd pressed his disfigured lips together in a parody of a smile. 'We shall take a care to not disturb him.'

At a signal from Kidd, Thynne's two men crossed the landing to go back inside the drying room. They reached up and smoothly took Elizabeth Thynne's portrait from the wall, as if they had practised the manoeuvre all day.

The various Assistants had followed them. 'You say you work for Mr. Thynne, but you give me no proof,' Jaspars said, tempering his natural fierceness with the placatory manner he adopted for clients. He sent an apprentice to fetch Sir Peter.

Having got what he wanted, Kidd stifled a snigger. The two men had the portrait between them, holding it by its unframed edges.

'Why does Mr. Thynne require it now?' Harry asked as they waited. 'It's still wet. He risks damage. It needs boxing to get safely to Cannon Row.'

Kidd looked at him suspiciously. 'How do you know to where it goes?'

'I worked on it,' Harry lied, aghast at his inadvertent slip. 'We spoke of Mrs. Thynne. Her husband's house was mentioned.'

Lankrink and Bokshoorn, who *had* worked on it, opened their mouths, but at Jaspars's fierce look of warning they soon shut them again.

'Spoke of her, did you?' Singer sounded unconvinced. 'Mr. Kidd, you accompanied Mr. Thynne's wife when she came here to be painted. You recollect this Assistant?'

'Too many of them to recall, Mr. Singer.' Kidd looked at each of the men in the drying room with him, sniffing the air as if on his master's grounds at Longleat. 'Like rabbits in a warren. Did we meet then, Mr. Jackson?'

Harry shook his head. 'Most likely, I was out of the house.' He looked at both men, receiving hard stares in return. If done to intimidate, it worked. Or if they stared because they disbelieved him, then he had little time before they picked his story apart, or caught out one of the Assistants, whom he could not expect to lie fluently on his behalf.

Footsteps approached from behind them. Looking most upset at being interrupted, Sir Peter came through from sketching Elizabeth Jones—the King's current favourite—in his studio. His Assistants moved aside for him in the crowded drying room.

'Dhr. Jaspars, Dhr. Lankrink, Dhr. Bokshoorn, Mr. Hunt,' he said. 'What is the problem here?'

CHAPTER FORTY-FOUR

THE HUNTSMEN'S PREY

Harry observed the momentary freezing of Kidd's expression, then, more slowly, the same thought passing through Singer's mind.

'Mr. Hunt?' Kidd repeated.

'You told us you was Jackson,' Singer said.

Thynne's men placed the portrait down and leaned it against the wall. Harry knew he had to run. If Sir John Reresby, or Joseph Fenn, had uncovered him, he was sure he could have explained himself to them without suffering extrajudicial damage. He had no confidence Thynne's Gamekeeper and Steward would show similar restraint.

'Where is Mr. Thynne's wife?' Kidd demanded.

Harry pushed his way backwards through Sir Peter's Assistants, knocking Bokshoorn and Lankrink aside, apologising as he did so.

Kidd and Singer were rougher, even pushing Sir Peter out of their way.

Harry ran out to the landing. He looked down the narrow back stairs. Then he looked up them, but considered his options more limited if he were to climb to the workshops on the next floor, or all the way up to the garrets. For a mad moment, he considered scrambling through the lucarne windows in the garrets and out to the roof, knowing the building next door, designed differently, had a flat roof he could jump to. But if he successfully made the jump—without smacking onto the piazza's pavement far below—Kidd and Singer, he reasoned, would simply wait for him. He must eventually have to come down and out from that building. And that was if he could get through a window in time, before they caught up with him in the garret.

Instead, Harry raced downstairs to the first floor. He could hear chasing feet on the grand staircase, but was unsure if he heard one pair or two.

Jumping from the last stair, he raced through the line of rooms facing the portico, including the one in which he spent most of the morning making the stretcher. From one of its shelves, he grabbed a long piece of timber—a reassuringly solid length of oak—as a way of defence. All he could think was that Kidd and Singer meant to do him harm; they would not try to charm intelligence from him. Also, he thought of their employer, and his reputation for violence.

Harry heard Singer, whose bulkiness gave him a trudging sound when he moved, emerge from the grand staircase and turn into the same room Harry had just been in. Stepping to the window, which had a balcony overlooking the piazza, Harry thought of jumping from it, but the height was too great. The Purbeck stone pavement would at the least smash his ankles. He could see no viable holds on the wall, between its bricks; they were mortared too cleanly and too close. Looking almost climbable was the chiselled stonework of the portico, but it began too far below him; the drop for a grip did not appeal. There were no other details on the house's facade he could use.

Instead, Harry went through a second door leading to another chamber, the end room of the first floor, where he considered hiding in its closet. Singer, though, was bound to look there, by which time Kidd would have joined him. Only two exits from this chamber. Two men chasing him. Singer, he knew, was in the room behind the door to his right, but where was Kidd?

Kidd was Thynne's Gamekeeper; Harry trembled at the thought of being chased by a professional hunter. He should just give himself up. Trust the two men would accept his word that he had no clue where Elizabeth Thynne was.

The door to Harry's right opened slowly, as if Singer expected Harry to jump at him. This caution gave Harry time to race to the second door, hoping Kidd was not immediately behind it. Shoving it open proved not, but he did stand at the top of the back stairs, having decided that whichever door Harry emerged from, he would wait there and be close enough to grab him.

Harry ran straight towards him, but at the last moment veered to one side, dodging Kidd and running up the grand staircase, back towards Sir Peter and his Assistants. But how much help could he expect from the elderly and unwell Sir Peter, or the equally elderly Jaspars? All the younger Assistants and apprentices were artists; you could hardly expect them to fight, even with the most disgruntled of customers.

When he reached the third floor, Harry ran into Bokshoorn's room, which had a balcony but no sensible way to the street below. He quickly reversed, to see Kidd and Singer arriving on the landing. As they turned towards him, Harry ducked the opposite way and ran inside the oils workroom.

Avoiding easels and obstacles, he reached the room's far end, where Jaspars had sat when Harry went to ask him for help. There was nowhere further Harry could go, so he stopped by Jaspars's easel. The table the apprentice had used to prepare pigments stood between him and the pair coming after him.

Neither of Thynne's men had brought weapons with them. Kidd took a maulstick from its rack and waved it threateningly. Singer located a long wooden rule.

'Where is Mr. Thynne's wife?' Kidd demanded again.

Harry said nothing, instead standing with his knees bent, ready to spring away if they lunged for him. His own panting sounded loud in his ears.

'We can beat the answer from you, son,' Singer said.

A searing dislike, hot in Harry's chest, arose for both men. He was tired of being hurt for information.

'I'd tell you willingly, but I don't believe you have her interests at heart. Only those of her husband.'

Kidd looked puzzled. 'What matters that to you? Why your interest in her?'

These were good questions, which Harry had not really thought through. Why *should* he help Elizabeth Thynne? Why his desire to protect her from these two men, and from her husband? It seemed something outside of himself compelled him. To do the best he could for a young woman he had never met, whose family riches kept her in circles far elevated from his own. Why should he care about her unsuitable marriage to a dislikable man? That Königsmarck was in love with her was self-evident, but Harry had no idea if she felt the same way about the Count.

But seeing her portrait in the drying room downstairs had cemented the feeling of being duty bound not to help Thynne's men.

'Well,' Harry answered slowly, thinking as he spoke, 'if a child in front of me fell into a fountain, and I knew I could save it from drowning, you'd think me a monster if I did not.'

Kidd shot an amused look at his partner and slapped the maulstick into his palm. 'Even if it meant your inconvenience?'

'It would cost me only some time. Spoil my clothes, perhaps. Not nuisance enough to stop me.'

Singer showed particular interest in Harry's example. 'That the fountain's in front of you is by the by. Why should the child's closeness matter? Your fancy obliges you to save all such clumsy children, in whichever fountain they fall.'

'I can never know about all such children,' Harry said. 'I'm obliged because I see it in front of me.'

'There's a line, surely, separating inconvenience and sacrifice,' Singer replied. 'Beyond which you'd no longer be willing to save your hypothetical infant.'

'In truth, I'm yet nowhere near that line.'

While talking to them, his hands hidden under the table, Harry had busied himself opening jars of pigment. Their lids were discs of metal sealed with wax; he needed time to unpick them. The last was a jar full of blue azurite, which the apprentice had crushed into powder.

With one swift move, Harry launched its contents over Singer's face. Kidd roared in anger at the sight of his partner being covered, then jumped over the table, waving the maulstick. For Kidd, lead-tin yellow. Harry unleashed the powder at him. It was finest-ground glass; Kidd immediately felt its sting.

The pigments blinded both men. They wiped at themselves in panic with their sleeves, desperately clearing the powder from their eyes so they could see again.

Harry took his chance to run past them. His thoughts ran so speedily he even had time to worry about the cost of replacing Sir Peter's pigments, and to hope no paintings were spoiled.

He rushed down the main stairs, pushing through a group of visitors come to look at the pictures. Some pigment had landed on him, colouring his shirt and face. He went on down to the ground floor. From behind him, he could hear pounding footsteps as Kidd and Singer brought themselves back to the chase.

Entering the large entrance lobby, Harry saw that the front doors were open, but a second group of visitors filled up the doorway, where they were being politely—and nerve-wrenchingly slowly—welcomed by Sir Peter's doorman.

Kidd reached the lobby, his eyes looking out wildly from his bright yellow face. The doorman saw him and swore loudly, and put himself between Kidd and the visitors, thinking to protect them from a mad painted man brandishing a maulstick.

Harry ran through to the parlour at the opposite end of the house. A private room—mostly used by the Assistants, rarely by Sir Peter himself—it owned all a parlour's usual furniture and an over-large fireplace. Although during the hot summer the fire had not been lit, a stack of logs occupied the hearth. Harry thought about hiding behind it, but Kidd and Singer would find him there straightaway. He tried the window, but it was locked. Sir Peter, he knew, kept the keys upstairs.

Like the room above it, a couple of doors at each end of one wall served the parlour. Both of them stayed closed. Harry knew Kidd and Singer would wait for him outside, in the passage by the servants' back stairs, not wanting to make the same mistake as before.

He needed to get past them, get out through the back door and into the yard. He would run through the stables to Hart Street. Hopefully, he could outrun Kidd and Singer. Faces full of pigment might slow them down.

Still, no one came into the parlour. As both were identical, the doors were no help in choosing which one to escape through.

No hint of a shadow or movement beyond them.

Harry could hear only shocked visitors being ushered upstairs by the doorman.

Why did Thynne's men wait? Harry decided there was no point in delaying any longer. The parlour's leftmost door was nearest the house's back door, but there was still a length of passage between them. He hoped the back door was unlocked. If it was not, he would have to go down to the basement kitchen and escape that way, through its door and up the stairs back to ground level.

Rather than do it tentatively, Harry burst through the left door with commitment, thinking it might clatter one of the men chasing him. It did not. The door swung wildly open and smashed into the wall behind it. Singer stood further off, anticipating the door might hit him. Harry continued, not pausing as he went through the door towards the man coloured blue. He did not dodge Singer this time, but lowered his shoulder and barged him as hard as he could. Even though the man was far bulkier than he was, Harry's momentum took him through him and over him as Singer fell backwards. Harry ran on towards the back door.

To his right, the bright yellow Kidd tried to catch up with him to block him off, but Harry had already reached the back door. He grabbed at the handle. The door would not release. A bolt was engaged high up. As Harry reached for it, Kidd took hold of his arm and pulled him over and onto the floor. Harry's shoulder slammed down on hard stone, the same Purbeck as out along the portico.

Harry rolled onto his back and kicked out at the enraged Kidd—whose pigment-stained eyes looked full of pain—and scrambled back on his haunches. Thinking to escape to the kitchen, he went towards the top of the stairs.

Singer had picked himself up, and came after him, slashing at him with the wooden rule. If he could see better, he would have made more connections. Only a couple of swipes met with Harry's head.

An apprentice and a cook, wondering about all the noise, had cautiously climbed the stairs. Harry pushed straight past them. When he reached the kitchen, he ran through it, past the larder, through Sir Peter's dairy, then through the scullery, where the same maid still scrubbed pots. She turned around, startled, as a man with a shaven head ran past her, then behind him, two more. One yellow, one blue.

Harry shouldered open the outside door, which allowed him into a narrow basement-level yard, not much more than a passage. The gloom of inside turned into the dazzling brightness of outside.

He sprinted for the steps leading back up to ground level.

CHAPTER FORTY-FIVE

THE BOGHOUSE SANCTUARY

Harry ran across the courtyard and kicked open the door to the house of office.

The building befitted those affluent enough to live in Covent Garden's piazza. Inside was a row of six lavatories, each fully enclosed by expensive hardwood. But despite its opulence, with the sun directly on it and no fresh air moving through it, the smell inside was atrocious.

None of the compartments were occupied; all had their doors ajar. Harry opted for the second one along and locked it behind him.

He heard Kidd's and Singer's boots scraping on cobbles; they slowed on the last of the steps leading up from the kitchen, confronted as they were by the empty courtyard.

The door of the compartment Harry hid in was substantial, but a stout kick—either Kidd or Singer could easily provide one—would break it open. The lavatory's seat boasted a smoothly polished surface for aristocratic rear ends, and was hinged for access by the soil men, whose visit was obviously due. Harry looked through its hole to the drop.

Gagging as he did so, Harry thought about hiding inside; he even opened the seat to look into the trench running under the six lavatories. The space was large enough to climb into; to do so, he would only have to put his distaste aside. Just unlock the door to his compartment, then climb in and pull the lid back down. If Kidd and Singer came in, they would see six open doors. They might scan the compartments to check they were empty. Harry doubted they would think of looking under the lids, especially as the smell was unpleasant.

He could not bring himself to do it. His own refusal made him think. If truly in fear of his life, he reasoned, he would not hesitate. The smell, or having to clean himself up afterwards, was scarcely considerable compared with rough questioning by Kidd and Singer.

His reluctance to climb in led to the conclusion that Thynne's men were not really a threat. Had they not been halfhearted when following him through Sir Peter's house? They had been careful, seemingly unwilling to incur injury. Rather than risk attack, they had not ventured into rooms he occupied. In the oils workshop, rather than try to capture him, they had engaged him in conversation. For military men, they displayed a surprising lack of bravery. Or— more likely, it now appeared to Harry—had they just realistically appraised his worth?

If Kidd and Singer had really wanted to catch him, they would have exerted themselves more fully, he decided. Which made him

think in turn that what he had supposed they looked for—Mrs. Elizabeth Thynne—was not what they wanted at all.

They had entered the house under the guise of collecting the
portrait. They had gone up to the drying room, which was usually
private. Afterwards, they had searched the printing workshop.
Harry remembered they looked around the room, not at the aquatints or mezzotints, or at the equipment used to make them. They
had looked along the shelves.

But Kidd asked Harry on the whereabouts of Elizabeth Thynne.
So, they did not know where she was, but finding her was obviously
secondary to finding something else.

Still expecting Thynne's men to enter the house of office, Harry
waited.

Even after five minutes or so of tense standing inside the cubicle,
hearing only his own breathing, trying not to take too much of the
stink into his nose, no one had come in.

At last, Harry risked venturing back outside.

Only a groom looked at him from his window above the stables,
wondering why anyone should need to spend so long in the boghouse.
Otherwise, the courtyard was empty.

CHAPTER FORTY-SIX

THE MERCENARIES' CALASH

Without the red coat to disguise him—left behind in Sir Peter's kitchen, and not reclaimed—Harry felt vulnerable. Fifty pounds dangled for his apprehending, even if Thomas Thynne no longer looked for his wife.

If ever he did, Harry thought, running through the permutations of that.

But now away from the house of office, Harry doubted his own reasoning. The place's stink, perhaps, had led him into error.

He scanned nervously around him. Hart Street was surprisingly quiet for the time of day. No one took an obvious interest in him.

He decided he would make his way to Gresham. As the shorter route presented a greater risk of recognition—too close to the Justice's house in Leicester Fields and his own in Bloomsbury Square—

Harry took a longer, more anonymous way along the crowded Strand. By Exeter Change, he sensed that a man watched him too closely. And past the entrance to Somerset House, he was sure another man followed. But both men turned in different directions, neither to reappear. For a while, Harry tried to merge with other people, insinuating himself into groups, which made them uncomfortable. As it risked drawing attention to himself—the opposite of what he wanted—he gave up. Instead, he stayed as close to the pavement's inside edge as possible, keeping to the walls of the Strand's grand houses.

Arundel House, where the Royal Society used to meet before it moved to Gresham College, was being demolished. Where it had stood was now a rubble-strewn square overlooking the Thames. In front of it waited a familiar calash. Its driver's face was shaded by his wide-brimmed grey felt hat. Its sole passenger wore a tricorne.

On seeing them, Harry walked straight towards the Count's men.

Kapitän Christoph Vratz, who had his snuffbox open on his lap, saluted him casually. 'Mr. Hunt! You are too easy to find.'

'So, how did you find me?' Harry obliged.

'We follow Thomas Thynne's men, hoping they take us to you. You did not see us in Russell Street, even as we drove right past you.'

Fearing the reappearance of Kidd and Singer, Harry's focus had been too much on pedestrians.

'You did not see Jerzy at Covent Garden, either,' Löjtnant Johann Stern told him.

'I did not,' Harry confessed.

He had not seen pedestrians either. It surprised him that the lumbering Boroski could conceal himself so well.

'You missed me, too, when I followed you along Little Drury Lane,' Count Königsmarck said, appearing next to Harry as if from the air.

Königsmarck concealed his long hair inside a flamboyant Cavalier-style hat, which looked far too hot for the day. The heat and the following had reddened his face.

'You don't punch me as your greeting this time,' Harry said.

'Perhaps next time?' Königsmarck gripped him by the hand and grinned. Then he gestured to Vratz to drive the calash away from the street and into the grounds of Arundel House. Vratz took it almost down to the river, finding some concealing shade beneath a plane tree.

'We have also watched Thomas Thynne, thinking his searching for Betty might take us to her,' Königsmarck told Harry. 'We saw him give directions to his men, outside his house in Cannon Row. It was done so urgently we felt we had to follow them.'

'They're his men we spoke of at Wapping,' Harry said. 'Kidd and Singer.'

'The men we met on the road to Strasbourg,' Vratz said grimly.

'We followed them into Covent Garden,' Königsmarck told Harry. 'We saw them go into one of the houses.'

'It's Sir Peter Lely's house,' Harry said. 'He let me stay there, out of sight.'

'The painter's? Had Thomas Thynne found out you were hiding there?'

Harry shook his head. 'It wasn't until they heard my name that they realised who I was. Sir Peter let it slip. They were there to make a search.'

'For Betty?' Königsmarck asked. 'They thought her there, too?'

'No, no. And she's not. At first I thought they wanted Sir Peter's portrait of her.'

'Thynne made her sit for it, to celebrate their marriage,' Königsmarck said, his face at first showing loathing, changing rapidly to disconsolation. 'We are still no closer to knowing where she is.'

Harry felt sorry for him; he knew well what infatuation felt like, and how painful it was to be apart from its cause. 'I wondered, as Kidd and Singer seemed to search for something else inside Sir Peter's house, if Thynne already knows where she is.'

'Then why proclaim of her kidnap?' Königsmarck asked. A second thought occurred to him, and he threw up his hands in indignation. 'And why lay the blame for it on me?'

'Fearing she had gone with you willingly, perhaps he preferred to think you had taken her. Or, she was kidnapped by others, but he has since found her. Unless she is still kidnapped, and he no longer cares.'

Harry saw Königsmarck's face fall even further. Vratz put his hand on the Count's shoulder to cheer him.

'I'm sorry,' Harry said. 'I make wild guesses. It doesn't help you find her.'

Jerzy Boroski joined them. He was without his musquetoon, and free of the large coat that served to hide it. He sent a look of apology towards Harry for the way they had previously treated him, a look which turned into a friendly, good-natured grin. On Prusom's Island, in Wapping, Harry had convinced Königsmarck and his men he had no part in kidnapping Elizabeth Thynne; they obviously all still believed it. Presumably, that was why they had transferred their attention to her husband and his men.

'Have you no other avenues to enquire along?' Harry asked.

'We spend more time hiding than looking,' Königsmarck complained. 'All of London thinks us the cruel kidnappers of a rich heiress. Thomas Thynne offers a hundred pounds for our finding.'

'A whole hundred? I'm only thought worth fifty.'

'I must remind you, Mr. Hunt, that I am a Count. Besides, the hundred is for all of us, I think.'

'Does he offer a further reward for finding his wife?'

Königsmarck stared at him, then looked more miserable than ever. 'So far as I know, he does not.'

'No, just for the men he accuses of kidnapping her,' Vratz said. Stern and Boroski murmured their assent, although Harry was unsure how much of the talking they had followed, as it was all conducted in English.

Harry took a long look at the men he was with. At the Count, Karl Johann von Königsmarck, very little older than he was, like him passionately enamoured with another man's wife, desperate for her return. At Kapitän Christoph Vratz, whose sanguine poise Harry could not help but admire, and whose loyalty to the Count was obvious. At Löjtnant Stern, who eyes constantly probed the demolition site around them, and who constantly fiddled with his hat. At Jerzy Boroski, solidly implacable, apparently imperturbable, and, Harry guessed, utterly dependable.

Harry made his decision. To all the other men's surprise, he clambered up into the calash.

'A shame there's no reward for her,' he said to them all. 'Let me take you to Mrs. Elizabeth Thynne.'

CHAPTER FORTY-SEVEN

THE BETHLEHEM RETURN

As they drove through Moorgate, Harry spotted the same disfigured beggar he had donated a sixpence to before, when going this way with Sir John and Joseph Fenn. The beggar had given Harry the idea of wearing a soldier's uniform to disguise himself; such men are invisible to most.

Vratz halted the calash at Bethlehem Hospital's gates. Under the watchful eyes of *Raving Madness* and *Melancholy Madness*, Harry, Königsmarck, and Vratz walked through them and up the steps. Stern and Boroski stayed behind with their vehicle, its horses drinking thirstily from a trough.

Joseph Matthews, the Porter, allowed them in through the penny-gate. He looked perplexed. Whenever Mr. Hunt had visited with Mr. Hooke, the architect, he always dressed plainly—usually in a brown leather coat, greatly bashed about. But the last time he had worn a waistcoat that probably cost a year of the Porter's wages. Now Hunt was shabby again. His head had recently been shaved— and what was that paint besmearing each side of it?

Inside the lobby was also Millicent Matthews, the Matron. Recognising Harry, she gave a start. 'You've not come back for William Jones? He's still aggrieved. How he suffered from being inside the Justice's lockup!'

'No, not for him,' Harry assured her, uncertain if he could trust Bethlehem's staff not to claim the fifty pounds. 'I wish to see one of your patients. Up on the female gallery.'

'A patient?' The Matron looked amazed. Her husband reassured her by squeezing her hand.

'Yes,' Harry said. 'With these men with me. I've no notion of the name you know her by. It will not be her real one, I'm sure. I remember the room she was in.'

Mr. Matthews, looking worried, seemed to make a mental calculation. He reached for his bunch of keys and motioned the visitors across the lobby, to where the stout iron gate at the bottom of the stairs was closed against them. He paused to think again.

'If you're unsure about letting us through, you could ask Dr. Allen,' Harry said.

Matthews shook his head. 'He's at his Finsbury madhouse.'

'Dr. Allen spends much of his time there,' Harry observed, having detected little respect in the Porter's tone towards the Physician. 'Perhaps the Apothecary, Mr. Lester, has authority?'

'I don't care to disturb him,' Matthews replied.

'He's a phlegmatic fellow. Does he catch up on his sleep, I wonder? The last time I was here, he seemed in need of it.'

'I shan't speak out of turn,' Matthews said, rolling his eyes complicitly. 'You're visitors, as any other visitors. Of course, I shall let you through.' He bent to unlock the gate, performed with a great clanking of metal on metal. The men left the Matron behind at the bottom of the stairs.

The Hospital seemed eerily silent.

'Last time I came here, a woman sang,' Harry said.

Matthews scowled. 'For a while, her singing was pleasant. But imagine such songs all day, and the day after, and all the days after that? We no longer allow it.'

'How have you silenced her?'

'We no longer allow it,' Matthews repeated, not looking back as he led them upstairs.

After Matthews had unlocked and relocked the upper gate, Harry pointed to the far end of the women's gallery. As he, Königsmarck, Vratz, and Matthews walked along it, golden evening sun raked in through the windows, angling across them. Only a few other visitors were in among the patients allowed the liberty of the gallery, who stood in their habitual desultory groups, apart from those preferring solitude.

Harry aimed for one of the rooms near the top of the western staircase, the one he had climbed with the Justice and Fenn. Its door stood wide open. The room was cool, just as Robert Hooke had designed it to be. Fresh air came in through its glassless window.

The room was empty.

'She was here,' Harry said to Matthews. 'Manacled. And gagged, because she uttered profanities, Dr. Allen told me. Bad enough to raise Satan's eyebrows, he said. She lay just there, on that mattress. The woman next door has straw.'

On seeing her portrait in Sir Peter Lely's drying room, Harry had recognised her straightaway. The same eyes—although when he first saw them, here in this room, they had been terrified. The same resolute chin, under the gag, and the same confident nose above it. Harry had thought her hair—in her portrait a shade darker than copper—had been shaved to make her scalp ready for blistering, but more likely it was to conceal her identity: Elizabeth Thynne, heiress to the Percy estates.

'The girl was only in for a short while, I recall,' Matthews replied. 'Her replacement is out in the gallery.' He went to the window and looked down into the exercise yard, as if he might find Elizabeth there. 'Was she even here for a night?' he asked himself.

'It was only ten days ago,' Harry pressed him. 'You must remember.'

'I do. The first time I saw her was when I came to the women's floor with you and the Justice.'

'You saw nothing of her arrival?'

Matthews shook his head earnestly. 'Nor of her leaving. I have little to do with the goings-on of the women's gallery. My wife has dominion over this floor.'

Königsmarck stared at the empty bed, willing Elizabeth to reappear on it. 'Where have they taken Betty?'

'Is she elsewhere in the building?' Harry asked Matthews. 'In another room?'

Matthews shook his head. 'Dr. Allen discharged her.'

'You've no notion where she is.'

'No notion at all. Remember, I'm but the Hospital's Porter.'

'We must find Dr. Allen,' Harry replied. 'Or we could ask the Apothecary. He may know of it.' His face darkened. 'I suspect others here know more.'

'What do you mean by that?' Matthews demanded. 'You questioned us before, when you thought we'd swapped two women. You accused us. The Justice arrested Jones, our Basketman. I've allowed you inside from my goodwill towards you, Mr. Hunt. Your association with Mr. Hooke lets you in. I know you're looked for. There's a reward.'

'I thank you for that, Mr. Matthews.' Harry let out his breath to gather himself. 'I don't accuse you. I know why Sebiliah Barton was led to self-slaughter. That's what angers me. She expected a child.'

Matthews looked genuinely dumbfounded. 'I didn't know that.' He paused, thinking through the consequences of Harry's informa-tion. 'Sebiliah didn't leave here for over a year.'

'It was not yet too apparent.'

'I'm sorry for it,' Matthews said.

'And the Hospital was willing to hold another woman against her will. I believe, only on the wishes of her husband.'

'Not the Hospital, Mr. Hunt,' Matthews said. 'It's the Physician, Dr. Allen, who elects who comes, and who goes.'

☿

THE GROUP OF MEN WENT BACK downstairs, the Porter doing his duty with his keys.

When they reached the lobby, the first thing Harry laid eyes on was a bright red coat. Following up it led to a zigzag nose, a gaunt face, and deep-set eyes.

Joseph Fenn, aiming a flintlock pistol, nodded to him.

Next to the Marshalman stood the Justice of Peace, Sir John Reresby, grim-faced and tapping his stick.

And, running through the penny-gate to join them, Kidd and Singer.

CHAPTER FORTY-EIGHT

THE WOUNDED CHERUB

'Those are the men!' Kidd shouted, pointing across the lobby, 'Henry Hunt! With him's the Swedish Count. And that, I'd hazard, is Vratz. Our master thinks they've taken with them his wife!'

Sir John flicked his nose. 'Your master being Mr. Thomas Thynne? Then you pair must be his Gamekeeper, Mr. Kidd, and his Steward, Mr. Singer. Who is who? Which is the yellow, and which the blue?'

'I'm Kidd,' said the man with the scar, whose face and shirt were streaked with lead-tin yellow. He moved past the Justice to take Harry by the arm. 'Mr. Thynne's eager to question them.'

The Justice looked askance at him and twitched his stick. 'As am I.'

Fenn turned his pistol a few degrees—far enough to redirect Kidd's attention.

Feeling threatened, Kidd stepped back.

Sir John inspected Harry, who was also marked with paint. 'I would never have known you, Henry Hunt, with your bald head and dishevelment. You are not the man I met at Gresham. You have done well to evade us so long, I credit you with that.'

Then he swivelled his head on his thick neck, looking at the other men with Harry. 'Three birds together. Count Königsmarck. Is this your Kapitän, Christoph Vratz?'

Königsmarck and Vratz both nodded curtly. Vratz eyed the penny-gate, trying to see if it was unlocked. The Steward, Carter, stood by it, having opened it at the Justice's knock. Kidd and Singer had arrived soon afterwards.

'But no Mrs. Thynne,' Sir John said.

Singer looked slyly at him. 'You know our master's importance, Justice. His influence. You've played your part to find these men, so be happy you've discharged your duty. I'm sure Mr. Thynne will recompense you for your time.'

Sir John's face flushed a deep, dark red. 'You must know your master well, since you presume to speak for him. You think you know me, too, as a magistrate to be bought.' The Justice's whole body quivered with indignation. 'And you threaten me with Mr. Thynne's clout.' His vowels had become even more northern; short, sharp— cuttingly so. 'You place him so far above the law he may take miscreants from its officials. Well, you are mistaken in all. Remember *my* influence, which comes from the King. Not from his bastard son, nor the seditious shits who support him. Even the shits in Parliament. Get you two gone to Cannon Row. Have no fear of this. If these men know of Mrs. Thynne, then they shall tell us soon enough.'

'They have her, Justice!' Singer protested. 'Everything they do shows it. Mr. Thynne's most anxious for his wife's return.'

'He's not, I think,' Harry said. 'Sir John, these two men barged into Sir Peter Lely's house, where they bullied him and his staff. They didn't seek Mrs. Thynne.'

'We never barged,' Singer said.

'Nor did we bully,' Kidd added. 'We looked for her.' He glowered ferociously at Harry. 'Of course we did.'

'Inside the printing workroom, you looked along shelves. Did you expect to discover her sitting upon one?'

'We tried to search all his house.' Kidd spoke to Harry but looked at the Justice. 'But you prevented us. You did your utmost to stop us finding her.'

'For what was your search?' Harry persisted. 'Not for the portrait, as you continued to look after I saw you with it. You sought something smaller.'

Kidd and Singer looked at each other, then at the Justice. 'Arrest these men, Sir John,' Kidd said, as if he gave the Justice permission. 'They're murderers and kidnappers.'

'Something smaller,' Harry continued. 'Perhaps for papers. Or a bo—'

The bang was so loud inside Bethlehem Hospital's lobby, it stunned all the men in it.

Pain in Harry's eardrums made him think they had burst. Smoke obscured his vision, although he was allowed a dim view of Fenn lying on his back with Kapitän Vratz on top of him. Vratz tried to pull himself away from the Marshalman; Fenn had locked his legs around him. Königsmarck pulled at Fenn's fingers, wishing to extricate the pistol from his grasp. The pistol could not shoot again, but it might be used as a club. When Vratz had grabbed at it, it had fired a bullet into one of the lobby's wooden cherubs, whose ear was shot away.

Gathering his senses, Sir John raised his blackthorn stick and charged towards Königsmarck, his limp barely slowing him down. The Count fended him off with a lurch to one side, and managed to wrap his arm around the stick and twist it away from the Justice's grip. Vratz finally scrabbled clear of Fenn, whose veering nose was bloody. As he did so, he kicked out at the pistol in Fenn's hand, which spun away from all of them.

Vratz got to his feet and ran to the penny-gate, pausing to check that Königsmarck followed. Carter—unwilling to risk injury— pushed open the gate to help them on their way. The two mercenaries ran off down the Hospital's steps. About halfway down, Königsmarck flung the Justice's stick behind them.

'Damn! Damn! Damn!' Sir John cursed, rubbing his aching thigh. Fenn sat up, blood dripping over his mouth and chin, and onto the lobby's floor.

'Their flight proves their guilt,' Kidd said. 'I told you they have Mr. Thynne's wife.'

'It proves nothing of the kind,' Harry said. 'More like, they're averse to arrest.'

'You did little to stop them, I noticed, Mr. Kidd,' Sir John said. 'You neither, Mr. Singer. Mr. Thynne described you to me as competent, soldierly men, yet you have little fight in you.'

'We've proved our mettle many a time,' Singer said, sneering at him.

'Yet today you are careful to avoid altercation.'

'I thought the same at Sir Peter Lely's house,' Harry said. 'You don't look for Elizabeth Thynne. Elizabeth Thynne, I say—I notice you only ever call her Mr. Thynne's wife.'

Singer turned his sneer towards Harry. Kidd wore a similar expression.

Sir John nodded to Fenn. Fenn undid a new, shining pair of manacles from his belt, dripping blood onto them. Harry, feeling numb, could only think what his arrest was likely to lead to. He had seen the Tyburn Fair procession. He had been caught up in it, in fact, when inside the Justice's coach, before Königsmarck's men took him. Was that really only nine days ago? He remembered a couple of white-suited men on one of the carts, and a woman badly gashed, as the crowd had taken against her.

In the eyes of the two men arresting him, Königsmarck's and Vratz's escape could only further confirm Harry's guilt, because of his association with them. Despondently, Harry put out his wrists; Fenn clasped the manacles over them.

After giving the manacles a shake to check they were fast, Fenn reclaimed his pistol from the floor. He reloaded it from the pouch on his belt, then raised it close to Harry's face. 'In case the Count and his men come back for you,' he said, in his rasping whisper.

'Get the intelligence out of him now,' Singer demanded, judging Sir John had composed himself. 'Then we may take the news to Mr. Thynne.'

'You mean bully it from him.' For a moment, Sir John looked ready for persuasion.

Kidd nodded vehemently, shaking lead-tin yellow to the floor. 'Nothing you've not done before.'

Sir John's expression darkened again. 'You are far from Longleat now.'

Kidd and Singer looked at one another, then both shrugged their acceptance of defeat.

'Get you gone,' Sir John said to them. 'When back at Cannon Row, together you may combine your colours. Your yellow, Mr. Kidd, and your blue, Mr. Singer, in commixture shall make the colour of your Green Ribbon Club. Of all those who support Monmouth in his bid to be king. The colour chosen by Shaftesbury, and his Brisk Boys.'

'We're not Brisk Boys,' Kidd said, scornfully. 'We only do our master's bidding.'

'As do I,' Sir John growled. 'Come, Fenn. Let us take our prisoner.'

They turned, Sir John with a last, somewhat consoling look at Kidd and Singer—he knew they would have to face their master's wrath—and walked through the penny-gate.

Fenn walked close behind Harry, pointing the pistol at his back.

☿

SIR JOHN RECLAIMED HIS STICK FROM the steps. By Bethlehem's gates, a pair of marshalmen wearing the same red as Fenn waited by the Justice's carriage. Both were armed, one with a pistol, one with a musket. Like Fenn, they also wore swords.

Harry almost laughed at the thought his arrest required such muscle, but then remembered it was not him they worried about, but Königsmarck and his men, especially the large, lumbering, musquetoon-wielding Boroski. They had been right to do so; Königsmarck and Vratz had shown some alacrity when making their escape.

Sir John scowled at the marshalmen as if they were at fault. But they had not realised that the pair hurrying out from the Hospital were two of the men he sought.

☿

IN THE JUSTICE'S COACH, ON REACHING St. Martin's Lane, the driver did not continue along Dirty Lane as Harry expected—this would have been the direct route to Sir John's home in Leicester Fields—but instead they turned south, towards Charing Cross.

Fenn grinned at him. Blood crusted his lips and lodged between his teeth. 'I nearly got you in Rotherhithe, Mr. Hunt. I saw you at the church. I was only just behind you. I lost you on the Bridge, when they pulled up the drawbridge behind you.'

'What took you there?'

'I found the woman you lodged with. She reported you.'

Harry suffered a sudden jolt, as if someone had seized under his ribs and pulled them. Surely Rachel had not reported him? At his look of alarm, the Marshalman supplied him with an answer he preferred.

'Unsworth's her name. Guessed you aren't who you told her. Thynne's pair, Kidd and Singer, found you out, too. They questioned everybody. I followed them through Rotherhithe more than once.'

Harry stared out of the carriage's window. 'Where are we going? Are we not headed to Leicester Fields?'

Sir John glared at him. 'You shall see. Soon enough.'

CHAPTER FORTY-NINE

THE BLACK
BOX

From Charing Cross, they turned into Whitehall.

Sir John whistled 'Dull Sir John,' the gleam in his eyes daring Harry to comment.

Harry stayed quiet.

Soldiers guarded the gate beyond the Banqueting House.

'His Majesty's whereabouts?' Sir John barked at a sergeant.

'Office o' Works, Justice,' the man replied. 'Consultin' with Sir Christopher.'

With a sharp tap of his stick on the roof, Sir John directed his driver to go there.

As they wheeled around in the road to go back the way they had come, Fenn laughed at Harry's expression. 'The King's called for you,

Mr. Hunt.' He leaned forwards, extracting the key for his manacles from his pocket. 'Sorry. For subterfuge.'

'His Majesty shall explain all,' Sir John said tightly, his unhappiness clear to see.

By the time they had returned up Whitehall as far as Middle Scotland Yard, Harry was freed from restraint and rubbing at his wrists.

Inside the Office of Works—a line of houses knocked through to become a series of interconnected offices—a man busy drawing told them the King spoke with Sir Christopher up on the first floor.

When they reached the top of the stairs, the King saw them; he beckoned them over to a large table covered with paper. At various desks, more draughtsmen worked on drawings, ranging from preparatory sketches to finely done presentation drawings for clients, and also detailed construction drawings, designed to be clear for the builders. One aide used Robert Hooke's copying machine to duplicate a large elevation of the new library at Trinity College, Cambridge, detailing its enormous windows.

Not for the first time, Harry thought of the similarity between Sir Peter Lely's business and Sir Christopher's, reliant as both were on an army of helpers.

Sir John and Harry made their bows to the King and Sir Christopher. Fenn hovered a little behind them, then, with nodded permission from Sir John, he went back outside to smoke a cheroot.

The King gripped Harry's hand as if worried he might run off. 'When I had news of a William Jackson staying in Rotherhithe, I wondered if he was you.'

'I washed up there after being hit on the head by a waterman, Your Majesty,' Harry said. 'He was annoyed I'd taken his boat. When asked for my name, William Jackson came first to mind. I cursed myself as I said it. It risked recognition, but by then I was saddled with it.'

'It must have been a hard moment, Harry,' Sir Christopher said. 'For I have never heard you curse.'

The King gave Harry a broad smile, which turned into a smirk. 'You know, as William gets older, he risks less, and laments it all the more. That he adds to his fund of stories much pleases me.'

Harry returned the smile, but more sheepishly. 'He thought he had found Mrs. Thynne. But when he went to Bethlehem Hospital, to release her from there, Sir John arrested him.'

'I arrested *you*, Henry Hunt, as His Majesty had commanded me to do,' Sir John said, still looking disgruntled.

Bewildered, the King ignored his Justice. 'Her kidnappers put her in Bedlam?'

'Kidnapper, I suspect,' Harry replied. 'Being her husband, he was well placed to do so.'

'Thomas Thynne?' The King did not pause for Harry's reply, but looked sharply at Sir John. 'You told me it was the Swedish Count, Königsmarck, who had her.'

'We saw the ransom letter from him, Your Majesty,' Sir John protested. 'Mr. Thynne showed it to us.'

'That letter only declared the Count's love for Mrs. Thynne,' Harry said. 'Königsmarck didn't write it—he confirmed it to me. He didn't write the ransom letter sent to Sir Benedict Cantley, either.'

'But both letters owned the Swedish style of writing,' the Justice protested.

'At the time, we said Scandinavian,' Harry pointed out, thinking on how remembering shifts to better suit the rememberer. 'The letter Thomas Thynne showed us names his wife as Elizabeth. Not as

Betty, as Königsmarck always calls her. And do you remember the way the nib spread the ink on the upstrokes? Neither Königsmarck nor his men have that habit as they write. All of them showed me.'

Sir John scoffed. 'You must tell me more of your doings with the Count and his men.'

'They took me from you, thinking I'd kidnapped her. Because you had arrested me for doing so.'

'I found you with them again, at Bedlam, before they made their escape.'

'We were there to find Mrs. Thynne.' Still bitter at Sir John's suspicion, Harry's voice rose as he struggled to keep his composure.

'Now, now, Harry,' the King said. 'That you met Königsmarck is fortunate. Hmm? If you have shown him innocent of kidnap and murder, I am glad of it, for he is highborn. I knew his father, vaguely, who was a Field Marshall. Blown up by his own side's cannon. Before that unhappy event, I met him at the Hague, when we both visited my brother-in-law.' The King's face clouded. 'At about the same time as the birth of my son. Who is the reason I asked Sir John to bring you to me.'

'You mean the Duke of Monmouth, Your Majesty?' Harry said, with the slightest of upwards inflections.

The King looked sternly at him. 'You seek clarification? Well, fair enough, I have others. But, yes, it is James who presently concerns me.'

Harry suddenly felt warm. The drawing office was airless and stuffy. 'Before you tell me more of him, Your Majesty, may I ask you a question?'

The King's assent was shown by his interested look. Harry steeled himself against his own timidity. 'Why should you take me at my word, and accept my accusations against Mr. Thynne?'

'Because I have knowledge denied to you,' the King replied mea-
suredly. 'Sir Christopher, I should like to speak with Harry and Sir
John in private.'

'Of course, Your Majesty,' Sir Christopher said. He led them to
his office at the far corner of the building. He bowed low, and left
them, shutting the door behind him.

☿

SOME ANIMOSITY STILL BETWEEN THEM, Sir John and Harry
looked at one another, then at the King.

'My intelligence is not so much about Thomas Thynne, but his
new wife,' the King started.

'You know what Mrs. Thynne had, and what her husband wanted from her,' Harry said. 'Something for which he put his own wife
inside Bethlehem Hospital, and had his men search Sir Peter Lely's
house. Something which concerns your son.'

That Harry had guessed what he was about to tell them placed
the King halfway between exasperation and admiration. 'Rare is
the day I feel anything so much as certainty,' he said. 'So *know* may
be too strong a word.'

Harry and Sir John waited for the King to continue. He made no
immediate effort to do so, preferring to absorb himself in the drawings piled on Sir Christopher's desk, sifting through them one by one.

After a long-seeming moment, he looked up at them and
coughed apologetically. 'Sir John, you spoke to me before of a box.
Hmm? One which causes great consternation, even though few people have ever seen it.'

Sir John looked disquieted. 'The so-called Black Box, Your Majesty? Made so much of by Shaftesbury, and the Green Ribboners?'

'Yes, that box,' the King said. 'I have to admit, I misled you. I told you it was a fiction, put about by those who wish it a fact. I told you my son's hopes are based only on air.'

Finding them suddenly engrossing, Sir John studied the toes of his boots.

'And now's the time to say otherwise,' Harry said. 'Since Mrs. Thynne's disappearance. Do you believe one to be linked to the other, Your Majesty?'

The King looked at them both, then back at the table of drawings, then drummed his fingers on his lips. He let out a lungful of breath, as if in defeat. 'It is not the box, of course, but what is supposedly inside it. Papers have been spoken of. I do not say that they exist. *If* they do, and *if* they come to light, then I would be eager to have them.'

Seeing Harry about to speak, the King shut him up by raising his palm. 'Their contents are neither here nor there, Harry, as they are my business, not yours. Papers. Important papers. Sensitive papers.'

'The Green Ribboners claim it contains proof of your marriage to Lucy Walter,' Harry said. 'Such proof exists, then.'

The King let loose a long, exaggerated sigh. 'Your use to me outweighs your impertinence, I have found. But take a care. You are too forthright. I have warned you in the past.'

Harry swallowed his reply and bowed his head.

'I do not say these papers prove anything,' the King went on. 'Only that, if they exist, I want them back. The box causes too much trouble. I am told Elizabeth had it. I am told her husband learned of it. Thynne has poured the news of it into my son's ear, and promised to obtain it for him.'

Sir John's expression lightened, as he saw reason for hope. 'But if you never married your son's mother, such papers can only be forgeries.'

The King arched his eyebrows, but said nothing.

Harry rubbed his hand over the stubble on his scalp. 'Mr. Thynne's men searched Sir Peter Lely's house, not for me—thinking I could lead them to their master's wife—but for something else. That they searched for the box is an easy fit with your news of Mrs. Thynne having it. Sir Peter painted her portrait recently. Perhaps she took the box with her there, then hid it.'

'Go back there and seek it,' the King commanded, looking unusually flustered. 'Straightaway. Sir John shall go with you.' The King's eyes widened. 'Do you think Thynne's men found it?'

'They may have returned to Sir Peter's house after being at Bethlehem. Where Sir John arrested me again, to bring me here.'

'Then there is no time to waste. Hmm?' The King put down the drawing he held, then found a fresh piece of paper and one of Sir Christopher's pens. He wrote out a short note in his expansive style and signed it with a flourish.

'Your pass, Harry, which you will need, as everyone still thinks you a villain. Fifty pounds, I have heard, for your apprehension. A tidy sum.'

He extended his hand for Harry to kiss. 'If Thynne's men have the box, then you must take it from them. When you have it, bring it to me. Harry. Sir John. You are among my most trusted of men. Tell no other souls of it.'

'Of course, Your Majesty,' Sir John said solemnly.

'No one shall know from my lips,' Harry promised. 'May I suggest something, Your Majesty, before we go?'

The King looked at him enquiringly.

'That Sir John goes to Covent Garden to search Sir Peter's house. I should like to find Mrs. Thynne. I wish her freedom restored to her as soon as possible. Besides, if she's where I think she is, she may tell us where she hid the box.'

'Where is she, Harry? Hmm?'

'I thought her at Bethlehem. Its Physician, Dr. Allen, had a hand in placing her there, against her will and well-being. Its Porter told me Dr. Allen's in Finsbury, at his private asylum for the mad. He spends much of his time there, which is why I think she's there. She's too important a person for him to leave unless he has to. He probably took her there straight after Sir John and I first went to Bethlehem, after Diana Cantley's dissection.'

'I am happy with that, Your Majesty, if you are,' Sir John said. 'If I, too, may suggest something. Why do we not go to arrest Thomas Thynne? If what Harry says is true, he put his own wife in Bedlam and lied about the Swede.'

'I think not,' the King said. 'Not yet. Support is too strong for my nephew. And Thynne is known as his great ally. The Country Party, Shaftesbury's Green Ribbon Club, the Brisk Boys—and all the other agitators against me—would take to the streets. We shall have riots all over London. I cannot risk that only on Harry's surmise, even though I think him to be right. No, Sir John, you go to Covent Garden. See if you can find Thynne's men and the Black Box there. Harry, you get yourself to the madhouse to recover Elizabeth Thynne.'

CHAPTER FIFTY

THE PERCY LION

For Harry's journey to Finsbury, the King gave use of a carriage and its driver. At Charing Cross, the man drove around the statue of Charles I; the King's father stared mournfully towards the site of his own execution. The statue had almost gone the same way as its subject. During Cromwell's rule, Parliament paid a blacksmith to melt it down. Instead, the man had hidden it until the Restoration.

As they turned into the Strand, Harry observed Northumberland House, residence of the Percy family when in London and the permanent home of the Dowager Countess, Elizabeth Thynne's grandmother. Over its gates prowled an enormous stone lion, the family's chosen symbol. The house's façade viewable from the road was only one side of an enormous square. Turrets topped each corner. Inigo Jones had added the fourth side to the square; the family now lived overlooking the river rather than the Strand.

In this house, just over twenty years before, General Monck had met with Edward Montagu, and Denzil Hollis and Sir William Waller, to secretly decide the limitations to be placed upon the King before his restoration. They had allowed him back because he promised toleration, and emancipation from the rule of sectaries and soldiers.

Sighting the by now familiar calash parked on the opposite side of the road from the gates, Harry told his driver to stop next to it.

Vratz was at first ready to whip his horse away from this strange vehicle pulling alongside; recognising Harry, he lifted his grey hat to him. Boroski and Stern both saluted—Harry was unsure how mocking their gestures were. Königsmarck kept low in the back, worried someone inside Northumberland House might recognise him.

'The King and the Justice now think us innocent,' Harry told them. 'The King has lent me this carriage.'

The men showed little joy at his news. The Count least of all. 'We saw Thomas Thynne and his men going inside.' Königsmarck pointed across the road to the house. 'But no sign of Betty.'

'Kidd and Singer? The same pair we saw at Bethlehem Hospital?'

'Yes, the same,' Vratz affirmed.

'So, they've not yet had time to go to Finsbury,' Harry said, mostly to himself. 'Did they carry anything with them?'

'Their carriage went straight through the gates,' Königsmarck said. 'They could have had anything with them.'

'I still hope to find Elizabeth Thynne before her husband does,'

Harry said, stepping out of the King's carriage and waving his thanks to its driver. 'I shall join you. We're going to Finsbury.'

'*Los!*' Vratz shouted, to set the horse off. '*Schneller!*'

Harry tapped him on the shoulder. 'Why do you speak in German to your animal, when you're from Pomerania?'

Vratz turned and looked at Harry in bewilderment, as if the question made no sense at all. 'This horse is German,' he replied.

CHAPTER FIFTY-ONE

THE FINSBURY MADHOUSE

Finsbury's windmills overlooked the Plague pits. The ground was now grown over, its wounds healed, but everyone knew what lay beneath.

Inside the maze of buildings west of the Artillery Ground stood Dr. Allen's private asylum. The house was tall and narrowly imposing; elderly timbers warped it out of true.

When Harry, Königsmarck, and Vratz were shown into Allen's office by a reticent aide—Boroski and Stern stayed with the calash—the Physician welcomed them from behind his desk with a pained and conciliatory expression. 'Mr. Hunt. I wondered when you would find us.'

'Us? So, she *is* here,' Harry said.

'Where is Betty? Königsmarck demanded hotly, leaning over the desk.

'She is completely well,' said Allen, alarmed. 'You have no need to worry.'

Vratz went around the desk and grabbed at Allen's shirtfront. Allen scraped back his chair, avoiding him.

'These men are Count Königsmarck and Kapitän Vratz.' Harry introduced them politely, as if they all enjoyed tea in the sunshine.

'We do not need this *commotion*,' Allen pleaded with the men threatening him. 'You risk upsetting my patients.'

'You took Elizabeth Thynne into Bethlehem,' Harry said. His voice sounded loud in his own ears. 'To be kept against her will.'

'Her husband bade me do so,' Allen replied.

Harry regarded him with open disdain. 'And that was reason enough to constrain her?'

The Physician's wig seemed even more overlarge than when Harry last met him; Allen pushed it back on his forehead. 'I cannot argue with such men,' he said, looking nervously between the three men confronting him. 'They are too powerful to rebuff.'

Harry felt the heat rising in his cheeks; he was at the very edge of maintaining his self-control.

'He offered more money than I could refuse,' Allen said, responding to Harry's accusatory stare. 'Not for me, but for the Hospital.'

'You call yourself a physician! Mrs. Thynne's well-being depended on you.'

'Where is Betty?' Königsmarck demanded again, placing his hand on the pommel of his sword.

Allen stood hastily. Without another word, he exited his office and led his three visitors upstairs to a comfortable and cosy withdrawing room.

Where Elizabeth Thynne sat reading on a sofa.

There could be no mistake—Harry felt a flash of relief for it—this woman in front of him was undoubtedly the subject of Sir Peter Lely's portrait. When Harry had last seen her, she wore Bethlehem Hospital blue; now she had on a dress of canary yellow. Her scalp was covered by a ginger-red fuzz; losing the abundant mane Sir Peter had depicted made her seem even younger than her fourteen years, and even more vulnerable. Seeing her made Harry touch his own hair, hardly grown back after Rachel had shaved him.

When Elizabeth saw the Count with this party of incoming men, she jumped up, dropping her book. 'Karl!'

Königsmarck and Elizabeth clung to each other. He kissed her forehead, her cheeks, her tears. He was close to crushing her, he held her so tightly.

'My love! My Betty, my Betty!'

Laughing and crying at the same time, Elizabeth had to push at him for space to draw breath. 'Karl! Karl! You have come for me!' Suddenly scared he had not, she looked panicked. 'You do? My husband is cruel!'

'We shall leave together, my love. For Amsterdam, for Rotterdam, for the Hague. Wherever you wish me to go, as long as it is with you. I shall protect you always, my Betty.'

He pulled her to him again.

'Who do you bring with you, Karl?' she whispered fearfully into Königsmarck's ear.

'This is Mr. Henry Hunt,' Königsmarck told her. 'He searched for you, and led us to you.'

Elizabeth's eyes narrowed; she shrugged Königsmarck away. 'Who is he, that he should do that for me?'

Harry answered for himself. 'The King commanded me to find you. I've performed similar tasks for him before.'

'Mr. Hunt was accused of kidnapping you himself,' Königsmarck said with some pride, as if he should take the credit.

Seeing Elizabeth's confusion, Harry cut him off. 'We've no time for all that. Mrs. Thynne—'

'Call me Elizabeth,' she said. 'I want no association with *that man*, least of all his name.'

'Elizabeth, then. To verify, was it your husband who placed you inside Bethlehem?'

'It was.'

'He misled us—me and the Justice of Peace, Sir John Reresby— into thinking the Count had kidnapped you. He said you left Northumberland House for the Royal Exchange, and its shops. Then for the Goldsmiths' Hall. He said your page looked for you, and that your grandmother sent out servants.'

'I'm sure she did not,' Elizabeth said. 'My grandmother benefits greatly from my marriage to Mr. Thynne. I never got as far as the Goldsmiths' Hall. Thynne found me by the Milk Street market and pulled me into his carriage.'

'The danger posed to Mrs. Thynne by her husband is why we brought her here,' Allen said.

'We? Who is we?' Harry asked.

'*We* is Dr. Allen and the Duke,' Elizabeth replied.

'The Duke of Monmouth?' In his confusion, Harry actually gawped at her. 'But the Duke asked for me and the Justice. Why want assistance to find you if he knew exactly where you were?'

Elizabeth sat back down on the sofa. Königsmarck knelt on the floor in front of her, having to swipe his sword out of the way to do so, and caressed the backs of her hands. Vratz leaned languidly against a bookshelf, looking as imperturbable as always.

'The past few days all merge together, so your question is a hard one,' Elizabeth answered Harry. 'At first—if we can believe what he told me—the Duke did not know. Thynne kept it secret from him. Only later did the Duke find out my husband had locked me away in Bedlam. He had me released as soon as he knew of it. That was when I was brought here.'

'I remember the Duke, not Thynne, asked for me,' Harry said. 'When Sir John and I met them both, at Cannon Row, your husband seemed averse to our help. He must have told the Duke after our visit.'

Elizabeth gazed at Königsmarck while she spoke to Harry. 'The Duke rescued me from my husband but makes demands of me himself. This madhouse is a prettier prison than Bedlam, but a prison nonetheless.'

'We placed you here to protect you,' Allen insisted. 'From your husband.'

'You can little pretend you've done your best for Elizabeth,' Harry told the Physician. 'You'd be hypocritical indeed.'

Elizabeth looked with approval at this stranger Karl brought with him. Although bespectacled, small, and poorly dressed, Henry Hunt had an intensity of gaze and a bombilating energy which made him quite formidable. She was glad he was friend rather than foe.

'The Duke placed me here, thinking to coerce from me what he wanted to know,' she said.

'That being the whereabouts of the Black Box,' Harry said.

'You know of it. Then, I presume, you look for it, too.'

'The King told me of it, wishing me to find it. His son told him you have it.'

Elizabeth's expression showed her disappointment. 'So, your search was not for me, but rather for the box, on the orders of the King. How dull of me to think otherwise.'

'No, no. Not on his orders. At least, not until a couple of hours or so ago. Although, as he's skilled at divulging only what he wishes to divulge, the box may have been behind his insistence I investigate Diana Cantley's murder.'

'So Diana *is* dead.' The words caught in Elizabeth's throat.

'She was your friend, I know. My sympathies to you.'

'Thomas Thynne told me of it. To frighten me, I suppose. I could not bring myself to believe him. Did he murder her?'

'I can't say,' Harry said. 'I wouldn't disbelieve it. He put it about that you'd been kidnapped, blaming the Count, yet he himself put you inside Bethlehem.'

He paced a circle in front of Elizabeth, rapping his chin gently with his knuckles.

'Do you remember when Mr. Thynne took you to Bethlehem?' he asked, after everyone else in the room had waited for his thoughts.

'As I say, the days all become like one.'

'What time of day, I mean? Was it in the evening?'

'It was, I remember.'

'Did you hear the Hospital's bell? The one rung at nine o'clock to clear the visitors.'

'I recollect a bell. I have no idea if it was nine or not. When I heard it, I was still outside in the carriage. Thynne employs a pair of men who seem always to be together. They waited with me while he went inside.'

'One with a scar through his mouth, the other far larger? Both of them owning skins darkened from too much sun?'

Elizabeth nodded.

'What colour's Mr. Thynne's carriage?'

'The one they took me in was blue.'

'With a large box for luggage, mounted over its front wheels?'

Elizabeth nodded again.

'Presumably, to avoid any visitors who came out after the bell, they took you to the back of the Hospital. The side which faces the Roman wall.'

Elizabeth looked at him as if Harry could see into her mind, but so far it was only simple reasoning.

'There are various doors to that side, for deliveries and so on. Was where you waited at the eastern end of the building, nearest to Little Moorgate? A door there has a sloped roof over it.'

'That is where the carriage waited. The men gagged me while I was still inside it, then placed a sack over me. When Thomas Thynne returned, they dragged me into Bethlehem. It was little distance, so it must have been the same door. I struggled against them, but they were three and I was one.'

'How long were you kept there?'

'Two nights. Dr. Allen brought me here on the morning of my second day.'

'I saw you on your first day, then. I only realised it was you when I saw your portrait at Sir Peter Lely's house, in the drying room there. So, I saw you in the morning, then met the Duke that evening, with Mr. Thynne. Afterwards, your husband must have told the Duke he had placed you inside the Hospital. You were released the day after.'

'Please, do not speak of him as my husband. I barely know the man. I know enough to judge him wicked.'

'You need never worry about him again,' Königsmarck told Elizabeth fervently, rubbing the back of her neck. 'We shall escape here, to wherever in Europe you please.'

'First, let us retrieve the Black Box,' Elizabeth said. 'It has been my bargaining tool with these men. With it, and the papers inside it, at least I am a voice in the conversation.'

'With these papers, the Duke of Monmouth may be King,' Königsmarck said.

'The Duke believes you have it?' Harry asked Elizabeth. 'And so, too, presumably, does Mr. Thynne.'

'They do believe it.' Elizabeth sent a knowing look at Königsmarck. 'Thomas Thynne tried to take it from me before, to give it to his friend the Duke. He wants the Duke to succeed his father, as he is Protestant.'

'As many do,' Harry said. 'The talk in London's of little else.'

'That's why his men attacked our coach near Strasbourg,' Vratz said. 'Kidd and Singer. They thought we had it then.'

Harry regarded the three men in the room, then Elizabeth. 'So, *do* you have the box, with these papers inside it?'

She looked at Königsmarck, who nodded that she could trust Harry. She, in turn, nodded at Harry. 'I do.'

'May I ask why you do?'

'It is a long tale.' Elizabeth was taken aback by Harry's question. Most men, she was sure, would have straightaway asked where she kept it. She wriggled herself down into the seat of the sofa, to make herself more comfortable for the telling. 'A shorter version is, that during Oliver Cromwell's time, the Duke's mother, Lucy Walter, was held in the Tower. Parliament thought her a spy. She had travelled to London from the Hague, bringing in a box the proofs of her marriage. She smuggled it to the Bishop of Durham, who had conducted the wedding ceremony. She remained close to the Bishop—Dr. Cozen—all her life. He took her last confession, in fact. He kept the box. Cromwell himself quizzed him, but by then Cozen was old, and his wits were gone. Although, his confusion may well have been pretence, for he passed the box to his son-in-law, Sir Gilbert Gerrard. Thinking it too incendiary to keep, and too important to destroy, Gerrard gave it to my father. After my father's death, my grandmother—most people know her as the Dowager Countess—kept it. As approval for the Duke of Monmouth rose, she calculated the box ever increased in value. She held on to it for as long as she could, but my grandmother has enormous debts. She's rarely away from a card table. So, she sold the box to the highest bidder. Thomas Thynne. His negotiations with her concerned the box as much as our marriage. Sadly for her, my grandmother is careless. She left the box to be found. So, I found it. Then I took it. Then I hid it.'

Elizabeth bent forwards to pick up her book from where she had knocked it onto the floor. *Parthenissa*, she said, showing them. 'There is no hurt in reading romances. *The Book of Martyrs* makes me melancholy. Dr. Allen, is my time here done?'

'It is done,' Königsmarck said, fending off the Physician's protestations. 'Come, my love. We must get you safely away.'

'Where's the box now?' Harry asked Elizabeth. 'Thynne's men searched for it at Sir Peter Lely's.'

'I shall not tell you here.' She glanced at Allen. 'Better to show you.'

Harry, Königsmarck, Vratz, and Elizabeth left Allen on his own. Only Harry turned as they went, to send the Physician a last, contemptuous look.

'Things go on at Bethlehem which you should stop,' Harry told him.

☿

WHEN THEIR LEADER EMERGED FROM THE madhouse with Elizabeth holding on to his arm, Stern and Boroski ran forwards to meet them. She hugged them both, and laughed at her newfound freedom—especially when Boroski, grinning his slowly spreading grin, patted the calash's seat for her to sit next to him. Königsmarck pretended a jealous outrage with the big Polonian.

Again, Vratz took up the driver's position. 'Covent Garden,' Elizabeth instructed him.

'The box *is* at Sir Peter's,' Harry said, as the carriage moved off, Vratz saying '*Hü!*' to the horse. 'Did you tell Sir Peter of its being there?'

Elizabeth shook her head vehemently. 'It would have been unfair to burden him with the knowledge.'

Königsmarck pointed at her head. 'Betty, we must hide your pate. It makes you conspicuous. Thynne and his men still search for you.'

Without looking behind him, Vratz passed back his hat for her, then whipped more speed from the horse.

CHAPTER FIFTY-TWO

THE OVERTURNED HOUSEHOLD

Rather than approach Sir Peter's house from the rear, this time Harry directed Vratz into the piazza. Again, Königsmarck instructed Boroski and Stern to stay with the calash.

Sir Peter's doorman—his misgivings plain—inspected the new visitors under the portico: two men who looked like soldiers; a young woman in a hat which had seen hard service; and Harry Hunt, who had caused so much trouble that morning.

'Let's find Sir Peter,' Harry said, steering his companions past the protesting doorman. He led them up the grand staircase and into the antechamber, the room with all its paintings and Venus by the window.

Joseph Bokshoorn was in there, inspecting the statue closely. On hearing visitors, he turned too hastily, as if caught in something shameful.

'She's so admirably done, she seems ready to step away from her plinth and speak to us,' Harry said by way of good day.

Bokshoorn looked relieved it was Harry. 'She waits for us to leave, so she may move again.' He started when he recognised Elizabeth. 'Pleased you are safe, Mrs. Thynne. We all worried for you.'

Elizabeth signalled her thanks to Bokshoorn with a brittle smile. 'Is Sir Peter busy? If not, I should like to speak with him.'

'In his studio, with the Duchess of Richmond,' Bokshoorn told her. 'Almost put her off. Men came this morning and rummaged through the house. Since then, Sir Peter's not felt himself.'

Harry grabbed Bokshoorn's arm. 'Did they take anything away?'

'Not had time to check. I called the Watch. Started a hue and cry. Half those in the piazza came inside. No surprise to me if things were taken.'

Bokshoorn left the room, then soon returned with the news Sir Peter would see them.

In his studio, the artist sat at his easel, making a preparatory sketch of the Duchess.

'Sir Peter, I must speak with you,' Harry said. The urgency in his voice persuaded Sir Peter to put down his chalk and make grovelling apologies to his sitter, who looked most put out at the interruption, and astonished that Sir Peter paid heed of it.

Sir Peter came out to the landing.

'Mrs. Thynne, my dear lady, you're safe!' Sir Peter said, out of breath from the walk. 'I'm so very glad of it.'

'Thanks be to this man, I am told.' She smiled across at Harry.

But Harry had no wish to waste time on pleasantries. 'Did Mr. Thynne's men make off with anything?'

'I know not, Harry,' Sir Peter said. 'It took all my Assistants to convince them to go. I'm so sorry I divulged your name. It was dunderheaded of me.' He clasped Harry's hands to underscore his apology.

At the sound of their voices, Lankrink had come out of one of the workrooms, shaking his head ruefully. 'They did not take the portrait, Harry, though I thought they would. They overturned much of the household. We've spent the whole time since fixing their mess.'

Elizabeth looked alarmed. 'May we go upstairs, Sir Peter?' she asked. 'Something of mine is up there.'

'Do you remember if the men came back in after I left, Dhr. Lankrink?' Harry asked. His feeling Kidd and Singer had too soon given up chasing him felt more and more justified. While running around the house after him, had they spotted the Black Box?

'All was confusion, Mr. Hunt,' Lankrink answered. 'I did not know you had gone until I knew you had gone.'

Lankrink looked so forlorn that Harry patted him on the back consolingly.

After Sir Peter had apologised again to the Duchess of Richmond, they all went upstairs together, following Elizabeth into the oils room. Sitting where he usually sat, Jaspars worked at his easel, although this time there was no apprentice with him.

He stood when he saw Sir Peter, bowed when he saw Elizabeth, frowned when he saw Königsmarck and Vratz, and scowled when he saw Harry. 'I've had apprentices tidying all afternoon,' he grumbled. 'Those men left nothing right side up.'

Elizabeth separated herself from Königsmarck's continued hold, then reached up to move aside some bottles and jars and tins high on a dresser. Her search along the shelf began confidently, then slowed, then died. When she gave up, shaking her head hopelessly, Königsmarck and Vratz took over, pulling out containers, and pointing at even the most unlikely candidates to be the Black Box. She shook her head to all of them.

'Everything is returned to its place,' Jaspars said heatedly. 'There is nothing there that should not be.'

They gave up their search, then—under Jaspars's austere gaze—put everything back.

To everyone's astonishment, Königsmarck let out a huge roar. His noise filled the oils room. Then he shouted, 'I will find it, Betty!'

When Königsmarck had calmed enough, Harry addressed Elizabeth. 'You told the Duke the box was here.'

'Eventually. He forced it from me. Days of captivity tired me. I no longer cared if he had it or not.'

'He must have told your husband—Mr. Thynne, I mean—who in turn told his men. They came to find it, but could not.'

'I told him not exactly where. Only that it was at Sir Peter's.'

'But searching again, they found it, and took it with them.' Harry paused, frowning. 'Why did Diana come here? I thought she came for the painting. Did she come instead for the box?'

Elizabeth made a strange expression, which Harry could not interpret.

'Did you ask her to reclaim the Black Box, before Mr. Thynne could find it?' he pressed. 'I think they found her here. She would not give it up to them when they demanded it. He or one of his men ran her through with a sword.'

'Did you see the portrait of me, Mr. Hunt?' Elizabeth asked him. 'Is that how you recognised me?'

'I saw it,' Harry said, looking at her curiously. 'As I said to you at Dr. Allen's madhouse. At first, I wondered if Diane came here to fetch it.'

'It was not to fetch it,' Elizabeth said. There was a pleading look in her eyes.

At last, Harry caught on. 'I see,' he said.

Vratz looked at him suspiciously. Königsmarck, still panting from frustration, looked only at Elizabeth.

'So, should we now try to reclaim the box?' Harry asked them.

CHAPTER FIFTY-THREE

THE MUSQUETOON'S THREAT

Upstairs in the Rhenish winehouse, Königsmarck and his men had found themselves a corner booth. It was relatively cool, being sheltered from the sunshine blasting through the window from the sultry day outside. Bottles of wine and various glasses littered their table.

They had left Elizabeth at Northumberland House—after checking neither Thynne nor his men were still there—to collect her luggage for a journey abroad and to keep away from her grandmother.

Stern loitered out in the street, keeping watch on Thomas Thynne's town house. They would swap the duty, Königsmarck had decided, one hour for each turn. Make themselves seem attached to the Admiralty Office, as various Navy functionaries came in and out of Derby House. The Count worried that Stern was likely to arouse suspicion; his fellow Swede's poor English might draw attention. Boroski had taken the first turn, though, able to stay unobtrusive.

Should Thynne appear, Stern was to report back to Königsmarck as soon as he could. Then they would intercept Thynne, force him inside his house, and reclaim the Black Box.

The house seemed quiet, giving no sign if Thynne was inside it or not. What if he never appeared?

In their booth, the three mercenaries rehearsed the possibilities and scenarios. Their conversation was detailed. Each man was listened to equally, despite their differences in rank. Being the most experienced, Vratz raised the problems. The final arbiter, though, was Königsmarck; once he had decided, there was no further argument.

They made a capable and self-sufficient unit. Harry found himself enjoying their company, even though they slipped between High Dutch, German, Swedish, and Polish, as much as they spoke in English.

Boroski wanted to know how he should load his musquetoon: buckshot or with multiple bullets?

'You've no need of that,' Harry insisted. 'Besides, you risk hurting bystanders. Or Mr. Thynne's servants. They don't deserve to be injured.'

Vratz translated for Boroski, then he and Boroski shared a look as if to say, what worry was that to them?

'I'm with Harry,' Königsmarck said. 'When Thynne sees all of us, he shall quickly cede the box.'

'Our numbers are enough,' Harry agreed, glad of the support. 'Reason shall persuade. There's no need for violence.'

'You've not fought your way across Europe,' Vratz said. 'I've seen plenty of need for it.'

Königsmarck grinned a feral grin at the Kapitän, then at Boroski. 'You may threaten him with the weapon, Jerzy. You must try your very best not to fire it.'

'*Tänk om Kidd och Singer är med honom?*' Vratz asked. Then he remembered Harry was with them. 'What if Kidd and Singer are with him?'

Boroski nodded. '*W takim razie potrzebny mi będzie mój muszkiet.*'

'Only to defend yourself,' Königsmarck said.

'Each of us has his sword,' Vratz added. 'I have my pistol.'

Königsmarck knocked back the contents of his glass, then poured himself another. 'I hope Thynne appears soon. Betty is desperate to leave, and wants the Black Box with her.'

'Not as desperate as I am,' Vratz replied. 'I am sick of London.'

Harry coughed to interrupt them. 'Please let me speak first with Mr. Thynne, to see if I can persuade him to give up the box.'

Königsmarck scratched at his ear, then shrugged. 'I think you will find he is a man immune to reason.'

'It may well be he's already delivered the box to the Duke,' Harry said.

'Then Betty shall have to accept defeat.' Königsmarck gazed sadly at him. 'I hope it does not change her mind. I wish her with me in Amsterdam.'

Mr. Prior, the winehouse's landlord, came to ask if they wanted more wine. He seemed apprehensive. These looked rough, tough men, and had untrustworthily foreign accents. One of them he thought he recognised. In his mind, Prior pictured the young man with the Justice, Sir John Reresby, but could not remember the occasion. He had a vague recollection of oysters.

Königsmarck ordered more wine. Boroski asked for *wódka*, and was happy Prior could oblige.

'We don't want to be raddled if we intend to take the box,' Harry warned them.

Boroski raised his glass. 'King Jan Three!' He belched impressively. 'Sobieski!'

'King Karl the Eleventh!' Königsmarck joined him.

'*Scheiß auf die Monarchie!*' Vratz said, to a loud guffaw from Königsmarck. Vratz raised his glass to Harry. 'It just sounds better in German.'

Although not understanding the words, Harry recognised the sentiment; he scanned the other customers to see if offence had been taken.

The three men with him looked expectantly at Harry. 'His Majesty, the King, Charles the Second!' he said dutifully. But the words felt false as he said them.

Boroski patted the musquetoon under his coat. 'I go load this *w wychodku*. I quick can be.'

'Your pistol's loaded, Christoph?' Königsmarck asked Vratz, after Boroski had left for the house of office. Vratz gave a nod in reply. Despite all their soldiering, Harry detected nervousness in both men.

They all waited anxiously. Time nagged at each of them. It was nearly time for Stern to swap over with Vratz, who kept going to the window; although from there, as it was around the corner, nothing could be seen of Thynne's house. Königsmarck kept lifting his hat to readjust his long hair, which was coiled up inside it. Boroski, once he had returned from outside, kept patting his concealed musquetoon.

In his own anxiety, Harry coughed repetitively, as irritating for him as for the other men with him. His fingers had a life of their own, drumming ceaselessly on the tabletop. When Königsmarck stared at him, Harry stopped them, but after a few minutes found they were tapping again. He tried whistling instead, Henry Purcell's 'They That Go Down to the Sea in Ships,' but even though he started as high as he could, he still failed to whistle the lowest notes. This time, Vratz looked viciously at him.

Footsteps running up the stairs told them Stern had arrived.

'Thynne is *naar buiten gekomen in zijn rijtuig*!' he informed them excitably. He dripped with sweat from not having found suitable shade to watch from.

'Thynne's leaving in his carriage,' Königsmarck translated for Harry.

Stern gave them more information, which again Königsmarck translated.

'He came out of his house, then returned inside. Johann thinks he forgot something.' Königsmarck paused, sending a significant look towards each of his men. 'It does not matter what it is. He's back out now. It is time to take the box.'

☿

AMID A FLURRY OF WEAPON AND clothing adjustment, they left their half-drunk drinks and some money—a mixture of Swedish riksdalers, Polish groszy, and Dutch stuivers—on the table and paced downstairs. As Königsmarck had rented a horse, he went with Vratz to the stables, where they had also left the calash. Its horse had been fed and watered; the stable boy was to keep it harnessed in case of a quick escape.

Harry waited for them on Cannon Row with Stern and Boroski. As soon as he had exited the winehouse he started to sweat. The late-afternoon sun was low, but still the heat was ferocious.

The three men had to press themselves into the wall when Thynne's carriage went past them. Harry recognised it from Josiah Keeling's description, so there was some truth to the man's story. It was painted dark blue and had a capacious luggage box—one large enough to transport a dead body inside.

They watched it take the turn towards Whitehall Palace.

Königsmarck emerged from the stables, encouraging his horse into a trot. Vratz drove the calash close behind, after Harry, Stern, and Boroski were all safely aboard. Going through Whitehall, they moved too fast for the traffic; other road users stared after them reproachfully.

They looked an interesting bunch. The sort of men who would not tolerate interference.

'If Thynne's going north,' Harry said, more to Vratz than either Stern or Boroski, 'I wonder if it's to the Duke's house in the Haymarket.'

'Thynne look arg,' Stern said. He searched for the English. 'Angry.'

'Why did he return inside his house?' Harry asked him.

'Come out with sword. I think for trouble.'

'He expects trouble, you mean.'

'Or looks for it,' Vratz said, slowing as the Count chose that moment to drop back level with them.

'Remember—Jerzy especially—we must not fire unless pro-voked,' Königsmarck said. 'What is your weapon, Jerzy?'

'Only *postraszyć*. Only to threaten,' Boroski replied dutifully. The *wódka* inside him slowed him—to slower than usual—but Harry knew this deliberation was deceptive. He had seen the quick soldier concealed inside his lumbering frame.

Königsmarck raised an approving thumb.

CHAPTER FIFTY-FOUR

THE PALL MALL
AMBUSH

Somewhere inside Northumberland House—there were many rooms to choose from—Elizabeth made herself ready. Her husband's carriage had not gone there; it did not wait outside its enormous gates. Königsmarck, up on his horse, was the first to sight him. Thynne's carriage had turned left towards Haymarket and was going past the Mews, where the royal stables were.

Königsmarck turned in his saddle and called back to Vratz. Then he heeled his horse forwards to catch up with Thynne. Vratz, seeing the distance increasing between them, flicked his reins to go after. The calash's wheels rattled and bounced on the road; its passengers reached for handholds to steady themselves.

Harry heard a shout. Thynne's postilion had seen them following. Thynne urged greater speed. His carriage went too close to another, which had to veer sideways. Its driver cursed heatedly at them all, thinking them bloods having sport.

Königsmarck brought his horse alongside Thynne's carriage. Vratz struggled to keep the same speed.

'Slow down!' Harry shouted. 'You'll turn us over!'

'What do you know of driving such vehicles?' Vratz asked, clearly enjoying himself. 'I have sat over wheels for thousands of miles.'

After turning into Pall Mall, going past its grand, lofty houses, and reaching the junction with St. Alban's Street, Königsmarck managed to get ahead of Thynne's carriage. He steered his horse in front of it, forcing its postilion to slow.

Vratz pulled up behind the carriage and reached for his pistol. Boroski produced his musquetoon. Stern, more reluctantly, withdrew his sword. Harry remembered Königsmarck assuring him that Stern had no such thing.

All three men jumped down to the road.

In front of Thynne's carriage, Königsmarck sat very upright on his mount, holding his sword high in the air. Boroski walked around the carriage, to its other side.

'No, no!' Harry cried, realising this could go very wrong.

'*Postraszyć!*' Boroski reassured him, continuing his walk. 'Threaten.'

Harry jumped from the calash and climbed onto Thynne's footplate, leaning in at his window. Thynne looked to be in the same black suit and white wig he had worn at their meeting in the library at Cannon Row.

'The very devil!' Thynne cried. 'You *do* work with these men!'

'Mr. Thynne,' Harry said, unable to deny it.

Opposite Thynne were Kidd and Singer. Kidd's scar looked livid in the evening sun, which painted the carriage's interior a radiant orange. All three had raised themselves from their seats to awkward squatting positions, but soon lowered themselves back down when Boroski appeared at the other window, levelling his musquetoon at them.

'You cannot be gentlemen!' Thynne exclaimed indignantly. 'You have gunpowder and bullets. I have only my sword.'

Harry was conscious of Königsmarck and Vratz pressing behind him—Stern having relieved Königsmarck of his horse—and also of Boroski on the opposite side of the carriage.

'You have a box,' he told Thynne, although Thynne knew it, perfectly well.

And Harry could see it. Next to Thynne, placed on the carriage's seat.

Harry had never paused to imagine it, yet was still surprised by its bulkiness. Obviously strongly made, it was a shineless grey blue—not the black the Brisk Boys put about. A blade of some kind had been used against it; it bore the scars of attack. Another dent by its keyhole showed the impact of a bullet.

Thynne ignored Harry's assertion.

'The box,' Harry repeated.

Thynne's asymmetric chin oscillated from side to side. 'What of it?' he snapped. As he spoke, the corners of his mouth drooped even more than Harry remembered.

'It's not yours,' Harry said. 'It was in your wife's possession. Kidd and Singer took it from Sir Peter Lely's house, where Diana Cantley had left it. Up in the oils workshop, was it not?'

'Our finding the box there does not make it Mrs. Thynne's,' Kidd said, sullenly.

Thynne eyed Königsmarck, who stood close behind Harry; a

look of hatred passed over his fleshy, wine-reddened features. 'My wife stole the box from her grandmother, I believe. Even if it were her property, as her husband I could contest that. Its contents, however, are not. They belong, unarguably, to the Duke.'

'Papers confirming his legitimacy, and his right to succeed,' Harry said. 'A certificate of marriage between his mother and father.'

'Exactly so,' Thynne replied. He looked to his men sitting opposite him, thinking Harry might be amenable to his view.

Kidd and Singer were unable to reassure him.

'Such papers are the King's property, then,' Harry said. 'To steal them must be treason.'

Thynne's face turned puce. His mouth had a couple of goes at starting his sentence. 'The King has always denied their existence, so can hardly object if I take them to his son.'

Harry turned around, to see Königsmarck, whose own face, conversely, had gone paper pale, and Vratz, who wore an expression of hard amusement. Boroski, expressionless at the other window, never wavered with his weapon.

'These are dangerous men with me,' Harry said, with a sense of foreboding. He suspected Thynne might decide to resist them. Kidd or Singer would not, he thought, as they seemed more circumspect than their employer.

'These foreign mercenaries have no right to the box or its contents at all, that I can fathom,' Thynne said.

'It's not worth risking trouble.'

'Yet for it, you chase me through Westminster.'

Standing behind Harry, Königsmarck grunted impatiently. 'Hand it over. I have promised its return.'

'You spoke rashly, then, Königsmarck,' Thynne said. 'Since I possess it, not you.'

Boroski angled his musquetoon to better show it to Thynne, providing clear sight of its flared, trumpetlike muzzle.

'Please, Mr. Thynne,' Harry begged. 'The Count and his men are prepared to take the box by force. Will you not peaceably hand it over?'

Thynne's heavy-lidded eyes blinked slowly, as if he was dazed by a punch and wanting to clear his head. Harry wondered how much wine he had imbibed that afternoon. As best he could, Thynne stood up inside the carriage, bending his head beneath its ceiling.

Without taking his eyes from Harry, he slowly drew his sword.

'They will have to take it from me.'

Thynne raised the sword to the horizontal, so it appeared foreshortened; its point was only a few inches from Harry's face.

'You've been unable to open it,' Harry said, trying his best to ignore the weapon. 'I can see your attempts to do so. You risk injury, perhaps your life, for a box which may be empty.'

'We'll get it open. If you stop me, you pave the way for Catholicism. You *must* support a Protestant King, even if those men with you do not.'

'I've never quizzed them on their religion,' Harry said. 'I'm little interested in how they pray. Whichever way they worship, I hold little sway over them. They've given me more time to reason with you than I thought they would. In truth, I don't much care for the box, or whatever's inside it. I do, though, care about Diana Cantley, whose murder the King commanded me to investigate. I suspected she was killed in Covent Garden, near Sir Peter Lely's house. I suspected it was your men who killed her. But your sword, I see, has an unusual cross-section, which matches the wound on her body. Diana refused to divulge where the box was, didn't she? Because she refused to bend to your will, you lost your temper. As you lose your temper now, so you behave against reason. Elizabeth asked her friend to hide the box. But Diana didn't do so well enough, for there it is, sitting on the seat beside you. You've not yet opened it, because you're missing its key. We found that on Diana's body. The Justice of Peace, Sir John Reresby, has it. You should have taken the time to search her after you killed her, or before taking her body to Bethlehem when you imprisoned Elizabeth there. You panicked, though, didn't you?'

Thynne took a step back inside the carriage, and lunged forwards with his sword at Harry.

'Harry!' Vratz warned him, his voice cracking with the shout.

But Harry had already seen the too-clearly signalled move and jumped from the carriage's footplate.

An explosion shocked his ears, the second they had suffered that afternoon.

CHAPTER FIFTY-FIVE

THE MINCED BELLY

Both of Thynne's horses reared, one kicking wildly. His postilion dismounted before he was thrown and ran to the other side of Pall Mall. Harry heard him shouting 'Murder!' as he went.

Inside the cloud of gunpowder smoke, Kidd and Singer had both drawn their swords. They sheathed them quickly once the smoke had cleared enough for them to discern Vratz pointing his pistol.

'What have you done?' Kidd cried, bending down to tend to his employer.

Thynne lay back in the seat, his legs stretched in front of him. His sword lay on the carriage's floor. Blood soaked the front of his shredded waistcoat and shirt. His eyelids were scrunched up in agony, his lips chalk white.

'I am wounded,' he groaned, sounding astonished. 'I am mortally wounded.'

Boroski mutely stared in through the carriage window, and lowered his musquetoon.

Harry opened the door. 'We must try to save him,' he said to Kidd and Singer. He put his hands into the mess Boroski had made of Thynne's torso, trying to extricate some damaged cloth which had worked deep into the wounds. Hot, wet blood ran over his fingers.

'How many bullets?' Harry asked Boroski.

'*Jestem po pas w gównie*,' Boroski replied sullenly. He put up the fingers and thumb of one hand, resting the musquetoon on the top of the carriage door to do so. Five bullets.

'He'll be lucky to survive,' Königsmarck said, standing in the carriage's doorway.

'Let's wish for some luck, then,' Harry said. As well as Thynne's lifeblood oozing, he could feel smashed bone.

'I am murdered,' Thynne said, his voice raw, and his breath coming in frantic heaves. His hands kept opening and closing to either side of him on the seat. He looked glassily at Harry. 'I am murdered,' he repeated, this time in quiet wonder, beginning to accept the fact.

'We must continue him on to the Duke's house,' Harry urged Kidd. 'It's close by.'

'Even so, I doubt he'd survive the journey,' Kidd replied.

'He either dies here, or there,' Harry said. 'There'll be water and cloth at the Duke's. At least there we can clean him and try to plug these holes.'

'Better to die in a bed, son, I suppose,' Singer said. Belying his words, he stared belligerently at the men surrounding him, looking as if he might spring at them. Any plan he might have of a fight-back was kept in check by Vratz, who had noticed it and shook his pistol at him.

'We shall hang for this,' Königsmarck said despairingly. 'Jerzy is my servant. I will be held responsible.'

'People are gathering, Karl,' Vratz told him. 'We must leave. Now. They will do their best to stop us.'

'We must try to save this man,' Harry insisted. 'Then it won't be murder.'

Königsmarck shook his head slowly. 'I go for Betty. And I will have that box.'

'Do you expect to get away?' Harry asked him, incredulous. 'You've shot Mr. Thynne. Every constable and soldier in London will be after you.'

'We've evaded them so far. We just need to keep our heads down until we get to the sea.' Königsmarck sounded as if he only half believed it.

By now, Harry had scraped away the remnants of tattered shirt from the wounds. Thynne's minced belly pulsed blood, reminding Harry of porridge bubbling in a pot. As best as he could, he pressed his hands over the holes, trying to stop at least some of the blood. Gore covered him as well as Thynne, and the seat, and the floor.

Thynne's panting was now even faster; each breath collected less and less air.

Arguing with Königsmarck would not save Thynne. Harry motioned to Kidd to take over the pressing of his employer's wounds, then stepped out of the carriage. He led the Count a distance away, beyond the hearing of Thynne's men.

'I know somewhere you could stay,' Harry told him. 'Get your-selves and Elizabeth on the Limehouse ferry to Rotherhithe. Meet me later on the causeway. It's at a place called Cuckold's Point—you'll see the pole with horns.' Harry saw Königsmarck's perplexity. 'Elizabeth will know. If you think you're being followed, there's a rope yard where you can hide. If you're not on the causeway, I'll look for you in there.'

As he returned to the coach, Harry could hear Thynne gasping with pain.

Harry reached across the stricken man and picked up the box from the seat. Neither Kidd nor Singer attempted to stop him.

Still looking through the far window, Boroski looked ashamedly contrite. Harry mouthed a goodbye to him. He turned and passed the box to Königsmarck.

'Goodbye,' Harry said to them all. He raised his blood-covered hands, to show why he did not shake theirs. Vratz saluted him. Stern, holding Königsmarck's horse, and keeping far enough away to avoid seeing the consequences of Boroski's discharge of the musquetoon, touched his tricorn hat to him.

Harry had a strong feeling he would see none of them again.

CHAPTER FIFTY-SIX

THE ROTHERHITHE ESCAPE

After only a short while a chirurgeon, Mr. Hobbs, had arrived to tend to Thomas Thynne, so Harry left the Duke's house in Hedge Lane, going out into the London night satisfied he had done all he could to make Thynne feel easier.

Thynne still clung to life, but no one was willing to say he could recover.

Although Harry had done his best to wash it away, he was still smeared copiously with Thynne's blood. Trying to hide it by bending forwards, walking as if he were wounded himself, he found a hackney in Haymarket. He urged its driver to be quick.

With so much gore down his shirtfront, he doubted the King's note would convince a member of the Watch, or soldier worth his salt, that he was innocent of any crime at all—and certainly not murder. He looked as if he had butchered a platoon. Besides, he worried, the King's signature was easy to forge. It would be seen as safer and more sensible to detain him.

The hackney driver was unwilling to go south of the river, so Harry paid him by the Morice water tower and ran across London Bridge. At this time of night, all was quiet. A couple of men conversing with the Bridge Warden looked as if they might be official; none of the three showed any interest in Harry after their cursory inspection. In the nighttime, it must have been difficult for them to distinguish the red.

He walked past the chapel of St. Thomas à Becket, then through Nonsuch House, passing under its painted splendour. Reaching Southwark, he took the turn to Rotherhithe. Pacing quickly, he soon reached St. Mary's church. Up on its tower, the flag Rachel had made still fluttered; the white looked eery in the moonlight. No one had yet noticed it—or if they had, they had not bothered to change it. Seeing the black *L* representing *H* for Harry felt like a portent; things would turn out well.

He walked along Jamaica Street to where he had arranged to meet Königsmarck and Elizabeth. Seeing the tall pole with its wooden horns, he descended the stairs between the riverside dwellings. The tide was half out, exposing much of the beach he had washed up on after being punished by oar. The causeway's stones reflected silver. It was later than Harry had surmised; he was unsurprised no one still waited. He went back, taking the same route he had taken before. Up by the rope yard—but not over the fence Harry had climbed to sleep inside there—he saw the Count standing half-concealed in a doorway. And Elizabeth standing beside him.

Königsmarck was resplendent in a pale suit with gold buttons, which Harry deemed a poor choice for going incognito. Elizabeth, more wisely, had chosen dark clothing. She no longer wore the hat Vratz had given her, but one of her own. At her feet were some of the Count's luggage—a portmanteau and a canvas snapsack—and her own.

Königsmarck held what was obviously the Black Box, its bulkiness contained inside a sturdy leather bag. He saw Harry's questioning look. 'I have had no time to open it, and I have not the means of doing so.'

'Where are your men?' Harry asked.

'They are to follow on after,' Königsmarck said. 'We thought it safer for us all.'

Seeing her husband's grume covering it, Elizabeth looked at Harry's shirt with distaste. Königsmarck moved in front of her, to protect her from the sight.

'Mr. Thynne's gravely wounded,' Harry told her. 'I doubt he will survive.'

'I should be sorry for the death of any man, most of all a husband,' Elizabeth said. 'I make no pretence to be so. Time might soften me towards him. Towards me, Thomas Thynne was only ever dislikable.'

'Where is this place of shelter you promised us, so I may make my escape with Betty?' Königsmarck asked.

Harry experienced a suffusing panic at the question. His promise to provide shelter had been hugely rash, suggested in a hot moment. Most of his moments since had been equally hot, giving him little time to reflect; how could he ask Rachel and Sarah to take in fugitives, one of whom had just taken part in a shooting? A shooting looking likely to kill the richest man in the country, which would be punished severely. Sarah would definitely refuse——she had reported him to Joseph Fenn. Perhaps Rachel, who had displayed a weakness for strays, might be able to persuade her.

Harry's best guess as to why Rachel had welcomed him was that since her husband's pressing into the Navy, she held no fondness for authority.

Despite his worries, and even though the place looked different again in the darkness, Harry led the couple to the building with the tailors' shop and up its stairs to the balcony. To knock hard would risk waking neighbours, so Harry tried soft. The women inside would most likely be in bed. His second knock, after a long wait, seemed horribly loud in the Rotherhithe night. Still, they heard no sound from within. Harry risked a third knock—harder again—which raised the ire of a local dog; its barks were shrill and insistently regular.

They heard footsteps across the wooden floor of the shop. Rachel's voice came cautiously through the door. 'Who knocks here so late?'

'Rachel,' Harry replied, 'it's William.'

Königsmarck and Elizabeth looked at him, then at one another, in puzzlement. He screwed up his face at them apologetically.

After a clanking of its bolt, the door opened. By Rachel's candle in its holder—giving out only a tiny light, but enough for her to navigate her own house—Harry could see that she trembled. The light flickered over the doorframe, and made her face glow a soft, glimmering amber. 'You have brought others with you,' she said, sounding wounded he had neglected to tell her.

'This is my friend Elizabeth, and with her, Count Königsmarck. He is from Sweden.' Harry looked to check if Rachel's expression changed. The fact it did not indicated she had heard nothing of the ambush on Thomas Thynne, nor of the search for his assailants.

'You sheltered me when I most needed it,' Harry told her. 'I ask for your help again. One night. Only one night. Then these people will be on their way. And this time, it won't be in return for apparel. We can pay you well.'

Harry prompted Königsmarck with a nod; the Count fumbled in his purse, searching uncertainly through the English money he had. Impatiently, Elizabeth took the purse from him and extracted a gold Guinea. She placed it into Rachel's hand and closed Rachel's fingers around it, brooking no refusal.

This sum of money astounded Rachel. She and Sarah between them would be lucky to earn that much in a week. Some months, even, they did not see so much.

Rachel allowed them in and closed the door gently behind them. Königsmarck and Elizabeth divested themselves of their luggage, including the Black Box, placing it all down on the floor.

'Sarah's awake,' Rachel whispered to Harry. 'She'll hate your being here.'

'I'm no longer in hiding, as I'm no longer looked for,' Harry answered, similarly quietly. 'I even have a letter from the King to tell her so. So, I can tell you my name isn't William.'

She looked at him with the direct and still gaze he was used to. 'That you weren't who you said you were was clear from when you first appeared at our door. Sarah minded it. I did not. At least, not so much. Sarah informed the Watch of your being here. Or a Marshalman, she thinks. He had a red coat, like the one I made for you. She feels some guilt about telling him.'

'She shouldn't,' Harry said. 'I could have brought serious trouble to you both. Sarah did her duty as one of the King's subjects.'

Rachel looked dubiously at him, unsure if he was being quite serious.

'I doubt she'll get any reward, though,' Harry continued. 'I'm now thought to be innocent, and the man who offered it is dangerously ill.'

'So, will you tell me your real name?'

Realising he had not, Harry grinned at her. 'It's Henry. Henry Hunt. Please call me Harry, as all my friends do.'

'Harry Hunt,' Rachel said slowly, trying it on for size.

Behind him, Elizabeth could not stifle a yawn. Harry registered how exhausted she must be, after her own rigours of the past few days. She leaned against the wall to support herself. He thought of all the turmoil her husband and the Duke had put her through.

Despite the money she had taken, Rachel seemed to waver. But then her face settled, decision made. 'Come through, you may sleep in my bed,' she told Elizabeth. She turned to Königsmarck. 'You may sleep in here . . .' Not sure how she should address a Swedish Count, she tailed off, then opted for not addressing him at all. 'I'll fetch some material to make your bed. Harry knows.'

'Where will you sleep, Rachel?' Harry asked.

She made no answer. Instead, she led Elizabeth to the door behind the shop's counter.

'Wait, Betty!' Königsmarck jumped forwards, and clasped Elizabeth into a tight hug, kissing her forehead, then her lips; his ardency took both Harry and Rachel by surprise. Both felt embarrassed by his display.

'Good night, my love. Good night!' Königsmarck said. 'Betty!'

Rachel held out her hand to speed the couple's separation. At last, the Count let Elizabeth go.

With an unreadable glance back at Harry, Rachel led Elizabeth into the private part of the house.

☿

IT WAS ELIZABETH WHO WOKE HARRY in the morning, not Rachel nor Sarah as he might have expected. It was before dawn, so still dark; no light at all eked its way around the shutters.

'It is as I suspected,' she said. 'Karl has gone. And taken the Black Box with him.'

Harry regarded her blearily and sat up. Moving too quickly from dream to Elizabeth's news made him stupid. He looked over to where Königsmarck's bed had been on the platform: it was empty. A look at the front door showed it was unbolted; Harry remembered bolting it himself before they had gone to sleep.

'That's why you wanted me to stop speaking of the portrait,' he said. 'You didn't trust him, did you?'

'Never quite. It was a test I hoped he would pass.' The muscles around her mouth were stiff as she spoke, and her eyes swam with angry tears. 'I thought his good nights were too effusive.'

'I'm sorry for it. I genuinely thought the Count loved you.'

'I think he still does. But not enough to stop him from taking the box.'

'How does it benefit him? Does he have someone to buy it?'

'Despite being a Count, Karl has little money. That's why he continues to sell his soldiering.'

'Is that why he separated himself from the Kapitän and the Löjt-nant, and Jerzy Boroski? They might disagree with him. Tell him to leave the box and stay with you.'

Elizabeth shrugged forlornly. 'On the whole,' she said, 'I find men a disappointment.'

'Did he tell you how he planned to escape?'

'He mentioned Gravesend, and a ship called *Hoppet*. It means *Hope*, he told me. Now I shouldn't wonder if he lied.'

Harry reached out for her hand, then stopped himself, remem-bering his station, and hers. 'Well, what does the Black Box and its contents mean to either of us? You're better off without it. It means most to the Duke, of course. And his supporters. The King's always denied its existence. You should just let the Count go.'

The door behind the counter swung open. Then Rachel, with her candle in its holder, followed closely by Sarah Unsworth, came through.

Sarah strode up onto the sewing platform and opened one of the shutters to peer into the darkness of the street below. 'Do you not hear those people?' she asked crossly, her face still pressed to the windowpane.

Harry had not; he had only just woken.

'I thought it the usual noise of Rotherhithe,' Elizabeth said. 'I am Elizabeth. Your friend allowed me to stay last night.'

'She's told me,' Sarah said, rudely. 'And *him* with you.'

She pointed resentfully at Harry. 'What misfortune do you now bring to our door?'

CHAPTER FIFTY-SEVEN

THE UNLOCKED BOX

Gravesend was like Rotherhithe, but with fresher air.

For the first time in days, cloud had come. The morning's sky was an undeviating Purbeck stone grey, the same flat tone from horizon to overhead. A cool breeze rippled puddles from the overnight rain. Windmills turned lazily up on the hill.

The horsemen rode along a track slicing through the rough, tussocky grass and dropping into the town: Harry, Sir John Reresby, Joseph Fenn, Thynne's men Richard Singer and John Kidd, and lastly, the Duke of Monmouth.

They made an odd alliance. Sir John perceived Harry as too close to the man they sought. He also disapproved of Monmouth. The Duke was with them because he was avid for the Black Box, not to capture the man who had taken it—even though it was his supporter Thomas Thynne whom Königsmarck's ambush had injured. Kidd and Singer, Harry presumed, aligned themselves with the Duke, but had formed a friendship with Fenn, speaking together of military matters. Fenn had even given out cheroots.

The rest of the men rode a short way ahead. Harry asked the Justice to relate the day's events.

Begrudgingly, Sir John obliged. 'Mr. Fenn and I were with the Duke—Kidd and Singer with us, too—searching into houses. All on the say-so of people wanting Thynne's one hundred pounds. That time was wasted. But then Vratz's whore—flower-seller, she calls herself, I use the more unvarnished term—came forwards. She told me where he was. Conveniently enough, near to my house in Leicester Fields. He lodged there with a doctor, who swears he knows nothing of the ambush in Pall Mall. I am inclined to believe it—we shall question him further. I arrested Vratz personally, which took no great bravery on my part. Given what we know of his soldiering, he was unexpectedly docile. I discovered him in bed, a careless distance from his sword, which lay upon his table. Mr. Fenn seized the weapon, and I seized the man. It was mystifying. Vratz appeared unconcerned, as if just giving himself up to fate.'

'If he lives or dies seems barely to bother him,' Harry said. 'He told me he died of his wounds at the siege of Mons. I thought he said it for effect, but perhaps he half believes it.'

'Mons was a grim engagement, so I have heard. Seeing your men die around you must cut away at least a part of your soul. But my sympathy for him will not free him from the gallows. Especially if the ambush turns into murder.'

'You think it will?'

Sir John shrugged. 'Thynne is too hurt, surely, to live much longer. Five bullets have torn his guts, wounding his liver and stomach and gall. One bullet has broken a rib. Another, his pelvis. One is lodged into his spine.'

'Have Johann and Jerzy been captured?'

Suspecting Harry of hoping they had not, the Justice subjected him to a close scrutiny. Careful to portray an innocent determination, Harry turned his face towards the town as if he thought only of catching Königsmarck.

'Constables from the Holborn Watch discovered them,' Sir John answered. 'Soon after we had arrested Vratz. Stern is full of sorrow, speaking of nothing but repentance. As for Boroski—when I can understand him—he makes no apology at all. He obeyed his superiors and feels duty bound to have done so. Mr. Thynne endangered you, he says, so he fired the weapon to save you. Vratz affects not to care, but he softens his role in the ambush, I am sure. He puts the blame on the other men with him. I could not question them for long, because the King sent men from the Palace to take them away. His Majesty wishes to quiz them himself. He insists you cannot be culpable, but will speak with you again.'

Harry raised his eyebrows. 'We know the King's concern. He worries upon the recovery of the Black Box.'

'Be careful, Mr. Hunt,' Sir John warned. 'It is not for you, nor I, to question what His Majesty worries upon. You must explain yourself to him, and your role in this matter. If Kidd and Singer had not spoken up for you, and if you had not insisted on accompanying Thynne to the Duke's house, you would now be alongside Königsmarck's men, standing accused with them.'

Harry looked suitably remorseful, saying nothing.

'For now, we must concern ourselves with finding the Count,' Sir John said, starting to ride ahead. 'We are lucky he was spotted in Rotherhithe. He is lucky to have escaped the mob.'

☿

THEY RODE INTO THE TOWN, REACHING the blockhouse, one of the device forts from Henry VIII's time. A flag fluttered over it; the tide lapped against it. Built opposite the Tilbury Fort, together they guarded this straight stretch of the Thames.

By now, Harry had moved alongside Kidd and Singer. They still rode with Fenn, who gripped his horse with his knees while setting on fire another cheroot. Joining their self-reliant military group made Harry feel self-conscious. He was glad he no longer wore the red army coat, which he had left behind at Sir Peter's house; he had no right to one, and could imagine the ex-soldiers' derision.

'I think, as Thynne's men, you can help me. I have questions for you.'

'Ask away, son,' Singer said, looking impishly at Kidd and Fenn.

'Indeed, Mr. Hunt, ask away,' Kidd said. 'You helped Mr. Thynne. You may have saved his life by your quick actions.'

'Note, we may never say the same to the Justice,' Singer warned. 'Whatever you repeat to him of this conversation, we could well deny.'

'I doubt you'll ever be asked to testify against your employer,' Harry said. 'I'm afraid his life's a measure beyond saving. Few shall want to pursue him for his crimes.'

Singer nodded gravely. 'What do you wish to ask us, son?'

'Firstly, then, was it Mr. Thynne who wrote the letter to Sir Benedict Cantley, pretending to be the Swedish Count?'

Kidd and Singer glanced at one another, then both shrugged simultaneously.

'I shall answer that one, Mr. Hunt,' Kidd said. 'I never saw him write it. He never let me read it. But he did entrust me with its delivery.'

'You saw he mimicked a Scandinavian style.'

'I know not their style. I did see it was not his own.'

Harry nodded, and thought for a second. 'Did either of you go to London Bridge, to collect the ransom from Sir Benedict?'

'Don't know about that,' Kidd said.

'Me neither,' Singer concurred.

Harry believed them. 'Presumably, then, that was Mr. Thynne.'

'How much was the ransom for?' Kidd enquired.

'Two hundred Guinea coins.'

'He's a funny bugger with money,' Kidd said. 'Got so much, but always wants more. For two hundred Guinea coins, I could see him thinking, why not?'

'What did you know of him killing Diana?' Harry asked them both.

Kidd sagged in his saddle. Singer shot him a warning look, to ask him to consider carefully his answer.

'I know it happened at Covent Garden,' Kidd replied. 'I saw her in the portico, in front of Sir Peter Lely's house.'

'Same here,' Singer said. 'The next time I set eyes on her, he asked me to help him carry her into Bedlam.'

'We both did,' Kidd said.

Singer nodded. 'She was dead by then.'

'He'd kept her in the carriage's luggage box,' Harry said.

Kidd, still holding his horse's reins, spread his palms. 'We can't be certain he killed her.'

'His sword matched the wound, I'm sure of it,' Harry said. 'That's something I can prove.'

Neither Kidd nor Singer looked as if they doubted him, so neither asked how he could do so.

'One last question, if I may. Was it you who delivered Sebiliah—the woman who died at Bethlehem—to my home in Bloomsbury Square?'

'Certainly was not, Mr. Hunt,' Kidd said.

'Never been to Bloomsbury Square, son,' Singer said.

☿

GRAVESEND'S QUAYSIDE WAS BUSY, SHIPS ROPED to it side by side. *Hoppet* was easy to find; its name was painted helpfully across its stern. It turned out to be a small brigantine, two-masted, snow-rigged, its deckhands making it ready to sail.

Spying a crewman by the rail, Sir John bellowed up to him. 'Do you have the Count Königsmarck aboard? We know he plans to be so.'

Harry had a moment of uncertainty. Königsmarck had proved dishonest; had he lied to Elizabeth about the name of the ship?

The sailor looked blankly down at the Justice and the riders with him, either not understanding, or else not knowing of the Count. He then disappeared without explanation, leaving the group all looking at each other, wondering if anyone would return.

An older man replaced him at the rail—perhaps the captain himself, for he looked weatherworn and competent—and called down. 'He is not aboard.'

'He is chiefly notable for his long, yellow hair,' the Justice shouted back to him.

'Oh, I know him,' the sailor replied, his accent strongly Swedish. 'I promise you, gentlemen, he is not here. If he wishes to embark with us, he must be so presently. We are out on the flood tide.'

Further along the quayside, one of the dockhands stared at the group of horsemen waiting by the *Hoppet*. At one man in particular. The dockhand nudged a workmate, who also started to stare.

'You're the Pro'estant Duke,' the first man called.

Turning his horse, Monmouth raised his hat at the man self-deprecatingly.

The dockhand was immediately charmed. 'I support yer, sir! I've no liking for Popery.'

'Thank you, my man,' Monmouth replied, flicking his eyes to either side of the dockhands, hoping for no more attention. But he was soon disappointed; another man joined his colleagues and saluted the Duke, then nodded affably to the other horsemen with him.

Another man bowed. 'The Duke!'

'Thank you, thank you,' Monmouth said. He looked regretfully at Sir John as more dockworkers approached to join their colleagues. 'We search for a Swedish gentleman,' he told them, deciding to turn the hindrance into an opportunity. His loud, clear voice carried even in the breeze. 'He has long, yellow hair. When last sighted, he wore a light-coloured suit, with gold buttons. There can be no missing him. We suspect him of shooting my friend—and it is soon likely to be murder, for he is hurt severely.'

The dockworkers looked at one another, amazed and happy to be helping the King's Protestant son.

The first man took it on himself to speak for them all. 'Most likely he stays a' the Red Lion, Yer Grace. Neares' brewhouse with rooms.' He pointed the direction further along the quayside, bending his wrist for the turn.

Armed with this new information, Monmouth thanked his new friends and spurred his horse to a trot. Being recognised by supporters, and by the possibility Königsmarck was near, invigorated him.

Cautious of how this scene would play out, Harry kept to the rear.

On finding the Red Lion, after tethering their animals the men barged their way in. Surly looks greeted them. The customers all shared the burly build and musculature gained through the loading and unloading of cargoes.

The landlord was tidying detritus from a table, whose smashed bottles and overturned cups told of recent trouble.

Wanting no repeat of the magnetism the Duke had displayed at the quayside, Sir John put himself in front of the group and pointed his stick at the landlord. 'We think you have a guest here. His true name is Königsmarck. He may use a false. He is a Swedish Count. He has perhaps the longest hair you have ever seen on a man.'

The landlord delicately dropped chunks of smashed glass into his cupped palm. 'I've no smoke if you mean him good or ill, so 'oo are you I should tell yer?'

'Why, we mean him justice,' Sir John said, stopping the man's work by taking firm hold of his chin. 'I am the Westminster Justice of Peace. This is the London Marshalman. This is the King's son, the Duke of Monmouth.'

Behind the Justice, Kidd and Singer stepped forwards, making an ostentatious show of gripping their swords as if ready to draw.

'And these two are Thomas Thynne's men,' Sir John continued. 'You have heard of him, I'm sure. You had better tell us if you harbour the man we seek.'

The landlord stared at Sir John, then at Monmouth, to whom he dipped his head. After Sir John released him with a derisive push, he set his mouth, then—as his hands were full of glass—pointed up the stairs with his elbow.

Immediately, there was a rattle of swords, each man checking his own. Fenn withdrew his pistol from the holster on his belt.

'No need for that, Mr. Fenn,' said Sir John. 'When Königsmarck sees our number, I'm sure he will give himself up.'

'He is a gentleman,' Monmouth said confidently. 'And shall behave as such.'

It was the Duke who led the way, creeping upstairs stealthily, everyone behind him treading as carefully. When the men reached the landing, they were faced by four doors, all of them closed. After an elaborate exchange of signals—points and nods—Sir John went to one, Fenn to another, Kidd and Singer stood by the third, and Monmouth covered the last. Not quite knowing his place, Harry stayed at the top of the stairs.

At a final nod from the Duke, all those at the doors hammered on them simultaneously.

One opened to reveal a scared-looking woman wrapped for travel. Another showed a man and his wife, also dressed for their journey, their bags just inside the door.

The door Fenn guarded moved on its hinges, then stopped.

'This one, I reckon,' Fenn whispered. Monmouth, Kidd, Singer, and Sir John all closed up to him. Fenn knocked again.

There was no sound from within.

Taking his permission from the Duke, and from a less eager Justice, Singer stepped away, then charged at the door shoulder first.

It exploded open, crashing backwards against the wall.

The men crowded around the doorway, from where they could see, at the room's centre, Count Königsmarck. Standing with his hands raised, he looked resigned to his arrest.

'Good day to you, gentleman,' Königsmarck said smoothly. 'Had you been a little more patient, I could have opened it for you.'

'We gave you time enough,' Monmouth said.

'You are Count Karl Johann von Königsmarck,' Sir John said. Although Königsmarck knew it, perfectly well. 'I recognise you from Bedlam.'

After the other men moved into the room, Harry took up the doorway, wondering if Königsmarck would try to deny who he was.

The Count made no attempt to do so. Instead, he bowed to them all, greeting them like welcome visitors. 'You will try to blame me, I am sure, for shooting Thomas Thynne,' he said. 'That circumstance was against my wishes and my orders. Mr. Hunt, there, shall verify it. He was with me when it happened. How is Mr. Thynne? I hope he makes a good recovery.'

'He will die, most likely,' Monmouth said, cutting across Sir John's move to answer. 'Five bullets through the belly would see off most men.'

'"Only for threat" was the instruction I gave. Was it not, Mr. Hunt?'

Before trying to reply, Harry thought through the sequence of events leading to Thynne's shooting. The Count had said those words, he remembered, but bore more responsibility than they let on.

The Justice answered for him. 'You could easily have forbidden any weapon at all. Let alone a musquetoon loaded with five bullets. By ordering your men to follow, as you chased Mr. Thynne to Pall Mall, you paved the way to violence. I have heard the story from these men here'—he pointed his stick at Kidd and Singer—'and from Mr. Hunt.' The stick was more cursorily waved in Harry's direction, as Sir John knew how well Königsmarck and Harry were acquainted.

'You know Thomas Thynne put Betty inside Bethlehem Hospital?' Königsmarck replied.

'Mr. Hunt has told me so. I have yet to decide the truth of it.'

'Oh, it is true. The Hospital's Physician admitted her, based only on a husband's word, and—of course—for his money. Thynne gagged her to stop her dissent. Dr. Allen shaved her head to disguise her. But who would ever guess the country's richest heiress was hidden inside Bethlehem? Her grandmother was complicit, willing to put money before kinship. And Monmouth, too.' Königsmarck bowed sarcastically to the Duke. 'You desired the Black Box. Thynne wanted nothing more than to give it to you. But Betty hid it from you both.'

'I find you mealymouthed, sir,' Monmouth said. 'You are the more Janus-faced. On learning of Elizabeth's duress, I straightaway released her.'

Stepping forwards into the room, Harry addressed the Duke. 'She was hardly released, was she? You and Dr. Allen moved her to his Finsbury asylum, not for Elizabeth's benefit, but your own. Perhaps you thought a softer regime would bring forth the answers you desired.'

Unused to being challenged—let alone by a commoner—Monmouth scowled darkly. 'In his hotheadedness, Thomas killed Diana. I wanted Elizabeth kept safe from harm.'

'You wanted the box,' Harry said bluntly. 'That's why you stayed silent on Thynne's murder of Diana.'

'I am sorry for that. Genuinely so. Thomas's temper gets him into trouble. I abhorred his behaviour towards both women. But you know the importance of the papers I seek. Of course I desired them, and so urged Elizabeth to tell me where they were. The fact I kept her safe and in comfort while I did so should not be held against me, surely.' The Duke turned to Königsmarck. 'You cannot claim any moral elevation above me. You betrayed Elizabeth, too, for the box. You inveigled your way into her affections. Your passion was all a masquerade. For you, I know, belong to the Knights of Saint John.'

'Who?' Königsmarck said. 'I know nothing of them.'

Monmouth looked disappointedly at him. 'The Order of Knights of the Hospital of Saint John of Jerusalem. To deny it is to betray your conscience. I have considerable support at the Post Office, and at the Office of Codebreaking. My intelligencers tell me that you would earn a sizeable fortune for the contents of this box. Seeking to promote the Catholic cause, you take your orders from Malta. You were given the task of taking the Black Box for the Pope. If he possesses these papers, then I do not. He desires a Catholic on England's throne after my father. Namely, my uncle James, Duke of York.'

Königsmarck sneered, as if the Duke was sadly mistaken, and as if, in any case, such a thing was inconsequential.

☿

HARRY COULD SEE THE BOX. It sat on the floor at the foot of the bed.

'You've not yet opened it,' he observed.

'I tried to, but it resisted,' Königsmarck replied. Even though he had been found out and prevented from escaping to Europe to claim his reward for the box, the Count still preserved an air of cheerfulness.

'Speaking of resisting, do we have an agreement that you will not?' Monmouth asked him.

Königsmarck smiled wryly at the men surrounding him. 'I am outnumbered. So, yes, as one gentleman to another, let us make that promise.'

Monmouth looked relieved, although, as the Count had pointed out, he had numbers on his side. He clasped Königsmarck by the shoulder. 'In any other circumstances, I am sure we would be friends. I shall speak to my father and do all I can for you.'

He switched his attention to the Justice. 'Let us try to open this box. Sir John, I trust you to report truthfully on what we find. Again, as gentlemen, one with another. You would not resort to subterfuge, I hope, to please my father.'

Sir John looked discomfited. 'On my honour, I would not. But I would prefer it to be opened in front of His Majesty.'

'He has always denied his marriage to my mother.' Monmouth could not quite keep bitterness from his tone. 'At the Palace, the truth would forever be obscured.'

'I believe you a man of honour, Your Grace,' Sir John said. 'As I pride myself to be. So, yes, let us try to open the box, here and now.'

'Mr. Hunt said you have the key, Sir John,' Königsmarck said. 'I heard him tell Thomas Thynne so at Pall Mall.'

'No, sir, not I,' Sir John replied. 'Why thought you that, Mr. Hunt?'

'I said it when trying to convince Mr. Thynne to give up the box. I wanted to save him from harm.'

Sir John looked at him mistrustfully, not understanding how it could have done.

Fenn, Kidd, and Singer all withdrew their pocketknives at the same time. As Kidd's looked the most substantial, he took on the role of box opener. He picked up the box and placed it onto Königsmarck's bed, then inserted his blade into the fine gap under the lid. He slid it around, feeling for the bolt, then tapped his knife on both its sides, to show those watching him how substantial a piece of metal it was. Far larger than anyone might expect for the size of the box.

'I cannot get through that,' Kidd said.

'Try to puncture one of the sides,' Monmouth suggested, his voice rising.

Taking a firm grip of his knife's handle, Kidd stabbed at the box. As had Thomas Thynne's efforts, it only removed a flake of paint.

'The Palace it must be, then,' Sir John said, with some relief. 'The King has men and tools to prise it apart. We can take the box there, as we take Count Königsmarck.'

Monmouth looked around the room, looking for anything that might open the lid. He was flushed, and his face was shiny with perspiration.

Seeing the Duke's obvious upset, Harry undid a button on the front of his shirt. 'Sir John,' he said. 'Your Grace. I have the key.'

'Why did you not say before?' Sir John demanded.

'I didn't know what best to do,' Harry replied. 'I've only just decided.'

The Justice looked despairingly at the Marshalman, Fenn, then back at Harry. 'You are an amphibious creature, Mr. Hunt. I have never known quite how to take you.'

'Take me as I am,' Harry replied. 'I seek to do what's right. Or, at least, that which is least wrong.' Harry took the chain from around his neck and held up the brass key to show them all. 'Diana Cantley had this with her when she was murdered. It was in with her clothes at Gresham College. I assume it's for the box.'

He made no mention of Thomas Crawley taking it for its silver chain.

'And you have had it ever since?' Sir John asked.

'Around my neck seemed the safest place to keep it.'

'Do not keep us on tenterhooks,' Monmouth urged Harry. 'Try it!' The Duke's nervousness was now agitation. He could not keep his hands still. Kidd and Singer, too, both twitched with fretful energy.

All the men pressed closer to Harry as he introduced the key to its hole.

With one full rotation, the bolt retracted smoothly.

Before opening it, Harry contemplated all the men crowded into the room with him. Monmouth was in a state of distraction, staring wide-eyed, his fingers curling open and closed repetitively. Königsmarck looked imploringly at Harry, desperate to know what was inside the box. Sir John glared at the box, looking sterner than Harry had ever seen him. Fenn's mouth twitched at the corners, and his eyes shone; he seemed amused by the situation. Only Kidd and Singer seemed unflustered, having less investment in the box's contents.

Harry lifted the lid. Inside was a package wrapped in paper and kept closed with red wax, a simple seal impressed into it.

Monmouth moved next to Harry to look at it. 'I do not recognise the mark,' he said. 'Not my father's. My mother never had such a thing, so far as I have seen. It is not the Walter seal her father used.'

Harry lifted the package out from the box and looked questioningly at the Justice.

'Give it to the Duke,' Sir John said. 'He should open it.'

Monmouth slid a shaking finger under the paper, breaking the seal. He unwrapped the package, dropping its covering onto the floor.

He stared at the contents for a long moment, without saying a word. His eyes were glassy, his face pale and sheeny, as if about to faint.

Slowly, he passed the package to Sir John.

It was not what any of the men expected a marriage certificate to resemble.

It was a book.

Sir John held it up for them all to see.

It was a copy of William Gouge's *Of Domesticall Duties*, describing the duties of husbands, and of their wives, and of the right conjunction between them.

CHAPTER FIFTY-EIGHT

THE UGLY
WORD

When Joseph Matthews recognised who it was, he looked wretchedly guilty.

'Alone this time, I see,' he said.

'I am,' Harry answered. 'Count Königsmarck and his men are held for Thomas Thynne's murder—Thynne died from his wounds last night—and the Justice is unconcerned by Sebiliah Barton's death. Or by what happened to her.'

'What happened to her?' Matthews said, through the bars of the the penny-gate as he unlocked it. 'Do you come to ask us, or to tell?'

After the searing heat and brightness outside, the lobby's coolness and relative gloom were welcome.

'A little of both,' Harry said. 'I know most of it, I think. Is your wife here?'

Bethlehem's Porter, Harry was learning, was a transparent man; the question obviously crushed him.

'She's told you,' Harry said.

'She has. Perhaps not all.'

'I'd like to speak to your daughter, too.'

Matthews took a pace one way, then the other, and for a second looked as if he would raise his fists to Harry. Instead, looking defeated, he went to find his family: his wife, the Hospital's Matron, and Hannah, one of its Nurses.

Overhearing them, the Steward, Carter, had appeared from his office. 'By what authority do you come to Bethlehem, Mr. Hunt, to speak with our staff?'

'Why, by the authority of what's right.'

Carter looked unpersuaded. 'I shall ask Dr. Allen for his say-so.'

'Is Mr. Lester here, too? Also, your Basketmen, Mr. Langdale and Mr. Jones.'

Grumbling loudly enough to ensure Harry heard him, Carter went across the lobby's polished floor to the Physician's office. Left alone for a moment, Harry looked around him, at the lobby, and at all its carved cherub heads. They, in turn, watched him, their blank eyes accusing—the one shot by Joseph Fenn's pistol the most accusing of all.

Carter reappeared and beckoned Harry into the office, where Thomas Allen sat in the big chair behind his desk, and Jeremy Lester perched on a stool at the old workbench.

Allen made no show of contrition for having confined Elizabeth Thynne at her husband's behest, nor for then taking her to his private asylum in Finsbury at the Duke's. Lester, the Apothecary, looked as lethargic as ever.

'Mr. Carter tells me you have asked for Mr. Jones and Mr. Langdale,' Allen said.

'Yes, and the Porter's wife and daughter,' Harry replied.

'She made no sign of her distress!'

'Sebiliah, you mean? You could not guess at it? I doubt that. No, you knew of it well, and put it aside. After all, your expertise is in identifying and assuaging distress. I wonder how much attention you paid to Sebiliah at all. She was quiet and caused no trouble. You knew she would not protest, whatever the abuse she suffered.'

Allen left the comfort of his chair and drew himself to the limit of his unexceptional height. He pushed back his wig from where it had slipped down his forehead. 'There are too many patients—'

'Too many patients, too many visitors, too few staff,' Harry interrupted. 'And too little money coming in. I remember you saying so in my elaboratory, when you identified Sebiliah. Nothing of that justifies mistreating the people in your care.'

A thump of his fist on the desk accompanied Allen's self-righteous look of outrage. Harry stared evenly at him, thinking his performance was more than half bluster. He could not bring himself to believe Allen really sought to justify such behaviour from his staff. If he left Allen to it, Harry thought, the Physician would ensure Jones and Langdale were punished, as long as Harry did not threaten to make public their abuse.

Anyways, there was more to come: Harry had not yet told Allen of the Matron's role in swapping Sebiliah Barton and Diana Cantley.

Allen huffed at Harry, then walked around his desk. 'We should take this up to the Court Room,' he said. 'More private there. Come with me, please, Mr. Carter. Mr. Lester, will you tell Mr. Matthews, on his return, where we have gone? And accompany him there after you do.'

☿

ALLEN USED HIS OWN KEY TO open the gates at the bottom, then the top, of the staircase. Once on the women's gallery, he turned immediately into the spacious Court Room, where the Hospital's committee meetings took place. Two impressive fireplaces faced each other under an intricately decorated ceiling. One wall displayed a pair of Robert Hooke's architectural drawings; one detailed Bethlehem's north elevation—the grander, more public-facing side—the other, plans of its galleries. On the opposite wall hung a Holbein portrait of Henry VIII, as oversized as its subject.

Allen ushered in Harry and Carter. This time, Harry noticed—unlike when he and Sir John had interviewed Allen before, downstairs in his office—the Physician was careful to close the door. Rather than sitting at the enormous table, Allen stood by the windows overlooking Moorfields.

'The Justice treated William Jones badly,' Allen complained, as Harry sat himself down. 'Then decided he was innocent of wrongdoing. Why should *you* need to speak with him?'

'Being held in the Justice's lockup scarcely compares with his treatment of Sebiliah.'

'Of what do you accuse Mr. Jones?' Allen demanded.

'Wait until he's here. Then act as his defender. Although, I've no authority. This isn't the Bench. Sebiliah killed herself, so the Justice's interest is nought. In a suicide, the culprit is clear. But I hold you the more responsible. You and your staff.'

At that moment, Jones and Langdale arrived with Matthews. They must have argued on the way; all three men were red-faced, their breathing quick. Jones and Langdale looked resentful. The Porter's face was grim. He motioned to Carter for him to take charge of the Basketmen. 'I'll find Millicent and Hannah,' he said, and left them.

William Jones eyed Harry belligerently. 'Already had time with the Justice, I did.' In his resentment, his Welsh accent sounded even stronger. 'He couldn't make me say I killed the rich man's daughter! Innocent, I am.'

'Have you not heard?' Harry asked. 'Thomas Thynne, a Member of Parliament for the Country Party, killed Diana Cantley. No, Mr. Jones, it's Sebiliah's death I hold you liable for. You and Mr. Langdale were the cause of her despair.'

'I never gave her the needle,' Langdale said dismissively.

'You gave her reason to put it into her own neck.'

'I've no need to listen to this.' Langdale turned to leave, but Carter prodded him in the back and glowered at him, making him sit at the table.

At a sign from Allen, Jones sat, too. He tipped back his chair petulantly, making the wood strain.

'Your abuse put Sebiliah into despair,' Harry accused the Basketmen. 'So much so, she committed suicide. Most think ending your own life's a sin, though the Bible says nothing against it. Corinthians, perhaps, with its talk of temples. You must see suicide as murder to be one. I for one do not. I bet, though, Sebiliah felt guilt for it. I bet she expected no better for her baby. She couldn't bear for it to suffer, as she had suffered. And besides, it was a bastard child, condemned to be looked down upon. I imagine she felt shame for it—even though she had no say in the child's conception.'

Harry felt his anger growing ever greater, and found he was

speaking ever faster. He had started to gabble. He remembered Sir John's words to him: *The word is* rape, *Mr. Hunt. An ugly word, but the right one.* He stopped his tirade and forced himself to calm, and to breathe more regularly.

'You cannot be sure it was either of these men,' Dr. Allen said, using his consoling doctor voice.

'I can be sure,' Harry replied. 'When I spoke to them last time, downstairs in your office, Hannah Matthews sent them a look. Both men refused to meet it.'

'That's a *look*, that is,' Jones said. 'Not proof, is it?' He rubbed his eyes brusquely. His usual satirical expression was missing. Despite his words, his face and posture showed only contrition.

Harry was not to be swayed. 'I remember you, Dr. Allen, had just told us Sebiliah's father was a widower, who died soon after her admittance into Bethlehem. She had no family or visitors, you said. Only the staff who ministered to her needs. I know not what brought Sebiliah here, but I know this Hospital brought her no comfort. She had the habit of pulling at her hair, so hard her scalp came away. I say habit, for she did this to herself over some time. Her skin was a mix of raw and healed.'

He looked at Jones, then at Langdale.

'No, you gave her no comfort. I can't know which of you is the father. I presume you both forced yourselves upon her. How many other patients along the women's gallery must dread your proximity?'

Neither Basketman answered.

Full of scorn, Harry turned from them to focus on the Physician.

'I used to think of you as kindly, Dr. Allen. As a man who cared for your patients. But money overrules your care. You accepted Mr. Thynne's money to confine his wife, then the Duke of Monmouth's to continue her captivity. You run your Finsbury asylum for profit. You're just as mercenary as Count Königsmarck and his men with their soldiering.'

A firm knock at the door prevented Allen's remonstration. The bulky form of the Matron, Millicent Matthews, came in, then her equally bulky husband, Joseph Matthews, followed by their daughter, Hannah. The Apothecary, Lester, came with them. They all found places at the table. Allen, at last, sat down, and Carter, too.

The last time Harry spoke to Hannah, he had been gentle with her. He used a far firmer tone now. 'You knew what these two Basketmen did to Sebiliah. But you said nothing of it.'

Although her lower lip trembled, Hannah answered him just as firmly. 'I don't remember you asking us of the *why* Sebiliah used a needle on her neck. You wanted only the details of the how, the when, and the where. Some wealthy woman she was swapped for at Gresham was far more on your mind.'

'I did not know then that Sebiliah expected a child. *You* all—' Harry stopped himself. 'You're quite right, Hannah,' he said, softening his voice. 'I did not think enough of the why. I knew Sebiliah to be melancholy and took the thought no further. Later, her body was transported to my home. Not something I wished for, I should be clear. That was when I discovered she was pregnant. Not until then did I concern myself with the why. For that, I'm sorry.'

'Where's her body now?' Hannah asked. Harry's apology had hardly mollified her.

'Buried. At St. Giles-in-the-Fields, in the churchyard there.'

What Harry did not add was that he had visited, but not for Sebiliah's sake. Instead, he went to see Diana Cantley's grave. An impressive monument, erected by Sir Benedict, had the details of

Diana's brief life inscribed under those of her mother; they lay together in the same plot.

Sebiliah's grave, unmarked, was in the furthest corner of the graveyard, the patch of ground set aside for paupers. Hooke and Grace had arranged her burial while Harry hid in Rotherhithe; Hooke's reputation had overcome the Rector's unwillingness to allow it.

He would pay for a stone himself, Harry decided, as he watched Hannah watching him. It fell to him to commemorate Sebiliah Barton's life; he chastised himself for not considering it before.

He turned his attention from daughter to mother.

'Mrs. Matthews, I think you turned a blind eye to what Jones and Langdale did. I also think you're capable of lying about swapping the dead women. And you're easily strong enough to carry a body.'

The Matron, shifting in her seat, looked pale, but made no protest. Her husband, Harry saw, did not disagree with any of this summation of his wife's abilities.

'Thomas Thynne—you all have heard of him, no doubt, after his being shot along Pall Mall—murdered a woman in Covent Garden. He bundled her body into his carriage's luggage box. He left her inside it, presumably while he thought of what to do with her. She was his wife's friend. Both women had kept from him something he wanted, which displeased him. A box, with some papers inside. Diana Cantley was the woman he killed. His wife, Elizabeth, he had placed into this building. Once given enough money to do so, Dr. Allen was happy to take her. To keep her out of sight, he instructed Thynne to pull up behind the Hospital, by the door closest to the mortuary. Thynne brought Elizabeth through it. Then he saw you, Mrs. Matthews, washing Sebiliah Barton, who had just killed herself. You told him she was meant for Gresham College, before her dissection. It was the opportunity Thynne needed. Diana was in his luggage box. You helped him to exchange their bodies. Diana for Sebiliah. You were the only person with time enough to do so. It was when William Jones had left you to change his clothes and wash himself, as he was covered in Sebiliah's blood, and when your husband had returned to his lodge. Thynne must have paid you, too, to convince you to assist him and then keep quiet. I wonder what your price was. Did he pay you with gold Guinea coins, I wonder? After all, he had plenty. He had taken them from Diana's father, promising to exchange her for them, despite having already killed her.'

Harry paused for the Matron to answer. She did not, but made no protest.

'Dr. Allen told me he keeps his anatomy room's key in his office. When Sir John and I were down on the basement floor, that room was locked, so we never saw inside it. You went from the mortuary up to Dr. Allen's office. Without disturbing Mr. Lester, you took the key. You, Mr. Lester, told us you stayed at your workbench all evening, but not that you were fast asleep.' Harry looked at the rest of the staff sitting around him. 'Your Apothecary ingests the medicines he prepares, the soporifics, which make him constantly drowsy.

'Dr. Allen was on his way from Finsbury to take receipt of Elizabeth Thynne. When he arrived, he went to receive her from her husband at the back door. Mr. Lester, of course, knew nothing of his movements. When I was here the other day, the back door was the only door I saw Dr. Allen open himself. You have its key, Dr. Allen. So Mr. Matthews, the Porter, knew nothing of it, either.

'Elizabeth told me her husband and his men put her inside a sack. She couldn't see anything of the Hospital until she'd been locked in her cell. She never saw you, Mrs. Matthews, while you cleaned Sebiliah's body. Dr. Allen, you took Elizabeth to the room in which you confined her. You placed manacles on her. You even shaved her head to make her less recognisable. Elizabeth uttered profanities, you told me. Nasty to hear, you said. But as her husband had already gagged her, inside his carriage, you never heard her speak. Thynne told his wife he had killed her friend, Diana. Think how terrified Elizabeth must have been, knowing what her husband had done.

'After you confined Elizabeth, you informed Mr. Hooke that Sebiliah's body was ready to take to Gresham College. When you looked inside the mortuary, you saw a woman's shrouded body, but it was Diana, not Sebiliah. You did not think to look more closely—why would you? Mr. Carter had informed you of Sebiliah's suicide, you came to Bethlehem to meet Mr. Thynne, and besides, Mrs. Matthews told you the body in the mortuary was Sebiliah. In fact, the Matron had carried her into the anatomy room, where she stayed until Thomas Thynne returned for her. He did so to take her to my house in Bloomsbury Square. By leaving her dead body there, he hoped to cause me trouble. Trouble enough to stop me from investigating further into Diana Cantley's death. His friend, the Duke, had nearly undone him by insisting I should help find his wife—who was here, inside Bethlehem, at your mercy as one of the patients.

'Mrs. Matthews, if Thynne hadn't seen you in the mortuary preparing Sebiliah, he would never have thought of swapping the two bodies. He would have quietly disposed of Diana later, I'm sure, throwing her away like rubbish. And I would not have recognised her at the dissection. After first coming here with the Justice I thought you might have had a hand in their exchange, as you were best placed. I became more sure when I returned with Count Königsmarck and Kapitän Vratz, looking for Elizabeth Thynne. We found only an empty room. I remember your husband saying that the women's floor is under your dominion. Yet you stayed downstairs. I presume you feared you had already been found out.'

Feeling suddenly bilious, Harry got up from his chair. He thought of going to the window for some air. After all the talking, he felt desperate for a drink.

These members of Bethlehem's staff—who had listened in various states of intrigue, disgust, shame, or disinterest—all stared at him. Eight pairs of eyes were focussed on him, and what he might do next. The behaviour of Dr. Allen, Mrs. Matthews, William Jones, and Edward Langdale was shameful. The others in this room, Harry thought, were guilty of wilful ignorance at best.

Yet he was the one who seemed the most ashamed.

He had had enough of these people. He would speak to Mr. Hooke. If Dr. Allen, as the Hospital's Physician, did not do the right thing, then Harry would see if its architect could bring his influence to bear.

CHAPTER FIFTY-NINE

THE MISSING PAPERS

By the clock on St. Paul's church, the time was just gone three. The afternoon sun seared Covent Garden piazza, making the bricks flame orange and the stone wincingly bright.

All the windows of Sir Peter's house were open, to stimulate some air to cool the rooms inside.

Next to her portrait in the drying room stood Elizabeth Thynne. To conceal her lack of hair, she wore a wig. She had chosen a bleached yellow colour; she looked like a sister of the red-haired woman in the painting.

With her were Harry, Robert Hooke, and Sir John Reresby.

Although it was so skillfully depicted, when Elizabeth looked at the picture, she felt nothing but dislike. 'I asked Diana to come here,' she said sorrowfully. 'Being my friend, she did so.'

'You must not blame yourself,' Sir John told her. 'It was your husband's sword thrust that killed her. His sword. His fault. His alone.'

She nodded her appreciation of the sentiment but looked as if she disagreed. 'I asked her to take the marriage papers from the Black Box and place them inside this painting.'

'I remember Sir Peter telling me of your interest in how the pictures are made,' Harry said.

'I asked him when I sat for him. So I knew there was room within the frame.'

'That's why you wanted me to say no more of the picture when Count Königsmarck and Vratz were here. You knew Diana had transferred the papers from the box. As they pretended to want it, I thought Kidd and Singer were here for the painting. Instead, they searched the rest of the house, until they found the box upstairs in the oils workshop.'

'Exactly so,' Elizabeth said. 'Thinking it was empty, I considered it no matter if Karl took the box. I never asked Diana to leave *Of Domesticall Duties* inside it. That was wholly her idea. She always enjoyed a prank.'

'You did not trust the Count?'

'I hoped to.'

'The Duke knew him to be a Knight of Saint John, desiring the box for the Pope.'

She looked at Harry, Sir John, and Hooke with sadness. 'I knew nothing at all of that.'

Hooke reached out for her hand with both of his. 'One day, my dear, you will find someone who will love you for yourself, and wish only to look after you.'

'Kind words, Mr. Hooke, but I doubt them. I think the Percy name does not allow it. And besides, I do not merely wish to be looked after.'

She said it with such charm, Hooke did not know if she chastised him or not. For the lack of anything else to say, he bowed his head to her.

Harry tilted his head questioningly at Elizabeth. By way of answer, she nodded.

Reaching up, he unhooked the portrait—rehung after Kidd's and Singer's visit—from the wainscot's ledge, then carefully leaned it against the wall, face in. They all peered into its back. Nothing was behind it. No papers lodged between the stretcher and the canvas, or tucked into one of its corners. There was a linen backing, which Harry carefully untacked from the stretcher. Once this was peeled away, it revealed the back of the canvas Sir Peter had painted upon.

No papers. Nothing at all.

At first, Elizabeth looked baffled, then her mouth trembled. She wiped her eyes angrily.

'You assured us, madam, the papers would be here,' Sir John said.

'I asked Diana to take them from the box. I said she should hide them behind this portrait. The box was where I left it, upstairs in the workroom. You told me the papers had gone from the box when you opened it at Gravesend.'

For once at a loss, Sir John looked pleadingly at Harry and Hooke. 'What shall we do? The papers are gone. Thomas Thynne did not have them. The Swedish Count did not have them. I am sure the Duke has not been duplicitous—I witnessed his great disappointment when we opened the box. Besides, if the Duke had them, all of London would have heard of it by now. The city would be in turmoil.'

'Somebody has them,' Harry said.

Sir John shot him an exasperated look, which said that was scarcely helpful. 'Then, that somebody holds the realm's future in their hands. You never moved them anywhere else, Mrs. Thynne? You lied convincingly to the Count when you kept from him the box's emptiness.'

Elizabeth looked as if he had slapped her. The Justice immediately looked contrite, putting up his palm in apology.

'Perhaps, finding herself unable to transfer them to the inside of this picture, Diana hid them elsewhere in this house,' Harry suggested.

'We cannot turn Sir Peter's house upside down,' Hooke said. 'It is only just tidy after Thynne's men.'

Sir John stuck out his chin. 'For papers as meaningful as these, we can overturn every shelf, unlock every drawer, and push aside every piece of furniture.'

'Then you can ask Sir Peter, not I,' Hooke said.

'I think His Majesty will command him,' Sir John said.

'It suits the King to have the papers disappeared,' Harry said. 'After all, he's never admitted to their existence, nor to the marriage.'

Sir John looked pensive rather than offended by Harry's opinion of the King. 'I shall consult with him.'

'Whom would he ask to conduct the search?' Hooke asked. 'Whom would he trust with the asking, or the finding?'

Sir John banged down his stick, making a resounding knock on the floorboards that must have been heard by Lely's Assistants downstairs. Then he looked deflated, losing height as he let his ribs relax. 'Well, before, His Majesty asked Henry Hunt.' He looked at Harry, and reached out to shake his hand. 'But you have been unable to find them. This is the time to say goodbye, I think. I am sorry for the nuisance I caused you, Mr. Hunt. I believed your detractors. For that, I am unfeignedly sorry.'

'It was easily done,' Harry said. 'Quite as easily, I accept your apology, and thank you for it. We believe those things which bring us comfort. We believe whatever suits our own preferences. And why should we not? The world's a confusing enough place. And the people in it are confusing creatures, often deceiving even themselves.'

The Justice seemed to accept this. 'Goodbye, Mr. Hunt. I'm sure our paths shall cross again.'

'I'm certain of it. Trouble seems to find me.'

'Mrs. Thynne—if I still call you that—shall we go?' Sir John put out his elbow for her to take.

Instead, Elizabeth took Harry's hand, squeezing it tightly as if worried he might scurry away. 'Goodbye, Mr. Hunt. I thank you. Profoundly, I thank you. You endeavoured to find my friend's murderer. In so doing, you became my rescuer. I am indebted to you.'

Harry released himself from her grip, then lifted Elizabeth's hand, but did not kiss it as she expected. Instead, they clasped hands in a more masculine way, as if a deal had been struck between them.

'You owe me nothing at all,' he told her.

Sir John made a decisive move towards the door. 'We must make our goodbyes to Sir Peter,' he said.

Each member of the group made their last bows and curtseys to one another, then Sir John and Elizabeth Thynne, née Percy, left the drying room, her portrait still leaning against the wall.

☿

HARRY RETACKED THE PAINTING'S BACKING.

Hooke bent to help him, holding out the tacks when Harry needed them.

'You must make things right again with Grace,' Hooke said, a gentle, unusually wistful tone in his voice. 'Without you, she is unhappy. I know she feels sorry for your last conversation, on the day of your arrest.'

Harry stopped his hammering. 'It wasn't the best of days, was it? I asked her to marry me. She detailed why she would not. Reasons I understand fully, for I treated her badly. I behaved selfishly. Then, Sebiliah's body was discovered in my elaboratory, and Sir John was convinced I had a hand in kidnapping, if not in murder.'

Hooke gave Harry an earnest look, pressing him to say more.

'I will speak with her, to apologise,' Harry promised him. 'I value her friendship above all others.'

'Her friendship?'

'For it to be any more, I would need to prove myself to her. She dislikes the man I have become.'

'She may be easier to convince than you think.'

The two friends resumed the work of putting back together the picture of Elizabeth Thynne, then they rehung it on the wall, to complete its drying in peace.

☿

THEY WALKED THROUGH TO THE ANTECHAMBER, where Sir Peter, surrounded by his art collection, sat on his sofa, demonstrating to an apprentice how the Duchess of Richmond's hands should be changed in the preparatory drawing of her.

'Harry! Robert! Sit yourselves down with me and tell me everything. Elizabeth Thynne's just now gone, the Justice with her. A delightful little thing, is she not? Let's hope she finds more happiness in life than yet she's been allowed.'

Sir Peter motioned to the apprentice to fetch a decanter and glasses from the sideboard. 'Let's drink together. It feels like it's been a long day.'

To both Sir Peter's and Hooke's surprise, Harry shook his head.

'First, I wonder if you'd assist me,' he said to them. 'I found this difficult before, when doing it on my own.'

'Of course,' Hooke said. 'But with what?'

'Give me one minute.' Harry went downstairs to the framing room to find a length of wood. He had also found some offcuts of canvas, which he brought back with him, too. By the time he returned to the antechamber, the other men with him were suitably intrigued.

He went over to the window and closed it against the day's heat. Then, he folded up some of the canvas into two pads and moved to the statue of Venus. He placed the length of wood between the statue and the windowsill, cushioning its ends with the canvas. 'Last time I did this, I was afraid she might topple. Would you hold her, to steady her?'

His expression showing he had guessed what Harry meant to do, Hooke stepped forwards to do so. Harry leaned with his back against Venus, then pushed with his legs. When she tipped, he lowered the length of wood further, so she rested against its length.

'Are you alright with the weight of her?' Harry asked Hooke.

'I have her.'

'A little more.'

'Joseph Bokshoorn was convinced she had moved,' Sir Peter said, now standing beside Hooke. 'I told him, only in his imagination.'

Harry jammed the wood down further still, increasing the space between the windowsill and the statue. Venus rested on the edge of the round base she squatted on. With enough gap opened up, Harry could withdraw what was beneath her.

It was a small package of papers, folded inside a larger piece. Its wax was imprinted with the royal seal. The King's seal. Nothing else on the outside showed what these papers were.

On the first afternoon he stayed at Sir Peter's house, after his friends Papin, Wylde, and Aubrey smuggled him there inside a barrel, Harry had recognised Elizabeth's portrait as one of the women he had seen in Bethlehem Hospital. When standing in the drying room with Hooke and Sir Peter, he noticed the picture was askew; Sir Peter himself had straightened it. Jan-Baptist Jaspars, Sir Peter's Senior Assistant, was such a perfectionist he would never have allowed it to be left hanging crookedly. Fearing his admonishment, whichever apprentice or Assistant who hung it would have been more meticulous. Someone, Harry had thought, must have knocked against it, or turned it on its cords. Or taken it off the wall then hurriedly rehung it.

Early the next morning he had gone down from his garret bedroom to look at it again. He had lifted down the portrait and searched behind it, and found the papers just where Diana left them, inside its backing. After retacking the linen, he needed somewhere to keep them safe. Finding the antechamber empty, and certain no one would look there, he placed them beneath the Roman statue of Venus.

'You must take *those* straight to the King,' Hooke said. His metallic eyes searched Harry's face, eager for agreement.

Harry slipped the papers into his pocket.

'Harry?' Hooke pressed.

'Will that be all?' Sir Peter asked them, sitting back down on his sofa. 'For I'm much fatigued. This house has been busy recently. My work seems never-ending. I wonder, how many more portraits do I have left in me?'

He waved his hand tiredly towards Harry's pocket.

'I hope that's what you think it is, Harry. I hope you know what best to do.'

CHAPTER SIXTY

THE MILE END GIBBET

Jerzy Boroski's body deteriorated. Crumbling and liquifying, it had collapsed against the gibbet's iron framework and made its slow escape through the spaces between. Birds had picked at it, leaving little of his face.

Harry, squinting in the hot sunshine as he looked up at him, remembered Boroski's slow, good-natured grin. The man had seemed to inhabit a private world, his imagination a more enjoyable place to spend time than this world; Harry could see an exposed part of the skull which used to contain it.

The Secretary of State, Sir Leoline Jenkins, had ordered that here at Mile End Green, by the side of Aldgate Street, was where Boroski's body should be displayed. The London-to-Colchester road was the route most used by Scandinavians, Germans, or Polonians travelling into London. It would be a warning to them.

Harry had watched the executions. Usually, he preferred to avoid them. He never enjoyed the spectacle, nor what viewing such violence did to people inside a crowd. It made them baser. It divorced them from their true natures—or, equally distastefully, perhaps it revealed them. He felt no need for an execution's supposed lesson; whether or not to commit a crime he would decide for himself. Justice, anyways, seemed so arbitrary that a hanging or a burning or a disembowelling provided little instruction of use.

He had gone to these executions from a sense of duty. An obligation towards the men who paid for ambushing Thomas Thynne with their lives. For if Harry had not inserted himself into the flow of events, perhaps Thynne and Königsmarck's men would still be alive.

Kapitän Christoph Vratz had shown no fear at all. In the cart from Newgate, alongside his comrades Johann Stern and Jerzy Boroski, and then at their place of execution—the gallows built precisely where Königsmarck had pulled in front of Thomas Thynne's carriage, by the junction of Pall Mall and St. Alban's Street—he looked completely sanguine. He even smiled at those gathered to see them die. Spotting Harry among them all, he sent him a friendly wave. Vratz had bowed deeply and seemingly sincerely to his captor, Sir John Reresby. When the cart pulled up beneath the gallows and Jack Ketch placed the rope around his neck, Vratz still appeared unperturbed. Those near Harry in the crowd all remarked on it. Some took it as his recognition before God he was guilty. Others thought it his certainty before God he was not.

Rarely did a man go to his death so cheerfully. When the presiding minister, Dr. Burnett, asked if he wished to make a speech, Vratz refused. Instead, he looked around him, to all appearances enjoying the sight of everyone lining the pavements and balconies of Pall Mall.

Johann Stern was far less serene; he spent his time in the cart praying for absolution. Full of woe and contrition, keen to let everyone know he was sorry before God, he trembled and wept. He seemed to regret his oncoming death. Heaven was unlikely, he had judged for himself, so he was fearful to his core.

Stolid as always, in mood Boroski was somewhere between the two others. His usual grin was absent; he looked sorry for his fate, but not guilty. He went to his death satisfied he had done his duty. He had followed an order from his Kapitän to fire upon Thynne. Boroski refused to believe, as Vratz and Stern both told him, that Vratz had actually shouted, 'Harry!'

At the appointed time, Ketch asked the three men under the gallows when they would signal for the cart to be pulled away. Vratz had answered for them. The last words he spoke were in English: 'Whenever it pleases the executioner.'

The great scandal was that Count Karl Johann von Königsmarck was not with them.

Visiting Bloomsbury Square to do so, Sir John had told Harry the story. After his arrest at Gravesend, Königsmarck was brought before the King at Whitehall Palace, where he performed with an exemplary self-assurance. The King responded favourably to his appearance—he still wore his light suit with the gold buttons— and his manner, which were everything a Count should exhibit. The King's and his Council's examination of Königsmarck was superficial, but afterwards the Lord Chief Justice, Sir Francis Pemberton, questioned him. Königsmarck confessed to nothing. When Sir Francis construed his fleeing immediately after Thomas

Thynne's shooting as evidence of his guilt, Königsmarck claimed that, as a foreigner in London, he had worried he would be accused of the crime; he could provide plenty of examples to show he was right to do so. Also, he said, not knowing the laws of the land he had thought it wise to make his escape. Advised that his friend Christoph Vratz was accused of the crime, along with Stern and Boroski, he said he was sorry for his men's behaviour, but they had acted against his wishes. The musquetoon, he told Pemberton, was only for show. He had not even known it was loaded.

The four men were tried together. To be fair towards them, the jury selected was half English and half foreign, which made their trial confusing. Evidence was given and repeated between witnesses and interpreters, the counsels and the Bench, swapping between English, French, Swedish, Polish, and High Dutch.

Thynne's men, Kidd and Singer, gave their evidence but were hampered by the Duke of Monmouth's instruction to make no mention of the Black Box. A messenger sent from Whitehall Palace repeated this requirement to them. Although His Majesty's name, for delicacy's sake, was not said, this messenger—a ginger-haired Captain of Foot named MacWilliam—made very clear that to speak of a box, or of a marriage certificate, would serve nobody well.

Königsmarck explained to the court that he had come to London to buy horses, being desirous to help in the siege of Strasbourg. The hope had been to buy a thousand; he had managed to buy only one. For this, he blamed illness and a poor grasp of English.

'But his English is very serviceable,' Harry pointed out.

'I protested that, too,' Sir John said. 'But I was silenced by the judge. Also, I am sure I read news of the siege being over. The prosecution did not think to mention it.'

Königsmarck's defence insinuated that Thomas Thynne's family had bribed witnesses to the ambush and to the Count's and his men's actions prior to it. Although the judge—Sir Francis Pemberton again, the Lord Chief Justice, placed there prudently by the King—ordered they must ignore such unproven allegations, the jurors could not unhear them. With Königsmarck's bearing and apparent honesty, the jury warmed to him. Especially when he told them how much he wanted to serve the English King—he had made enquiries about fighting for him in Tangiers—and how much he loved England, the English, London, and Londoners, and how very glad he was, as a Protestant, to be having his trial in a Protestant country.

'But according to the Duke, Königsmarck's a Knight of Saint John,' Harry interrupted. 'Working for the interests of the Pope.'

'We heard little of the truth in that courtroom,' Sir John said bitterly. 'Königsmarck reinvented himself, there on the stand.'

Summing up after everyone and everything had been heard, Sir Francis told the jury that if a gentleman's servants—from too much zeal—acted to protect their master's honour—misguided though that might be—then their master should not be accused of any guilt at all.

To Sir John's disgust—although he would never criticise the King's decision-making openly—Königsmarck's verdict of innocent meant he could leave the country, provided he never returned.

'The Duke pleaded Königsmarck's case to his father,' Harry said. 'Having made a gentleman's agreement, which he did at Gravesend—Königsmarck's life in return for the Black Box—he felt obliged to uphold the promise. No matter that the box proved empty of the documents he had hoped for.'

Sir John had shrugged at him, not so much noncommittally but in a more-than-half concordance.

Looking up at Boroski's decaying body, Harry wondered if the King had spoken to his son about the box and its contents. As everybody knew, Monmouth was the King's great favourite, but so far the King had refused to change his mind on the succession. His Catholic brother, James, should inherit the throne, not his supposedly illegitimate son. Otherwise, it made the succession a matter of favour. It gave any monarch the power to put anyone into the role, or opened the way for a popular vote. A monarch might be nominated by a political faction.

The monarchy would fall.

Christoph Vratz's body had been embalmed and returned to his home in Germany. For a criminal, such consideration was unheard of and caused more consternation. His guilt could not be in doubt; he admitted he left his pistol at the scene of the ambush. After his behaviour at his execution, though, many saw Vratz as a hero.

It little mattered what happened to the Kapitän's body, Harry thought. It was not as if Vratz could feel more punished than he had already been.

No matter: the King had given his permission for it. Harry guessed his son had asked for the favour to be extended to the Count's man.

After the hanging, men claiming to be his friends took Johann Stern's body. Actually, Harry knew, it was driven straight to the College of Physicians, where students of anatomy needed a subject.

Jerzy Boroski, on the other hand—a poor man, only a servant, and, after all, the man who pulled the trigger—was displayed inside a gibbet.

As for Harry's own appearance as a witness, it had been surprisingly brief. Everyone was happy he spoke English, aside from the six foreign jurors. No one seemed willing to place him with four foreign mercenaries. It was far easier to view Harry as a witness to the ambush, rather than as an active participant. None of the men on trial sought to implicate him. Even Boroski, who could have used the fact that Thomas Thynne had drawn his sword and was about to run Harry through, preferred to tell only that he followed an order from his superior. He would not have it be known that he did not follow his duty. Kidd and Singer both explained Harry's presence on Pall Mall as that of a bystander who had tried his best to help Thynne after the attack. With the Duke's say-so, and—Harry presumed—the King's quiet prompting, the Lord Chief Justice kept from persuading the jurors otherwise. Although Prior, the landlord of the Rhenish winehouse, was present to give evidence, he was never called. So the court never heard of Harry spending the afternoon before the ambush with the mercenaries.

One other thing that eased the way to Harry's exemption from any closer study of his time with Königsmarck and his men was that London's newssheets did their best to blame Elizabeth Thynne. They speculated—or else they flatly stated—that she had planned her husband's murder and used as her weapon to kill him a besotted Swedish Count.

That the Count had betrayed her, following his orders as a Knight of Saint John, was carefully withheld from the story.

CHAPTER SIXTY-ONE

THE BLOOMSBURY HOMECOMING

The only one of Harry's household who remained was his maid-servant, Janet Webb.

His cook, Hubert Dieudonne, had stayed for a while, doing his best to drink his way through the wine cellar. It was only spared when another offer enticed him away. His leaving could hardly surprise Harry; the last time Hubert had seen him, Harry was manacled after his arrest by the Justice of Peace for Westminster, and a dead woman lay in his elaboratory.

Oliver Shandois, too, had left. The first night after Harry's arrest. When Janet first told Harry of it, he had resented Oliver's disloyalty, and his ingratitude. Then he caught himself, realising what little had kept Oliver there. After mulling it over, Harry decided he should wish Oliver only the very best of fortune.

Harry had used him as little more than a tool. He had wanted his servant to better represent himself, and had followed the fashion of keeping a black boy. When he thought of how little he had paid for Oliver's servitude, he shrank from the shame of it.

Harry wondered if Oliver might go abroad. Get himself to the docks—at Rotherhithe, perhaps—and find a place on a voyage far to sea. What opportunities might arise for him? Harry hoped he would evade suspicion of having escaped a master's employ and be allowed to make his own way in the world.

Rather than stay on in an otherwise empty house, Janet had returned to her family. Strangely enough, that was near Sir Peter Lely, although Seven Dials was far rougher than Covent Garden piazza. She was careful to lock up, and had returned regularly to Bloomsbury Square, to check on Harry's house. Harry owed her for three months' wages, so that, too, had been on her mind.

She stood at the workbench, preparing a simple salad. She had made aristippus; Harry, drinking it at his kitchen table, watched her lazily in the evening light.

He preferred to sit here rather than anywhere else in his house, he had decided. It was a cool sanctuary from the summer heat. His pots and pans hung neatly, the cupboards stored everything logically, and the sights and smells of the kitchen pleased him. Everything in it had a reason to be there. Everything in it was *useful*. Like at Sir Peter's house, Harry's kitchen was in the basement, but enough light entered from Bloomsbury Square to allow him to read. In the evenings, he liked to read here by candlelight, enjoying the way all the metal in his kitchen softly glinted.

Now—although his attention wandered—he used needle and thread to mend his old brown leather coat. Scarred by his earlier adventures, he had no hope of restoring it completely, but its rips could be stitched, and the lining redone. He might never wear it again; he knew only his fondness for it.

The withdrawing room, which used to be his favourite room—the room from where he could survey Bloomsbury Square and enjoy the sense of superiority it gave him—now showed to him his folly. Every choice he had made for it was vulgar. Every object in it seemed facile. None of the colours went together. It was an improvident, pompous room, only reminding him how much money he had spent. It stabbed him to think how much money he had wasted. The ridiculous purple sofa, his India screen, the Turkish carpet, the teak cabinets, the glass decanters, the silver candlesticks, and the Thomas Tompion walnut longcase clock. The wallpaper, which reminded him of his fallout with Grace, and her accusations he had wasted her time and ignored her opinions.

He should have gone with her choices. Although, Harry wondered, after the past two months or so since Diana Cantley's death—the trial coming two weeks after Thynne's murder, the executions for it two weeks after that, and the time of Boroski swinging in his cage—he might now dislike those as well. Mentally, Harry had compiled lists of what to sell. One idea was to leave the Square. He could live comfortably for a quarter of its cost.

Grace was right to be disenchanted with him. Having money made him selfish; it made him insensitive towards her. It could have bought so much more. Changed things for the better—not just for him, but for those around him.

He had resented Grace doubting him, but why should she not? Josiah Keeling had seemed utterly convincing. Perhaps the man had believed himself as he related seeing Harry take Sebiliah over his wall. Grace knew now that Keeling was a liar, but she had not known it then. Sir John promised to watch out for Keeling, who was now allied with Titus Oates and Israel Tonge, as they exposed yet more details of the Popish Plot. Sir John would not arrest the man for his false statement against Harry, for he thought it a sincere mistake. Harry suspected Sir John was unwilling to expose further that he had so readily believed him.

That Keeling had described Thomas Thynne's coach so exactly—a dark blue chariot with servants' seats at the back, a large luggage box over the front wheels, and steered by a man riding a postilion—meant he must have seen it. Harry—who had not taken Sebiliah's body over his garden wall, from Königsmarck or anyone else—thought this meant Thynne had paid Keeling to say so. By then, Thynne was in a state of panic. He had murdered Elizabeth's friend Diana, then hidden her body in his carriage's luggage box. When he fortuitously found Millicent Matthews preparing Sebiliah Barton's body in Bethlehem's mortuary, as he went to arrange with Dr. Allen the taking in of his wife, the Matron had been Thynne's answer. But then his friend the Duke engaged Harry to find his wife, after Thynne himself had hidden her.

Nevertheless, Grace's look of doubt had broken someth—ahh, he made too much of it.

Anyone would have doubted him.

A knock at the front door sounded far away from down in the basement.

Harry had mounted a lantern clock with a pendulum and a spring mechanism on the kitchen wall; it told him she was exactly punctual. He had so much he wanted to say to her. He wanted, most of all, to apologise for what he had put her through over these last few weeks.

'Would you answer that, Janet, please? And would you bring her down here to the kitchen?'

Janet looked doubtful. 'Not up in the withdrawing room, sir?'

'I think she'd prefer to see us as she finds us.'

Harry put down his coat and placed the needle and thread on top of it. Feeling suddenly nervous, he got up from his chair. While he waited, he straightened pans that were already straight and wiped imaginary grime from surfaces Janet had left gleaming.

He could feel how fast the pulse in his neck was beating.

Two pairs of footsteps came down the stairs. Janet, he could tell, led the way.

As she came into the kitchen, his visitor seemed as shy as Harry felt. Rather than look at him, she stood looking around the room, paying close attention to it, as if trying to memorise everything in there.

The window, a horizontal slot just above the level of Bloomsbury Square's cobbles outside, showed a sky whose blue was darkening, and allowed a slab of late-afternoon light over her. It dusted her with gold. The sun was so bright on her skin it bleached away all detail, and made her pale green dress glow.

'Thank you, Janet, that will be all,' Harry said.

Left alone together, the hazy late-afternoon light warming them both, Harry moved towards her and held her to him.

'I'm so happy you've come. I worried you would not.'

'Harry,' she said, and kissed him firmly on the mouth.

Harry held her by the shoulders, stepping back and straightening his arms to take a better look at her.

'There's so much I want to say to you, Rachel,' he said.

AUTHOR'S NOTE

All named characters are fictional versions of real people apart from Janet Webb, Hubert Dieudonne, Oliver Shandois, Sir Benedict Cantley, Diana Cantley, Sebiliah Barton, Rachel Lejbowiczowa, Sarah Unsworth, and Kill-sin Abbott. These are fictional versions of themselves.

As in the previous books in the Hunt and Hooke series, *The Bloodless Boy* and *The Poison Machine*, for a more coherent narrative I felt the need to simplify historical events and remove historical actors. I've brought forwards in time—to the summer of 1681 rather than February of 1682—the incident on Pall Mall which brought together Count Königsmarck and Thomas Thynne so calamitously. This is for the prosaic reason that *The Bloodless Boy* was set in winter, and I wanted the contrast. Besides, a hot summer seemed to fit the themes better.

For a full description of the ambush and the circumstances around it—and, perhaps, to better understand my decision to simplify it—*Lady Bette and the Murder of Mr Thynn* by N. A. Pickford is a fascinating read. The notes of the trial, too, are well worth looking at, and are available online.

I'm grateful to Jonathan Andrews for allowing me to use his thesis *Bedlam Revisited: A History of Bethlem Hospital 1634–1770*. From this I found the names of the staff at the Hospital at the time this story is set. The two Basketmen, William Jones and Edward Langdale, in fact impregnated two women patients, Mary Loveland and Esther Smyth. Both men were expelled. Bethlehem's governors agreed to pay towards the upkeep of the children. The Porter and Matron, Joseph and Millicent Matthews, were 'admonished' for allowing such abuse to occur. It was decided that two locks should be placed on the cell doors on the women's floor, presumably with different keys.

At the Tyburn Fair, when Harry is arrested by Sir John, the crimes of the condemned are from the Old Bailey's records of 1681 and 1682. I put them together for a representative execution day. The Tyburn gallows could hold twenty-four people at a time, one more than I include.

In case you're wondering about the timeline when Harry looks up at Jerzy Boroski's decaying body in its gibbet, justice in those days was swift. The trial of the men accused of murdering Thomas Thynne took place just two weeks after the event, and the executions were carried out two weeks after that.

To answer the question Sir Peter Lely poses, 'I wonder how many more portraits do I have left in me?' the portrait of Elizabeth Thynne, née Percy, was his last.

ACKNOWLEDGEMENTS
AND THANKS

For reading drafts and good advice: Rob Little, Sonia Little, Kate Lloyd, Stan Lloyd, Kym Berry, and Lydia Berry.

For translation: Swedish, Susanne Alm; French, Pascal Lelièvre and Anne Schiller; German, Christoph Muelders; Polish, Anna Spittle-house and Aleksandra Waszkiewicz; Dutch, Yvonne van de Velde.

For his advice on what money could buy in the late seventeenth century: Professor Sir Roderick Floud.

For advice (and great conversation) on seventeenth-century music, and for the lute tablature that serves as the epigram for this book: Chris Susans. Sir John Reresby was an accomplished musician, including playing the lute. He would have recognised and been able to play 'A Health to Betty' from Chris's tablature.

For all at Melville House: Dennis Johnson, Valerie Merians, Carl Bromley, Michael Barson, Beste M. Doğan, Peter Kranitz, Sofia Demopolos, and a managing editor who prefers anonymity.

For being my formidable literary agent: Gaia Banks at Sheil Land Associates.

At the end of my last two books, I thanked Christopher Fowler for his role in their finding a publisher, and for his encouragement and friendship. I see no reason for this to change, despite his death in March 2023. Many, many thanks to you, Chris.

ABOUT THE
AUTHOR

Robert J. Lloyd, the son of parents who worked in
the British Foreign Office, grew up in South London, Innsbruck, and Kinshasa. He studied for a
Fine Art degree, as a painter, photographer, and
installation artist, but it was while studying for his
MA degree in the History of Ideas that he first
read Robert Hooke's diary, detailing the life and
experiments of this extraordinary man. After a
twenty-year career as a secondary school teacher,
he has now returned to painting and writing, and
is working on the fourth book in the Hunt and
Hooke series. He has a wife and three children,
and lives in the Bannau Brycheiniog in Wales.